Tangled THREADS

TANGLED IN TIME BOOK 1

CAROLINE CORVIN

First published in 2022 by Grenwyvern Publishing

Auckland, New Zealand

Cover design © Covers by Jules

www.carolinecorvin.com

Content Warning

"...when you have eliminated the impossible,
whatever remains, however improbable,
must be the truth."

Sir Arthur Conan Doyle, *The Sign of Four*

Uninvited

Kate

Auckland, New Zealand - March 2020

SHE DARED TO OPEN her eyes, and pain confronted her. The glaringly bright ceiling, the walls, everything hurt. Through the window, shards of sunlight stabbed at her eyes, while the cheerful blue sky offered a callous affront to the grey shroud of her grief. She clamped her lids down, drawing shutters on the pain.

This was how she'd survived those first days after the accident, barricaded against the dazzling whiteness of the sterile world. People came and went, and she let them. They spoke to her, and she ignored them. Most of the time, she dozed, plunging back into the calm darkness. Drifting in the warm, deep waters cushioned her from the drumming pain in her head and the vicious rawness of her damaged throat. She reluctantly surfaced for long enough to comply with requests to eat this, swallow that; and then dived back into the soothing caress of sleep.

Only once had she taken part in conversation. It was the morning of the second or third day—she wasn't sure. She had, without thinking, opened her eyes in response to a doctor's tentative inquiry, and then felt obliged to engage further.

"Kate? It's Doctor Lee. I've come to check on you again. Could you open your eyes for me?"

Oh, how she wished she'd stayed strong, not allowing herself to be tricked into the compliant habits of normal society. She should have refused the polite request, should have ignored the question—then she would have avoided what came next.

"Well, Kate. It's great to see you awake. How are you feeling today?"

The young doctor's voice had that silky tone people used before they told you something you didn't want to hear. Thoughts tumbled through Kate's mind, but the ability to pluck out the ones she needed eluded her at first. And then one pushed itself forward from the writhing mass and formed into words.

"My husband?" she asked. The name came to her. "Alex?"

A puzzled expression flashed across the doctor's face and disappeared, replaced with the sympathetic mask of calm.

"Kate, do you remember what happened? Do you know why you're here?"

She remembered. A winding road washed with sheets of heavy rain. Headlights veering towards her and then sliding, spinning—and the sound. The excruciating scream of metal was unlike anything else she had ever heard.

"Yes, I remember," she said, her voice toneless. "It was raining. There was an accident." She asked the doctor again. "But what about Alex? Where's Alex?"

The doctor, ignoring her plaintive query, patiently explained. "Yes, Kate, you were in an accident." She hesitated, frowned a little, inhaled a slow deep breath, and continued. "Kate, I'm so very sorry. Your husband—James Beckett—he didn't make it. They worked extremely hard to save him, but his injuries were too severe. I am so sorry," she repeated.

Kate lay back and closed her eyes and his face was in her mind; James Beckett, her husband. A sweep of dark hair, a wide cheeky smile. Laughing. Yes, he laughed a lot.

Although the doctor spoke with gentle, carefully chosen words, they caused pain far beyond what she'd endured physically. To dull bodily pain was simple. Whenever it grew too much to bear, with a press of the button, the pump oozed blessed morphine into her veins. But the doctor confirmed what she'd suspected—she had survived, James had not. The only respite from this new anguish was to seek refuge back in her dark world. She vowed that no-one should spoil it for her again.

Therefore, a rush of annoyance surged through her body when, one afternoon, they lured her into opening her eyes again. Lying there, simply listening to the sounds of the hospital ward, provided a soothing constancy. After days of shutting out all other senses, her hearing had become noticeably more acute.

The care assistants who shuffled along in Crocs knew not to venture into room 16 with offers of tea. The squeaky-wheeled trolleys trundled past her door, not bothering to stop. She caught snippets of cheery conversations as they moved on to her neighbours.

Nurses walked by on brisk, sneakered feet. So much to do, so many patients. She didn't mind them shunning her to attend to others.

In the mornings doctors came with steady, confident steps. They'd stop to ponder her charts, murmur to the nurses, and leave. She was usually safe from their scrutiny for the rest of the day.

She had developed a strange pride in her ability to separate out the passing parade by the sound of their footsteps. But this time she couldn't identify the measured tread approaching her room. She knew for certain that it wasn't any of the usual ward inhabitants.

Curiosity piqued, her eyes flew open without thinking. Two uniformed figures stood in the doorway. Navy and blue; police officers. Tricked again, she met their inquiring gaze and confirmed she was awake.

"Mrs Beckett, we're sorry to trouble you, but we're trying to establish the facts surrounding your accident. We've got a few questions. Is it OK if we come in?"

They didn't appear sorry, not that it was possible to read their faces, since masks obscured all but their eyes. *Why the masks?* She pondered for a moment before her brain retrieved the words: Covid.

While the accident had changed her world forever, outside these walls, the virus had altered the world in unimaginable ways. She'd overheard the concerned chatter in the corridors. The looming threat of a global pandemic was now a reality. While locked down inside her traumatised body, the entire country had also locked down tight. Some conversations sounded hopeful. Perhaps this disease might spare the little island nation she called home from its worst.

Maybe for others in the city beyond these walls there was light at the end of the tunnel, but there was no escape for her. Her husband was dead, she had suffered a serious head injury, and a lonely future stretched endlessly ahead of her.

The officers appeared satisfied with her mumbled recount of the accident. With a single exception.

"Mrs Beckett, there's one other question," said the younger man. "The doctor told us you asked about someone called Alex. Was there someone else in the car with you? Was Alex with you in the car?"

She gazed out the window, replaying the earlier conversation with Doctor Lee. Her brain was immersed in a billowing fog.

"Yes, my husband... no...," she hesitated, confused by the question. Then, mercifully, a few misty strands cleared. "No," she said, meeting the police officer's eyes, more confident now. "No, it was only my husband and I in the car. My husband—James," she answered. "Not Alex."

Part One - Here

CHAPTER 1

Tomorrow

Auckland, New Zealand - May 2007

"CHOIR PRACTICE TONIGHT?"

Nicky's tousled dark head poked around the corner of Kate's classroom door.

"Yeah, count me in. I'll be there with bells on."

She grinned at the invitation. Unaware that 'choir practice' was teacher code for 'drinks at the pub after school', the two little girls sitting on the mat playing with Lego exchanged wide-eyed looks, clearly impressed by this new revelation that their teacher could not only sing but had other musical abilities.

"Meet me in the car park at three. I'll just need to grab the twins and we can head down there straight away."

Nicky bustled off to her classroom, while Kate turned to the whiteboard to finish writing up the day's timetable. Pride washed over her at the realisation she'd survived this first week back without crashing. And grateful—for the school principal who'd given her leave to nurse her dying grandmother; for these women, her colleagues and friends who'd checked in with her all the way along that arduous journey, including those terrible last days when her grandmother's life ebbed away. And now wrapping her up in their warm, supportive kindness as she returned to work. The prospect of ending the day, relaxing with them at their favourite local bar, offered a reassuring sense of normality after a tumultuous year.

One advantage of a busy teaching day was that three o'clock rolled around quickly, and by three-thirty she was sipping a glass of fruity white wine at an outdoor table. Although April had rolled into May, it was a balmy late autumn day, with no hint of winter waiting just around the corner.

Sitting in the bar, gazing across the road at the beach, the lively breeze and sparkling sea reminded her that there were other things she'd put aside for the last six months while Nan was ill. Tonight she'd give her friend Ange a call, see if she and Tony were going out on the boat this weekend. She'd lived so much of her life on the water, and the waves called to her, beckoning the sailor back to the sea.

"Right, that's them sorted."

Nicky slid onto the bench seat next to her, joining the cluster of eager teachers in a well-earned end of week drink.

"They look happy," said Kate. In a well-practised drill, Nicky had installed her six-year-old twin boys in a convenient play area, with a fizzy drink and a packet of chips each. "You know," she added, "I'm still amazed at how you do it."

"Well, it's a case of having to, really. If I want a life." Nicky hadn't let the inconvenience of falling pregnant six months into her second year of teaching, or the resulting lively twins, hold back either her career or her social life. "They are hard work. Not sure how I ended up with two such naughty little monkeys. But I wouldn't be without them." She cast a doting look at her offspring, who were, as twins often are, completely happy as long as they were together.

It would be easy to be envious of Nicky. She had it all. These two sweet boys. A partner who adored her, and who she loved despite the many flaws she seemed to find in him. She moaned about Chris all the time, but it was tongue in cheek. Everyone could see they were the picture perfect family. Kate wondered if they would eventually get around to the big wedding that Nicky said he owed her. In her teaching career, Nicky had also jumped on the fast track to success. A team leader now, she already had her eye on the Deputy Principal's job.

"So how was it? First week back ticked off?" Nicky asked, in her usual upbeat way.

Kate, pulled from her thoughts, almost gave her the expected polite answer, to say it was fine. But underneath, it wasn't—and this was Nicky. She could tell her the truth.

"I survived. But to be honest, this time away, it's made me realise I don't want to do this anymore. I'm going nowhere fast."

"Something to do with turning over another birthday?"

Nicky was so damn astute. Kate's thirtieth birthday celebration a few months ago had been a low-key affair, given the circumstances. But as the decade of her twenties faded from view, niggling worries had surfaced. Sitting at her grandmother's bedside, she'd had time to think. All her friends the same age seemed to have done so much with their lives: husbands, children, careers, travel. Whereas she was just marking time, caught in some grey in-between, the whirl of competitive sailing, university days and the exciting first steps into teaching behind her. Tomorrow was just a vague nothing.

"Yeah, a bit. I think I need a change. A big change."

"Like what?"

"Well, I wondered if I should do the OE thing? You know, go to London. See a bit of the world. I've been places with the sailing comps, but that's history now. And even then, outside of the racing, we only saw the inside of a hotel or a gym."

"You should go for it, Kate. Did it myself a few years ago." Marnie Perry, Kate's own team leader, leaned across the table having overheard their conversation. "I won't lie—it can be bloody hard work in some schools. Some of the inner city ones are concrete jungles. The kids were pretty wild, too," she laughed, rolling her eyes. "But if you get into a good school, well, it's fabulous. The holidays are great. Every six weeks, you get a term break. Lots of bank holiday weekends. And Europe on your doorstep."

"So how do you get started?" Kate asked, encouraged by Marnie's enthusiasm.

"The big agencies have people over here. They do presentations every so often. You just go along and before you know it, you're signed up, guaranteed a job. You know we'd be sad to lose you, having only just got you back. But I've come to realise this is just a job. Life comes first. If you think you want to do it, I say go for it."

"Thanks Marnie, I'll look into it."

Kate felt relief at Marnie's support. It would help to assuage her guilt if she was to up and leave the workplace that had supported her so whole-heartedly through the dark months.

"One other benefit, of course," Marnie added with a smug smile. "The English men are adorable, and there's so many of them. Worked for me." She winked and threw an appreciative glance at the attractive blonde-haired man seated at the far end of the long table.

It certainly *had* worked for Marnie. She'd met her teacher husband, Phillip, in a school in Kent. And seeing him there, in animated conversation with another colleague, his appealing Yorkshire accent drifting across the room, Kate saw a glimpse of possibility. Maybe this could be how her own happily ever after story might end.

CHAPTER 2

On The Way

Auckland, New Zealand - May 2007

KATE STOPPED MID-STRIDE AND took a hasty step back from the door, embarrassed heat spreading across her cheeks as she realised her mistake. In her hurry to make it on time, she'd blundered into the wrong room. The inhabitants of Seminar Room 4 in no way resembled likely candidates for a presentation on 'Teaching in the UK'. Their faces registered surprise, too. She was not who they expected, either.

She'd bustled her students out the door and leapt into her car at exactly 3.07 p.m., according to the dashboard clock, but she was still running late. The traffic had been horrendous. The slightest drop of rain and Aucklanders rushed to their cars, clogging the motorways.

She stopped to catch her breath and read the sign on the door: 'Getting Started on Your Family History'. That explained the gaggle of silver-haired women in the room who'd stopped their chatter to stare at this intruder.

"Don't think I need to get started on that," she muttered, as she trailed through the maze of corridors, hoping to find the correct room on this floor of the Plaza Hotel.

Today was her first brave step towards breaking free of her past, to make her own way in the world. It was time to put herself out there. Find someone. 'If you do what you've always done, you'll get what you've always got.' That's what the conventional wisdom said. And what she'd always got was loneliness and disappointment. So this time, she was going to do something different. She wouldn't be the first Kiwi girl to bring home the perfect man from the UK. Goodness knows she hadn't met anyone here that came close to being Mr Right.

After five minutes trailing around the hotel corridors, Kate located the room: 14, not 4. She berated herself for not checking more carefully in her haste. Noticing a spare seat in the back row, where her lateness wouldn't be obvious, she slipped into it, another hopeful face amongst rows of others. All eyes focused on the glowing screen, intent on the possibilities that awaited them in England. Forty-five minutes later, she'd signed up.

"I think that's everything we need for now." There was a note of triumph in the agent's voice as she handed over a thick folder of information, no doubt pleased at the commission she'd receive for recruiting each keen young teacher. "We'll keep in touch by email so you'll know to look out for the rest of the paperwork in the mail."

Leafing through the swag of papers, Kate experienced her own small surge of victory. They'd promised her a job in London by the start of the new British school year and help to get herself established. She hadn't chickened out, although it would have been easy to do so. Two months and then this was happening.

She slid the folder into her bag to protect it from the still falling rain and made a run for the car. Ripping the door open, she flung herself inside, relieved to find shelter. A gift sat on the passenger's seat, the stylish wrapping hinting at its contents. Intricate paisley patterned paper echoed the swirling designs etched on the Moroccan bracelet nestled underneath. An explosive gold tulle bow provided the final flourish. Her hunt for the perfect gift had taken her all over the city, and she hoped her friend Tracey would appreciate her choice when she freed it from the nest of magenta tissue inside.

After fighting her way across town in rush hour traffic, the universe smiled on her. Finding a park on this busy Ponsonby street was always problematic. She jerked the wheel in a sharp u-turn, claiming a newly-vacated space right opposite Tracey's apartment block. Tucking the precious present into her coat, she braced herself for the rain and dived out of the door. In the apartment block's entry foyer, she studied her bedraggled appearance in a strategically placed mirror. A quick flick of a comb, a touch of lip gloss, and she looked respectable enough to take the lift to the third floor.

Tracey swung the door wide, a glass of bubbly in hand.

"Happy birthday. Looks like the celebration has begun," Kate said, swapping the gift for a proffered glass.

"Not every day you turn thirty," said Tracey. "Thanks for coming. I know we've got the party on Saturday, but I so wanted to do something today."

They were unlikely friends. Tracey, an in-demand makeup artist with her own line of products, an upmarket clientele and a love of fashion and night-clubbing; Kate, a fresh-faced athlete, most at home in shorts and trainers. They'd met in the A&E department one Saturday evening four years ago, both nursing suspected broken ankles—Tracey from falling from the heights of her heels at an afternoon cocktail party, Kate from a less glamorous tumble off slippery jetty steps. The incredibly slow rate at which patients trickled through triage provided enough time to share their life stories. Three hours later, with their injuries pronounced as only bad sprains, a firm friendship had been born.

"Katie, Katie, Katie!" The urgent voice bubbled up from the small person now wrapped around her legs like shackles, rendering her unable to move. She bent down and scooped the little girl into her arms.

"Well hello there, little Miss Brooke. How are you this evening?"

She adored Tracey's three-year-old, and the feeling was mutual. Brooke gave off a sweet, freshly washed smell, her still damp curls fragrant with fruity shampoo. Her chubby face glowed a delicate pink, flushed from the warmth of her evening bath. She drank in the smell, enjoying the comforting weight of the child enfolded in her arms. Brooke's innocent adoration spoke to a longing deep inside her. One day, it would be her own child.

"I'm good. Mummy's birthday," Brooke said, pointing at her mother. In the past few weeks, Brooke had discovered her ability to use speech as a magnet for the attention of others, turning into a veritable chatterbox in her attempts to monopolise the conversation.

"Yes, Mummy's birthday. Did you have cake?"

"Yes, I had cake. Yummy." One little hand pointed towards a white frosting swirled creation on the kitchen bench, while the other attempted to wipe away the sticky evidence smeared around her mouth.

"I promised she could stay up until you arrived," said Tracey. "Right, my darling, shall we get Kate to pop you into bed and then she can come and have a drink with the grownups?"

Having extracted a solemn promise from Brooke that she would stay in bed, they wandered out to where Tracey's boyfriend and the other guests clustered in small groups. Introductions made, Tracey waved her into a comfortable white leather chair and sat opposite, her face expectant.

"Now, tell me—how did it go?" Tracey couldn't hide her impatience. She'd been nagging Kate to do something about the idea ever since she'd mentioned going overseas in casual conversation a month ago.

"So, I did it. It's all arranged with the agency. I'm going."

"Good on you." She stretched out a hand, giving Kate's a squeeze of approval. "It's about time you put yourself first. You did right by your grandparents, but now it's your time."

"I only did what anyone would have."

"No," Tracey said, shaking her head in disagreement. "I don't know anyone else of our age who would have thrown in the job they loved to care for their sick grandmother. You are one in a million. Remember, it's your turn. You deserve this."

At the time her grandmother became ill six months ago, Kate saw no other option. The struggle had left her exhausted and emotionally drained. All those appointments, with this doctor, that specialist, each contributing their knowledge to prolonging her grandmother's life. And sitting next to her in the chemo sessions, amidst the rows of armchairs, next to each a bag of fluid, dripping little beads of hope into a desperate arm; around them a room full of cancer patients, the sound of quiet chatter, an unexpected chirpiness considering their plight. Cancer hit everyone hard, but for an old lady in her seventies, it was insurmountable. In the end Vera insisted the treatment stop, choosing to fade away, quietly drifting off to meet her beloved Bill again, wrapped in a cloud of morphine to dull the pain.

"Well, I bet she and Grandad will both be looking down with big smiles. They'd approve of me going. It's like I know the country even though I've never been there. All my childhood, I listened to their stories of 'the motherland'."

"Yeah, I remember hearing a few of them myself," said Tracey. "You couldn't stop old Bill when he was in full flight telling a yarn."

"And at last I've got something of value from my father. That British passport—it means I can stay as long as I want."

"Cheers to that," said Tracey, tapping her glass against Kate's with a clink. "Come on, let's tell the others your news."

After dallying at the party for longer than planned, it was already after midnight when she crawled into bed. Sleep eluded her, even though she wanted nothing more than to rest. Tomorrow was a school day. She couldn't afford to arrive tired and jaded to front a class of eight-year-olds. Little people were demanding.

But despite trying to deflect them, thoughts bubbled to the surface. So much to prepare. Only two months to get her life here in order so she could leave it behind. In the end, she surrendered to her need to organise. Crawling out of bed, she rummaged in her desk for pen and paper and began a list. Scrambling back into bed an hour later, the clock warning her it was now two a.m., she felt a quiet satisfaction with her scrawled list, and excitement that each one ticked off was a step towards her new life.

But sleep still danced out of reach. Despite the comfort of her list, a small niggle of disquiet remained. In the classroom, she took charge naturally, and never questioned her own competence. She'd understood the end goal and had known from the first day at university how she would attain it. Through her years in the sailing world, she'd displayed a dogged determination, and a ruthless fearlessness, spurred on by a strong competitive streak.

Visualising what she needed to do to succeed had always come easily. She mapped out the most effective route to the end point and went for it. The love from her students, the praise from parents and colleagues, the wins and trophies—all those things stood as proof of what she could accomplish. But this was different. This wasn't a job. This wasn't a sport. This was her life. And she had no clear vision of the endgame, let alone whether this road would lead her to it.

No Going Back Now

London, England - August 2007

"THIS IS IT, LOVE," droned the taxi driver.

"I think it's down there." Kate pointed at a gap between the houses, where a narrow right-of-way was only just visible, a tunnel beneath gloomy overhanging trees.

"It may well be love, but you'll have to get out here." He met her gaze without blinking, steely resolve in his eyes. "Won't take the cab down there, I'm afraid. Half these places there's not enough room to swing a cat, let alone turn a car."

With a sigh, she thrust a twenty-pound note at him. He made no move to help her unload the cases, and she immediately regretted not insisting on change. He didn't deserve a tip on top of the sixteen pound fare. She hefted the two enormous suitcases from the depths of the cab and lugged them onto the high-sided kerb, hoping it wasn't too far down the driveway. Manoeuvering both of them would be a challenge.

She stopped for a moment to survey the street. Grand terrace houses flanked the pavement. Their elaborate frontages reminded her of white icing on a wedding cake. She'd spent many evenings watching her grandmother creating swirling edible decorations that transformed a brandy-soaked fruit cake into the stunning centrepiece of someone's special day. Kate had marvelled as her deft hands wove intricate lace, delicate lattice patterns, and twirling scrolls. The window frames and balconies of the houses surrounding her sported the same elegant flourishes.

The tang of rain hung in the air. She scanned the looming grey sky. Right on cue, large staccato drops peppered her upturned face, spurring her into action. She was strong for a woman of her size, the product of years of sailing. Hauling on lines and wrestling with steering a boat built muscle that came in handy. She set off down the driveway, wrangling an unruly case in each hand.

Tucked in behind the glorious Georgian terraces was a row of 70s townhouses. Finding her way to the far end of the five units, she stood in front of her new flat. In their day, real estate agents would have described them as a 'smart entry level opportunity' in an inner London suburb. The exteriors, now tired and jaded, gave them a sad, unloved appearance.

"You'll love it," the room's previous occupant had enthused when organising the handover by phone. "Two minutes' walk from Earls Court station."

She'd been so lucky to find this place through the informal network of Kiwi teachers who flowed back and forth between London and New Zealand. The location was perfect, and up close, the flat itself wasn't too bad either. The second-floor balcony provided a handy refuge from the now insistent rain. Her knock on the door prompted a tumble of footsteps on stairs. A slim blonde-haired girl flung it open in welcome.

"Kate, come in," she said, her Australian accent broad. "I'm Sophie. Great to meet you." She sized up the two enormous suitcases. "Well, the good news is you don't have to lug *them* upstairs. This is your room right here." She motioned to a glass sliding door. "Wait here. I'll zip through and unlock it."

Kate stood facing a wall of glass. A cascade of gauzy fabric masked the interior. This must have once been a garage, like that of the neighbouring unit. Sophie appeared through the glass, whisking back the curtains and sliding open the huge door.

"This is a great room," said Sophie. "I think you'll like it. Matt and I considered moving down here, but decided it was too much effort."

The glass frontage, white painted interior and pale wooden floor created an airiness.

"It's nice." In fact, it was far better than she'd expected. Not at all like the stereotypical dingy flats of a London OE.

"It is. You're the only one of us on the ground floor," said Sophie. "Only downside is you might hear us clomping around upstairs."

"Oh—it's got a bathroom."

She ventured past the low bed into a tiny ensuite. Compact for sure, but at least it was all hers. She'd never flatted before, so this would be a gentle introduction to sharing a space with strangers.

"Yeah, back in the day someone did short-term holiday lets. Put in the bathroom and somewhere you can make a coffee. The main kitchen's upstairs. And there's a decent lounge there too, if you want."

Flopping down on the bed, she found it was more comfortable than it appeared.

"I love it already," she said, and it was true.

"I know you're probably shattered after the flight, but you should come up and say hi. Not often we're all home at the same time, so it's a good chance to get the introductions over," said Sophie. She led the way upstairs, where they found the other occupants scattered across the kitchen and adjoining lounge.

"So, can I interest you in a glass of wine? Or a beer?"

The young man standing in the kitchen had a distinctive Irish lilt. His conservative dark suit was a stark contrast to the wild, stalky hair and a pair of Nike trainers that peeped out from underneath the too-long trousers pooled around his feet.

"A beer would be great. Thanks."

"I'm Damian," he said, flicking the cap off the bottle in one swift movement. "From Dublin." He handed her the beer, then shed his suit jacket and plonked himself on the bar stool next to her. "Cheers," he said, clinking his own bottle against hers. "Welcome to the flat."

She sipped at the dark ale, its thick bitterness surprisingly refreshing. She hadn't realised how thirsty she was. Solely focused on getting from the airport to the flat, she hadn't bothered to stop for a drink. After a forty-minute journey on the train and nearly that again in the cab, she was starving as well. Without food in her stomach, while fighting a creeping tiredness, and disoriented from the effects of the beer, she had to make a conscious effort to follow the chatter between her new flat mates.

Soon Sophie and her boyfriend Matt made a move to leave, heading off to their bar jobs. "Doesn't pay too well," she said. "But having the days free means we've seen heaps of the city."

"Plus, while we're working behind the bar, we're not spending money on the other side of it," Matt added. "Not like the other Aussies—swimming in so much alcohol they won't remember most of their time here."

Jenny, the fourth flatmate, wore nurse's scrubs. "Great to have another New Zealander," she said, as she too prepared to leave for her evening shift. "Maybe tomorrow you can catch me up on things from home."

She pulled on a heavy jacket, grabbed a large, colourful tote bag and headed for the train station, leaving Damian in charge of the rest of Kate's induction.

"Let me cook you dinner," he offered. "Since it's your first night. You look exhausted."

Although a little odd, he was friendly. She sat on a high stool at the kitchen bench while he set to work. A plate of beans on toast wasn't quite what she'd expected. But she'd been awake for close to twenty-four hours and the ordinariness of sitting here while he pottered at the stove made her immediately feel at home.

"So what do you do, Damian?" she asked.

"I'm in IT," he said. "Pays well. And, although I have to wear a monkey suit, most of the time I deal with the clients remotely, so I get away with wearing these." He pointed at his incongruous footwear. "You're a teacher?" he asked.

"Yeah, one more week of the school holidays and then it's game on."

"Couldn't pay me enough," he said. "Shit, the kids would all have left by the end of the day if I was in charge."

Her laughter and confident smile hid an unsettled lurch in her stomach, provoked by thoughts of the new job. She tried to put the nervousness aside and focused on attacking the puddle of baked beans that flowed across a small mountain of hot buttered toast. Comfort food. It was exactly what she needed.

CHAPTER 4

Sister

London, England - August 2007

KATE ARRIVED DISHEVELLED FROM the crush of a rush-hour tube ride. The sad looking inner-city school wasn't the least bit inviting. It resembled a prison compound, with imposing security fences surrounding a concrete playground. There wasn't a single tree or blade of grass. The contrast between this and the sprawling grassy fields of the school she'd left behind couldn't be greater.

Nagging doubts eroded the thrill of being on her big adventure. In her heart, she knew she was a capable teacher, and one whose students liked and respected her. But Marnie's warnings about London schools that looked just like this, inhabited by feral children, echoed in her brain. But she also recalled the soothing words of the recruitment consultant and the brochure's cheerful testimonials: 'good pay and teacher-friendly schools', 'a remarkable experience'. Well, now she would find out which was the reality.

She stepped through the door to a friendly welcome from the receptionist. To be met with a smile was a positive sign. She'd worked in some schools where ferocious, intimidating women inhabited the admin area, but Deena was obviously not from that mold. A mass of spectacular braids, gleaming oily black, intricately woven and accented with beads, framed a cheerful face.

"Come with me," she said. "Your classroom's in this block. Very handy, in fact—staffroom's there, copier room next door and the bathroom on the other side. You'll appreciate that on a wet day."

Although well-located, the classroom was dismal. She put on a brave smile, masking the dismay that overcame her as Deena ushered her through the door, where a nasty, musty smell lurked. Deena wrinkled her nose in distaste as the odour engulfed them.

"A bit stale in here. Been locked up for weeks, of course."

"No worries. I'll open the windows and let some fresh air in. It'll be fine."

"Well, anything you need, you pop down and see me."

She made a mental note to keep in with Deena. Not only had she been genuinely helpful, it was well-known that the office staff were the centre of a school and keeping them onside was the first rule of a harmonious workplace. She was pleased they'd made a good start.

"The head will be in soon. I'll bring her over to meet you."

She hoped to make a good impression on the head teacher, too. They'd exchanged emails, but their first in-person meeting would be important. She smoothed her hair and straightened her clothes in preparation.

She surveyed the room. These four walls would form the limits of her workday world for the next year. The bare blue pin-boards framed by paintwork of drab brown added to the gloomy atmosphere. With only a sliver of natural light from a bank of small high windows, it was hard to summon enthusiasm for the place—not at all welcoming for a group of eight-year-olds returning from the long summer break. *We'll soon fix that.* She could already imagine an art project to both win over the kids and brighten the space. She set about emptying her backpack, arranging pens and pencils on the top of a battle-scarred desk.

She jerked her head away from the task at the sound of the door flinging open. A wild-looking woman, hair askew and outlandishly dressed, burst into the room. At first Kate wondered if this was some irate parent, about to lecture her about something for which she couldn't yet be held responsible. She took shelter behind the small desk and prepared to defend herself. But realising that the speed with which the woman had propelled herself into the room was enthusiasm, not anger, she relaxed.

"Hi there. So excited to meet you," she gushed. "I'm Ellie Beckett—your neighbour across the corridor—Room 3B, Grade 3 like you. And you must be Kate?"

It looked as if Ellie Beckett had attempted to tame her sunburst of red hair by pulling it into a messy bun. It might have passed for a kind of scruffy chic on a young lawyer in a smart suit, or a doctor in a white coat with clipboard in hand. Instead, matched with floral Doc Martens, flowing skirts and a hand-knitted cowl, she looked like some anachronistic hippie. A rainbow of chunky jewellery adorned her hands, wrists and neck, completing the picture. But from the amiable smile and the welcoming eyes, Kate sensed that this was someone who she would be pleased to have in her life.

"Well, you'll be super busy before the kids arrive, so I'll leave you to it. But how about I swing by and take you over to morning tea? Good luck." And then she flitted off in a whirl of colour, like a youthful fairy godmother.

As the blare of the morning tea bell died away, Ellie appeared in the doorway as promised.

"Come on, if we're quick, we can be first to the coffee machine. Right here near the staffroom is the best thing about these classrooms. Call it payback for sticking us in the grotty old part of the school."

She followed Ellie, her earlier nervousness all but drained. It helped that she'd made a positive start with the headteacher. Priyanka Sharma, a diminutive woman in high heels and an air of kind authority, had popped in for a brief conversation and then, having seemingly judged Kate to be as competent in person as she appeared on paper, moved on to the next class.

Kate's students were a diverse bunch representing a multitude of ethnicities and cultures, as was to be expected in this vast city. But kids were kids, and she knew how to build relationships with them—in fact, was very good at it—and the first two hours had passed smoothly. However, she was thankful to have Ellie alongside to help her navigate the next hurdle of being a newbie—meeting her workmates.

True to Ellie's prediction, they arrived before anyone else. Perched on two of the battered vinyl chairs, they watched others sigh as they joined the coffee queue snaking back to the door. The room was a sea of unfamiliar faces. Some looked at her with blank disinterest. Others shot polite, curious glances. There were smiles of welcome from others, and some of these drifted in to join them, their chairs drawn up to circle an ageing faux wood coffee table.

"Kate's first day in an English school. All the way from New Zealand." Ellie made the effort to introduce her to each new person and by the time the bell signalled their return to class, a small happy buzz had replaced her gnawing uncertainty. This felt like a place she could belong.

Ellie Beckett was one of those people who it was easy to get to know. She freely shared about herself, invited questions and in the space of one lunchtime, Kate already felt like they'd established the beginnings of a friendship.

"I grew up here, in London. Over in Bethnal Green. A genuine East Ender. It's a pretty hip part of town these days, but we're still a down-to-earth lot."

That explained the accent. Kate's ears were already becoming attuned to the multitude of dialects that were conveniently lumped together as English. In this one room alone, she might have picked out ten different lilting accents, rising and falling in the hubbub of the first day of term conversations.

"So, does your family still live there?"

"Mum does. Won't ever get her to leave that house of hers. She loves it there. Dad buggered off years ago. To be honest, we don't miss him." Despite her words, Kate saw a fleeting look of sadness, perhaps recognising her own feelings about absent parents in her new friend's eyes.

"And then there's James, my brother. Well, you'd never find him living back in the East End, no matter how many magazine articles try to sell it as up-and-coming. He's certainly left all that behind. No, James lives in Bayswater, very upmarket. And traitor that I am to my modest roots, I'm living there with him." Her face came alive as she talked about her brother, evidence of the bond between siblings that, as an only child, Kate would never experience or understand. "Well, that's when he's home. He travels a lot. He's a TV producer. Don't ask me exactly what that means. All I know is it keeps him very busy and pays him a shitload of money."

By the end of the day, Ellie had established that they took the same tube line, informed her that no one stayed and worked late onsite in these schools, escorted her to the station, synchronised their plans for the train journey the next morning, and waved enthusiastically from the carriage window as Kate hopped off at her stop.

She arrived at her empty flat, tired but euphoric. Her first day had gone far better than she'd expected in so many ways. What she hadn't expected was to make a friend. She poured herself a wine to celebrate and set to marking the thirty books she'd lugged home in her backpack.

On Friday, Ellie insisted Kate come out with her, and they went from an after school session at the pub, to a huge group table at a cheap and cheerful Indian restaurant, ending up at a heaving Notting Hill bar where Kate found herself surrounded by Ellie's massive circle of friends. Perhaps a solar system would be more apt: Ellie, the sun in the centre, with her flaming hair and flamboyant clothes, orbited by a diverse group of people, all caught in the gravitational pull of her carefree laugh, quirky conversation, and irrepressible sense of fun. Tall and striking, she dominated the room, both with her appearance and her personality.

Kate noticed the intriguing way Ellie drew the men of the group to her like moths to a flame, yet appeared to have no particular attachment to any of them. Admirers surrounded her, all intently listening to her latest anecdote, adoration in their eyes. Even when animated, Ellie's features were more handsome than pretty, but those unusual cat-like amber eyes beckoned them in. However, not one of them seemed anything more than a friend. It surprised her that such a vibrant woman should be thirty-two and unattached.

As they walked along the dark streets, winding their way back to the train station, Kate's curiosity got the better of her. She kept her tone light and teasing. "So no one special there, Ellie? A couple of those guys seemed to pay you an awful lot of attention. Not to mention buying you flash drinks."

Ellie's laugh was hollow as she quickly brushed aside the question. "Nah. They're good fun, but that's about it. We all know each other too well to be anything more than drinking mates."

Something in her words made Kate suspect that Ellie's confident exterior masked doubt. Why she should doubt that someone would love the real her, Kate couldn't understand. Even having only known her a week, she would describe Ellie Beckett as one of the most loveable people she had ever met. In fact, meeting her was like finding a long-lost sister.

CHAPTER 5

Girls' Night In

London, England - September 2007

"Wow, so you really don't have any family? That's tough."

Ellie's voice was sympathetic, but she couldn't hide the curiosity on her face. Clad in retro striped flannelette pyjamas and fluffy slippers that resembled two dead cats, her outfit was at odds with the stylish, expensive-looking couch where she perched. She clutched a bowl-shaped glass in one hand, half filled with liquid the colour of ripe plums.

They'd already made a large dent in the bottle of wine. It sat on a huge rustic chest that could have come from a pirate ship, with its massive iron hinges and rough-hewn timber sides. It made a rather spectacular coffee table. With her other hand, she scrabbled around in an enormous bowl heaped with popcorn. Kate too munched on a hand full of fluffy kernels, the buttery saltiness bringing back childhood memories.

'Big girls' sleepover' they'd called it. On an autumn night so unseasonably cold out that even the pub was an unappealing prospect, they'd settled in to eat, drink, and watch movies. And talk. Spending time here with Ellie, in this huge sprawling house, provided an attractive alternative to her own more modest flat, even though with flatmates either working or clubbing, they would have had it to themselves .

"Yeah, that sums it up," said Kate from the depths of an oversized armchair. It was like being embraced in a warm hug, the leather softly curled around her. Explaining her family circumstances was hard, the memories raw, even after all these years; memories of a four-year-old who had recognised her parents' pleasure when Nana Vera and Grandad Bill arrived on their doorstep one day.

She still heard her grandfather's voice. "We can't stand by and do nothing any longer. Katie's coming with us." Bill was insistent. Her parents hadn't argued. Even through the haze that enveloped their drug-addled brains, they'd registered an arrangement that left them free of any responsibilities.

"Get her things," directed Vera. They'd loaded thin pale wee Kate, one supermarket bag of scruffy clothes and two sad-looking teddies into the Holden Kingswood and sped off without a backward glance.

Relieved of their small burden, Kate's parents wasted no time in leaving the country. The last anyone knew, they were still in Bali. She sometimes wondered how they'd avoided jail all these years. But she was grateful for that. Not for any love of them; she couldn't have borne the media furor that always ensued when the Balinese authorities caught Kiwis with drugs and threw them into their frightening jails. She imagined herself on the front page of the New Zealand Herald: 'Abandoned child still hasn't forgiven her parents—says they can rot in hell.'

She twirled the ruby and diamond ring she wore on her right hand. That engagement ring must have cost a tremendous amount for her grandfather, back when he was a labourer on minimum wage. But he had never skimped on the woman he loved. On her middle finger sat a man's signet ring. The engraved letters were hard to see, polished smooth from years of wear. But it soothed her to run her fingers across it, the initials '*WM*' faintly discernible to her touch.

The thought of her grandparents brought both the sweetest memories and tangible pain. Her childhood without parents or siblings had still been a happy one. Vera and Bill had been more than enough. Perhaps their disappointment and outright shame at their son's willing surrender of his child led them to overcompensate. They had wrapped her in love, provided well for her material needs, as well as encouraging her to aim for the stars. But now they were gone. Realising she'd ignored Ellie while lost in thought, she snapped back into the moment, responding to her new friend's expectation of more details.

"Well, my parents—as far as I know—are alive. Though I doubt you could say alive and well. You can't expect your body to hold out forever when you've spent that many years putting shit into it. I've been told that my mother runs a stall in a beach market, selling junk to tourists. And my father works in a bar."

"They say Bali's beautiful," Ellie mused. "But your mum and dad are crazy to be doing drugs there. God, even here that Schapelle Corby woman was on the news every night."

"Exactly," said Kate. "Somehow they've sailed above it—or perhaps more appropriately slid below it. God knows how. Local knowledge perhaps. They've been there almost thirty years."

"But your grandparents, they were like parents to you, weren't they?"

"Yeah." She smiled, thinking of them. "Best of British they were. Lots of you Poms came to New Zealand in the 50s. It was pretty hard for their generation—born in the depression, grew up during the war. And after the war, things were tough here. They ran promotions encouraging people to immigrate—'come to the promised land' type of stuff."

"And was it? The promised land?" Ellie asked.

"Oh yeah, they never regretted it. They moved from a council house in a dingy part of Manchester to their own little house by the sea in Auckland." That house was hers now. And she'd left it. She quickly brushed the thought away, determined not to let homesickness spoil this adventure. She kept on talking to keep her mind off it. "And Grandad had steady, well-paid work. On construction sites. Hard work, but it suited him."

"What about your grandmother? She was happy there?"

"She loved it. Once my father was at school, she decided she wanted a job. Worked in the corner store for thirty years. She was in her element—all the people coming in, daily chit-chat, the gossip. She knew *everything* that went on it that community."

"Like Coronation Street?" Ellie laughed.

"That's it," said Kate. "You know her name was Vera? Like Vera Duckworth? But she looked more like Betty Turpin. We used to tease her about that."

Kate could still picture her. Dark hair laced with silver, always arranged in neat waves. Lively eyes, topped with expressive brows. A firm mouth to match her determination. God, she missed them.

"And with them being from Manchester, you could have picked them up and dropped them into the Rovers Return and they would have fitted in perfectly."

"Made them nostalgic for the old country, I suppose," Ellie said.

"Yes, it was compulsory viewing. To be honest, I quite liked it. How embarrassing. But it was something we did together. "

"Don't worry, so did we," confessed Ellie. "My mum is proud to be Scottish, but I remember when we were kids she was addicted to English soaps. Still is, I think. Coro, East Enders, Emmerdale—she loved them all."

"I can't wait to meet her. She sounds like a strong lady, raising you two on her own."

"Yeah, she did a great job. Jamie and I weren't easy at times. Never in real trouble, but we didn't exactly conform. And with our dad taking off before we were in our teens, she had the worst of it on her own," Ellie said. "She was called in to school a fair few times. She still can't believe I'm a teacher. Says she hopes I'm getting payback for all the grief I gave to my teachers." From the spark of mischief in her eyes, Kate could imagine that was true. "But she was never on her own. We had two lots of grandparents, aunties and uncles and a swag of cousins. There was always the option of packing us off for a visit with someone when things got too much."

"I have to say I'm a little envious of that," Kate admitted. "Some of my friends had big extended families. They'd go off camping in the summer and come back with stories of the fun they had. I didn't miss my parents, but I think I would have liked to have brothers and sisters, and some cousins." Then she added, "Well, I have cousins—but my mother's family wanted nothing to do with me, so I wouldn't know them if I fell over them."

"But why?" Ellie asked, brows raised in shock.

"My other grandparents blamed my father. Said he led their daughter astray. Maybe the drugs were his idea, but I guarantee the money was hers. They're old money—well, for New Zealand they're old money. They live in a massive house in Epsom. That's about as grand a suburb as you'll find in Auckland. But yeah, they washed their hands of her—and me included."

She hated the tinge of bitterness that crept into her voice when she spoke of them. Hated that even now she had a lingering curiosity about them. Hated that perhaps, deep inside her, she even longed for them to reach out one day; to welcome her back into the family. But these were childish longings. The adult Kate knew it would never happen.

"But how could they hold that against you? You were only a little girl." Ellie shook her head in disbelief.

"You know what's ironic? I have my grandmother's name: Katherine." A brittle laugh spilled out. "The only thing she gave me. Although I've always been called Kate. I imagine no one ever shortens hers. From what I've heard, she's way too snobby for that."

"Well, you must spend some time with *my* family," Ellie said. "You should come with me to mum's place one Sunday. She loves an excuse to make a roast dinner. It's always 'more the merrier' at her house. It's pretty humble compared to this," she said, "but it's home."

"Yeah, well, this place *is* pretty posh." She scanned the elaborate room.

"Ah—yes," Ellie agreed. "Not where I ever imagined us living. But I have to give credit to my brother. James has worked so hard and last year it finally paid off big time. Here's to *Prestonwood Cross*," she said, raising her glass.

"I've seen it," exclaimed Kate. "Oh my god, it was riveting. I couldn't wait to watch it every week. He worked on that?" The dark whodunnit had captivated everyone; the hot topic of conversation at work after each new episode aired.

"Yes, he was the executive producer. They knew it was good, but there was no way they expected it to go all the way. Three BAFTAs," said Ellie, with an obvious hint of pride. "So he thought he'd celebrate by buying his first home. Some first home, isn't it?" she said, waving her hand at the elegant, expansive room, a wry smile on her face.

The enormous period house *was* an unlikely first home. With five bedrooms, it sprawled over three levels crowned by a rooftop terrace. It even sported a surprising patio that spilled down onto a walled garden. They sat in one of the spacious high-ceilinged lounges, furnished with oversized modern couches large enough to double as beds.

The house also showcased Ellie's natural flair for the bold and intriguing. She described how, armed with James's unlimited credit card, she'd relished the task of furnishing it for her brother. On the walls, vibrant artworks enlivened the vast expanse of white. Above Ellie's head was a kaleidoscopic Romero Britto print titled 'Night Out'. Its dancing couple in all their pop art glory might have been plucked out of a London club. Opposite, a Banksy print was equally at home. Obsessed with the elusive street artist, James planned to spend his next big pay check on an original. For now, the print must suffice. Flamboyant rugs made the open wood-floored living spaces cosy. Kate wiggled her toes in one, the luxurious depths resembling the coat of an iridescent yak.

"You've done an amazing job," she said. "That room you've put me in is beautiful."

"It's come out quite well, I think." Ellie's smile was modest, but she looked pleased at the compliment. "It's pretty much a mirror of mine. I love that they both have a window overlooking the garden. And as for having your own bathroom and that big walk-in wardrobe—it's bliss."

Kate had fallen in love with the high-ceilinged room the moment Ellie swung open the heavy door. It was bright and super modern, but somehow still captured the essence of its Victorian era birth.

"Until a few weeks ago, a work friend of James's rented it. But she hooked up with a guy who lives in Richmond and moved in with him. So it's nice you came over to stay. I've been rattling around here on my own."

"Well, it's great to escape the flat," Kate admitted. "I know it's a fantastic setup; privacy if I want, company if I prefer. But this is far more fun on a Friday night."

"Absolutely," agreed Ellie, topping up their wine glasses. It was a velvety French red from Bordeaux she'd raided from James's stash. Kate savoured its earthy flavour, letting it roll around in her mouth. "Here's to girl's nights in," Ellie suggested, raising her glass, and the tinkle of crystal as their glasses met sounded like the flutter of happiness in Kate's chest.

CHAPTER 6

Family Reunion

London, England - October 2007

"GET A MOVE ON Katie, love, we're going to miss the tube."

Ellie's lightly freckled face peered around the classroom doorway, framed with that wild tumble of red hair that spoke to her Scottish lineage. As did her unpronounceable birth name: Ealasaid. Apparently, her mother had insisted upon it, only to have it immediately and permanently abbreviated to the more user-friendly version by which everyone knew her. But the accent was pure Londoner, and Ellie Beckett was a Londoner through and through.

Kate grabbed her coat and bag and hurried after her. Ellie fizzed with excitement. Her brother, James, had flown in from Prague that morning.

While working overseas for the past few months, Ellie had missed him desperately. Not having siblings, Kate couldn't relate to that feeling, but it was obvious that for Ellie, her world was less than complete when James wasn't around.

They emerged from Bayswater tube station into fast disappearing daylight. The clouds hung low overhead, small wispy tentacles stretching towards them. A steady rain fell—a 'dreich' day, Ellie would say, dropping into the idiom of her Scottish mother.

Crowds of people flowed along the streets at a faster than normal pace, faces grim, fixated on reaching their destinations without getting soaked. They marched in single file, hoods pulled low. Ducking between the oncoming umbrellas, only agile manoeuvres avoided eyes being poked out. The dampness heightened the smells of the streets:the ever-present car fumes, a dropped takeaway container with abandoned curry spilling onto the pavement, the people like woolly wet dogs, and a faint whiff of sewage that was inescapable in the city, even in this stylish neighbourhood.

A few blocks from the station, the two women dived into a less frantic side street. Ahead, the black and gold doorway of The Swan was a welcome sight.

"Remember," warned Ellie, "outside the family, he's James, not Jamie. He'd never forgive me if either of us called him that. The little boy's name doesn't sit well with his image." She pushed open the tall, heavy door, and they plunged into the welcoming dark warmth.

Kate was unprepared for the niggle of dislike triggered by her first sight of James Beckett. After all, he was the brother of someone who had fast become a good friend. However, she'd always had a natural wariness of cocky men. And that was the first adjective that sprang to mind when her gaze fell on him, holding court at one of the high tables in The Swan on this dreary Friday night.

He was the centre of a group, regaling them with some story, his face alive with the telling. Expansive hand gestures punctuated his sentences. Even from across the bar, his voice rang out clear and confident. To someone who didn't know his family background, the faint touch of an East End accent was at odds with his appearance.

He had a shock of brown hair swept into a glossy wave, and shaved close on either side in the latest fashion. He sported a neatly sculpted beard, most likely the product of the same hip barber who had created the hairstyle. And his dress was the epitome of a stylish thirty-something: a simple but expensive crew-neck jumper, topped with an elegantly casual jacket and not-your-ordinary jeans. From his appearance, it was no surprise that he was a partner in the rising-star film production company. He looked like someone born to be in charge.

A stern voice in Kate's head told her to keep an open mind. Surely if he was Ellie's brother, he couldn't be that bad. She would be polite and friendly. She wasn't about to spoil her friend's evening by acting frosty towards her brother, especially based on such a hasty and, she had to admit, rather superficial judgment.

Ellie called out his name and waved wildly across the crowded room. Hearing her, he turned, and his gaze lit upon them. There was no doubt that James Beckett was a good-looking man. And there was no doubt that he knew it.

"Ellie!"

He pushed through the scrum of people around him and wrapped his sister in a hug, velvet brown eyes shining with obvious delight at the sight of her.

"And this is my friend Kate," said Ellie.

Kate stiffened, feeling awkward and angular, as he wrapped her in an obligatory welcome hug and brushed a kiss on her cheek. He smelled of beer and the underlying spicy scent of some men's perfume.

The circle of men opened to make space for the two women. Quick introductions made, they turned back to the bar to get a drink. Ellie ordered a dark viscous beer for herself. That wasn't her usual choice, but it mirrored what James had in front of him. Spotting its distinctive purple bottle, Kate requested her latest favourite gin with tonic. While the barman splashed the mixture into a large fishbowl shaped glass, she surveyed James from a distance.

She kept her gaze discreet, attempting to prevent her curiosity from showing. He appeared younger than she knew him to be. Ellie had only last week celebrated her thirty-third birthday, and he was her older brother by a year or two. In contrast to his impeccable dress, he had a relaxed, casual manner. Although he showed little physical resemblance to Ellie, it was obvious that he shared her gregarious personality. The group of men gathered around the table hung on his words, with James definitely the centre of the blokey banter.

There was a football match on the multiple big screens scattered round the bar. They'd come in during a break, but on the restart, their presence subsided into the background. England were playing Croatia, and on track to lose. James and his friends sat engrossed in the drama of the beautiful game. With sighs of frustration and yelps of outrage at the referee, they lived every moment like they were on the sidelines. Kate had zero interest in ball sports and found the male obsession with them tedious. But she couldn't abandon Ellie, and she obviously didn't want to be parted from her brother, despite the fact he was ignoring her. So the two women hovered on the edge of the conversation.

She knew Ellie had counted the days until his return, after three months working on a project in the Czech Republic. Although Prague was a quick plane trip from London, he either hadn't made the time or sensed the need to come home for a weekend. And he had deterred Ellie from going to see him, pleading long hours on set and a lack of spare time. Now he was home—and it appeared her brother didn't fully reciprocate Ellie's joy at seeing him. She didn't seem concerned that he took little notice of her, his attention fixated on the football. Maybe this was their normal way of being. Maybe this is how siblings existed. Kate didn't have any experience from which to judge.

Once the game ended, some of the group drifted off, citing the need to get home to wives, children, girlfriends. The rest set about drowning their disappointment at the football result with more beer. Their pub meals arrived and with a gnawing hunger in her stomach and a slight wooziness from two gins, she tucked into the steamy steak pie with enthusiasm, even enjoying the pile of peas and mashed potato that surrounded it.

While she ate, she listened to the conversation, with James at last devoting some attention to his sister, although still preoccupied with the ongoing post mortem of the game. He nodded and made comments to Ellie, while simultaneously taking part in mourning the English team's lacklustre display.

Kate felt a rising annoyance at his blindness to Ellie's desperate need to connect. She was like a hungry puppy, pawing at his feet, waiting to snatch every tiny morsel of attention he tossed her way. Meanwhile, the bloody football still dominated his mind.

When one of the other men sidled over to Kate, striking up a conversation, the distraction was welcome. He was pleasant enough, not bad-looking, although the cigarette that dangled from his lips ruled him out for a serious flirtation. There were some vices she could live with in a potential date, but smoking wasn't one of them.

She quickly identified a second reason not to pursue anything beyond this conversation. He worked on the trading floor in the stock exchange. Not that this was bad of itself, but his attempt to explain what the job entailed with talk of selling short and hedge funds left Kate struggling to prevent her eyes glazing over with boredom. She maintained a polite mask, covering her total disinterest in the subject, which had the unfortunate effect of encouraging him further. She wished she was better at this game, envying those women who could give a guy the brush off without him realising it until after they'd neatly dispensed with him. At last, Ellie came to her rescue.

"Shall we head back to mine?" Ellie suggested. "James will be on his way any minute and we can have a drink back there."

"Sure," said Kate, grabbing the opportunity to escape from trader-guy. Drinks with Ellie and James provided a convenient excuse. She tossed him a quick goodbye and an apologetic look, disguising her relief to have escaped his clutches. But once out on the street, she changed her mind. "You know what? I think I'll go to my place. You two can have some time to catch up without me in the way." Ellie deserved a reunion with her brother and his undivided attention.

"Oh no, you won't be in the way," Ellie protested. "And besides, I don't want you to walk to the station alone."

"I'll be fine, and you know it. The streets are so busy. It's perfectly safe."

"Please. Come and stay over. There's no need for our 'girls' nights in' to end just because James is home." Her face mirrored the plea in her voice. There'd been little opportunity for either of them to really talk to James, and it seemed important to Ellie that Kate get to know him.

"But I didn't bring anything with me."

"Not a problem. I have a gorgeous new set of pyjamas that I will let you have the pleasure of wearing. Although they're too pretty to say you can keep them. And a brand new toothbrush. You needn't give *that* back," she laughed.

At that moment, James toppled out of the pub doors behind them.

"Right ladies," he said, placing an arm around both their shoulders. "Back to mine for a drink." It was a statement, not a question. Kate opened her mouth to protest, but sensing her objection, he cut her short. "Come on, Kate, the night is young. And we've only just met. Seems about time I got to know the new best friend my sister's been blethering on about for weeks."

"See, you're not about to spoil our sibling reunion." She found it hard to say no to Ellie a third time, and with the force of James's insistence behind it, she capitulated to their demands.

"OK," she said with a half-hearted smile, all the while kicking herself for being so easily swayed.

"Great," he said, as he released his grasp on them to rummage in his pocket, soon producing a bunch of keys. "Wait till you try the Czech booze

I've brought home. Bloody rocket fuel, but once you've got a taste for it, it's just the thing on a cold night."

"You're driving?" Ellie could see as well as Kate that James had far too much alcohol on board to drive.

"Hoped you would?" He held out the keys to her. "You've only had a couple."

"But it's only a few blocks and the rain's stopped," Kate suggested. The night air had that sweet, freshly-washed smell, the odorous streets cleansed by the rain. She felt like a walk after being in the crush of the pub, and she wasn't one hundred percent sure Ellie was safe to drive, either.

"Don't really want to leave the car overnight, though. Some bastard will probably steal the wheels," he said.

"Give me the keys, then." Ellie extended her hand with a sigh. They strolled around the corner to where a large shiny BMW sat parked on a loading zone.

"My pride and joy," he said with a wave at the car. "Bought it with my first decent pay check. Can't leave this beauty out on the mean streets of Bayswater all night."

Ellie climbed into the driver's seat, while James joined her in the front after removing a parking ticket from beneath the windscreen wiper with a flourish.

"Only twenty quid. Cheapest way to get parking around here," he said with a grin, glancing at Kate in the back seat before tucking it neatly into the back pocket of his jeans.

Ellie fired up the engine, and the car emitted a refined rumble as she carefully edged its large nose into the street, and crawled the few blocks, before tucking it into the parking space out front of the house.

"Good girl," he said. "Thanks love." He planted a kiss on her cheek. "I know you don't like driving this beast, but if you handle her gently, she's not a problem. Just like me."

He laughed at his little joke before leaping out to drag two enormous cases and a chunky briefcase from the car boot. Kate wasn't an expert on designer luggage, but she knew enough to recognise the '*LV*' logo meant Louis Vuitton, and it wouldn't have been cheap. Inside, he trundled the cases down the hallway while Kate and Ellie settled in the lounge.

"So, what do you think? He's fun, isn't he? I'm so pleased to have him home."

"Yes, he's a bit of an extrovert." Kate chose her words carefully, concealing her doubts behind a smile.

The extrovert in question bounced into the lounge and lay back on a sofa, two enormous feet resting on the arm. Kate cringed inwardly, as too many years of Nana's rules about feet and furniture echoed in her head. But it was his house, his furniture and so his rules.

"Louboutins," he said, noticing her gaze on his feet. The shiny black leather shoes sported incongruous bright red soles. "Expensive but so bloody comfortable they're worth it."

"Good to know," she said, wondering at what someone in his position might deem expensive.

"So, where's that celebratory drink you promised us?" said Ellie.

"Oooh, nearly forgot. Rustle up some glasses, love, and I'll grab it from my carry-on."

The girls moved to the kitchen where Ellie lined up three tumblers and they sat on high stools clustered around the massive marble island. James deposited a tall green bottle in front of them. The label said '*Becherovka*' in lettering of blue and gold as strident as the smell of the clear liquid he sloshed into their glasses. Kate took a sip, finding it unusual, but not unpleasant, with a hint of cloves reminiscent of Christmas tantalising her tongue.

"So Kate," he said. "Another teacher. Tell me—I always ask this of Ellie's teacher friends—what made you choose the job? Apart from the holidays, I can't get my head around it. Stroppy kids, grotty classrooms and then there's the pay."

It was a question she'd been asked many times, though never before with the disparaging comments. And so, still reeling from his negative spin on it, she gave the answer she always did.

"I guess I wanted to do something that made a difference."

He came straight back at her. "Yeah, but there are other ways of doing that." He gave a snort, shaking his head. "Take what I do, for example. Make some good telly. Get paid ridiculous amounts of money for it. Makes a difference to loads of people. Gives them an escape from their boring lives."

"I suppose I wanted to do something that helped kids grow into people who don't have boring lives. To have lives they don't need to escape from."

He regarded her thoughtfully. "Hmm. You may have a point." And then, as if wanting to change the subject, rather than admit she'd bested him, he knocked back his glass in one gulp. "So another one?"

An hour later, lying in the comfortable bed she almost thought of as hers, she snuggled into the delicious borrowed pyjamas, but sleep wouldn't come. Her brain insisted on mulling over the evening's events. Unsure as to precisely what she thought of James Beckett, who was now most likely snoring his head off downstairs after consuming too much alcohol, he was all she could think of.

Physical exterior: definitely attractive. Personality: undecided. He exuded a boyish energy that was compelling and infectious. But there was definitely something superficial about him she really didn't like. She thought of the sharp clothes and immaculate grooming. The flash car, designer luggage and expensive shoes made her wonder if there was anything of substance under that shiny exterior.

And she couldn't help replaying the two hours in the pub and the offhand way he'd treated his sister. That annoyed her, as did the way he'd belittled her career choice, although she was proud to have not let him get away with it. She had made him stop and think. Perhaps the most annoying thing was that James Beckett had preoccupied her thoughts all night, and even now wasn't prepared to go away and let her sleep in peace.

CHAPTER 7

Sunday Lunch

London, England - October 2007

"IT'S WARM, CONSIDERING IT'S almost November," Ellie said as they emerged from the confines of Bethnal Green station. It was only a few stops on the underground, and on a Sunday morning, the emptiness of the train and the uncrowded platforms were a pleasant contrast to their weekday commute.

"You think so?" said Kate. "I wouldn't say it's warm. I'm definitely very attached to this woolly coat and my beanie."

She had forgotten her gloves, so instead kept her hands tucked deep into the pockets of the cobalt blue coat. It was one of Ellie's serendipitous op shop finds. Ellie was a master secondhand shopper, always discovering treasures others had missed. She'd plucked it from amongst a row of dull blacks, greys, and browns with a triumphant flourish, to find it was exactly Kate's size.

"Is James meeting us there?" Kate asked, keeping her voice neutral as she mentally prepared herself for her next encounter with the man. The rational part of her suggested she give him another chance, but it was difficult to ignore her gut response to his obnoxious behaviour.

"Nah, he's begged off lunch today. Going to catch up with some friends. He had dinner with Mum last night, so at least she's seen him. God, one time he was back an entire week before he went round home. Work, of course. Swore me to secrecy. I told him I'd never do that again. After all, you've only got one mother."

Kate's steps became instantly lighter. She suppressed a small, pleased smile. Looking forward to meeting Mary Beckett without the prospect of James's irritating presence, the day seemed better already.

Bethnal Green was as colourful as its name, not what she expected from an inner city suburb. They took a shortcut through a park. A few steps away from the harsh pavements, they strolled across a neatly mown field. She peered at the sickly winter sun trickling through trees, which by spring would be verdant green. The leaves underfoot retained a slight crispiness, although the recent rain made them slick in places. The smell of decaying foliage reminded her of walking in the bush pathways as a child, once again triggering a pang of longing for home.

They wove their way through a maze of streets, at last heading down a narrow cul-de-sac where 1950s terrace houses faced an old churchyard. Teetering headstones, overgrown with moss and populated with frills of lichen, clustered in untidy rows in front of the church. St Stephen's, a large brick edifice, looked more castle than church, its turreted tower topped by a flagpole where a Union Jack flopped in lazy surrender to the windless winter air. Kate revelled in her surroundings, drinking in the sight of these buildings, so different from New Zealand, where nothing was truly old.

Ellie stopped at the last house in the row. "Home sweet home," she announced.

There was a small cottage garden, captured within a low scalloped wrought-iron fence. A narrow path led to the heavy wooden front door. Unusual feature panels of multi-coloured bricks flanked the door, their mottled, glossy surface reminiscent of scaled lizard skin. Before Ellie could knock, the door swung open in welcome. Mary had been watching for them.

It was immediately obvious that Ellie's height was a gift from her mother. Mary MacNeill Beckett had a tall, slender form accentuated by a fine-featured face and long, stick-thin arms that wrapped her daughter in an exuberant embrace. Ellie's luxurious red hair was also a mirror of her mother's, although Mary's was lighter with age. However, while Ellie allowed hers to spill down her back in an uninhibited tumble, Mary had tamed her hair into a neat bun. She released Ellie from her welcoming hug and scooped Kate into her arms as if she was her own.

"Come in, love. Ellie's told me all about you. About time she brought you over for a meal." She still had the trace of a lilting Scottish burr, even after living in England for many years.

The divine smells of a traditional Sunday roast filled the house. Fragrant beef sizzled in the oven, and Mary confirmed that Yorkshire pudding and gravy would accompany it. No doubt there would be peas. Despite being raised by English grandparents, Kate marvelled at the ubiquitous presence of the humble pea at every meal.

Ellie pottered in the kitchen, lifting lids on various saucepans to investigate what simmered inside, then dodged a rush of hot steam that billowed from the oven, as she checked the progress of the meat. She punctuated each bit of attention to the meal with a sip of wine. Kate, installed on a stool at the counter, enjoyed her own glass of red. Meanwhile, Mary, due on an afternoon duty at four p.m., poured herself a glass of a vivid orange, fizzy drink. A matching bright orange and blue label proudly proclaimed the contents to be IRN BRU.

"You should try some," Ellie encouraged her. "It's Scotland's national drink."

"I thought that was whisky?" replied Kate.

"Oh that too," laughed Ellie, half-filling a glass. "Here, try some."

It had an odd flavour, not unpleasant, but no competition for the wine.

"So I thought you were off these late shifts?" Ellie frowned at her mother.

"They were short this week, so I said I'd do two," Mary replied. "Don't worry, I'll get a cab home."

"Good to hear it," said Ellie, relief clear on her face. "I don't like to think of you walking home late from the tube. And before you say that *I* do—yes, you're right. But in my case, it's a one-minute walk. And there's always people around, and—"

"And it's a better area," said Mary with a bemused smile. "You forget I grew up in Glasgow. And that I began my nursing in Aberdeen. I'm not afraid to be out in the less posh parts of the city."

"But you could run faster back then," joked Ellie. "And in Aberdeen, I bet you didn't walk on your own too often. From what he said, Dad was always there to meet you. Trying to woo you."

"Ah yes, he did that. But remember, he was often offshore. So there were many a night I took the bus on my own."

"Well, make sure you're careful, Mum. We worry about you," said Ellie, peering into the oven. "Right, things are looking good in there."

"How about I set the table?" offered Kate.

She laid out cutlery on a broad, heavy oak dining table. Arranged above the matching sideboard, a collection of framed photographs caught her eye. In the first a castle, bold and brutal, stood guard over a small island. There was a statue in the next picture, a Madonna and child standing on a windswept hill where the tussock grass lay almost horizontal, surrounded by purple heather in full bloom. And beside that was the photo of a beach, the white sand dunes, also rippled by the persistent touch of wind, and the water beyond a surreal shade of blue. The last picture captured a traditional

Scottish Highland house, white-washed walls punctuated with a bright red door.

Mary came into the room bearing the first of several large dishes, a bowl with roasted vegetables, steam wafting off them. Mary smiled, noticing Kate's gaze on the photographs.

"Home," she said. "Scotland."

"Whereabouts? I had no idea Scotland had beaches like that."

"It's Barra, in the Outer Hebrides. The MacNeill homeland," she said. "I wasn't born there, nor were my parents, but we always thought of ourselves as coming from Barra."

"It's beautiful."

"Yes, I miss it. We used to go there to visit family when I was young. But after I married Ron, perhaps two or three times. Never took Ellie and Jamie. I should have."

"Perhaps you'll still go sometime."

"Yes, perhaps I will. Life flies by. You forget to make time to do these things."

"So, tell me about these places."

"Well, the house is my grandmother's. One day, when she was a widow in her fifties, she announced she was going back. After living for thirty years on the mainland. We'd go to the island, stay with her for a few weeks every year after that. Often at Christmas. And we'd stay on for New Year. That was the real celebration—Hogmanay. You've never experienced a proper New Year's until you've been to Scotland."

"I'll add that to my list. Though seeing that beach, a summer visit is tempting."

"Yes," said Mary. "You don't really think of Scotland and beach in the same sentence, do you? That one's the best on the island. Hardly anyone on it, too. Sometimes we'd go across in the summer holidays. I spent hours pottering around there with my cousins."

"The castle's pretty impressive."

"It's called Kisimul," said Mary. "In Castle Bay. You can only get there by boat. It wasn't in great shape when I was a child, but I hear they've restored it. Tourists love a castle."

"And the statue?"

"Our Lady of the Sea. She stands watch over the bay from high on a hill. A steep climb, but the view from there is amazing. As kids, we used to race each other to the top. Not sure I could even walk it now. I've got old." A wistful expression crossed her face.

Although Kate knew Mary was in her sixties, when she'd opened the door, Kate had sensed a youthful energy about her. But now, as she spoke of her distant childhood, it was if the weight of the years descended on her.

"Right, better get the rest of that food on the table before it gets cold," said Mary, the shadow disappearing almost as swiftly as it had come as she hurried back to the kitchen.

Over lunch, she discovered Mary had the same sparkling personality as her daughter, full of quirky humour and lively conversation. Wrapped in the warmth of a family, Kate basked in a happiness that she hadn't experienced in a long time.

"Oh my goodness, where's the afternoon gone? Almost time for work," Mary said, as jangling Westminster chimes from the mantlepiece clock marked the hour.

"You get ready and go, Mum," said Ellie. "We'll take care of this."

"Yes, let us do the cleaning up. You did all the hard work cooking it," said Kate.

Mary bustled off to her bedroom, reappearing soon in navy nurse's scrubs and clutching a warm coat. She wrapped her daughter in a hug, then Kate too, and set off for the station.

"Thanks for inviting me," said Kate, up to her elbows in hot water, scrubbing away at a stubbornly greasy plate. "I really like her."

"And she really liked you, too," said Ellie. "I knew she would. Mum only had two children, but she would've been mother enough for ten. She's always loved us bringing home our friends, made them part of the family. Now you are too. An honorary Beckett."

"You know, I think I might quite like being a Beckett," said Kate, with a thrill of delight at the thought.

CHAPTER 8

Moving In

London, England - November 2007

KATE STOOD AT THE photocopier, hands on hips, silently cursing the machine. For some reason, it always saved its worst for her, and it particularly enjoyed making her Monday mornings an extra challenge. Today it had jammed on the first sheet.

When Ellie arrived, she found Kate on hands and knees with every drawer and flap hanging open and still no sign of the beast being appeased. There were smudges of toner on her hands from the one crumpled sheet she'd wrestled free. However, a strident, pulsing error message still taunted her.

Ellie shot it an evil look. "Bloody thing. It always does this at the start of the week."

She waded in, opening still more hidden compartments. After much muttering, she produced a concertinaed piece of paper, gave a victorious wave and then, with harsh plastic clicks, slammed everything shut. The lights stopped flashing, and the errant beast whirred in contentment, producing the copies with an innocent hum.

"OK, now that's fixed, I need to talk to you," she said. "Come on, let's grab a coffee."

They made their way to the dingy staffroom. Its only redeeming feature was the surprisingly good coffee machine that perched on the bench, from which Ellie extracted two presentable flat whites, and they plonked down on a pair of ugly striped chairs.

"So?" Kate asked. She was already used to Ellie's schemes; always planning something. Life was never dull when Ellie Beckett was your best friend.

"So—James and I had a fantastic idea over the weekend." Kate could see Ellie's eyes sparkle. She took a deep breath, trying to ward off a twinge of nervousness that, whatever it was, it also involved James.

"You could move in with us," she blurted. "We've so many empty rooms, and it would be nice to have you living there. You know what it's like with James—never can tell if he's going to be home or away."

Thoughts of permanently living in the beautiful, high-ceilinged bedroom that already felt like hers dangled tantalisingly before her. She had to admit the idea had merit. She and Ellie spent a lot of time together out of work, and even after James's return a month ago, she stayed over often, at least once a week.

But then there was the James factor. She'd not warmed to him at their first meeting, and since then, every time she'd encountered him, that first impression coloured her view: arrogant, way too confident. And the way he dressed; that uber-cool, immaculate veneer was off-putting.

She considered what it might be like to share a house with him. Not appealing—but possibly not difficult. As Ellie had said, he was away more than he was home. And it was a big house. It wouldn't be hard to avoid him. She tried to keep her expression neutral, not betraying any doubt on her face.

"So James is OK with the idea?"

Kate tried to sound casual. She was unsure of what he thought of her. They'd hardly exchanged more than a few words, with him always flitting in and out of the house whenever she visited.

"James thinks it's a great idea. I know he feels guilty about leaving me home alone so much."

Well, she hadn't seen any signs that his lack of attention to his sister bothered James one bit. But, hey who was she to know what went on between the two of them when she wasn't there? And although it irked her that, by moving in, she might be indirectly letting him off the hook, enabling him to carry on neglecting Ellie guilt-free, if she didn't take up the offer, it was Ellie who suffered.

"Well, it's a bit of a surprise." Accepting there was no good reason to say no, she pushed aside her reservations. "But how could I turn down the offer of one endless girl's night in with you?"

Ellie's arms wrapped around her in an exuberant hug, a broad grin lighting up her face as her eyes danced with excitement.

"You can move in straight away if you want. It's practically your room already."

"Yeah, it might depend on me finding someone to take my place. The flatmates are a good bunch. I wouldn't want to leave them in the lurch."

It had been a very loose arrangement when she'd moved into her current flat. Jenny was the only original housemate. The others paid her their share, and she took care of the rent. Kate wasn't comfortable about moving if it would cause her a problem. However, there was a constant ebb and flow of young people through London.

Word went out across the networks of friends and acquaintances and she quickly found another recently arrived Kiwi keen to take her place. As she slid the door across, leaving her little room for the last time, she felt a small twinge of regret. The Earl's Court flat had been a great place to start. But Ellie's offer was too good to refuse.

The first night in the Bayswater house, she lay cocooned in the warmth of the massive bed. She had treated herself to some high-quality sheets and luxuriated in their new, freshly-washed smell. There were still the sounds of the city, but they were more subdued here. Even the street-lights were a little friendlier, their ambient glow penetrating the cloudlike white curtains that were so long they made gentle pools where they met the floor. In the half-dark she could pick out the ornate plaster rose that surrounded a minimalist modern light. It was the most beautiful room she'd ever slept in, and now she wasn't merely a guest in it. This was home.

Kate leaned on the kitchen counter, munching toast and inhaling the scent of fresh coffee. There were definite advantages to living here, including the coffee machine.

"Morning."

James pranced into the kitchen, a towel around his waist. He had a well-toned torso and muscular arms that she couldn't help but admire, although with a discreet glance. It didn't seem right to ogle her friend's brother openly.

"That coffee smells so damn good. I might even have one myself for a change." He ambled over to the machine.

After two weeks, her initial wariness at living with James had somewhat subsided. Lots of things about him still annoyed her. He could never walk into a room, even his own kitchen clad in a towel, without projecting the aura of a grand entrance. As always, the smell of the designer aftershave he'd slathered himself in preceded him. Although she had to admit the unexpected bright lemony fragrance was rather pleasant.

"You smell pretty good too," she said. "What is that? I could almost wear it myself."

"Versace Pour Homme," he replied, as he filled a cup with dark viscous liquid. "You're welcome to it if you like. Help yourself. Inside the cabinet in my bathroom." James spent more time in the bathroom than even her most high maintenance friends. It was fortunate she and Ellie each had their own ensuite, otherwise it would be near impossible to get a shower. "Just don't tell Ryan. Always acts like he owns the place when he's here. I'm sure he uses my stuff in there."

James was quick to judge people and was open in his disdain for some of Ellie's friends. Ryan, in particular, seemed to rub him up the wrong way. Tried too hard. That was his problem. James didn't take to people-pleasers. But Kate suspected he didn't mind her presence. However, she knew he was most interested in her being in the house for Ellie. He owned the house outright and didn't need her money. The rent was ridiculously low, a token amount towards the outgoings. On every level, moving in was the right decision, even if she had to tolerate James Beckett.

"So, what are you girls up to today? More scoping out other people's trash for Ellie to bring home as treasure?"

"Yeah, I think I've agreed to Camden Markets today. I'll do my best to restrain her from the really hideous finds."

"I'll hold you to that," he said. "No crappy retro chic, please." He wagged a commanding finger at her. "And if you fail in your mission—" He folded his bare brawny arms across his chest. "—and she does indeed buy things that look like that—" He glared at the row of gaudy orange and avocado green 1960s plates arranged on the sideboard. "I expect you to tell Ellie you love it so much you absolutely must have it for *your* room. Because we've got quite enough of it lurking around here."

"Mission accepted," she said with a grin. "I think I know her well enough to be persuasive."

"Good girl," he said. "Succeed and I'll buy you dinner."

This was the disconcerting thing about living with James. Whenever she encountered him on her own at the house, like this, they slipped into an easy banter. Under that brash exterior, he and Ellie were more alike than different. There was an inherent likeability about both Beckett siblings.

Perhaps that was why this unexpected camaraderie had developed between her and James. She realised now that she had never *really* loathed him. And she might even be forced to admit she actually quite liked him. Ellie would be pleased. And to her surprise, she kind of was, too.

CHAPTER 9

Mi Casa, Su Casa

London, England - November 2007

JAMES'S FOOTSTEPS POUNDED ON the treadmill in time to the rhythm of the music in his headphones. Noticing Kate enter the room, he pulled them off.

"OK if I hop on the bike?" she asked.

"Sure, go for it," he said. "Mi casa, su casa. Quite nice to have some company for a change. Hell would freeze over before we saw Ellie in here."

"Ah, yep," she agreed. "Your sister has lots of things going on, but exercise isn't one of them."

He watched as she climbed onto the seat and, finding her feet dangling over the pedals, leapt off again. As she bent over to adjust it, he tried not to look at that attractive rounded arse. Didn't want her to think he was perving at his flatmate.

"It's great that you've got this set up. Three months over here and my fitness has really gone backwards."

"You're welcome to use it any time," he said.

James's extensive home gym occupied a small sunny room off the back of the house. He'd given Kate the full guided tour of the place when she moved in and seen the pleasant surprise on her face when he'd opened the door to reveal the array of gleaming machines and rainbow coloured rows of weights.

He watched, trying to keep his gaze unobtrusive, as Kate swept her shoulder-length blonde hair into a messy ponytail before climbing onto the spin bike beside him. The strands that escaped framed her high cheekbones and so relieved her face from appearing somewhat severe in its angularity. As he ran, he couldn't help his mind straying to the other attributes of their new flatmate. The mirrored wall in front of them allowed him to steal glances at her without it being obvious.

Her mouth, while a little too large for her face, also hinted at softness. When she smiled, she displayed a slight overbite and less than perfect teeth. The fact they'd never had corrective work suggested she wasn't from an affluent home. However, the lack of perfection was almost a welcome relief to an otherwise elegant symmetry.

As was the nondescript blue of her eyes. Large and long-lashed, had they been a more compelling colour, it would have been almost impossible to break away from her gaze. Too-perfect women made him nervous. He met a lot in his line of work and he avoided making them anything more than work.

Kate's immaculately groomed brows spoke of someone who took care of herself. He noticed her large hands gripping the bars, with nails that, although a practical length, had a precise manicured appearance. The pale pink polish appeared conservative, perhaps even boring, until the light caught the flash of glittering nail art.

Her workout clothes revealed an athlete's body. Not the lean, honed figure of say a runner or a gymnast. The generous breasts would most likely have impeded those sporting choices. He let his thoughts wander, imagining what they would feel like. In his mind he ran his hands over them, firm and round as apples, topped with perky wee nipples.

He jerked himself back to reality, worried that should she turn towards him, she'd see these lascivious thoughts written on his face. However, his treacherous brain almost immediately flitted back to that gorgeous shapely bottom and his eyes followed his thoughts. He checked himself for a moment, but there was no suppressing his curiosity.

He allowed his gaze to drift surreptitiously down to where the sweet tight cheeks met those lovely lycra-clad legs. The curves of her limbs were more muscle than softness. In particular, her arms and shoulders implied a strength that dwelled within. He'd not realised how much of an attractive package she was when he'd suggested to Ellie that she move in. Now, with the outer wrapping removed, Kate had caught his attention.

"So, do you only train for fun? Or is there a sport you're into?" he inquired while trying to keep pace with the machine. God, he'd better not let her distract him too much—one mis-step and that bloody treadmill would fire him off the back like a bullet. It had happened before, but there had been no one to witness his humiliation.

"Yeah. I'm a sailor."

The unexpected answer jolted his concentration, causing him to lose the rhythm of his stride. He steadied himself just in time to prevent a fall.

"A sailor?" he repeated.

He had a sudden vision of navy recruits in those ridiculous white outfits: flared pants and flat caps with a chin strap. No, not that sort of sailor, he realised. Sailing sometimes popped up on the sports channels. If he remembered correctly, those New Zealanders were pretty damn good at it.

"What do you sail?" he asked, regretting the question the moment it came out of his mouth. *What a stupid question—a boat, of course, you idiot.* Luckily, she didn't notice his discomfort.

"A Laser," she replied. "It's a single-handed yacht. They even have an Olympic class for them now."

"Wow, that's impressive. I don't think I've ever met a girl who knows how to sail a boat."

"Growing up where I did, sailing's something lots of kids get into," she explained. "They call it a rich person's sport, but you don't have to be. Plenty of people are keen to get kids involved. I spent hours down at the yacht club. It was a kind of second home for me."

"So, are you good?"

"Actually, I am," she said, without hesitation. He was a little taken aback at this. From what he knew of her so far, he would have expected more modesty. "Well, I was," she laughed. "When I was younger, I won a few national titles and placed at the world junior event twice."

"Bloody hell," he said. "Dark horse, eh? Well, remind me to never challenge you to a boat race."

"At least not a sailboat race," she agreed, as she pulled on some earbuds attached to an iPod.

James had decided it was a good thing that Kate had accepted the invite to move in. He didn't need the rent money, but having someone else in the house helped to damp down his guilt about being out so much. He worked hard, and he played hard. Which meant that since their other flatmate left, he'd often left Ellie here alone. She was a grown woman with loads of friends and a social life. Even so, he felt he owed it to her to be home more. The adulation she'd showered him with as a small child still lingered, creating a sense of obligation on his part. Kate's presence helped to diminish that obligation. Plus, she was easygoing and, as a bonus, also easy on the eye. The perfect solution.

He relaxed back into his workout, the steady rhythm of his footfalls contrasting with the whirr of the bike. As he upped the pace, he breathed more heavily with the exertion, and once again, an acute awareness of the woman beside him took over. He drank in the fresh tang of whatever perfume she wore, mixed with her own female smell as it drifted across.

Best not go there, mate. Not sure she even likes you, let alone would let you near that body. But that didn't mean he wouldn't be in with a chance should he ever decide to pursue the attraction. He liked a challenge.

CHAPTER 10

Christmas Magic

London, England - December 2007

KATE LEFT THE LAWYER'S office in a sad haze. Signing the papers to finalise her grandmother's estate felt like adding the full stop to her past life. And as December marched on relentlessly towards Christmas, the reality of facing her first holiday season without family loomed over her. Sensing grief hovering close at her shoulder, she determined to do something more cheerful with the rest of the afternoon; may as well make the most of the pay she'd sacrificed to take care of the legal stuff.

So instead of heading for the tube, she made for Knightsbridge in search of more of the legendary London Christmas magic. Last weekend she'd lingered in shops in Regent Street, not buying; simply enjoying the Christmas buzz. Her favourite had been the multi-storied Hamley's toy store, losing an hour there revisiting childhood. Afterwards, heading for the tube, she'd spun in delight as the overhead lights flickered into life, turning an ordinary city street into a fairyland.

Today, mesmerised by the animated window displays at Harrods, she joined the trails of shoppers lured by the promise of the wonderland awaiting them. She wandered through the floors, marvelling at the variety. It was beyond anything she'd imagined. She could understand how the stunning displays of merchandise, virtually anything you might desire, tempted people to open their wallets. Today she made a purchase herself; a set of Christmas cookie cutters that she hoped to put to use in Mary Beckett's kitchen tomorrow.

Allowing the Beckett family's whirl of festive preparation to sweep her along helped to take the edge off the sadness. True to Ellie's prediction, Mary Beckett had immediately promoted Kate to family status. She assumed all Christmas preparations would include her and that she'd spend Christmas Day with them.

Tomorrow she and Ellie had been summoned, like all good daughters, to help Mary with the Christmas baking. She had already decided to make her own contribution, some Christmas shortbread; and now she had the means to shape them as he grandmother had taught her.

By late Saturday afternoon, the air in the Beckett house hung heavy with the sweet aromas of sugar and spices. Kate's shortbread waited to cool in neat rows on a baking tray. Next to them on a wooden board, sat a cake drenched with whisky; baked for hours on a gentle heat, it engulfed the house with a thick, warm smell. Two dense fruity puddings, fragrant with spices and including a penny for luck, still bubbled in pans. Trays of dainty Christmas mince pies lined up on racks; their golden brown pastry so tempting that Mary announced they should take a tea break to sample some.

"These are good," Kate said, her mouth crammed full of sweet pastry.

"The secret," Mary said, "is to prepare the fruit mince well ahead. It's been sitting in the fridge for a month."

"Delicious," she mumbled through a mouthful. "It's the best I've ever tasted."

The cup of strong tea and a little taste of the baking were well-earned. The final job was to wrap everything, then place it in cheerful Christmas tins. Mary stacked them on shelves in the pantry, where they patiently awaited their grand entrance on Christmas Day.

But the preparation wasn't complete yet. The following weekend Mary insisted they should come again on Saturday to help decorate the house. So once more they took the train to Bethnal Green, braving the increasingly chilly walk to Mary's house.

Stripping off coats and scarves, they settled into the warmth of the lounge where in one corner Mary ahd already assembled a rather realistic artificial fir tree. The stacks of boxes around it contained treasures waiting to be taken for their annual outing. Mary's face was as excited as a little child's as she unwrapped ornaments, revealing each one with care, greeting it like an old friend. Kate thought of all the boxes in storage in her house back in Auckland. In some of them she'd tucked away her own precious memories of Christmas past, safely waiting until the day she was ready to face them again.

"Oh, look at this one." Mary held out a delicate glass bauble laced with gold that was nested in layers of tissue. It held a minute winter scene, a cottage surrounded by snow with deer grazing nearby. "I remember buying this one year in Edinburgh. We'd gone to visit my auntie and one afternoon we took a stroll down the Royal Mile. I couldn't help but pop into a little shop selling Christmas things, and when I spotted this, I had to have it." With gentle fingers, she plucked it from the paper and hung it in a specially selected spot.

"This is one James bought you, isn't it?" asked Ellie, holding a dear little Christmas-themed bear which had 'Harrods' embellished on its winter scarf.

"Yes, it is," said Mary, turning to Kate. "He knows how much I love Christmas. It started one year when he was still a little boy—he took his pocket money and bought me a decoration. He could see how much I loved that gift. And so every year since, without fail, he finds another. Soon I'm going to need a bigger tree."

"That's lovely," Kate said. She would never have picked James as someone who would indulge in such sentimental gestures as still buying these little gifts year after year to delight his mother. She'd have thought him more of the grand gesture kind of guy, who'd find something big and expensive in an attempt to outdo everyone else's gifts. She suppressed a frown at her irritation with the man. James seemed to possess an annoying ability to keep proving her wrong.

Accompanied by wine, laughter and stories of Christmases past, they worked until the tree was heavy with a glittering array of beautiful ornaments, swathed in tinsel and topped with an exquisite angel. Her gown of green and gold satin glowed under the tiny fairy lights, while her serene white porcelain face smiled beneficently down on their completed work.

"She's stunning." Kate adjusted the angel to sit more steadily on her perch, ensuring she wouldn't topple.

"Isn't she," agreed Mary. "Another one Jamie found for me."

They'd only just sat down to have lunch before embarking on the next task—dressing the house in its Christmas finery—when the door swung open and James strode in, a toolbox in one hand. There'd been no suggestion he was joining them, but it seemed Mary had been expecting him.

"Hello love. Want some lunch? I held off thinking you might have a bit with us," she said. He leaned over and planted a kiss on her cheek.

"No Mum, I'm all good. Had brunch with some friends. I couldn't eat another thing. I'm here to do the lights for you, just like I promised."

He disappeared upstairs and mysterious bumps and thumps sounded from the attic overhead. Finally, emerging with a large box, he headed outside into the chill of the afternoon. As they settled back to their own work, Kate could hear the odd bang and intermittent hammering from outside.

Meanwhile, the three women carried on opening boxes, retrieving more decorative pieces from their depths; garlands to be strung along the mantlepiece, an antique nativity scene, bunches of holly and even a sprig of mistletoe above the doorway. When they stood back and surveyed their completed handiwork, Kate couldn't help but marvel how in a few brief hours they had transformed the modest house into a magazine-worthy showpiece.

They were just enjoying the cup of tea that seemed to be the obligatory full stop on any task in the Beckett household when James burst into the room, rubbing his hands together in a furious attempt to restore circulation.

"Shit, it's cold out there. OK, Mum, time to come and see what I've been doing out there, besides freezing my balls off."

Not only was it surprising that James had made time in his busy whirl of work and social life to do this, but the competence with which he'd completed the task was also unexpected. She hadn't taken him for a man who could wield hammers and electric drills with skill—let alone produce the complex lighting display that now rambled across the entire front of Mary's house. It framed the windows and door, trailed along the eaves and looped along the front fence.

Although only around four in the afternoon, the sun had set and to the east the sky was darkening. The twilight tinted the street sepia, the trees muted green, the red bricked houses now a dull orange, and rooftops already blackening as if it were night. It was far removed from the long summer evenings of a Southern Hemisphere Christmas.

"Right, Mum, time to do the honours," James said, inviting Mary to turn the switch.

Without even a flicker of hesitation, the lights burst into life, pushing back the encroaching darkness. The simple terrace house, moments earlier identical to the others in the street, was now a unique blaze of beauty. A cascade of tiny white lights dripped from the edge of the roof, glowing electric icicles. A dazzling Santa's sleigh, with a full complement of reindeer, picked out in green, red and gold, skimmed along the front fence. By some trick of electrical wizardry, the old gent's hand waved in a cheery salute.

Children across the road laughed and pointed in glee at a snowman next to the front door, whose stick arms rose and fell in a glittering dance. And Mary stood, her face crinkled in a broad smile and speechless with pleasure.

But it wasn't the delighted expression on Mary's face that stuck in Kate's mind afterwards. It was the way James watched his mother; the love written there for all to see. The tenderness with which he then placed his arm around Mary and hugged her to him sent a jab of regret that she'd never had a mother worthy of such love.

But as usual, she pushed away those thoughts, and reminded herself that she *was* lucky. She'd loved people like that. She'd had people in her life who she would have done anything for, in the same way that James would do anything for Mary. Once more, she accepted there was common ground between herself and this man. Strange that someone she considered her total opposite was in fact much the same as her when it came down to the things that really counted: home, family, loyalty, love.

CHAPTER 11

O Christmas Tree

London, England - December 2007

KATE LOUNGED AROUND IN her pyjamas even though it was nearly lunchtime on Christmas Eve. She'd slept late, only surfacing when the need for food and coffee became greater than the need for sleep. The busy flurry of school events before the Christmas break had left her exhausted. But now two weeks of holidays stretched in front of her.

When the ornate grandfather clock in the hallway chimed two, shame at her slovenliness propelled her to the shower and proper clothes. After, she felt much more human, and settled in her usual comfortable chair in the lounge, engrossed in a book. Ellie lay on the couch doing the same. It was a pleasant indulgence to sit and read for hours on end.

In the corner, Ellie's Christmas tree, a triumphant declaration of what one could achieve in a short time at Harrods with a sizeable amount of money, twinkled merrily, its tiny lights bouncing off the gaudy pink and purple ornaments. The stunning detail of the lush branches was so realistic only the presence of a pine-scented candle issuing its distinctive Christmassy aroma gave any hint that the tree hadn't been cut from the forest that very day.

Around four, James stumbled in, laden with boxes and bags.

"I thought you went to the office," said Ellie.

"Only stopped in for a few of hours—then I had to get onto this lot."

"Ooh, hope there's one for me there."

"Oh no. I forgot about yours," he said, adding his purchases to the small stack under the tree.

"That's OK, I forgot about yours too." She pretended to ignore him and read her book.

Within a day of the tree arriving, several artfully wrapped parcels had appeared beneath it. Kate had seen two with her name on the outside. She'd added her own contributions; for Ellie, an exquisite Chanel scarf she'd found in a vintage shop, and for James, a tea selection from Fortnum and Mason. Although the kitchen sported a coffee machine so advanced that it resembled the Tardis, James was true to his English roots in that he actually preferred tea—as long as it was quality, not your regular PG Tips.

"You girls keen for a few drinks at The Swan?" James suggested as they cleared dinner dishes. "Got a few friends calling in there. Why don't you come too?"

"Great idea," said Ellie. "Give me five minutes to tidy up a bit."

"You too Kate?" he asked. "Can't spend your first Christmas Eve in London watching reruns of Christmas movies."

That was exactly what she'd planned to do. However, much as it was tempting to curl up with *Love Actually*, Kate knew that if she was going to settle here in London, she needed to push herself to get out more.

"Yeah, why not?" she said. "Just need to do a quick change."

Hordes of people packed The Swan. No live football blared out from the giant televisions, although soundless recordings of matches past still flowed across the screens. Instead, the room had a distinctive festive atmosphere; the bar decked in shiny garlands.

Kate could hear Christmas music above the lively chatter, the faint strains of The Pogues' *Fairytale of New York* providing a nod to the season. The earlier arrivals had staked out a large corner, and Kate followed James and Ellie into the group huddle.

Crowded in as they were, there wasn't much opportunity to mingle further, which Kate decided was fortunate when she spied Mr Forex Trader eyeing her speculatively. But trapped on the opposite side of the bar, he made no move to escape. There were, however, some more promising men in James's circle of friends. Freed from the usual distraction of football games, several struck up conversations with her, including one who appeared as interested in her as she was in him.

"Teacher?" he said. "Me too. Glad the holidays are here at last. I'm Steven." It surprised her to find a teacher amongst the group, given James's low opinion of the job. He had warm brown eyes, an untidy shock of curly hair, and a mesmerising northern accent that made her think of Marnie's English husband.

"Yeah, don't mind admitting I'm pretty exhausted after the term. It's been a bit of a culture shock."

"Enjoying it though?"

"Loving it. To my surprise."

"Yeah, it's not a bad lark, especially the holidays. As long as you like kids. How about I buy you another drink to celebrate your first term?"

She found herself agreeing and settled into a pleasant conversation with Steven. He wasn't the most captivating guy she'd met, sort of ordinary, but he was a definite improvement from trader-guy who had obviously decided it wasn't worth fighting his way over to compete for her attention.

As the evening wore on, she noticed the increasing effects of the pub's Christmas themed cocktail menu. She'd worked her way through several of them. The sweet, spicy flavours masked the alcohol content, but its warmth glowed in her veins. Therefore, it was probably a good thing when Ellie wiggled her way through the crowd and leaned in close to her ear.

"Time to go home?" she yelled over the noise.

"Yeah, suppose so," Kate agreed, although there was a twinge of disappointment at breaking away from her conversation. She and Steven were getting on well, but no doubt she'd see him again. She tossed him a final wave as they threaded their way towards the door, but he didn't notice. Seeing him already cozying up to another woman, maybe she wouldn't be seeing him again after all.

CHAPTER 12

The Gift

London, England - December 2007

THE FRONT STEPS WERE icy, and they clung to each other like climbers on an ascent of Everest. That the two girls were both slightly tipsy added to the precariousness of their journey home. *If one goes down, we're all going down*, James thought to himself. So he took a firm grip on the rail and dragged Ellie after him, hoping the momentum would bring Kate along too.

Ellie's psychedelic Christmas tree blinked happily in the corner, as if pleased to see them home. She lay on the couch staring, hypnotised by its glow.

"I love this tree. It's fucking amazing." Her words were a little slurred.

"You did a great job," he agreed. "A unique tree. Now can I get everyone a drink? Or maybe not you Ellie—you've already had at least one too many of those Christmas cocktails."

"They were bloody good," she said, propping herself on one elbow in a brave attempt to appear sober. "That last one was like a posh hot toddy. But I wouldn't say no to a wee dram of that latest whisky you brought home."

"Kate? You want one?" he asked.

"Sure," she said. "I don't think I've ever drunk whisky. But I'll give it a go."

That was no surprise. He'd thought Kate more likely to be a wine or gin girl since down in the tropics the weather wasn't exactly conducive to whisky.

Once he'd poured the drinks, they sat sipping in silence, as if all three were now in the thrall of the Dalek tree in the corner. He should have known a monstrosity like this would result from letting Ellie loose on the Christmas decorating.

"So, Kate—what do you think?" he asked, nodding at the glass.

"Surprisingly good," she said, sniffing at it. "I expected it to be just a big hit of alcohol, but there are a lot of different flavours there. Quite subtle."

"Ah, well, that's a good start. Maybe you have the palate for it. We might make a whisky connoisseur out of you yet."

"It's Christmas!" Ellie leapt to her feet, interrupting their discussion.

"Of course it's bloody Christmas. Has been for weeks if you hadn't noticed," he said.

"No, I mean it's after midnight. It's actually Christmas Day. Let's open a present. Only one each." She rummaged under the tree. "One for you, James. Here's one with Kate on it." She deposited a parcel on each of their laps. "And I think I'll have this one for me."

"You go first," he said, seeing the little child springing from his grown-up sister.

"OK—and it's from Kate," she read off the tag. She ripped the paper open to reveal an expensive-looking scarf. He knew enough to recognise

Chanel logos entwined in the patterned fabric. Vintage designer; typical Ellie style.

"Kate, it's stunning," she gushed. "I love it. These are almost impossible to find. Seems I've taught you well these past months. That shop in Notting Hill?"

Kate nodded, modest pleasure on her face. She'd chosen well.

The gift he held intrigued James. He read the neatly handwritten label: *To James, from Kate.* He wondered if she'd studied him as well as she'd studied his sister. Wanting to find out the contents, he jumped in.

"My turn," he said.

Such an exquisitely wrapped gift could only have come from one of the upmarket stores. He had clients who wooed his favour with parcels like this. A discreet little sticker proclaimed the source–Fortnum and Mason. Pulling aside the wrapping to find a stylishly packaged exotic tea selection, he realised this girl knew him far more than she'd let on. What an astute gift. Being a tea drinker made him an anomaly amongst their coffee-worshipping generation, but she had noticed.

"That's spot on Kate. Thank you," he said, rising to plant a polite kiss on her cheek. This close, she smelt good; that same fresh perfume that lingered in the gym room long after she'd gone. She blushed a little. He wasn't sure whether the pleasure of having chosen well, or the brush of his lips, had triggered the sudden heat in her face. Either way, it added a sweet soft glow that emphasised the high cheekbones and stormy grey-blue eyes.

Looking at the tea, a twinge of guilt niggled at him. She'd gone to so much trouble choosing something she knew he would like, while he'd asked Rhonda, his PA, to go out shopping on his behalf. Both the presents for Ellie that still sat under the tree and the gift that Kate held in her hand resulted from his instructions.

"Go get them something pretty, something girls would like. Pick something you'd like and I'm sure they'll like it too."

As a result, he had absolutely no idea what was in the parcel. He hoped she would think it was something he'd chosen himself; that he'd made a little effort. However, a moment later, when the contents emerged, he was happy to confess the exact opposite.

Inside the wrapping, also upmarket department store style, was a long narrow box. Kate lifted the lid, parted the layers of tissue, and held up a dainty camisole. Made of a fabric that flowed like liquid silver and edged in lace, it screamed sexy. Its plunging neckline would leave little to the imagination. Then, when he thought it couldn't get any worse, she produced a second matching item. The tiniest of g-strings dangled from her outstretched hand. The type of lingerie you'd buy your lover. Not your flatmate.

"Oh!" was all she said, but her face flushed red. This time there was no doubting her discomfort.

"Oh my god," said Ellie. "It's beautiful, but not what I expected."

"Not what I expected either," he said, realising that he would now have to admit to being the slack bastard who sent other people to do his Christmas shopping. He scrabbled to retrieve the situation. "So, you've found me out. All right?" He took a breath. "OK, I have to admit, the only gift I buy at Christmas is for mum. Ellie—all those things you've had over the years? Thank Rhonda and her impeccable taste. She's never got it wrong—till now."

Bloody Rhonda. What the hell had she been thinking? If she wasn't such an amazing PA, he'd fire her for making him look so damn stupid.

Ellie tried to stifle a giggle and failed. That provoked a burst of giggles from Kate. Before he knew it, the pair of them were in an uproar, sprawled on the couch, spluttering with laughter. Each time he thought they might stop, one would glance at him or the other and fall about laughing some more. It was contagious. In the face of it, he couldn't help but let go, and join in the laughter; his mortification evaporated as he saw how hilarious the situation was. Just as long as they didn't tell anyone else.

As their cackling finally subsided, Kate stretched out her hand to the silky puddle of lingerie. Whether it was the lingering alcohol or the loosening effect of the laughter, he could tell from the wicked expression on her face that her inhibitions were definitely down. She picked up the camisole, and with a naughty grin, pressed it tightly against her. He gulped as she pulled it closer, in a voluptuous pose that showed her every curve outlined in the silvery satin.

"So, James," she said with mock seriousness and a flirty wink, "what I *really* want to know is—how come you know my size?"

"Ew, creepy," said Ellie. "James, have you been going through her laundry? Or her underwear drawer?"

The two girls rolled around, laughing some more. James laughed too, trying to fend off the images of Kate dressed in only the skimpy lingerie. It was a coincidence that it was her size, a lucky guess on Rhonda's part. But he'd paid sufficient attention to her rather lovely body while they worked out, side-by-side in the gym, that he may well have been able to guess its dimensions correctly.

Meanwhile, unwelcome flashes of her wearing that camisole and knickers continued to play havoc with his body. He hoped it didn't show on his face as he fought valiantly to damp down the quickening in his groin. He'd already come dangerously close to overstepping the line. The last thing he needed was an obvious hard-on drawing attention to the lustful thoughts whirling in his mind. His sister would never forgive him.

CHAPTER 13

Mistletoe and Wine

London, England - December 2007

"KATE, MAKE IT GO, please?"

Tiny three-year-old Annie's voice was pleading as she presented Kate with a plush unicorn. It had wide eyes set in pale, plush fur and an extravagant tail. She loved how children, from the moment they met you, would accept you into their universe without any question.

She'd been sitting drinking in the atmosphere, immersed, for the first time in her life, in a genuine family Christmas. With her grandparents, Christmas was a wonderful time. Sweet memories of their little traditions would be with her forever. But there had always been only the three of them. Now surrounded by three generations of a family who had swept her into their celebrations as if one of their own, it was a special day.

"It's going to need some batteries, sweetie."

She'd groped around to find a hidden zipper under the animal's stomach, an empty plastic cavity beneath. She took the velvety toy in one hand and that of the little girl in her other.

"Come on, we'll go see Auntie Mary and see what she's got."

Mary was, in fact, great-auntie to this little poppet. Today she had a permanent smile on her face, enjoying every minute of her sister's grandchildren romping through the house.

"Ah, yes, I remembered this year." Mary pulled open a kitchen drawer to reveal a large stash of batteries. "Everything seems to need batteries now."

Within minutes, the unicorn sprang to life. The little girl raced off, dancing happily, the toy clutched to her chest now also performing its own jerky dance.

"These kids make it feel like Christmas, don't they?" Mary observed.

"Yeah, it's kind of magical, isn't it? They believe in it wholeheartedly," Kate replied.

"It's partly selfish reasons when I invite Rose over for Christmas. I get to enjoy her grandkids, which is a real treat since it doesn't seem Ellie or Jamie are going to provide me with some anytime soon."

Kate smiled. "You never know. Maybe this year they'll meet the love of their life and before you know it, you'll have a whole swarm of little ones."

She wondered if she was, in fact, voicing her own hope that the next year might bring things that deep down she wished for; things that this new start in a new place might deliver.

"Maybe," said Mary. "Not that I want to pressure them. They have to live their own lives. As long as they're happy, that's the main thing."

"What's the main thing?" asked James, appearing in the kitchen.

"That you're happy," Mary replied. "That's the only gift I want for Christmas, that my children are happy."

"Very happy, Mum." James wrapped her in a hug. She was almost as tall as he, but her slender frame made her appear fragile in his arms. "But I have another gift for you. Come and see."

"OK, let me check this oven first. I'll be through in a few minutes."

"Hope you know what's inside this one?" Kate said with raised eyebrows as she followed him through to the lounge.

"You're not going to let me forget that for a while, are you?"

"Nope, I think I deserve to get some mileage out of that stuff up."

"Well, it wasn't a total stuff up was it? It fits you and it's a rather lovely if inappropriate gift?" He quirked a brow at her, and she couldn't help but smile.

"Agreed. It is lovely. Thank you, even if it wasn't quite what either of us expected."

They made their way into the lounge, overflowing with people. At least the children were elsewhere, easing the crush a little. Mary had years of experience in family Christmas gatherings and had put together a children's table covered in treats at one end of the dining room next door. This acted as a magnet for the kids, who played with new Christmas toys and ate sweets unchecked while happy to be free of boring adult conversation.

Kate found a spare chair and James, seeing nowhere else, perched beside her on the wide arm. There was lively chatter and much laughter. The greatest hilarity stemmed from the progress of one stray child as she made her way around the room.

About eight years old, she had snuck back in from the dining room and everyone was indulging her fascination with the tradition of kissing under the mistletoe. Clutching a sprig in her hand, she first popped up behind her parents, waving the greenery above their heads. They smiled and obliged with a kiss, then propelled her towards an aunt and uncle to do the same.

Kate, lulled by the warmth of the room and the contented atmosphere, realised too late what was about to happen. If she'd been more wide awake, she could have—and would have—averted it. Just as she savoured the first fragrant mouthful of her mulled wine, a delighted squeal sounded by her ear.

"Your turn," a little voice said.

She and James both turned to see the child leaning over them, arm raised as high as it could go and the damn mistletoe dangling from it.

"Your turn," the girl repeated.

James realised before she did that the easiest, least embarrassing way out of this awkward moment was simply to get it over with. He leaned over and kissed her full on the mouth. A long, slow kiss. Satisfied, the little girl moved on in search of new victims. Kate sat, stunned. It hadn't been unpleasant. In fact, it troubled her to admit that she'd even quite enjoyed it. But trust James to take a chance at giving her a good pash rather than the chaste peck on the cheek that might have sufficed.

"Sorry," he said. "Merry Christmas."

Cheeky bugger, he's not sorry at all. The audacity of the man overwhelmed her. But that was James; absolutely no shame.

"Kids!" she said, rolling her eyes in an attempt to diffuse her embarrassment.

"Yeah, that little girl's having a ball. Looks like she's about to do a second round."

He winked at her. Then, seeing his mother come into the room, he rose to his feet. He took Mary by the hand and led her over to the tree, where underneath a few unwrapped presents remained. James was quite a showman. Kate had seen him in action a few times. She knew he loved to be the centre of attention and fully expected him to make a show of this too, giving his mother a gift in front of the entire family so that all could see what a loving son he was. But to her surprise, he didn't.

"You need to open it in there," she heard him say, voice quiet, as he directed Mary to the dining room.

They disappeared through the door, and it intrigued Kate that he should let go of an opportunity for a grand gesture. After a little while, they returned. Mary walked over to the tree and hung a new decoration. James nodded his approval at its placement and wrapped his mother in another hug. He could be a jerk sometimes, but where his mother was concerned, he appeared to get it right.

"Let's feed these children first," suggested Mary, to the mothers of the little ones. "Then we can enjoy a bit of quiet ourselves while they're busy eating."

Ellie and Kate joined the women, following Mary to the kitchen, and began the process of ferrying food to the dining room. Kate balanced a bowl heaped with the small scarlet saveloys which at home they called 'cheerios' or 'little boys', marvelling at how children the world over enjoyed the bright coloured, but bland tasting treats. Ellie placed a second bowl, this one brimming with curly fries, as the children all sat, faces eager, prepared to swoop.

"Notice anything?" Mary asked, as the children pounced on the food, the previous flow of chattering and giggles replaced by chewing.

"Like what?" said Ellie.

"Look, there." Kate and Ellie both followed her eyes to the wall above the sideboard.

The four photographs of Barra had now become five. The newest addition showed the same cottage as the first; Mary's grandmother's house. Six children of various ages posed in front of it. There was a small girl, perhaps five years old, atop a sturdy Shetland pony, another tall thin older girl holding its lead. Two more girls stood awkwardly looking into the camera with shy smiles, their eyes squinting into the sun. And next to them, two cheeky boys who were obviously struggling to rein in the boundless energy of all small boys long enough for the photograph to be taken.

"Oh wow," said Ellie. "That's lovely Mum. From James?"

"Yes, your brother, for all his faults, can be very thoughtful. It must have taken a lot of ringing around family to get a copy of that."

"So, tell me, who are they?" asked Kate.

"Well, that's me on the pony. Riding on the ponies was one highlight of our visits. I still remember that one. Her name was Bonnie. I loved her so much even though she was a feisty wee thing. I used to ask for a pony every Christmas and birthday, and was disappointed every year. Not surprising—no room for a pony in a backyard in the middle of Glasgow. The girl holding her is my cousin Jenny."

"Oh, yes, I can see it now." Ellie peered at it more closely. "She visited last year, didn't she? She hasn't changed all that much."

"I'm sure she'd find it flattering to hear you say that," said Mary. "And then there's my two sisters, Rose and Fiona. My brother David and my cousin Angus. Look at the pair of them, mischief in their eyes. They were always in trouble." She smiled. "Such good days. We didn't have big expensive holidays like the kids these days, off to Europe at the drop of a hat. But they were wonderful."

On the way home, Kate half-dozed in the back of the car, basking in contentment after the long day. The food and the company had been rather blissful. Even James had acquitted himself well as a doting son, even if she hadn't quite forgiven him for taking advantage of her with the mistletoe.

"So how did you like your first English Christmas?" Ellie asked.

"I loved it," she answered, and meant it.

CHAPTER 14

Diagnosis

London, England - May 2008

"RIGHT, YOU NEED TO go," Kate told the 'three amigos' as she bustled them out the door. "Hurry or you'll miss your bus."

That was the pet name she gave to her personal fan club, three little girls who were of the age that they adored their teacher and loved nothing better than having extra time to chat once the other children had left. She loved teaching these kids, and they were teaching her.

There was Aamenah, her sparkling eyes and heart-shaped face framed in a colourful hijab. Her best friends were Billie, whose family had come with the wave of Jamaican immigrants in the 1960s, and Salma, with parents who ran a popular Bangladeshi restaurant. Experiencing this diversity of cultures was another reason she loved London. She'd chalked up almost three terms now and as she'd found her feet in this job, and settled into life with Ellie and James, the pull of home had subsided to an irregular fleeting feeling.

She followed the trio into the corridor, heading across to Ellie's classroom, hoping to borrow some extra red paint, as the kids had exhausted her supplies. To her surprise, there was no-one there. Thinking that maybe Ellie had been hanging out for a three p.m. coffee, she made her way to the staff room only to find it empty, too.

"Have you seen Ellie?" she asked Deena at reception. "She's disappeared."

"Gone," said Deena. "She took off right on the dot of three. Not like her to be out the door so quick, not like some others who nearly run over the kids to beat them out of here," she said, rolling her eyes. "Didn't even stop to say goodbye. In a rush to get somewhere, I think."

"OK, thanks, Deena," she said, remaining calm despite a small niggle of worry.

It certainly wasn't like Ellie. Kate abandoned the few jobs she'd planned to do before leaving, grabbed a pile of books to mark at home, and set off for the tube. At least there would be plenty of seats if she left early.

She knew before she opened the door that there was no-one else in the house. And three hours later, when she was still there alone, the flickers of concern had escalated into a certainty that there was something extremely wrong. She'd resisted sending Ellie a text, but decided it was time.

'You OK?' An hour later, the message tag still said 'Delivered' but not 'Read'. By now, Kate wondered if she should contact James. She didn't like to bother him if it wasn't necessary, as she knew he was always busy. Late as it was, he would often still be working. And she didn't want him to think her an idiot, worrying about Ellie when there was probably a perfectly good explanation for her whereabouts. While she had left school in a hurry, it wasn't as if someone had abducted her.

Fortunately, she didn't need to dither any longer. Bright headlights announced James was home. But it was Ellie who burst into the room first, with James trailing in her wake. Her eyes were red and puffy, surrounded by smudges of mascara. Her face had a grim set to it. She flung her bag onto the couch and ripped her coat off, dumping that as well.

"Ellie, what's wrong?"

"Ask him." Ellie's eyes flashed as she waved her hand at James, his face set in an exasperated grimace. "He's the one who knows all about it. He's the one who's making all the decisions."

And she turned and marched off to her room, the door slamming behind her. Kate had known Ellie for seven months now. She was a person who didn't hide her emotions. Kate had seen her happy, sad, frustrated, disappointed, mildly pissed off (usually with James); but she'd never seen her like this. This was full-on anger, disturbing in its intensity.

James slumped in a chair. She'd also never seen him like this. He was always so buoyant, confident, without a care in the world. This was a man with the weight of the world on his shoulders. Defeated.

"James, what's wrong?"

He took a deep breath and she could see pain in his eyes. "It's mum," he said. "She's been feeling tired for ages. And even in the time you've known her, you'll have noticed her weight dropping. Last time I gave her a hug, it was like hugging a feather. About a month ago, after I don't know how many visits to her doctor, he finally ran some tests. The results came back. It's cancer."

"Oh, James," she said. "I'm so sorry. Is it treatable?"

He shook his head. "No, not really. They think it started in her pancreas, which is extremely hard to detect. That's why it has spread. Any treatment is going to be hard on her, and the chances of it giving her much longer, let alone cure her, are tiny. That's why she's decided." He swallowed hard. "She won't have any treatment. That's why Ellie's like she is."

"She's angry at your mother?"

"And me," he sighed. "Mum asked me to go with her to an appointment about two weeks ago. A few days later, she told me to come over to her house. Just me. She told me she'd decided to opt for palliative care only; when things get bad. And that's probably going to happen sooner rather than later," he said with a resigned shake of his head. "I told her I'd support her with her choice. After all, it's her life, her choice."

"So, I guess Ellie only found out today?"

"Yeah, and she's got this crazy idea that without my support, Mum will change her mind. But she won't. And I won't do that to her. I don't want to lose her, but I have to stand by her when she needs me. Even if it means my sister hates me for it."

"Give her time. This has been a tremendous shock for her."

"That's another reason she's pissed off with me. She thinks I should have told her straight away. But mum asked me not to. She wanted to tell Ellie herself, in her own time. I think she knew Ellie would want her to take the treatment. To fight."

"Yeah, Ellie would. She'd always choose to fight. But, as I said, give her time."

"We don't have time. Ellie needs to get her head around the situation quickly if she wants to make the most of what Mum has left. I don't care if Ellie's pissed off at me. She can be as angry as she wants with me if that helps. We've got years ahead of us to patch things up if we need it. But she can't go on being angry with Mum. Mum needs her."

"Well, I'm here for all of you. Anything I can do, you only have to ask."

"Thanks," he said. "Mum really likes you."

"Your mum is a darling, and she's been so kind to me. I'm so sorry, so sad to think this is happening. It's a journey I've been on before and it's a tough one."

"Your grandmother?" he asked.

"Yeah. She made the same decision eventually, to not have treatment. They started, but it was brutal. There came a point where it was no longer worth going through that to have a little more time. She said it had been a long life, and a happy life—and she knew Grandad was waiting for her to join him.”

“Mum’s thinking the same. She would rather be well enough to do a few things that are important to her, rather than spend half her time recovering from chemo treatments that, in the end, won’t beat this.”

They sat with the TV on, neither actually watching, rather allowing it to fill the void with mindless noise. Kate microwaved two frozen dinners. Thank god for Sainsburys, comfort food in minutes. She’d just finished her feeble attempt at eating when she heard soft footsteps. Ellie leaned in the doorway. She made her way to the couch, hair still wild and clothes dishevelled. But her face appeared more relaxed now, her expression almost suggesting calm resignation. Had she heard their earlier conversation? She sat beside James, maybe offering a slight gesture of forgiveness.

“So, Kate,” she said, fixing her with an intense look. “You know what’s coming. Tell us, what do we do now?”

CHAPTER 15

Goodbye

London, England - June 2008

WHAT THEY DID WAS shove everything else aside. Ellie organised leave and a substitute teacher appeared as Kate's new classroom neighbour. James enlisted the help of his PA in delegating all he could. Rhonda proved she was adept at doing more than Christmas shopping on James's behalf. And he learned that, to his surprise, he could relax his grip on work and the world wouldn't end.

"Just me," Kate called out as she jostled shopping bags through Mary's front door. It was Saturday morning, and she was running errands. She'd settled into her role as family backup. By quietly taking care of the small mundane tasks, Ellie and James could focus on spending time with their mother.

"A few things Ellie said you needed. She'll be over soon."

"Kate, darling, thank you so much." Mary appeared in the kitchen doorway.

"You needn't have got up. I know where everything goes."

"No, but I like to keep busy. I spend far too much time sitting in my chair these days. It's good for me to get out of it and do a few little things."

Mary walked across the polished wood with slow, measured steps, the placement of each foot hesitant, as if unsure that it would hold her. Kate stood, ready to grab her if necessary. Once she would have struggled to support a woman as tall as Mary. But now, she was a shadow of the person she'd been when they met, not even a year ago. The disease, once uncovered, was flaunting its presence.

"I hear you've been on some outings this week?" said Kate.

"Yes, it's been lovely. I suppose he told you? James bought a wheelchair. I have to admit, I protested at first." Kate noticed how thin her voice had become. Another sign of her diminishing strength. She couldn't imagine Mary having the ability to protest anything too loudly anymore. Especially when it involved James. He was so damn single-minded. "But I suppose I didn't want to face the fact that I'm not up to doing much walking any more. Once I accepted that, it was fine."

"So, where did you go?"

"Well, he insisted we try it out straight away. So on Tuesday we drove to a little cafe I like down in Greenwich. And Ellie took me for a walk in the park on Thursday."

"It's lovely over there, isn't it?"

"Yes, summer's coming early this year. These last few weeks the weather's been beautiful." Kate gazed out at the clear sky. It was going to be another perfect day, quite at odds with the usual London weather. And the grim situation. It was wrong for the world to be so full of life and promise while Mary hurtled into dark times. "That's why James insisted we go out yesterday as well. To make the most of the fine weather. We drove down to Rose's in Brighton."

Brighton! Kate couldn't believe it. It had to be at least two hours in each direction. Longer if the traffic was bad. No wonder Mary looked exhausted. She couldn't understand how James could be so bloody stupid.

"Wow, that's quite a journey," she said, struggling to keep the disapproval from her voice.

"Yes, but it was nice to see her. Although I'm paying the price for it today. Had to have a sleep in. Still a little wobbly, to be honest."

Mary rested one frail hand on the kitchen bench, steadying herself. Her breathing was shallow. There were tense lines etched on her face from the effort of keeping herself upright. Kate swiftly stepped across to slip one arm around her waist and guided her into the nearest chair.

"Best you sit down and have a rest while I make us a cup of tea." She tried to sound upbeat and cheerful, but behind her smile, she harboured serious worries. Thank god Mary hadn't fallen. "You take a rest there and I'll put the kettle on."

She turned so Mary couldn't see the anger in her face. That idiot James. How could he fail to see that well-meaning or not, he wasn't helping his mother if he exhausted her like this? She wouldn't stand by and see him charge around the countryside with her like the hero of the moment. She'd never taken James on about anything before. But this time she must.

Her opportunity came that evening. She was pottering in the kitchen at the house when he arrived home, flinging down his briefcase and collapsing into the nearest chair.

"Long day?" she asked.

"Yeah, had to drive up to Cardiff. Location manager insisted I do the final sign off on some locations. Honestly, I'd have much preferred it if I'd been able to decide from the photos. That's what a producer normally does." He sighed. "But I guess that's why they pay me the big bucks."

"Cup of tea?" she offered, trying to buy some time while she decided how to broach the subject, and mustered the courage to do it.

"Yeah, that'd be great, thanks. I'm exhausted. I usually love driving, but with all that's going on, today it seemed a real drag. Travelling can take it out of you."

Thank god, she thought—the perfect opening.

"Well—speaking of travelling—there's something I need to talk to you about."

"A-ha." He sat flipping through the newspaper lying on the table, paying little heed to her.

She took a deep breath and counted to three.

"I saw your mum today. She wasn't in a good way. James—you can't go taking her on such big outings. She just can't cope anymore."

He jerked his head around. The hawk-like glare of his attention was now directed at her. He dropped the paper and fired straight back. It took her by surprise, as lately they'd had such a good rapport over things to do with Mary. She'd felt appreciated and her input welcome.

"When I suggested it, she agreed it was a good idea! She *wanted* to go."

His voice had risen, and she could sense his irritation. Self-righteous shit. He hated anyone challenging him. But she had to brave this, for Mary's sake.

"James, you obviously haven't noticed, but your mother isn't one to stand up to you. She'll always go along with your suggestions." A note of exasperation crept into her voice, despite her vow to keep calm.

"Mum had a brilliant day yesterday," he argued. "She and Rose had a great time."

"But she's paying the price for it today. Wait till you get over there. You'll see what I mean." Her voice lifted to match his, determined to make him see.

He rose from the chair and took a step towards her. "Are you saying we should deny her the chance to enjoy what time she's got left?"

His dark eyes blazed, and the anger contorted his handsome mouth into an aggressive scowl. Something had triggered this reaction—no this over-reaction—but she told herself to stay the course.

"No—that's not it at all!"

"You'd have us just let her fade away inside that house, seeing no one? Well, damned if I'm going to let her spend her last days like that. She needs to cram a lot of living into a short time and I'm going to make sure she does!"

"Have you ever thought to ask her what she wants? What *she* really wants? Perhaps it's time you stopped making this all about you."

She immediately wondered if she'd gone too far. His face was incredulous, in disbelief that she would even think of speaking to him like that. He took another step towards her, and she shrank back, retreating from the waves of anger radiating off him. James naturally had a huge physical presence, but now, towering over her, he was truly intimidating. She closed her eyes and prepared herself for another barrage.

But it didn't come. She opened them to see him poised there, mouth open as if the words wouldn't come. And then he simply turned and walked away.

Still shaking, Kate made herself go through the familiar motions of making the tea. She stood for a long time, holding the cup in hand, staring out the window, studying the people drifting by on the street. She liked people-watching. Wondering about their stories. Where had they come from? Where were they going? Were they happy? Or sad? Or neither—living some beige existence? Meanwhile, the tea went cold, and she poured it away down the sink.

After a time, regrets about being so assertive with James surfaced. He was in as much pain as Ellie, although he hid it well behind that facade, not wanting to admit that he, who usually controlled things, was faced with something he couldn't control. She needed to be kinder, treat him with greater understanding.

"Does the offer still stand? Tea?" His voice startled her. She hadn't heard him approach. It surprised her that such a big man could move almost without a sound. Like a giant panther, light on his feet but poised to spring into action if riled. "Looks like you need another one too," he said. "I'll make us both one."

She nodded, still wary after their skirmish, and continued to stare out at the passersby.

"I need to apologise. My behaviour was absolutely out of line. I'm sorry." His capitulation was unexpected. She'd witnessed quite a few confrontations between James and Ellie. And she'd never once seen him back down. And certainly never apologise. She said nothing. "You didn't deserve that. Not someone who's doing so much for this family. And you're right—I've been selfish. I should have noticed what it was doing to mum."

"It's OK," she said. "Sometimes when it's happening, you can't see what's in front of your eyes. I think it's our mind's way of protecting us from things that are too hard to face."

"It's still no excuse. I am sorry. Please forgive me." Only a short time ago, his eyes had been dark with anger. Now she read the sincerity of his words and perhaps regret in their mellowed mahogany hue.

"I'm sorry too. I was out of line. Said things I shouldn't have. And it's OK, she's been resting today and she'll be better again tomorrow," she reassured him. "Perhaps you need to get her friends and the family to come to see her," she suggested, adding gently, "I think the time for making lots of new memories might have passed. Give them time to talk with her about the memories they already have. She'd love that. I know my grandmother did. And now I treasure those conversations we had."

"I will," he said. "Thanks Kate. I *do* appreciate all the help you're giving us, and her."

"It's what people do at times like this. And with Mary—she's been so good to me. To be honest, I feel quite useless, but if I can help in some little way and make things easier, then that's great."

"Well, she loves you, too. I know she enjoys the time you spend with her. Talking helps keep her mind off all the other shitty stuff."

As she lay in bed, she heard the front door close with a soft click and the throaty rumble of a car engine. James was taking the night shift. He'd resume his place by Mary's bedside, and Ellie would head home. She decided there was one positive thing to come out of this bleak situation. James had stepped up and was finally putting his family ahead of his work. Behind that brash facade was a decent person. She'd seen the first glimpses of it at Christmas. He wasn't afraid to show the world how much he adored his mother. And while he'd previously appeared offhand with his sister, now, when it mattered, you could see that he cared for her. He was the strong one, holding Ellie's head above water. So she didn't drown in the enormity of what they were facing. Holding his mother's hand as she journeyed to a place where they couldn't follow.

She realised that her previous disdain for James had been slowly chipped away. He was in many ways a good man, a kind man. Not a perfect one, but then those didn't exist, anyway. He was very different from her, but she liked him.

They fell into a grim routine, Ellie and James ensuring that one of them was always at Mary's side. Kate was there often, and strangely enjoyed her visits. Despite the seriousness of the situation, there was lots of chatter and laughter, and it was a privilege to be included in their conversations.

"Oh my god Mum, do you remember that Christmas when you bought Ellie that little pink bike? And she'd gone to bed, and I was still up, helping you be Santa Claus?"

Mary choked with laughter.

"God, Kate, you should have seen her. I think she was a little drunk. Probably on Santa's glass of sherry. Anyway, here's this grown woman on a five-year-old's bike, riding up and down the street outside our house, and ringing the bell. It was almost midnight. The neighbours must have thought you were crazy."

"No, Mum, that wasn't the worst holiday. The worst holiday was that year you took us to Cornwall. Do you remember we were in that tiny little caravan, and it rained and rained and rained for days?"

"Oh, how could I forget!" said Mary. "And then the one day it was fine, we walked down to the beach and the waves were so big. I didn't want you to go in the water, but of course James insisted, and then he nearly drowned."

"That's right! I'd forgotten about that. You know, back then I think I hated him so much, I wouldn't have cared if he'd drowned."

"Oh Ellie, that's awful," Kate laughed.

"But it's true! I truly hated him back then. He teased me mercilessly and pulled my hair. You don't realise how lucky you were to be an only child. Not having an older brother who picked on you."

"We did some stupid things, didn't we Ellie? Do you remember when we lit that fire in the backyard? I'm sure it was your idea to roast chestnuts on our own bonfire. And the neighbours called the fire truck? I don't know how you put up with us sometimes, Mum."

"It was a bit of a bumpy ride with you two," said Mary, "but I wouldn't have changed it for the world. Children are the best. At the risk of sounding bossy, you need to all get on and have some. You won't regret it, I promise."

Her watery eyes met Kate's, and she gave a gentle smile, as if Mary knew of the desire for a husband and family that she thought she'd hidden deep down inside.

Even the time for talking was over sooner than expected. At the beginning, the cancer had been slow and insidious. Now it quickened the pace of its march as if time itself had fallen in step alongside the disease so that soon they were hurtling towards the inevitable conclusion.

The nurses visited each day, giving their guidance, ensuring Mary was comfortable and pain free. She was a model patient, graciously accepting the care that she herself had given to so many in her nursing career. Never demanding, never making a fuss. And that was how she left them.

It had been a tough day. Mary was struggling and the nurses for the first time mentioned the word hospice. Exhaustion was Ellie's permanent state of being, but this fresh development tipped her over the edge. She'd gone straight to bed the moment they'd arrived home.

Kate sat in a chair, the TV functioning as background noise. Her phone rang. It was odd how a sound so cheerful and full of anticipation could equally convey an ominous sense of dread. Seeing it was James calling, she knew it wasn't good.

"She's gone," he said. "She was sleeping. Her breathing was a bit ragged, but no more than usual. And I was just sitting there, reading my book. Then I noticed the silence."

"Oh, James, I'm so sorry," she said. Tears welled in her eyes.

"Ellie's phone went straight to voicemail."

"She's in bed. Do you want me to wake her?"

"No. I'll come. I want to be the one to tell her. The doctor's on his way. But after that, I'll come."

Kate poured herself a massive slosh of gin, and lay back on the sofa, staring at the ceiling, waiting for him to arrive.

CHAPTER 16

Wake

London, England - June 2008

"OH GOD, I'M PISSED," mumbled Ellie, from where she slumped in the back seat.

"You're allowed," Kate replied, flicking her gaze to the rear-view mirror, which confirmed that Ellie did indeed appear very drunk.

She edged James's white Beemer into the traffic. It was raining again, the droplets on the windscreen splintered by the lights of oncoming cars.

"It's OK baby, close your eyes and have a little sleep," soothed James. "Kate's going to get both of us drunken bums home safely."

"Thanks Katie, love you," she said, drifting off.

"Love you too."

"Yeah, thanks Kate," he echoed. "It's been a shit day."

"Sure has," she agreed.

"At least they all came," he said. "So many people. A bloody good send off."

"Yes," said Kate. "I thought we'd never get them on their way. Everyone just wanted to talk about her. God, I could never hope to have that many friends even if I live to be a hundred."

He grinned. "Yeah, a proper wake, it was. She would have loved it."

Arriving at the house, Kate took care not to nudge the wall as she nosed the big car into the narrow parking space out front. She and James extracted Ellie and flanked her as they made their way up the steps.

"I'm OK, I'm OK," she reassured them, as James flicked on the lights. "Need bed."

"Sure love, way you go. See you in the morning." James hugged her and pointed her toward the stairs. She wove her way towards them, her gait unsteady.

"Goodnight sweetie. I'll be up soon. I'll come and check on you, yeah?" Kate called after her, then turned to James and asked under her breath, "Is she OK on her own, do you think?"

"Yeah, she'll be good. I think it's as much the tiredness as the alcohol," he reassured her. "What a week. You know, I think I need the drinks she's had," he said. "Want one?"

Without waiting for her answer, he pulled out a bottle of whisky and two glasses, placing them on the granite bench top.

"Why not?" she said. "Seems only fitting to have a wee dram for Mary."

"Yeah," he said. "She'd be all for it." He splashed a generous amount into each glass. "Shame they don't make it on her beloved Barra. That would have been the ultimate." He surveyed the bottle in his hand. It was one of his favourite Islay whiskies; an expensive Lagavulin. "Well, this will have to do and it's no poor substitute, anyway."

The whisky was a burnished amber, not unlike the eyes of the man handing her the glass. As she raised it to her lips, she breathed in the sweet smoky aroma, the smell of Scotland.

"To Mary, to Mum." He raised his glass. "Slàinte mhath."

"To Mary. Slàinte mhath," she echoed, clinking her glass against his.

The whisky's peaty chocolate flavour filled her mouth, delivering a warm, medicinal hit as she swallowed. Appropriate in the circumstances. Medicine to heal them. They stood by the counter, sipping their drinks, each wrapped in their own thoughts. The ticking of the antique clock echoed off their silence, marking the void in their conversation with its steady beat.

"It's so bloody unfair." His voice was harsh. "Fucking useless doctors." He turned to her, eyes blazing, his voice bitter. "You know, you have to wonder how they could send her home all those times, saying it was nothing. Prescribed her some Vitamin B shots. Useless bastards."

He shook his head, muttering curses under his breath. He tossed back the whisky, the grip of his hand on the glass so tight, jaw set in a tense line, struggling to control the anger coiled tight inside.

"Fuck them all."

His voice trailed away, despondent, defeated. He crumpled over to lean on the bench, resting his head on his arms.

Six months ago, it would have surprised Kate to discover that anything could reduce James Beckett to tears. And six months ago, she would have never thought she would do what she did next.

Placing her glass on the counter, she stepped towards him, wrapping her arms around him from behind as he wept in silence. She let her own tears fall, dampening the crisp white linen of his shirt as her cheek lay on his shoulder.

He smelled good. That musky scent of a man. She hadn't been close enough to one to inhale it like this for a long time. Mixed with it was the distinctive fragrance that he always wore—the one he kept tucked away in the downstairs bathroom. It always wafted into a room when he entered and lingered after he had gone. Up close like this, combined with his own unique aroma, it was intoxicating.

Pressed against the length of his body, he also felt good. After spending many hours in the gym room together, Kate knew the shape of this man. Whenever their workouts coincided, she couldn't help but sneak a glance across at the muscular legs, the powerful arms and shapely buttocks.

Like Ellie, he was tall, but whereas she was lean, he was substantial. With his shirt off, he had the physique of a rugby player. He reminded her of the beautiful men she'd covertly ogled back in New Zealand, when her class's swimming lessons at the Millennium Pool had coincided with a training session of the professional rugby league team. Unable to show overt interest in front of a group of seven-year-olds, she had still taken the opportunity to admire them discreetly.

James had a similar sculpted body, pushed to hardness by determination and commitment. And now, she couldn't help but be aroused by how well her own fit against it.

He turned to meet her embrace, at first careful, almost hesitant, enveloping her gently in his arms, but then, perhaps sensing the desire welling up in her, clasped her close against him.

She'd heard it said that a rush of lust often accompanied the presence of death. There was no doubt the crippling grief that had possessed them had been replaced by another urge.

She desperately wanted him to make love to her. Not gently. Oh no, she wanted him to take her quickly, roughly, maybe as a way to knock the sharp edges off their pain.

He lifted her head from where it lay damp against his shoulder and kissed her—hard. She reciprocated his kiss with the same ferocity. He'd sensed the desperate need in her.

His mouth tasted of the smoky sweetness of the whisky, and a hint of saltiness from their tears. He plunged one hand into the front of her shirt and cupped the curve of her breast. A small cry of both pleasure and pain erupted from deep within her, as he squeezed one of her large erect nipples, the traitorous pair signalling her arousal.

An exquisite combination of sensations engulfed her—the thrilling firmness of one large hand on her breast accompanied by his soft impatient mouth working down from lips to neck, while his other hand unbuttoned the front of her shirt, tracing the smooth line of her stomach.

"Not here," she mumbled through his kisses. If she let this continue, he would take her here against the countertop. Despite their sudden overwhelming need, somehow she wanted this to be more, to mean more.

"Come on, then," he urged, taking her hand and pulling her towards his bedroom, then pausing. "If you're sure, that is. If you want this."

He scanned her face, his own serious; eyes darting, dark pupils dilated with desire.

"Yes, I want this."

She said it without hesitation, but felt pleased that he'd checked. They both needed to know there'd be no regrets come morning.

The bedside lamps bathed his bedroom in a golden light. Kate strangely felt no desire to ask him to switch them off, as she might normally do with a first time. Usually she took courage from the darkness, gratefully allowing it to swathe her body, keeping one last barrier between her and a man. But months of living in the same house had created an unexpected intimacy, and she felt no trace of awkwardness at revealing all of herself to him.

While her own lack of inhibition was a little surprising, the confidence with which James discarded the last of his clothes and stood before her, allowing her eyes to wander across the beauty of his body, was not unexpected. He was a man very comfortable in his own skin.

In the early days, she'd thought him arrogant. But now she understood he was one of those rare individuals who seemed to know who he was, both his strengths and his flaws, and accepted them. It didn't bother him if others did the same or not. James was brave enough to simply say 'take it or leave it'. And she knew which she wanted.

Rummaging in his suitcase, he produced a strip of condoms.

"Never go away unprepared," he said with a grin, tossing them onto the bedside table.

"Just as well," she said, relieved, as it had been a while and she was unsure whether any still hid in the depths of her handbag.

He stood beside the fire, and the play of light and dark from the flickering gas flames outlined the curves and valleys of his muscular body. With his face in shadow, she couldn't read his expression. He extended his hand.

"Come here," he said.

She placed her hand in his and stepped towards him. The warm caress of the fire mingled with the warmth of his touch as she let him trace the outline of her body. As he ran a finger over her lips, followed the curve of her chin, outlined the hollow of her neck, traced the narrow path between her breasts, she marvelled at how delicately those large hands moved across her, lulled by the gentleness of this interlude.

She shivered as his hand grazed her thigh, exploring further, fingers circling, causing her breath to quicken, her body leaning into the pressure of his touch.

His lips roved across her breast, licking, and sucking and nipping until with one hard tug of her nipple, his teeth demanding, he catapulted them back into the frenzy that had engulfed them in the kitchen.

Kate's previous lovers had been without exception considerate, but predictable, unimaginative. Boring. But with James, there was a wildness, a sense there was no map for where this might go.

Her heart thudded in time to his rapid breathing as he shoved her back onto the bed. He moved to lie across her, pinning her with his weight, his thigh nudging between her legs, his erection huge between them.

"Do you trust me?" he asked, his eyes bright with anticipation.

She nodded, but felt a little shiver at the strength that now pulsed in his hands and the tension of his body pressed hard against her.

"Then let me do this," he said, his voice a whisper.

With eyes closed, she let him explore at will, surrendering to him, allowing him to lead her body wherever he desired it to go. Big hands roved down her length, a finger circled lazily at her centre, another finding its way deep inside her and then a second, causing her to gasp in pleasure. Feral groans echoed across the room and she didn't recognise her own voice separate from his, as they moved against each other.

He dropped to his knees, trailing his lips across her stomach, fluttering his tongue against the tender skin of her thigh, moving inch by inch towards her centre, sucking and nipping and licking, the sensation building to a ball of heat at her core.

And then, just as she thought that her need for him was so great that she might beg him not to stop, he drew back. Reaching for the condom, James tore it open with deft hands and offered it to her. She eased it over the length of him, seeing him shudder as her hand traced his erection. He lifted her hips, sliding a pillow beneath her, laying her out before him, and she let her legs fall open in invitation, an offer to let him use her as he wanted.

She coaxed him inside eagerly, and within moments, the friction of his rhythmic thrusts sent her back into a dizzying whirl of pleasure. She opened her eyes and met his, watching her, reading every flicker of her heightening arousal, and only giving into his own shattering orgasm moments after her own.

Afterwards, they lay in silence for ages. He flicked off the lights, and they bathed in the blissful afterglow of their lovemaking, his arm wrapped around her waist, her head cradled against his broad shoulder.

He spoke first, his voice quiet and low in the darkness.

"Tell me, how is it that a woman like you hasn't already hooked up with someone?" he murmured, stroking the curve of her hip.

"Never been the right person," she sighed. "And I've never been anyone's right person."

"I find that hard to believe. How can that be?"

"Ah," she said, "well, I have given that some thought. Ellie and I have a theory: Fatal Flaw Syndrome."

"What? What the hell is Fatal Flaw Syndrome?" He gave a soft chuckle .

"Ellie and I both have it. We've talked about it at length. Both of us show it in different ways, but in the end it's two sides of the same thing."

"OK, tell me then." He pressed an amused smile against her hair.

"All right. Well, with Ellie, she's always open to people. She falls fast and hard. But then, before you know it, there it is. Some 'Fatal Flaw', which means she can't possibly be with them. Remember Anthony?"

"Yes," he said, "seemed a nice guy. She even took him round to meet Mum."

"Yep," said Kate, "But fatal flaw—he was vegetarian. Ellie decided he'd either try to convert her or judge her. End of relationship."

"Probably true."

"Yeah, but he was perfect for her in every other way. People work through far bigger things than that to be together."

"OK. Next," he said.

"Mark, you know, the one from Cornwall? The artist?"

"Yeah, now I thought he *was* going to become my brother-in-law."

"Well, he almost did. He adored her, and he certainly fitted Ellie's bohemian aesthetic. But no, suddenly she decided he was too homegrown. Too down-to-earth. She had this fear she'd blink and find herself living in some rural artist's community, dying of boredom. She decided she wanted someone more exotic—definitely not English, definitely not rural. Fatal flaw, out he goes."

"But there have been others."

"Yeah, but guaranteed every one of them, when it got serious, there was some unsurmountable reason not to go any further. She has a theory that it works in reverse too—told me there's been several she wanted more from, but then they ended things. She consoles herself by believing that they discovered a fatal flaw in her, and so, heartbroken as she was, it was for the best."

"So tell me about you?" he said. "What fatal flaws have you uncovered?"

"I never let them stay long enough for me to find out." It had been her protection, effective at preventing heartbreak. "With most of them, I don't go beyond a few dates, maybe a bit of casual sex, have some fun and then move on. If I don't get too attached, then I can't be disappointed."

"So, is that what this is?" he asked. "Will we do this a few times and then it's thanks, James, but no thanks?" He was so direct. Somehow, because she expected it, it didn't throw her.

"Would that bother you?"

She rolled towards him, seeking truth in his eyes. His return gaze was intense, his eyes sparking, even in the dimness of the room.

"If you'd asked me this morning whether I'd be happy with a quick fuck to help us work through our mutual grief and then afterwards carry on like before—yeah, I would have said that's fine by me. Because that's how it's always been with me. No commitments, no worries."

"Your fatal flaw?" she suggested. "Can't commit?"

"Perhaps." A slight smile played around his mouth. "Though it sounds like it might be yours, too?"

"Fair call," she replied. She deflected the conversation back to him. "So there aren't others?'

He laughed. "Yes, and no..." He hesitated, as if judging how much he should reveal to her. But as he continued, she read a sincerity in his eyes that she'd doubted possible in the early days of knowing him. "I have to be honest, with my job, there's hardly ever been a time when I haven't had a woman by my side. I've never lacked options for my plus one at all the parties and events. But I never bring them home. Not one of them has been in this house. Or met my family."

"Wow, that's quite some record."

"Well, most of them are smart enough to read my lack of serious long-term interest correctly and drift off to more promising prospects. I know everyone thinks I'm shallow, a party boy. Out to have fun and fun to be with, but expect nothing more. But something's changed," he said. There was vulnerability in his face. "I've changed. And I think it's happened in subtle ways I hadn't noticed. But tonight it jumped out and smacked me over the head. Like someone said, you fucking idiot James, what you need, she's right there in front of you, why aren't you doing something about it? For the first time, I think I do need more. I want more. I want you."

He leaned in and kissed her. In that questioning kiss, Kate understood what he wanted to know—would she, could she, give him what he needed? She responded without hesitation, her mouth seeking his, deepening the kiss in an unreserved yes to his invitation. She didn't know where this was going, where it would end up, but she wanted more too. Now they had ventured down this pathway, she knew exploring each other physically wouldn't be enough.

Their first frantic lovemaking was like being roughly tumbled in a rogue wave. Later, as they moved more gently in the ebb and flow of a slow, deliberate coming together, she delighted in scrutinising his body more closely, checking its response to the touch of her hands, her mouth.

And in return, he analysed her body's reaction like a scientist, having trapped some exotic new specimen, now wanting to understand everything about it. She wasn't unnerved by this intense study, but revelled in it. It reminded her of the old-fashioned wedding vows: 'with my body I thee worship'. He reverently attended to each part of her, testing what he could do with it, what he could make it do in response.

But the overwhelming physicality was only the beginning. They had lived in the same house for nine months, and would have said they knew each other reasonably well. However, now they had moved into this uncharted territory, it was as if they were new to each other again. He had questions.

"So, you've never been in a proper relationship?"

She lay there, curled against him, running her hand absentmindedly across the dark curled hairs of his chest. "Only once—one that I thought would be forever."

"So why wasn't it?"

"I was too young. Just nineteen. He was ten years older. An American. He came over to join one of the sailing development programmes. The first few times I saw him at the yacht club, he had a group of girls around him—like moths to a flame. He was charming, and he was different. They were all hoping he'd single them out for individual attention."

"And you?"

"No, I was so focused on my sailing at the time that I only drifted through the club. I didn't have a boyfriend, and I wasn't looking for one. My whole life revolved around training and competing. Qualifying for the big events was everything."

"But you ended up with him anyway..."

"Yeah, it sort of happened by accident. I was in the club carpark one night and my car had a flat tyre. I had set about changing it. Always took pride in being independent. But he noticed me struggling to loosen off the wheel nuts and came over to help. Afterwards, I offered to buy him a drink to thank him for rescuing me. Within a week, we were inseparable."

"Love at first sight?" Even in the darkness, she could tell he was smiling, as if he didn't believe in the concept.

"Well, as close as you can get," she replied. "And I did love him, totally and hopelessly. We were together for almost a year. But as it came closer to the time for him to go home—his contract was ending—I got scared. He assumed that I'd be going with him. Like I said, I was too young for such a big decision. To go with him would have been huge. So I broke it off before the time came."

"And he let you?"

"Yeah, walked away without looking back. It threw me. He just cut me off. Made no attempt to change my mind. It was like we had never been."

He stroked her hair, his hands light, the touch soothing.

"I realised that I'd never questioned whether he felt the same way about me as I felt for him. In the month before he left, he started seeing one of the other girls. And she went with him." She couldn't stop the remembered hurt from seeping into her voice.

"I couldn't understand how he went from planning our life together in San Diego to taking someone else to live that life. I felt like an idiot, that I'd made more of it than it was. Since then, I haven't been able to trust myself to make good judgments about men."

He had been lying on his back, listening to her talk. He rolled towards her, brushing her hair aside.

"You should," he said in a husky voice. "Trust yourself."

And as he made love to her once more, this time slow and gentle, she did as he said. She let go of the doubts, trusting the perfect fit of their bodies, the primal rhythm of their dance, and the expression in the eyes of this flawed but beautiful man.

CHAPTER 17

Morning After

London, England - June 2008

SOUNDS FROM THE STREET—A car starting, a door closing, distant voices—all hinted that it was morning. Moving in tiny increments, from being asleep to awake, Kate eventually opened her eyes. They paused on the elaborate plaster rose in the centre of the white ceiling and then closed again. She knew without checking that this was, in fact, not her ceiling, not her room, not her bed.

Although not touching him, she sensed James's presence next to her, the relaxed rise and fall of his breathing, the tiny movements as his body adjusted itself into a more comfortable position, and then his arm sleepily reached for her, laying across her waist. This blissful semi-awake state was spoiled by the imposition of her body's sudden need to pee, and she eased his arm away. After using the bathroom, she slid back in beside him. Even half-asleep, he sensed she'd returned and gathered her to him once again. She lay in a comfortable doze until her inconvenient body presented its next demand. Now it wanted water.

She voted against strolling around the house naked, although she had heard no sounds hinting Ellie had surfaced. Leaning over the side of the bed, she began rummaging in the pile of discarded clothing. Retrieving her shirt, she looked at the length and rejected it. Not a good look to have her bum hanging out the bottom. On her next attempt, she found James's and pulled it over her head, glancing down to check it was of sufficient length to ensure she was decent.

Kate padded down the hallway, her steps light. The patterned Turkish runner provided a buffer between her feet and the cool wooden floor, and also muffled her footsteps. She pushed open the door to the kitchen, only to find Ellie nonchalantly leaning against the countertop. The whisky glasses that she and James had abandoned were still sitting there. She was thankful they'd detoured to the bedroom, so she didn't have to think of what else would have happened on that counter.

"How's your head?" Kate said. Last time she'd seen Ellie, she was heading for a massive hangover.

"Unexpectedly good. And how are you?" she asked with a knowing grin.

"The same," Kate replied noncommittally, while realising that it was obvious where and how she'd spent the night, given she was standing there in a man's shirt.

"I think it's great," Ellie said. "In fact, it's a relief. Not having to live with all that pent up sexual tension between the two of you anymore."

"What?" The events of last night had come as a surprise to Kate. Yet somehow Ellie had predicted this would happen.

"I would say it was more of a spur-of-the-moment thing."

"Oh no," Ellie assured her. "All roads have been leading to this for a few months now. Only neither of you could see it. I didn't want to say anything in case I jinxed it. I think it's bloody marvellous."

Kate sculled a glass of water and then set to making coffee for her, tea for James.

"I'm off for a walk," said Ellie. "I'll bring back doughnuts." It was a tradition that at least once in the weekend someone would do a trip to the little Italian bakery a few blocks over. Their doughnuts were sublime.

"Yes, please," Kate said. "You know which ones." Infused with a thick caramel, to which they added a delicious hint of salt. They were her favourites and were addictive.

After Ellie left, she downed her coffee and headed back to the bedroom, depositing the tea next to James and then tiptoeing back around the bed to snuggle in beside him. She pressed herself along the length of his muscular back and slid her arm under his to rest her hand on his chest. She twined her fingers in the strands of dark hair, stroking him as she might a cat. He stirred from his sleep, making small contented noises.

"Tea there for you." She whispered in his ear. He rolled to face her, seeking out a kiss.

"Coffee there," he said. "You taste of it."

"Doughnuts also coming soon. Ellie's gone for them."

"Then we have time."

There was playfulness in those whisky-coloured eyes a few inches away from hers. His hand moved down her back, across her hip, and settled to rest between her legs. His fingers probed further, carefully searching for just the right spot. She groaned as, having located it, he stroked back and forth with exquisite gentle pressure.

"Bet I can before she gets back," he said, nuzzling against her neck.

For a man with such big hands, he could use them with surprising precision. She didn't accept the bet, but she would have lost. Her final tiny gasps of pleasure coincided with the sound of Ellie's Doc Martens clunking on the front steps. He smiled smugly as he unwound his body from hers and reached over to take a sip of the now lukewarm tea.

"Now, off you go. Get me a doughnut to say thank you," he said, patting her bare bottom, encouraging her to venture out from the tangle of sheets.

"My pleasure," she said.

"Yes, I think it was," he replied with a satisfied grin.

CHAPTER 18

A Proposal

Kent, England - December 2008

THERE WERE CARS SCATTERED along both sides of the driveway and down the country lane. James edged his BMW into a spot that had gone unnoticed. They came to a stop on a concrete pad in front of the barn.

"Sorry, it's a bit further to walk, but at least you ladies will make it into the house without sinking in the mire."

It had been raining for weeks. In fact, James struggled to recall many days without rain since Mary's funeral way back in June, and here it was Christmas. The mutterings about climate change might well be right. The fields were awash and there was more mud than grass in the parts that weren't under water.

"It's fine," Kate said, hauling on a raincoat.

"The car's much safer over here, too."

"Definitely," Ellie agreed with a wry grin. She'd been to enough Beckett Christmases to know.

On more than one occasion, there'd been damage done to vehicles at the Beckett Christmas bash. Overindulgence in Christmas spirit was dangerous when coupled with the rambunctious Beckett personality. The uncles, aunties and cousins acted as if drink-drive rules didn't apply at Christmas time. He'd known them to play dodgems when trying to extract a car from a tight spot. Definitely a good idea to park well away from the rest of them.

With hoods pulled up against the endless wet, they dived into the back, unloading the vast supply of food and alcohol organised by Ellie. They headed for the house like packhorses on a week-long trail ride, burdened with bags and boxes, an excessive amount, given that there were only the three of them. But it went without saying that people would contribute generous amounts of food and drink to the biannual gathering.

James was thankful that this was the year of the big family 'Christmas do'. It would have been overwhelmingly sad to have spent this first Christmas without their mother at the house. At least this way, the craziness of the large extended family would sweep them along and take their minds off her empty place at the table. Despite their father, Ron, abandoning them, the remaining Becketts had always gone out of their way to keep Mary and her children in the fold.

When James was thirteen, Ron had announced he was going back to Aberdeen to work the North Sea oil rigs. His four brothers couldn't understand the 'daft bastard', but money to support his family continued to flow. They expressed open scepticism when he took a job down in Indonesia, even if it was well-paid. Although he still provided for Mary and the children, they could see the writing on the wall. Mary attempted to shield them from the truth, but James and Ellie were old enough to realise he wasn't coming back.

In the end, the contact stopped. When they eventually discovered he had a new family with a young Indonesian woman, her Beckett in-laws decided he was beyond help and rallied behind Mary and the kids. They'd all moved on and rarely mentioned his name. At the biannual Christmas gatherings, they blended seamlessly with the rest of the family, as if he had never existed.

Over the years, various family members decreed new traditions. As a kid, he'd been reluctant to take part, but always complied to keep his mother happy. And as an adult, he'd continued to indulge her by going along with the ridiculous ideas. It was worth it to see her enjoyment. This year he'd done it for Ellie, and he was wearing the result.

As a tribute to the movie '*Bridget Jones' Diary*', the four senior Beckett wives had declared ugly Christmas jumpers compulsory this year. There was to be a prize for the ugliest, voted on by all present. Kate's incredulous face when he'd produced one for her suggested that Ellie's selection might well be the winner.

"I'm not bloody wearing that," she'd said.

But Ellie had insisted Kate counted as family, and that's what family did, silencing her feeble protests. Little did either of them know he had plans for today that would bind Kate even more closely to this family. In his pocket was a small velvet box containing a ring.

He watched Kate trailing Ellie into the kitchen where a flock of aunties met them, eager to take charge of the overflowing bags. James still marvelled at this woman and their relationship. Neither of them had anything like it in their past. Both had a string of past lovers. Both recalled brief dazzling flashes of passion that faded with the realisation that there was nothing of substance to sustain it. The last year had been the worst of his life, but it had also been the best. It had taken the death of his mother to strip back the layers of his life to see what was important—and that was Kate.

"James." There was a booming male voice. "Good to see you, lad, and your sister."

A large hand clapped him on the back, a fond gesture from the man who'd replaced his absent father. Keith was the eldest of his four uncles, and the one with the biggest personality. Which was saying something in a family of confident extroverts.

"And this is your lovely lady?"

He sidled over to Kate, sliding an arm around her waist. James hoped she wouldn't take offence. What might be judged overfamiliar to some was a friendly normal in the Beckett clan. But Kate, in her usual easygoing way, smiled and was soon engaged in animated conversation with Keith as if they'd known each other forever.

The day passed in a pleasant blur of food, alcohol, and lively conversation. He genuinely liked these people. Not everyone could say that about their extended family. He knew lots of people dreaded these types of family Christmas gatherings. But he felt an ease amid his family that didn't happen anywhere else. This was the one place he felt he truly belonged. And today it was obvious the family had decided Kate also belonged.

By mid-afternoon, there was a slight bustle as some gathered their belongings, preparing to leave. Keith called the group to attention with a jangling of a spoon against a glass.

"Before you all slope off, as the oldest, I get to say a few words. No bloody arguing or moaning. Until I decide to turn up my toes, you're stuck with me." He turned an authoritative glare on a pair of his brothers, who were sniggering.

"And you young ones, make sure you pay attention when your elders have something to say," he said with mock-severity, pointing towards some of the youngest cousins, who giggled nervously, still a little unsure whether that frown on his face was genuine.

"Now, I'm not going to take too much of your time, but some things need to be said. Firstly, thank you all for coming along. If it wasn't good to see you, it was good to see the food and booze you brought. And we certainly made a large dent in that."

He waved at the tables, once heaving with food, now a rubble of discarded plates and leftovers.

"Secondly, thanks to Graham and Wendy for opening your house to all of us again. You're bloody brave, letting all this lot in. Let's raise a glass to say so."

His aunt and uncle stood beaming while all toasted their hospitality. Owners of the large rambling farmhouse, they were pleased to open its many rooms to the family for the occasion.

"And finally, as you know, while we celebrate all who could be here, we always take a moment to remember those who aren't with us. And this year..."

He paused for a moment, struggling to hold back the emotion.

"This year, we are, of course, without the lovely Mary. Ellie and James—and Kate—she would have been so pleased that you came today, even though it's hard doing that without her. You know we loved her too. You know we miss her. So let's take a moment to drink to her. To Mary."

Although James had known it would happen, a family tradition, the toast overwhelmed him. The loss of his mother was still raw. In places like this, Mary's absence was painful. However, knowing a reply was expected, he steeled himself, cleared his throat, and spoke.

"Thank you. You know she loved you all, too. It's bloody hard, especially on days like today. Not only because I'd give anything to have another Christmas with my mum, but also because—" His voice caught with emotion, "—there are some things I'd have loved her to see. And this is one of them." He stopped, searched the room, and then found her. "Kate, come here."

She wore a puzzled expression, but putting her glass down, wove her way through the crowd, stormy blue eyes fixed on him.

He reached into his pocket, retrieving the small box, resting it on his open palm. Realisation dawned on her face. Her eyes grew wide, and he scanned for signs this was going to go how he hoped it would. No going back now, not in front of the entire family. Which was one reason he'd chosen to do it this way. He couldn't chicken out. She stood awkwardly beside him, and fear surged through him. Was she going to reject him?

There was a collective hush in the room, as if they, too, were waiting for the answer to that question. It was too late to stop. No choice but to be brave, so he abandoned his practised speech and said the words that came into his head.

"Kate, you've met all the family now, and I hope it hasn't put you off. I love you and if anything good is going to come out of this year, I hope it's going to be that you say yes. Will you marry me? Join the Beckett clan?"

She gulped in a huge breath, and he could see waves of emotion wash across her face. Maybe she could see the fear that lurked behind his eyes, because she smiled a small reassuring smile and took his hand.

"Yes," she said simply. "Yes."

Whoops, cheers and applause filled the room as he scooped her up and kissed her. Remembering the ring, he plucked it from its satiny nest and threaded it onto her finger. He hoped she would like it. He'd spent hours with the designer, mulling over ideas, examining a dazzling array of stones, and then having selected one, waited patiently for the man to work his magic, crafting this unique piece.

Ellie pushed her way through the mob, who had pressed in around them to offer congratulations. She wrapped both of them in a massive hug and shrieked with delight.

"About time," she said. "Thank you, James—you found me a sister, and she's a bloody good one."

Those who'd been intending to leave paused in their goodbyes, staying to indulge in the freely-flowing champagne.

"Where did this come from?" Ellie asked, already on her second glass.

"Snuck it into the car when you weren't paying attention and got it out the same way," he said with a smug smile.

"Looks like you've been up to lots behind my back. But all of it good. You did quite well, considering it was without my usual help."

"Ah, well, we might still need some of that—there's a wedding to plan now, isn't there Kate?" he said, turning to his new fiancée. Such a strange old-fashioned word, but somehow he found it unexpectedly appealing.

"Yes, we have."

Gazing back at him, her face appeared happy, but he still had uncomfortable doubts. He couldn't put his finger on exactly what or why, but it was as if other thoughts simmered beneath the surface, her smile not so dazzling as he'd have expected. Maybe he was imagining it. Perhaps it reflected how bloody nervous he had been. But she'd said yes, so he needed to relax and enjoy his new status as a person engaged to be married.

It was almost an hour before they dragged themselves away from the well-wishers and joined the stream of family, all heading for their homes. Kate drove. She wasn't a big drinker and was confident in handling his big car, weaving through the narrow lanes, navigating the busy motorway, and finally crawling along the brightly Christmas-lit streets of central London.

"I'm exhausted," she said as they dumped the remains of the day in the kitchen.

"I'll make you a coffee if you like," he offered.

"Nah, I think I might head for bed," she said, kissing him lightly and padding off down to their bedroom. There it was again, that nagging hint of something unsaid. Again, he brushed it off. She's just tired, he reassured himself.

"Ellie? Coffee?" he asked.

"Yes, please," she said, flopping into the nearest chair. "Well, a big day in the Beckett family. I'm so pleased for you both." She tugged off her boots, propped her woolly sock-clad feet on the coffee table and sprawled back in the chair.

"Do you think she's OK?" he asked from the kitchen. "That she really wants this?"

"Of course she does," said Ellie. "There's nothing Kate wants more than a husband and a family. You know, she always brushes off what her parents did to her. And she'll tell you she's adjusted to losing her grandparents. But from the time I first met her, there's been this undercurrent of sadness there. I felt so sorry for her—she's been pretty much alone in the world. But now she has you."

"And you," he said. "And a whole great tribe of Becketts and Mac-Neills."

"But it's you who's made her feel like she belongs to them."

"Well, I haven't been too good at relationships till now. But I'm bloody determined to make this one work. To be a good husband to her."

"I'll kick your arse if you're not," she said. "Even if you are my brother, she's my friend, and she deserves to be happy. Promise me you won't fuck this up?"

"No, I won't. I used to think that finding 'the one' was a load of bollocks. But she is the one. And I'm going to get this right."

Boxing Day inched by at glacial speed. Kate and Ellie, ever the bookworms, sat and indulged in the new titles they'd purchased for each other. He noticed Kate's bare hand flipping the pages of her book. She wasn't wearing the engagement ring. He tried to tell himself that it was just her getting used to a new thing, so easy to forget to put it on, not yet a habit.

He sat, flicking through TV channels, but only found game shows and reruns of terrible old movies on their annual outing. With nothing else to occupy his mind, he found himself questioning Kate's response to the proposal. He worked his way through every moment since then, and the doubts loomed even larger. He berated himself for being so stupid as to put her on the spot like that. Usually so careful in his planning, perhaps this time he'd overlooked the most important part of the plan—Kate herself.

At lunchtime, Ellie produced leftovers from the Christmas feast, which left him overfull, but still dissatisfied, not with hunger, but with his mood. He sought refuge, as he often did, in running.

"See you in a while," he said, tying on his shoes.

"OK love, have fun. I'd join you but I'm still so tired. Yesterday was such a big day."

James felt a brief glimmer of hope in her words and her smile, but the insecurity swirled around him again as he pounded along the Bayswater streets and into Kensington Gardens. It was not a familiar feeling, and with each footfall he pushed back at it, replaying in his head her every word, every gesture, searching for clues that she really wanted to marry him. He strode past Kensington Palace, and on through the Royal Parks, then down The Mall, dodging the ever present tourists, before finally looping back through Mayfair and home.

He sat on the doorstep, muscles taut, his body slick with the effort, but his mind had stilled, and his confidence returned. When he sat on the couch, newly showered, she came and lay alongside him, book still in hand but relaxed in his embrace.

"Why do you always smell so good?" she said, nuzzling into his neck, tracing the lines of his cheek with her long fingers. As he stroked her hand, she suddenly sat bolt upright.

"Oh, my god. My ring. I forgot to put it on." She headed straight for the bedroom and returned with it, extending her hand to admire it. "That's better," she said, resuming her place next to him and retrieving her book.

Dinner was another round of leftovers, followed by all of them, he included, retreating into books.

"Done. The end," Kate said, dumping the book on a coffee table with a thud.

"And?" said Ellie, looking up from hers.

"Brilliant. You'll love it. Hurry up and finish yours so we can swap."

And with that, she announced she was going to have another early night. He left it for a while, then made his way to their room. As he slipped into bed beside her, he sensed she was awake. He lay along the length of her body, dotting gentle kisses down her neck, and allowing his hand to caress her thigh.

"You're not asleep yet, future Mrs Beckett?" he whispered, trying out the words for the first time. She rolled to face him.

"No, I'm not Mr Beckett." In the light from the street, he could see there was a glimmer of a smile on her face.

"Still OK with becoming Mrs Beckett sometime soon?" He had to know if she had doubts she wasn't sharing, even though the thought scared the shit out of him.

She paused before replying. Only seconds, but it was an eternity.

"Yes, I am."

"I worried you were having second thoughts. You were a bit... I don't know... like there was something not quite right."

"No, not second thoughts. Although, I suppose I was slightly pissed off that you asked me like that in front of your family. What if I'd wanted to say no? You didn't really leave me any option but to say yes."

He considered her words for a moment.

"You know what? You're right. I was terrified you'd turn me down. I suppose in my head the family was an extra insurance against you saying no. I'm sorry."

"It's OK. Maybe I was overwhelmed, like it was too good to be true. I was never going to turn you down. I do love you, you know—in spite of your faults."

"Oh, and there are many. But fortunately, I think they might be redeemed by my talents."

His hand slid across between her legs, and his fingers sought the warmth there.

"Can I remind you of some?"

"Hmm, I think you could." She let her thighs fall open, inviting him to continue what he had begun. He relaxed into the moment, reassured that she wanted him, not only in this way. He would be her husband, her partner, for life. He'd not let those doubts snipe at him again.

CHAPTER 19

The Wedding Planner

London, England - January 2009

"Do WE HAVE TO start this now?" James wore a grumpy frown. "I've got a hell of a headache and my mouth tastes like the dog pissed in it."

"We haven't got a dog, and we *do* need to get started." Ellie tilted a determined chin at her brother. "It's important we get all the bookings done as soon as the businesses open after New Year. Spring weddings are popular, so we need to be quick or you'll miss out."

"I appreciated you driving us to the party last night, Ellie. But you should be grateful that as the sober driver, you're the only one feeling chirpy this morning. So please, go easy on us. Let's leave this till after dinner."

It was already lunchtime, and since they hadn't arrived home until almost three, it was a miracle they'd surfaced this early.

"Yeah, how about we do that?" Kate intervened, desperate to keep the peace between the siblings. The two of them arguing wouldn't help her thumping headache. "Let's order in some takeaways tonight and maybe we can start on the master plan then."

Seeing that it was two against one, Ellie agreed, although there was a definite deflated sag of her shoulders. She was more excited about the wedding than they were. Disappointment written on her face, she placed her notebook and pen in a prominent place on the coffee table as a sign she was ready to resume wedding planner duties later on.

"OK," she said, in a more conciliatory tone, "we'll do that. And, since it appears I'm the only one capable, I'll do the doughnut run and make us all coffee when I get back. Even without a hangover, I'm still pretty shattered by the lack of sleep. I could do with a nice caffeine and sugar hit."

She pulled on her coat and a pair of shaggy fur-topped boots and set off into the bleak day.

"Apart from the hangover, I had the best night," Kate said.

James's director friend threw legendary New Year's Eve parties at his sprawling country house. This year's superhero themed one had, however, become a de facto engagement celebration for them. The newly-engaged couple had been the centre of attention with endless hugs of congratulations and much gushing over the dazzling ring.

"Me too," he said. "And you were stunning. Linda Carter never filled out her Wonder Woman costume as attractively as you did. I wanted to punch a couple of those guys for being too friendly in their congratulations."

"Well, I'm glad you didn't, Batman. I don't need you going all macho on me in situations like that. I can look after myself, you know. In my sailing days, I learned far more than how to handle a boat. When you're a young woman in a male-dominated sport, you soon learn how to divert the ones who step over the line."

"OK, suppose I'll have to stick to saving Gotham City if you won't let me save you. But I can't promise not to be jealous, only that I won't hit anyone."

"Guess I'll have to do the same. I wasn't too happy with some of those women ogling you in your tight costume." She hadn't been the only one admiring how his body, toned by the daily workout regime, along with his unflagging confidence, allowed him to carry off a costume that left little to the imagination. "You looked way too sexy. I'm sure there were a few women hoping they still might persuade you to reconsider your decision."

"Nothing could make me do that," he said. "Asking you to marry me is the best decision I ever made."

"Ditto," she said.

"And we should do it soon?"

"Definitely. You know, I don't get the concept of a lengthy engagement," she mused. "I've always thought it kind of odd. You either want to get married or you don't and if you do, then you should just get on and do it."

A week later, reflecting on this conversation, she realised how she'd unwittingly given James permission to launch them headlong into a wedding.

———

Kate and Ellie had survived their first day back at school. The kids had been pretty lively, still filled with all the excitement that Christmas brings to eight-year-olds. But overall, it wasn't too bad. They'd made their usual quick escape and now, just after four in the afternoon, Kate was nestled in a chair by the fire marking books. Ellie sat next to her in companionable silence doing the same, the only sound the crackling fire and the scratch of their red pens correcting errors.

The open fire was one of the original features retained in the otherwise modernised house. True, it was a hassle carting wood in from the stash on the back porch. And it took a while to warm the vast high-ceilinged room.

But the intermingled fragrances of pine resin and smoke were intoxicating. And the flames were mesmerising. Even the fanciest gas fire was a poor imitation, unable to replicate the leaping flashes of colour or the pops of tiny embers drifting up the chimney.

She wasn't expecting James to arrive home early from the office. He'd been restless the last few days. He thrived on the pace of work and, although he wouldn't admit it, was keen to get back to the multitude of tasks that made up his hectic job.

"Good day?" she asked as he bounded into the room. He had an air of excitement about him that suggested it had been.

"Very good. In fact, so good, you need to put those books down. I've got a surprise for you."

With a flourish, he produced a large bottle of champagne from his bag.

"What? Tonight? But it's Monday. You know I don't like to drink on school nights."

She immediately regretted the comment, not wanting to sound peevish, or reignite the tense conversation they'd had only yesterday about how her teaching job would limit the future life James had mapped out for them.

"You know you don't need to work," he'd said. "Now that I'm established, the money's going to keep flowing in."

"But what would I do all day? Ellie and you would be at work, and then you're away so much."

"You could do some casual days, or volunteer work. And travel with me when you want. Think about it."

"OK, I'll think about it."

She had only agreed to put an end to the debate. But she knew what her decision would be. While it was tough sometimes and not particularly well paid, she loved teaching. She never tired of the thrill of seeing kids discover the world of learning. But it also meant that from Sunday to Thursday, she needed to lay off the booze. Thirty lively eight-year-olds and a hangover were an unwise combination.

"Nothing wrong with starting the week with a celebration. I'll get some glasses."

Once James had made up his mind, he wasn't easily deterred. She gathered the books into her tote bag with a resigned sigh, wondering what on earth they were celebrating on a regular Monday evening in January. Ellie, curiosity also piqued, stopped her marking and dumped the pile of exercise books on the floor beside her. They waited, watching the door, anticipating his return and a usual flamboyant James-style revelation of the surprise.

James sloshed a generous measure of champagne in each glass, distributed one to each of them, then reached into his briefcase. He handed her a heavy cream leather folder embellished with gold.

"Open it and you'll see."

On the first page in bold letters she read 'Wedding Celebration Prepared for Miss Kate Moreton & Mr James Beckett'. What followed were pages of details—flights, accommodation, food, decorations—for a small but elaborate wedding on a Greek island.

"It's booked for the mid-term break."

"That's only a few weeks away."

"Six," he said. "Surely that's enough time for you to find a dress?"

"I'll help," said Ellie. Looking somewhat peeved that James had usurped her role as wedding planner extraordinaire, she was quick to leap in and grab any jobs that were left. "I've already made a list of potential shops for us to check out."

Of course she had.

"And after the wedding, I've booked a few days for us," he said. "I've chartered a yacht—one with sails—so if you feel like it, you can give the crew a few pointers. It won't be the honeymoon I'd like to take you on, since you'll have to get back to school. But I promise in the summer we'll have a proper holiday."

"So you didn't stop to think I might like to have had some say in the matter?" It wasn't easy to have your voice heard when you had a bull-headed Beckett to contend with, but she'd hoped on this topic he might have at least asked her first.

"It's not set in stone," he added quickly, seeing the narrowing of her eyes. "You can change anything you want. But I thought rather than start with a blank page, this would be easier on you." He did have a valid point. "Especially with work. It's not like you can get away during the day to sort things."

"I might have made time. If I'd been allowed."

It wasn't quite how she'd imagined preparing for her wedding. It felt odd that, apart from choosing a dress and turning up, there wasn't much else for her to do. But then she'd seen some of her friends almost driven mad by the preparations, arriving at their big day overwhelmed by relief that it would soon be over. Maybe this *was* a better way.

He studied her face with a look that reminded her of a loyal dog, eager to please its owner, wanting a sign that it was, in fact, a good boy.

She sighed and gave it to him. Putting the folder down, she stood and folded into his waiting arms, allowing him to wrap her in one of his enormous hugs. She still loved the way she fitted under the curve of his shoulder, and the reassuring protection of his bulk. Snuggling into him, she felt an unspoken relief in the press of his lips to her head, as the tension he'd hidden so well ebbed from him. She could tell behind the bravado he'd harboured doubts, but it wasn't in his nature to show them, not even to her.

"Thank you," she said. "It's going to be beautiful."

A broad grin of pride spread across his face, any last shred of worry that he'd done the wrong thing slipping away.

"And you, my love, will be the most beautiful part of it," he said, his kiss radiating an infectious happiness. As always, she let herself bask in his optimism, tossing away any doubts of her own.

CHAPTER 20

Time to Leave

London, England - June 2009

KATE SAT SURVEYING HERSELF in the mirror, admiring Ellie's capable hands working magic on her hair. She herself always struggled with the fine slipperiness of its length and opted for simple solutions, leaving it loose or caught in a sporty ponytail. Four months had passed since the last time she'd had Ellie go to this much trouble. That was for her wedding.

The shock of having James take over the wedding plans had faded, and they'd spent an idyllic week in Greece. The wedding itself, with only a few close friends and family, was perfect. Simple, no fuss, and only the people that mattered to them. Kate's friends back in New Zealand wouldn't have come, anyway. All struggling with young families and mortgages, the short notice gave them a convenient out.

She'd settled for the few days' sailing afterwards as a honeymoon. The promised longer vacation hadn't materialised. James always had work commitments, so they confined holidays to short jaunts, although they'd been reasonably frequent. With Europe on their doorstep, Kate had ticked off many must-see destinations, as well as special places that most people had never heard of. James always loved being one step ahead of the crowd. He knew what would be on trend before it happened. Yes, despite James taking over, it had been perfect. And while married life would never be perfect—that would be an unrealistic expectation—life was good.

She watched as Ellie's deft fingers wove an elegant updo worthy of the upmarket restaurant she and James would dine at tonight. She always felt guilty about leaving Ellie behind. Often, the three of them would head out together. But today he had summoned her via a mysterious text. *'Meet you at Julien's at 8. Huge news. Can't wait to share the surprise with you.'* Both the message content and the choice of restaurant suggested this was not a night to invite Ellie to join them for a family dinner.

Julien's was a tiny French bistro that had become their special date night venue. Tucked away at the top of a set of shabby stairs, it was a hidden jewel. It was impossible to get a table there at short notice, but James had been going there for years, long before it had become an icon of the local dining scene. The owner, Julien himself, was a friend. He would always find a way of squeezing them in.

"So, what do you think he's up to?" Ellie asked.

"Absolutely no idea. Perhaps it's something to do with where he's been this week."

James had spent several days in Glasgow and was due on an early evening flight. Kate paid little attention to his work—not because she wasn't interested, but because she struggled to follow the whirlwind that was James's work-life with so many projects on the go, from almost completed ones to others that were just the germ of an idea.

"I suppose I'll have to wait and see," she mused. "To be honest, I've learned to be a little wary of James's surprises."

"Don't blame you," Ellie laughed. "His proposal alone would've made anyone worried about what would come next."

"And the wedding. He gets so caught up in the excitement of his brilliant ideas that he doesn't stop to think that we might not think it's so brilliant."

"You have forgiven him for that, though?"

"Oh, for sure. He's like a bloody great puppy—he chews up your favourite shoes, but you love him all the same. And now, looking back, if I had the chance, I wouldn't change a thing."

She stood, surveying her appearance in the full-length mirror. She'd chosen a special outfit to match the mysterious special occasion. The dress was new, and it was perfect. Shopping with Ellie was like having your own personal stylist. She had an innate sense of what would work, quite at odds with her own eclectic and rather bizarre wardrobe. And she made it her mission to know all the up-and-coming designers where treasures could be found, often at good prices. Not that price mattered when James dispatched them with his credit card and told them to have fun. This unique dress was the highlight of their latest successful expedition.

"Told you it was perfect." Ellie wore a satisfied smirk. "It's the oddest colour, not blue, not grey. But it's like they invented it for you."

It was, in fact, almost the exact shade of Kate's eyes, and the perfect accent for her blonde hair.

"Neckline's a bit daring." Kate nervously arranged the narrow fabric strips on either side of the plunging 'V' neckline.

"Go on you, you've got great boobs. Show them off! Show that brother of mine what he's missing when he buggers off on work trips all the time."

The toot of the taxi left no time for further deliberation. Kate threw a wrap around her shoulders. It would provide a touch of modesty for the journey between the house and the restaurant, plus a barrier between her bare skin and the slight chill outside. Although officially summer, there was still a hint of the unsettled spring weather lingering in the evening air.

If you hadn't known it was there, Julien's would be almost impossible to find. The entrance was to one side of a non-descript menswear store. You entered by pushing open heavy glass doors that led into a 1970s tiled foyer. Here the options were a bland lift or a narrow set of tired vinyl-clad stairs. But a treasure awaited those who dared to make the ascent to the first floor. Dining at Julien's was perfection—the food, the ambience, and the staff who took pride in meeting your every whim.

"Kate, so lovely to see you," gushed Julien, as he welcomed her in his exuberant French style with a kiss on each cheek. "Your husband has told me it's a special occasion, so come with me. I've set a table for you in the room down the back."

He was a man you wouldn't look at twice in the street. Medium height, average build, pleasant features, but nothing that stood out. But behind the plain facade, he was a conjuror who had created this perfect place where it was possible to escape from the world.

She followed him past white-clothed tables, where candlelight sparkled on silver and crystal, as he led her to a tiny room with only one table encircled by a buttoned velvet couch.

"James, your stunning wife is here. Of course, if you'd rather, she can dine with me instead."

Julien and James had a running joke that should Kate ever tire of her marriage, Julien would take her in a heartbeat. Of course, there was the slight inconvenience that would need to be overcome in that eventuality—Julien's partner, Thomas. Kate always maintained that she could do a lot worse than become part of a ménage à trois with Julien and Thomas. Both men were so much fun. Life with them would never be dull.

"Not tonight, Julien. Back off." James warned him with mock threat. He rose to his feet, meeting her eyes with a sparkle of mischief, and kissed her cheek.

"Oh, well, you know I'm an extremely patient man, and this one is worth waiting for," said Julien, steadying her as she slid into the seat.

"Thank you, Julien," she said, smiling at the familiar banter.

He leaned over to extract a bottle of champagne from the elegant ice bucket perched beside the table. He opened it with a dash of theatre, its resounding pop echoing in the little room. It was fresh and light on her tongue, with a slight caress of sweetness. And a delicious yeasty fragrance wafted from the tiny explosions of bubbles as she sipped it.

"Now, James has already ordered for you," Julien said, "so you can relax and enjoy." And he slipped away to supervise the preparation.

James's odd habit of choosing her food in restaurants was a topic of conversation amongst her friends. There was the night when Sophie, a romantic at heart, whispered across the table to her, "You know it's rather sweet the way he does that, even though it's dreadfully old-fashioned." The accompanying wistful expression suggested that Sophie secretly longed for someone to do the same for her.

Then there was the lunch at which Izzie had pulled her aside. Ever on the alert for women receiving less-than equal treatment, Izzie had given her a stern talking to. "Kate, you really should stand up for yourself and tell him no. You might think it's a little thing—but if you let him get away with that, where's it going to end?"

"Don't be so ridiculous," she'd replied. "To be honest, I'm lazy when it comes to food. James, on the other hand, makes a study of it. At least when he orders, I know I'm going to get something decent."

She didn't admit it to Izzie, but she was also happy to defer to her husband because of the pleasure it gave him. When it came to food, he was the teacher and she the student. He schooled her on the provenance of the ingredients, the intricacies of the cooking methods. She'd glance from her plate to see his attention focused on her. And then see the sheer delight written on his face, knowing he'd pleased her with his selections. There was a strange intimacy between them at these times. Something sensuous in their shared enjoyment of the food—almost a kind of foreplay before they moved on to other sources of mutual pleasure.

They chatted away over the first two courses, updating each other on the minutiae of their days apart. But that line of conversation drifted to a close as Julien delivered dessert. It was so exquisitely presented that she was hesitant to destroy it with a spoon.

As she took the plunge, diving into the layers of pastry and custard, Kate decided it was time to put James out of his misery and also plunge into the reason for them being here. All evening she'd seen that he was dying for her to ask what the surprise was.

"So, tell me. What's the special occasion?"

At the opportunity, he leapt straight in, his eyes excited.

"Well, while I was in Glasgow, we signed a deal for a new mini-series. It's going to be amazing. Based on a book that won the Man Booker Prize."

"And...?"

"And it was written by a New Zealander. She's done the screenplay. It's superb."

"And so...?"

"And so you and I, my love, are off to New Zealand!" he finished. She sat in stunned silence while he topped up her glass. "I'm taking you home! Let's drink to that."

"But this is home for me. Yes, I own a house in New Zealand, but it's not home anymore."

She tried to keep her voice even, but under the table she clenched her hands tight. Just when she thought he knew her, he blundered in and did something like this that made her doubt he ever would. How could he be so blind? She had an amazing house to live in, a small but loyal group of friends. And then there was Ellie and the several younger Beckett and MacNeill relations that they met socially on a regular basis. For the first time in her life, she had a large family to call her own. And above all, she had a job she loved. Now he wanted her to quit it. While she loved him desperately, she often wondered if she should stand up to his more outlandish ideas. Like this one.

"I thought you'd be happy," he said. "I'm sorry. I didn't think you were so attached to this place. And wouldn't you love to be back there for summer, while here it's winter and dark at three p.m.?" She sighed. What was there to say? It sounded like a done deal. "It won't be forever. We can come back here in between projects. I'll keep the house, of course."

"In between projects? I thought we were talking one mini-series." She could no longer keep her voice steady and the shrillness even grated on her own ears.

"Yes, well, it's a long-term partnership between us and a production house over there," he said, looking sheepish. "If things go well with this series, we see other opportunities opening up." He paused for a moment, a thoughtful expression on his face—and then cleverly played his trump card. "But it's not all about work. Wouldn't you rather bring up our kids in New Zealand? I thought you said it was a paradise for families?"

She surrendered at that. He'd outmanoeuvred her.

Kate had made it clear from the start that she wanted to try for a baby as soon as possible. Neither of them were especially young, and if they were going to have three, which they'd decided was the perfect number, they should start soon. And they had tried.

She'd immediately stopped taking the pill and whenever they made love, the thought that this might be the start of their very own little Beckett added an extra thrill. The notion of becoming a father filled James with a tangible sense of elation. He was absolutely determined to be better than his own father. They'd talked for hours about the life their kids would have. And yes, she had gone on about the idyllic childhood to be had in New Zealand. It was her own fault.

"Ok," she said, deliberately trying to inject a cheerful note in her voice. "You're right. Let's have some Kiwi babies."

The relief was obvious on his face.

"And we can come back here lots so they get to meet all the family. It's only a day away, after all."

Hmm, a very long day, even if you only count the hours in the air. Kate shuddered inwardly at the idea of navigating planes and airports with a baby in tow. But of course, they would always be in business class, so perhaps it wouldn't be a total nightmare.

He leaned over and poured the dessert wine. It resembled liquid gold and gave off the syrupy smell of raisins. She raised her glass.

"To our Kiwi babies," she said, the clinking of the crystal signalling her acceptance of the deal.

"Drink that quickly. Let's go home and see if we can make one."

He gave her a flirty wink. She couldn't help but forgive him anything when he flashed that boyish grin. She wondered if it would work the same magic on Ellie when they broke the news to her.

CHAPTER 21

Barra

Kate

London, England - July 2009

ELLIE WASN'T A NATURALLY secretive person—exactly the opposite, her thoughts and feelings often spilling across her face before she could rein them in. It was both a blessing and a curse. Her openness and honesty were part of what endeared Ellie to her friends. Such sincerity and lack of guile were rare qualities. However, her inability to tell polite little white lies could be confronting.

So, while Ellie had done a good job, battling to conceal whatever was currently bothering her, failure was inevitable. For days Kate had known there was a turmoil inside of her friend, like a roiling storm cloud that darkened her face when she thought no one was watching. And it had something to do with James. Several times she'd appeared on the verge of saying something to him and then hesitated. Finally, one night at dinner, it poured out.

"There's something we need to do before you go." Ellie casually dropped the remark in between mouthfuls of tortellini. Being Ellie's turn to cook, predictably, dinner had arrived from Marks and Spencer. Kate was in awe of the marvels to be found on its shelves. Many nights, it saved them from the risk of either starving or eating one of Ellie's frightening culinary attempts. She would miss it when they returned to New Zealand.

There was an undercurrent in Ellie's voice tonight. Sensing trouble, Kate feigned nonchalance by continuing to pursue a rogue piece of pasta that was trying to avoid her fork.

James also noticed the slight edge to Ellie's remark. Over the years, he'd learned to read the subtleties of his sister's moods. He paused, his next mouthful still balanced in mid-air, and turned his full attention on her.

"What's that?" He rested his fork against his plate and waited.

"We need to take mum home," Ellie said. "To Barra."

He sat and thought for a moment, perhaps weighing up how to reject this suggestion without it developing into an argument.

"Ellie, it's a lovely idea," he said carefully. "But you know I've got a hell of a lot to sort out with work before we go. You can't expect me to drop everything and race off to Barra." There was a defensiveness in his tone that didn't go down well. Ellie's eyes widened as she fixed her brother with a glare. "Besides," he said, fuelling the fire, "it's a bit of a mission to get there."

Ellie's thunderous face showed exactly what she thought of his excuses. She slammed her fork down. It bounced across the table and clattered onto the floor. She ignored it, instead turning on her brother.

"What do you mean 'a mission'? It's not the bloody end of the earth, you know. We'd fly to Glasgow and then take the plane from there. Surely you could spare a few days from your precious work for Mum?"

Kate said nothing. She'd seen them fight before and knew not to get in between two fired-up Becketts. It could get ugly, but the outcome was predictable. Ellie would yell, scream, sometimes cry, but in the end, give in to James. Until now.

Kate could see from her determined expression that this time Ellie intended to stand her ground. This time, she was going to take him on. Today, there would be no surrender. Best to let them slug it out until James faced the inevitable. She carried on eating while their voices rose around her.

She was right. Once he realised that no amount of emotion or logic would move his sister even a millimetre on this one, James capitulated.

"OK, but I can only spare two days. You make the bookings, then tell Rhonda. Get her to shuffle my schedule. I'll be there."

Kate finished up her last days at school, leaving behind the place she'd been unsure of at first with deep regret. A few days into the summer holidays, and they were at Heathrow boarding a flight to Glasgow.

Ellie carefully placed the elegantly simple wooden box which held her mother's ashes in her hand luggage. Neither she nor James had ever been to Barra. But Mary had filled their lives with her reminiscences, tales of visits to the remnants of family on the remote island. She'd always said they'd go together some day. Little did she know that someday wouldn't come.

Arriving in Glasgow, they hurried to follow the directions to the departure gate, located in a far-flung extremity of the terminal.

"Why such a tight connection?" James complained as they sprinted down the long corridors.

"There was no other option. The Barra flight is earlier today because of the tide," said Ellie.

"What? The tide? Why the tide?" There was confusion on his face.

"They need to land when the tide is right—so there's enough beach. We land on the beach."

"Holy shit," he said under his breath, "I can't believe I'm only hearing this now." Kate knew Ellie had mentioned it. But James, preoccupied with their imminent departure for New Zealand, hadn't been paying attention. "Is it too late to take a boat?" His voice was hopeful.

"Yes, it is," said Ellie. "You wanted to be there and back in two days. We're going to Barra and we're going on this plane."

They barrelled through the last exit, where only a stencilled number 58 on the corrugated iron walls showed it was an airport gate. There was no air bridge, no waiting bus to ferry them to the plane. The plane itself sat on the tarmac, patiently awaiting its passengers. It was a sparrow perched amongst hawks, tiny and insignificant next to the larger planes. Proudly sporting a blue and white Scottish flag on its tail, it was at least modern.

"You weren't exaggerating when you said it was a little plane." Kate regarded it sceptically.

"If I'd known it was this small, I'd have spent some time in the bar," joked James, attempting to make light of the situation, an attempt to conceal his dislike of flying.

It was one surprising gap in James's otherwise fearless nature. He usually embraced things that terrified others, such as driving high-performance cars to their limits. He'd even gone so far as organising a weekend away with friends, to experience the thrill of laps around the treacherous Nürburgring. It had been a relief when he arrived home unscathed, not another notch on the circuit's tally of deaths. At one time he'd raced motorbikes. Kate had seen the video, and it was frightening. Leaning into the corners at speed, his knee almost grazing the pavement, you could sense his absolute faith in the bike and his ability to control it.

But despite his total trust in other forms of machinery, James was suspicious of planes. She'd pondered on the reasons and decided it was probably because he was such a control freak. It was the unknown human factor that bothered him. James wasn't comfortable entrusting his safety to anyone else. Perhaps she should get him flying lessons.

He tolerated trips on the big jets that were necessary for his work. Ensconced in business class with attentive staff, he could pretend he wasn't actually in the air. However, there would be no such pretence in a plane so small that you'd be able to see the pilot's every move.

"Don't be such a baby," said Ellie. "It's completely safe, and it's a beautiful day for flying."

She was right. Overhead, the sky was a perfect arch of blue. At the front of the plane, a narrow set of steps led to the tiny doorway. A smiling face peered out at them and beckoned them forward with a friendly wave.

Getting on board was challenging for the two lanky siblings, but once folded into their seats, the compact plane had a comforting cosiness. The co-pilot, who doubled as steward, checked that all eighteen passengers were buckled in. Next came the obligatory safety briefing and an update on the conditions. Blue sky all the way, with maybe a few puffs of cloud. No wind. They were in for a smooth ride.

The plane was efficient at getting itself airborne. After a ridiculously short run-up, it was aloft and climbing towards the sun. Kate chattered away to James. She hoped discussing mundane details about their move would occupy his mind, so he couldn't dwell on the horrifying distance between himself and terra firma. It wasn't easy over the insistent drone of the whirring propellers that were keeping them aloft.

Sitting in the window seat, she followed their passage. Below, fingers of the mainland coast soon gave way to jewel-like islands dotted in an iridescent sea. And finally, they were simply suspended above the endless blue, with no land at all in sight.

After almost an hour, the plane began its descent. Islands reappeared below them and it became obvious that the largest one was their destination. It was disconcerting to be hurtling towards the beach below. Even though Kate knew the beach landing was planned, the lack of a proper runway unsettled her, making it seem more like an emergency landing. As they descended, each small gust of wind buffeted the plane, rising and falling as it rode the breeze. She could see a cluster of dark-roofed white buildings marking their target.

When they touched down on the mushroom-coloured sand, it was surprisingly gentle. The beach was like a mirror, slick with water. Spray fanned from the wheels as they swung back around to taxi towards the small control tower and tiny terminal.

The baggage handlers swooped on the plane the moment it came to a standstill. They watched as two burly men unloaded their luggage, slinging it effortlessly into a small jeep-like vehicle.

"Thank god." James rose from his seat as soon as the seat belt light flicked off. He was determined to be first off.

The two women stood on cue to follow him. The door of the plane swung back to reveal a narrow set of steps and a breath of tangy salt air. They stepped out onto firm sand, marching like a line of crabs towards the terminal.

"Wait," Ellie called, "let me take a picture. We might never come here again." She'd already whipped out the tiny Nikon that was her constant companion, recording her life as it happened.

James kept walking, ignoring her plea. He was never a fan of having his photo taken. But Kate, ever-obliging, posed for the picture, then snapped one of Ellie while the other passengers politely waited for them. A kindly older man stepped forward, offering to take one of the two of them, arms wrapped around each other, still smiling from the exhilaration of the flight, with the brave little plane behind them.

James and Kate wandered over to collect the luggage from what resembled a bus stop. No flash baggage carousel here. Ellie returned with the keys to their rental car. She tossed them to James, and they loaded the bags. Soon they were following the single loop road that circled the tiny island, heading for their beachside hotel.

"That's unbelievable." Kate gasped in delight as they surged over a crest and caught sight of an exquisite little bay. "Except for the temperature, you'd swear you were on some Pacific Island."

The crescent of white sand framed water of a surreal blue. On the hill overlooking the bay was a hotel. It was the traditional Hebridean white with black-slate roof, but that was where the resemblance to the island architecture ended. A cascade of modernity along the shoreline, with large angular windows, its lines echoed the sharp hills behind. A welcoming sign informed them of its claim to fame as Britain's most westerly hotel. Out beyond the bay, the Atlantic ocean surged endlessly, with nothing but its icy waters stretching all the way to Canada.

After lunch, Ellie declared she was going to her room to have a nap.

"Don't you dare call it a nana nap," she said. "You know why I'm so damn tired and it's not old age."

They did. She was still exhausted from the gruelling last week of the school year. Ellie had been frantic after making the mistake of offering to direct the Grade 3 musical. The challenges of coordinating kids, teachers, and an army of parent volunteers had taken its toll on her. The evening had been a triumph. They had showered her with flowers, wine, and sincere thanks. But she wouldn't volunteer for that job again.

"No, you get some rest," said Kate. "We'll go for a walk. Let's catch up for a drink before dinner."

Kate and James threw on jackets and headed down onto the beach. It was still warm for Scotland, but the sea breeze was lively.

"Do you think Ellie's going to make it to the top of the hill tomorrow?" Kate asked.

Her concern was genuine. Ellie's idea of exercise was a stroll in the market in Portobello Road. Tomorrow they would scatter Mary's ashes from Heaval, a hill high above Castle Bay. Ellie remembered her mother's accounts of climbing to the statue of the Virgin and Child. It was the perfect place to set her free. But what Ellie had forgotten was that Mary's memories were those of a child, young and full of boundless energy. Kate's copy of *Lonely Planet: Scotland's Highlands and Islands* said the walk wasn't long—but it was steep.

"I dunno," said James. "I hope so. She's too bloody big for us to carry. I suppose we'll just have to take our time. Glad I brought my iPod. I can play some music to drown out the sound of her moaning."

"At least the weather is going to be good."

Kate had never lost her sailor's habit of checking the forecast. The morning would be clear, although there was mention of possible thunderstorms later in the day. She hoped they didn't eventuate. Even she wouldn't want to be on that little plane during a storm. As for James, he'd probably need sedation.

"Yeah, thank god," he said. "Don't fancy a long walk in Scotland's liquid sunshine. And let's hope that early in the day, the fecking midgies won't be out yet."

*

They rose in the dark. The plan was to be at their destination soon after dawn. By six a.m. they were already trekking upwards. As predicted, Ellie struggled on the climb, but she didn't complain once. This was her idea, and she was determined to see it through.

Finally, they stood alongside the statue. Her white marble robes glowed with an unearthly light in the early morning sun. The water far below them was like a vast golden mirror. However, the lady of the sea was oblivious to the stunning view of the bay, her gaze fixed on the child she bore on her shoulder. He, in turn, stared into the heavens, from which he'd plucked a star that was now clasped tightly in a chubby hand.

There was the faintest whisper of a breeze. It carried the damp smell of dew-laden grass, overlaid with a slight hint of the sea. There was an overwhelming sense of peace as she gazed across the grassy hill to the bay and the endless ocean beyond.

"Great choice Ellie," she said. "It's perfect."

"OK, Mum." James removed the little box from his backpack. "You're home now."

It was hard to believe this was the only remainder of such a vibrant woman. Kate's grief was not only for Mary, but her grandparents. Their ashes were interred in a peaceful lawn cemetery back in New Zealand. She wondered if she'd asked would they too have wanted to return to the country of their birth? She hadn't asked; they hadn't said, so now she would never know.

They'd agreed that James would scatter the ashes while Ellie's words would accompany her mother as she flew free to lie amidst the earth of her true home. Ellie pulled a crumpled piece of paper from the inner pocket of her jacket. It had obviously been folded and unfolded many times to prepare for this moment. Kate knew she had spent hours searching for the right words.

Neither James nor Kate considered themselves religious. But Ellie had a strong spiritual side to her nature, in private delving more deeply into the old religions. Her mother's death had solidified her beliefs, and she now discreetly observed worship of the goddess. Kate found it intriguing, although it wasn't a path she was drawn to herself.

Ellie had developed a friendship with a gentle young woman, Ceridwen, born of pagan parents and herself a practising Wiccan. She had gifted a simple Celtic farewell used at her own mother's funeral rite for Ellie to read. It seemed rather appropriate that she should invoke the goddess, while standing alongside a statue of the most revered woman in Christianity, as she bid farewell to a woman who had meant so much to them all.

As the ashes whirled away from James, carried on the morning breeze, Ellie's high, clear voice also drifted in the air. When it was done, the three of them drew together and stood wordlessly locked in a sad embrace.

CHAPTER 22

Castle

Barra, Scotland - August 2009

BY THE TIME THEY'D made their way down the hill to the waterfront, the sun was high in the sky. Kate gave silent thanks for its warmth after the early morning chill that had taken up residence in her bones.

Cheerful outside tables decked out in red tartan tablecloths signalled that the little cafe had opened for the day. They were inviting, a happy contrast to the whitewashed walls. As they stepped inside, the young owner's eyes glowed with welcome.

"Nice to have people here so early in the day. What can I get you?"

All three ordered the full cooked Scottish breakfast. Their early start had meant no chance of anything, not even a coffee at the hotel. The moment it arrived, Kate attacked the mound of food, eager to dispel her hunger. Crispy bacon flanked two deep golden eggs. She chomped her way through those as well as slices of black pudding and square sausage, both with an appealing, coarse texture and spicy flavour. However, she pushed aside the accompanying haggis. James pounced on it, having finished his own.

"You don't know what you're missing," he said. "It's delicious."

"Well, actually, I do know what I'm missing. Knowing what's in there is the reason I'm not eating it."

"Your loss, my gain." He speared the last slice with his fork.

They sat letting the food digest, staring out at the castle, which gave the illusion of being close enough to touch. Separated by a small stretch of water, it dominated the small bay.

"There next," said Ellie. "We wouldn't be proper MacNeills if we didn't visit the clan headquarters. Do you know I read that the clan chief leased it for a pound and a bottle of whisky a year?"

"My sort of deal," said James. "Being paid in whisky. Hope it was a good one. Although I can see why he didn't want to live there. Looks too rustic to me."

"Well, rustic or not, let's get ourselves over there soon. Need to be at the airport by three."

It took longer to get in the boat than to make the crossing. Five minutes out into the bay, they scrambled up metal steps onto a small jetty that protruded from the island's rocky shoreline. Up close, the castle was even more impressive, with stout square walls that could repel any invader with ease.

After making a circuit right around the base, Ellie left them to it.

"If you don't mind," she said, "I thought I'd do a bit of fossicking by the water."

Kate and James wandered into the sunny, sheltered courtyard. Studying the reconstructed buildings, she could imagine she'd travelled back in time.

"Let's go onto the wall walk." She considered walking the battlements a must-do when visiting a castle.

"Ah, no—I think this is where we part ways."

She'd forgotten. Along with his strange mistrust of flying, James also had an incongruous fear of heights. He wasn't the sort of person you expected to have any phobias. And he kept quiet about them unless forced to admit it. The only exception he made to his 'no high places' rule was the ski lifts. He considered them a necessary evil if he was to have the thrill of speeding down snowy slopes at breakneck speed.

"You go," he said. "No need for you to miss the view just because I won't go. I'll meet you back by the jetty."

Kate headed for the stairs that spiralled upwards at the far end of the courtyard. She strode along the walkway atop the curtain wall. The wind had risen. No longer simply brisk, it clawed at her hair, grabbing tendrils from beneath her hat and whipping them against her cheeks. A glance overhead explained why. The forecast thunderstorm was on its way. Billowing towers of dark clouds had drifted from inland and were fighting the sun for control of the visible sky.

She looked away from them, out across Castle Bay, taking in the stunning view. It was every bit as spectacular as promised. With the threatening clouds tucked behind her, there was a vision of blue as far as she could see. Sky and sea both shimmered, and she inhaled the saltiness carried invisibly on the unsettled air.

She could see Ellie below, near the shoreline, no doubt scouring the beach for sea glass. It fascinated her, and she had an intriguing collection of opaque treasures, smoothed and sculpted by the waves. James came into view below the wall as he made his way to join his sister. He was so handsome, more so like this, relaxed in jeans, and his shirt hanging loose. He glanced up and smiled, the wave of his hand reaffirming that he was happy for her to continue exploring without him. A few steps further, and he disappeared from view.

She stood at the foot of the lofty stone tower. The boatman had urged them to take advantage of the opportunity to climb to the top. Apparently, it contained some narrow and tricky walkways and had been inaccessible to the public. But a group of local enthusiasts had worked to make it safe, blocking off the more treacherous areas so that at least for now one could explore its hidden secrets.

Kate stopped beside the entranceway and surveyed the structure looming above her. The blunt squareness of it reminded her of the brutalist 1970s architecture that had dominated her university. However, the severity of the tower was relieved by the rough-hewn stones of endless shapes and sizes from which some medieval craftsman had created this formidable defensive advantage for his laird.

It began as an uneasiness that crept across her body. Then, starting with her arms, it was as if a million tiny insects were dancing on her skin, their needle-like feet tapping out a crazy rhythm. She shuddered at the accompanying chill that crawled systematically down the length of her body. It was as if a shadow had wiped out the sun, taking all warmth with it. Compelled to look skyward, the tower drew itself upwards to its full height, radiating menace.

Then she experienced a sensation akin to falling. It was as if she was plummeting downwards, yet the tower leered over her, threatening to crush her. Instinct drove her to drop to the ground. She drew up her knees, curled into a foetal position, and closed her eyes. The earthy smell of the stones beneath aggressively assailed her nostrils. Her body was deathly cold, and so heavy, as if its entire weight was dragging her down into the wall.

Then there was a massive explosion, a thunderous boom that reverberated off the ancient walls and echoed in every part of her being. It was like standing close to a massive speaker at a rock concert; the sound not only surrounding her, but vibrating in each cell of her body. With a breathless sob, she protectively hugged herself even tighter. As the sound circled closer and closer, she tried to fight back, attempted to thrust it away with the force of her thoughts; but it was futile, as she slumped under the weight of its unyielding pressure.

Part Two - There

CHAPTER 23

Angel

Barra, Scotland - August 2009

"Are you alright there?" The question, in a velvet Scottish-accented voice, was so close that it must be directed at her.

She opened her eyes and squinted up in its direction. At first he was a blank silhouette against the sky, but slowly the details of a man emerged from the glare. A stray beam of sunlight lit his blond hair like a halo. Was he an angel come to save her? He was extremely tall, and Kate had to crane her neck to make eye contact. He wore a concerned expression as he repeated the question.

"Are you alright?"

"I think so."

But she was uncertain, still fearful of the disturbing sensations that had possessed her body. She was disoriented, like waking from sleep in the middle of the day. And completely unsure what had just happened. He stretched out a hand towards her.

"Can I help you up?" His query was tentative, as if not wanting to alarm her with overfamiliarity.

"Thank you, yes."

She reached out, placing her hand in his. With one powerful tug, he pulled her to her feet. Once upright, she set about smoothing her rumpled clothes. She stood, still shaky, and now overwhelmed with embarrassment.

"I'm not sure what came over me," she explained, not wanting to meet his eyes.

"Ah well," he said, his voice soothing, "maybe you haven't had enough to eat today? Why don't we go down to the little shop by the entrance and you could get a coffee and some food?"

"Did you hear that noise?"

"Noise? The thunder? Yes, it was fairly impressive. Another good reason to get down off this wall, I think. Won't be long before those clouds drop a lot of water on us. And even if the odds of being hit by lightning aren't high, I'd rather not take a chance."

A sweet, pungent aroma lay over the damp air. The smell of ozone suggested the storm was about to descend on them. She followed him back along the wall and down the tight spiralled staircase leading to the main courtyard. He left her at the door to the shop that sold wrapped snacks and coffees.

"Thank you," she said. "That was nice of you to stop."

"Not at all. It's what anyone would do to help a visitor."

"You're from here?" she asked.

"Aww no, not exactly from here," he said, "but you know, I'm Scottish and I can tell that you're not. Australian?" he asked.

"No, a Kiwi."

"A Kiwi?" He raised one eyebrow inquiringly, unsure of the word.

She noticed he was good-looking in a boyish way, although he appeared of a similar age to her. Apart from his modern attire, a white t-shirt and jeans, he could have fallen out of one of the paintings in the National Gallery depicting a perfectly formed Greek god. She realised with a start that she had been staring at him, thinking these thoughts, and hadn't responded.

"Oh, yes, a Kiwi—it means someone from New Zealand. It comes from the name of our national bird—flightless, long beak, with whiskers like a cat." *God, I'm babbling now.* The feeling of awkwardness in his presence was driving her mouth to get ahead of her brain.

He laughed. "Well, you learn something new every day. It sounds bizarre."

She laughed too. "Yeah, it is a bit strange, I suppose."

"OK," he said, "well, I'm Alex. It was nice to meet you...?" He paused, extending his hand.

"Kate," she said, allowing him to clasp her hand in his. There was an inexplicable ease, his touch comfortable, although he was a stranger. Perhaps it was the charming smile that seemed to radiate reassurance, confirming he was a genuinely nice person. Or was it because he'd handled her awkward episode with such grace? It was weird that someone she'd never met before had seen her at such a vulnerable moment, and yet her discomfort had somehow faded away.

"Right, well, I thought I'd catch the next boat. Are you sure you're OK? I feel like I shouldn't leave you here on you own."

"Oh, yes, I'll be fine, really. And I'm not on my own. My friend Ellie's here too, down on the beach. But thank you again."

"You're very welcome, Kiwi Kate." With a smile, he turned to amble off down the pathway that wound around to the small jetty. It struck her that for such a tall, even gangly man, he moved with an effortless grace.

Kate bought two coffees and a large bar of chocolate, then made her way down a rocky path to where Ellie was still combing the shoreline for treasure, oblivious to the drama that had just occurred. When Kate tried to explain it, even to her own ears, it sounded ridiculous. A fuss about nothing.

Ellie was more excited to hear the details of her rescuer than the strange goings on beneath the tower. Somehow it diminished the crippling fear until it almost seemed as if maybe it hadn't happened. By the time they had drunk their coffees, dispatched the chocolate, walked a little more and then caught the next boat back to the mainland, Kate was once again wrapped in the comfortable cloak of normality.

CHAPTER 24

Flight

Barra, Scotland - August 2009

"Oh, God, I hate being last on," Ellie fussed. "Everyone gives you dirty looks for holding them up."

Somehow, they had lingered too long in a cute gift shop, not allowing enough time for the drive to the airport. Ridiculous considering the island was tiny and no one part was far from another. Arriving late at the airport terminal, they slung their luggage on a cart a moment before it departed with its last load. They followed it out to the plane, relieved at being allowed to board. Ellie hurried across the sand. Kate followed her as she sprinted up the stairs to duck through the compact doorway.

The co-pilot directed Ellie into a single seat on the left-hand side. Kate's was the last empty one in the pairs to the right of the aisle. To her relief, rather than being greeted by annoyance, she was met with a wide smile. Sitting in the window seat was the man who had helped her out of the castle.

"Well, hello again, Kiwi Kate," he said.

Ellie, overhearing, gave her a questioning glance.

"Hi Alex." Kate took her place beside him and fastened her seatbelt.

"Ellie, this is Alex who I told you was kind enough to help me when I felt unwell in the castle. Alex, meet my friend Ellie." She introduced them across the aisle.

"Hi Alex." Ellie's small wave and rueful smile said it all. Kate knew what she was thinking: '*How is it you get to sit by the good-looking guy?*'

"I can't thank you enough for before," Kate fumbled, a little of her embarrassment returning. "I still don't know what came over me."

"Hey, we all have things that scare us," he said. "Like this, trapped inside a flying pencil for an hour. I don't like these little planes," he admitted.

"So what made you come here, then? If you had to fly on this plane?"

"Doing some research."

"Research? You're writing a book?"

"No, nothing like that. No—I'm an actor. I've got a part in a TV series set here. A murder mystery. None of the filming will actually happen on the island. Most of it on a lot near Glasgow, locations closer to civilisation."

This intrigued Kate. She'd met a few actors who hung around with Ellie's brother, James. But she'd exchanged more words with this one than all of them put together. She had no real idea what the job entailed.

"So do you always put this much effort into preparing?"

"Sometimes. This one I wanted to. It's a book adaptation. When I read it, it seemed as if the island was almost another character. I thought I owed it to the part to get better acquainted with the place."

His captivating blue eyes sparkled with life. His dark blonde hair fell in an unruly tumble almost to his shoulders. If she'd encountered him at home in New Zealand, she'd have thought him a surfie.

"Do you surf?" She surprised herself when the idea made its way from her brain to her lips. She hadn't meant to say it out loud. *Idiot.*

He looked confused.

"Ah, no, absolutely not. Water sports aren't really my thing." He grinned at her..

"Oh," said Kate, "ah... I thought... just the hair..."

"Oh yeah, I get it," he said, automatically running his hand through it to push it back off his face.

"Not how I would choose to wear it, but I've just finished a period drama—eighteenth century. Could have had a wig, but they itch like hell. So I convinced them I should let my hair grow. Go natural. Time to get it lopped off now before we start this new shoot."

"Sounds like you put a lot into your job."

"I suppose so. And you—what do you do in Kiwi-land? And what brings you all the way out here?"

He was not only easy on the eye, but easy to talk to. Kate relaxed into the conversation. She told him about her time in the UK—the challenge of her students; her travels in Europe and her friendship with Ellie; the sad reason for their trip to Barra. And that this was her last week before she returned home.

"Well, I might look you up sometime." Seeing her puzzled expression, he explained.

"My agent has put me forward for something down your way. It's a great role. But outside my usual. Somehow I've been pigeon-holed as Mr Nice Guy."

She could see why, with his beautifully sculpted features, dimpled chin and soft mouth that seemed to turn up at the corners in a permanent hint of a smile.

"This time I'd get to be the bad boy, although with a few redeeming features, of course." She smiled at that. "And if I get it—well, it's a part that would get me noticed outside the UK."

"What is it?"

"Top secret for now, I'm afraid. If I told you, I'd have to kill you," he joked. "But give me your email. If I come down, we could catch up. And by then I might even be allowed to talk about it."

Kate rummaged in her handbag, trying not to open it too wide and so reveal the rubble that lurked within. She found a scrap of paper and a pen and handed him her email address. Maybe he will, maybe he won't, she thought. But she had already decided that if he contacted her, she definitely wouldn't mind.

Landing in Glasgow, they said goodbyes as he went in search of a taxi and they headed to the gate for the return flight to London. The moment he was out of earshot, Ellie began her interrogation.

"You sure got lucky there. He's gorgeous! Now if that had been my seat number, I bet it would have been some bore, and I'd have had to put on my headphones and pretend to be asleep."

"Yeah, but he's an actor. Bound to have all the bees around the honey-pot."

"But if he comes to New Zealand—you'll have that honeypot all to yourself."

"If," said Kate. "I won't get my hopes up, but if it happens, yeah, I'd give it a go."

"So tell me all," said Ellie, as they buckled into their seats on the next plane. "We've got an hour, so you don't need to leave anything out."

"Well, his last name's MacLeod," she began.

"Oh my god, maybe he's Connor's brother! Connor MacLeod..." said Ellie.

"... of the Clan MacLeod," they chorused. Then burst into fits of un-controlled laughter, to the annoyance of their fellow passengers.

"Bloody hell, you went to a castle and fell into the Highlander movie!"

It was fantasy fan Ellie's favourite movie, and she'd made Kate watch it with her several times. Together they'd shed tears over Heather's death, and Connor's eternal loneliness, and basked in the warmth of the happy ending. OK, they were fictional characters, but that's what a good story did—made you believe.

By the time they began the descent into Heathrow, Ellie had extracted sufficient information to move on from the topic of Alex MacLeod.

"You know Kate—you're the best. God, I'm going to miss you. No one else would come all this way with me to take Mum home. Including that bloody useless brother of mine."

Ellie adored her brother James, but her disappointment at his decision to stay in London was still raw. He was reluctant to accompany Mary's ashes to Barra, giving flimsy excuses for not making the trip, culminating in a massive argument followed by uncomfortable silences between the two of them. Ellie said she'd given up trying to change his mind and simply stopped talking about it altogether.

Kate had welcomed the opportunity to go on this pilgrimage. Not only had it helped Ellie, giving her a supporter at a tough time, they'd been able to have some fun together before she left. Who knew when they'd see each other again?

But after two years away, it was time. She'd left New Zealand hoping that coming here might help her turn her life around. In some ways, it had. She wouldn't return the same Kate who'd left. She was more outgoing, more at ease with new people, and resolved to make the most of that back in Auckland. As Ellie, with her firm belief in new age philosophies, would say, "Ask the universe for what you want and it will send you what you need." No more sitting waiting for the future to come to her. She was going to be open to whatever opportunities the universe sent her way.

CHAPTER 25

Homecoming

Auckland, New Zealand - August 2009

THE TAXI SIDLED UP to the curb and a slight jolt pulled Kate from her doze into reality. She was home. The young driver leapt out more enthusiastically than she'd expected and heaved her cases from the boot of the Prius. The car drifted away silently, leaving her studying her house with mingled joy and disappointment.

She should be content. This was her happy place. But leaving here two years ago, she had imagined a quite different homecoming. One where she didn't return alone. This house didn't sit easily with a solitary occupant. Its walls held memories of a family, her family. And more than anything else, she wanted a family. She had planned on returning to this house, hand in hand with someone, ready to create a new chapter in her life. Somehow, she'd failed to do that.

Kate was grateful for the property manager, who'd suggested she rent the house fully furnished in her absence. She could walk back in like she'd never been away. Apart from unpacking the small stack of boxes in the shed, there was little to do. Teachers were in high demand, but full-time work wasn't something she needed or even wanted. She had the house, which, although old and tired, was valuable real estate. As children of the depression and a war, her grandparents lived frugally. After their deaths, Kate inherited an unexpectedly large sum of money. A friend's astute guidance meant that despite the Global Financial Crisis, her well-placed investments had weathered the years better than most.

From the barrage of job offers, she handpicked a regular two days at her old school. It would ease her sadness at leaving her London job. While challenging, she'd grown to love it, and missed everyone already. With five other days at her disposal, she threw herself into the task of bringing the house into the twenty-first century.

The first job on her list was removing the garish patterned 1970s wallpaper from the living room. It was a geometric floral in tones of orange and brown. Years after selecting it, Nana continued to tell visitors how much she loved it. "My favourite colours, and so cheerful," she would say. Vera took their polite nods as endorsement of her choice and never noticed the discreet smirks, particularly from Kate's friends.

Several times during the day, Kate cursed her grandfather's commitment to the mantra of his generation: *'If a job's worth doing, it's worth doing well'*. She battled with the well-glued paper, wielding a palette knife like a weapon. It was a warm day, too warm to be enveloped in clouds of steam like some dragon of legend. But the steamer was her friend, and without it, progress would have been painfully slow.

As the sun went down, she sprawled in a chair, drinking a well-deserved beer. The bottle of Steinlager was quintessentially Kiwi, and the cool lager was just what she needed. She smiled as she thought of her grandfather.

'Weasel piss' was what he called these light, summery beers. "Give me a good dark porter," he'd say. "Now that's what I call beer."

"Sorry, Grandad," she said, apologising for both her beer choice and the day spent undoing his handiwork.

Kate flipped open the laptop on the dining room table to check her email. The messages from Ellie were coming thick and fast. She appeared to have fallen head over heels in love. The start of the English school year had coincided with the arrival of a new PE teacher. He and Ellie had embarked on an intense, covert relationship. So far, they had kept it from the head, although many of their colleagues knew and were apparently delighted. Kate was delighted, too. Ellie was a treasure that too many men had overlooked.

However, today's first email wasn't from Ellie. The universe had sent her Alex MacLeod. To her surprise, he had been true to his word. He was probably coming to New Zealand later in the year and he'd reached out to her.

Kate thought back to their brief, bizarre encounter at Kisimul Castle. The memory still disturbed her. When she thought of it, it made her skin prickle as if she was rolling on spiky sea grass. And if she dwelled on the thought too long, she relived the unsettling moment when the entire world skewed onto its edge for an instant and then jolted her back to earth. It reminded her of watching stunt drivers race onto a ramp at speed, catapulting their car onto two wheels and then plunging down onto all four with a crash.

She and Alex hadn't spoken about it when she'd found herself next to him on the plane. Perhaps he'd wanted to spare her the awkwardness. She'd been glad of it. On the hour long flight to Glasgow he'd talked about his life as an actor, and in return he'd seemed interested in hers. And now, in this email, he'd restarted the conversation as if they were still sitting next to each other.

Hello there Kiwi Kate, Hope you don't
mind me making contact. After all,
our friendship only amounts to a
conversation at a castle and an hour
on a plane. But it did feel like the
start of a friendship. I found your
email and decided I'd check how things
are going for you now you're home.
Me, I've been busy but an actor never
complains about having work. Always
need to make the most of it. Once
you've lived through the lean times,
you know to grab what's offered. And
the job in New Zealand is looking
more promising by the day, so I'll be
definitely taking that one if it comes
through. So anyway, back to you…

It was a friendly email, and she didn't hesitate to reply. It was odd for her to feel this type of instant connection with someone, but there it was. She pushed send and immediately sensed impatience for his next response. Over the next few days, she checked her emails more frequently. She told herself it was boredom, that she needed to find more to do. But she was lying to herself, and the rush of excitement when his next message arrived two days later was evidence of that. The correspondence quickly exploded from a couple of times a week to daily.

Ellie was jubilant. "You go for it, girl."

Kate had confessed to her new long distance friendship after listening to almost fifteen minutes of Ellie relating the latest progress with the athletic Hugh. It had to be love when Ellie was willingly accompanying him on hikes in the country.

"That Alex is a seriously good-looking man," Ellie said. "And if he is as nice as he sounds, then you need to get out of the friend zone."

The first step towards that arrived in the form of a new message:

```
Can we talk? Really talk? Here's my
number. How about 7 p.m. your time
tomorrow? It'll be 7 a.m. here. I
think I can manage to be up in time.
```

She laughed at that. He'd been moaning about the early calls for his current project—cars arriving at four a.m. and in the makeup chair by five. The actor's life wasn't the charmed existence everyone thought. The hours were demanding. Hard to live any kind of normal life around a filming schedule.

```
Yes, let's talk, that would be fun.
Call you at 7. Set your alarm!
```

And so a new routine began. Now they talked every day, sometimes for hours on end, weaving time together around his work. Her phone bill skyrocketed.

"Just friends, eh?" Tracey teased her. "Sounds like more than friends to me."

"Don't be silly. Hard to be more than friends over the phone."

"I dunno. There is such a thing as phone sex."

"Interesting concept—but no. No phone sex. Just talking."

Soon, Alex had a new idea. Something called Skype.

"Have you got any techie friends? If they help you set it up, we could talk properly. I use it for work, but no reason we couldn't use it for fun."

Yes, she had techie friends. She summoned Ange's husband Tony that weekend and after a few minutes of his tinkering he declared her computer ready.

Monday dragged as she waited for seven p.m. to roll around. She had an early dinner accompanied by two gins to steady her nerves. Why *was* she so nervous? She told herself it was ridiculous, as she sat staring at a blank screen. As the clock in the corner of the screen displayed 7:00PM, a bizarre sound issued from her computer, as if there was a telephone trapped underwater, the ringing struggling to bubble to the surface. She clicked on the small green icon, the bubbles stopped, and the screen lit up.

They might have been in the same room. His boyish face appeared almost life-sized on the screen, although a little fuzzy around the edges. Realising he could see her in the same way she could see him, she had an urge to check her hair. She stopped herself in time, thinking it would look vain, but vowed to tidy herself beforehand next time.

He was every bit as good-looking as she remembered. Neatly sculptured features, a lazy grin and eyes of a deep intense blue that even the hazy video link couldn't dull. The expressions rolling across his face captivated her as he talked, laughed, questioned.

Maybe Tracey was right—they had become more than just friends. The conversation flowed like wine, and they revelled in the sweetness of this novel way of being together. But rather than satisfying their thirst for contact with the other, Skype seemed to exacerbate it. The daily calls became essential.

One night, she was running late. The offer of taking a few after school sailing lessons with kids down at the club had been too tempting to refuse. But that day, some idiot had parked his car blocking their access to the boat sheds. After much cursing and a call to a towing company, they'd hauled the little boats safely inside, but it had chewed up all the time she'd planned to make herself presentable for Alex. There was no way out of it. He'd have to see her as she was, her hair a salty mess and the sheen of sweat lighting her face.

His raised eyebrows, as the video kicked in, said it all.

"New look? Very au naturel."

"Ah, yes, things went a bit awry down at the yacht club. It's a long story."

"Well, I like it. Now I know your champion sailor claim wasn't just to impress me."

"No, I'm the real deal."

"That you are," he said softly, with a strange look on his face. "Well," he said, snapping back into his usual smiley self, "apart from the trials and tribulations of the yacht club, what else has been happening in your world?"

Alex was mainly doing promo work now. They'd wrapped filming, and his days were often free. Free to talk to her. He lounged on a sofa in his Glasgow apartment, thin rays of sunshine struggling to make an impact, attempting to ward off the fast-approaching chill. She sat in bed, covered with only a crisp sheet, windows flung wide and the sound of evening cricket song. And oh, how they talked. She'd gone to work over-tired some days, scolding herself for not hanging up sooner. But she didn't regret it. This intense connection that had sprung from an accidental meeting was blossoming into something shiny and new. And soon the connection would be in person. He was coming.

CHAPTER 26

Connection

Auckland, New Zealand - December 2009

KATE SAT ON THE hard utilitarian chairs in the arrivals hall. She decided they'd deliberately designed them as a disincentive for loitering. The arrivals board above announced that Flight NZL 570 had landed and was processing. He was in business class, so he should emerge near the front of the trickle of passengers.

She stifled a yawn. It was the earliest she'd been up for a long time. The flights from London via LA always arrived at the ungodly hour of five-thirty am. And she'd allowed extra time to make herself presentable, which took a concentrated effort. Sure, in her sailing days, she'd have been heading for the water early. But there was a vast difference between tugging on a t-shirt and shorts while throwing her hair in a ponytail, and preparing to meet Alex.

At least in December, it was already becoming light. Through large windows behind her, the night sky was peeling back to reveal a honey-coloured dawn. She turned her attention back to the doors.

And there he was. A full head taller than anyone else, sandy sleep-tousled hair and a flash of a smile that lit his face as he caught sight of her. He'd long since lopped off the long hair he'd sported when she met him, now with a modern crop reminiscent of a model from a fashion magazine. However, his simple white t-shirt and jeans spoke of a person who wasn't the least bit interested in the latest trends.

"Kiwi!" he called out. "How are you?"

Alex abandoned his baggage trolley and wrapped her in a hug. It was oddly intimate considering they'd only met in person once before, and that only a few months ago. But through the emails and phone calls, Kate felt she knew him.

However, there were things she couldn't have known. Only now could she describe the warm, solid feel of his arms encircling her. Only now could she inhale the smell of him, masculine but overlaid with the spicy scent of something he'd used to freshen up before getting off the plane.

"Alex." She smiled at him. "Welcome to New Zealand."

He was excited to be here. Of course he would be. They had flown him down to meet with the casting team for a television series. The film industry was thriving in New Zealand, with homegrown big names like Peter Jackson drawing others to consider basing themselves down under. They'd loved his audition tape, so they had invited Alex to meet them in person and do a 'chemistry test' with the Kiwi actress who had won the lead role. But Kate hoped that perhaps a little of the excitement was because he would get to spend time with her.

There was another drawback of the flight arriving so early. The journey home dropped them into heavy commuter traffic. For a small city,

Auckland had disproportionately large traffic problems. But for once, Kate didn't mind.

From the moment they loaded his bags in the back, they launched into the same easy conversation that had kept her up late many nights. She let his beautiful voice, with that soft Scottish accent, wash over her. She could listen to him all day.

Added to that, his simply being here triggered an unexpected response. It wasn't only his presence, his tall frame overflowing the seat, filling the car. He brought something bigger than his physical self. Perhaps this was what made him a talented actor, what set him apart from dozens of others.

Having him here sitting beside her awoke something. It thrummed inside her, like the beating wings of a small, hopeful bird, insistently hammering against the bars of its cage.

———

Kate sat alongside the cottage garden she'd created at the front of her house, pulling weeds that dared to compete with the dazzle of colour that was blooming there. She inhaled the delicate fragrance that drifted upwards from the last few violets. She loved the petite flowers, nestled in a nest of downy, heart-shaped leaves, and mourned that their time was ending. Now she would patiently await their return the next spring.

It was the third day since Alex had arrived, and for him, an important one. He'd left early in the day, heading to the studio out west. He'd been optimistic, but then that seemed to be his natural state of being, always exuding a youthful aura of joy. Kate marvelled at his ability to wake each morning and be instantly ready to face the day. It was a stark contrast to her own struggle to drag herself from the clutches of sleep, fuelled by a hit of dark coffee. Talking late into the night with him was taking its toll.

The late afternoon summer sun bathed her bare arms and legs. In the background, the ever-present sound of the sea soothed her. It was high tide and below the house, the waves rumbled against the rock wall. But there was a depth to the rumble that wasn't the sea and it was getting louder.

"Kate!" Hearing her name, she turned to see the source of the sound.

"Come for a ride." He was behind the wheel of an outrageous yellow sports car. He laughed, and his happiness was contagious.

"I'm filthy," she called back, wiping the dirt from her hands on the front of her shorts.

"Go get changed then. I'll wait."

Within five minutes she'd installed herself in the passenger seat and they were off, the wind ruffling her hair.

"Where are we going?"

"I thought we might go for an early dinner. Have a bottle of bubbles to celebrate."

"You got the part, then? Congratulations."

"Yes, looks like you'll be seeing more of me. Filming starts in March. It'll be four months at least."

"That's great!"

"You didn't ask about the car..."

"Well, I knew you'd tell me eventually," she said with a giggle.

"Rental car," he said.

"No," she said in disbelief. They didn't rent out cars like this. "You're lying."

"It is," he protested. "I thought we could have a bit of fun in it for a few days. A road trip up north. You up for that?"

"Why not?" she said. "Great choice—Northland is beautiful."

"Yeah, well, one of the assistant directors—we worked together once before—he has a beach house. Gave me the key and said to take a few days there before I go back."

"Good guy to know," she said, already thinking about what to pack. And about what it would be like to have this dazzling man all to herself.

CHAPTER 27

Road Trip

Northland, New Zealand - December 2009

KATE SAVOURED THE EXHILARATING sense of freedom as they whizzed along the motorway, leaving the city behind. She had always loved this part of the country and often imagined what it would be like to live there. Every day would seem like a holiday.

They'd both been up early that morning, buzzing with a shared excitement about the trip. After squashing bags into the compact rear of the car, they headed north.

With the map book on her lap, Kate acted as navigator. After an hour, the roads became more basic, the towns smaller. After another hour, she directed him off onto a narrow winding road where the bush came right to the edge, as if it was waiting for the opportunity to seize back what humans had taken from it. Above them, the trees arched across the road on either side, creating a high vaulted ceiling, like a cathedral of nature.

Here and there a driveway disappeared between the trees into the dimness, a letterbox the only hint that there was something beyond. Most looked as if someone had simply hacked a path into the primeval forest. The odd one was a little wider, maybe with a gate. They swept around corners, over blind brows of hills and the odd tight hairpin bend. She finally glimpsed a wooden gatepost with the number they'd been given. A metalled driveway led upwards in gentle curves between the trees.

"Thank god for that," he said, sounding relieved. "This car is so low, I worried we wouldn't get it up the driveway. Some of them are pretty rough."

"Yes," she agreed. "You'd need a four-wheel drive for a few of them."

He eased the car carefully up the slope, being sure to avoid the fingers of trees that reached out, almost touching them. With the roof down, she could smell the distinctive damp greenness of the New Zealand bush. It was cool and fresh. And then, as if by magic, the trees parted to reveal a surprising house.

Its facade soared above them, reaching for the sky. The bold modern lines might have been jarring in this environment except for the warm timber walls and expansive glass, which created the illusion that the house was simply an extension of the bush. Once inside, there was another surprise. The opposite side of the house was all glass, revealing its clifftop perch. Below and beyond was the sparkling sea, lit by the intense glow of the midday sun.

"Oh," Kate said in a whisper, rendered almost speechless by the sight. She never tired of the sea. It was her soul, its ever-changing moods an endless source of fascination. Today it sparkled like a woman decked out in a sequined dress, anticipating a party.

"That's impressive." Alex sauntered into the kitchen and confirmed that, as promised, someone had magically stocked it with everything they needed, including beer. He flicked the top off one and offered it to Kate.

"Don't mind if I do."

She took it, stepping towards the massive doors that led onto a deck. She unlocked one and rolled it back. It slid open noiselessly, allowing the world outside to pour in. She closed her eyes and breathed the intoxicating sea breeze, overlaid with the fragrance of the bush which embraced the house on three sides.

They sat in large comfortable chairs, drinking in the view. Kate tipped her head back, eyes closed, and let the sun and the warm breeze caress her face. Alex disappeared inside, and she could hear him clattering around in the kitchen. He emerged a while later, proudly carrying a large platter arrayed with all kinds of tempting food.

"And this," he said, placing it on the table with a flourish, "is the full extent of my meal preparation skills."

"Looks pretty good to me," she said, scooping a generous dollop of runny cheese with a piece of crusty bread. She wrinkled her nose at its pungent aroma, but it didn't deter her from taking a bite. "Oh my god, that smells foul but tastes divine."

"I think this might go well with it," he suggested, pouring a generous measure of wine into two glasses. It was a Gisborne Chardonnay, all buttery and delicious. Two glasses later, aided by the food and the heat, it was tempting to give in to the languid feeling which had crept over her and lounge there for the rest of the day. But Alex wasn't having it.

"OK, time to walk off lunch," he announced. "The beach awaits."

Off the deck, a half-hidden track meandered down through the trees. Tantalising glimpses of the sea peeked through beneath the pohutukawa. They were in full flower, their fiery red bristles scraping the sky. This abundant flowering was the sign of a long, hot summer, according to local lore. The spiky cabbage trees were also laden with flowers like rosary beads cascading from their lamppost trunks.

The clattering of cicadas above was deafening. From time to time one dropped from its perch, jostled from an overcrowded branch. Kate brushed the insects off, their serrated legs and papery wings scratchy on her bare arms. A few hundred metres in, she heard a gasp from in front of her.

"Shit!" Alex exclaimed. "That bloody hurts!" There were pinpricks of blood where the skin had been pierced. His attackers, a cluster of nasty-looking barbs, were still attached to the hairs on his legs. "You told me there was nothing that could hurt you in the New Zealand bush," he said, his face indignant.

"Only if you've shaved your legs," she retorted. "It's hook grass. Sit down over there and I'll pull them off."

He did as she directed. Even though she tried to be gentle, there was the odd grimace as she extracted a particularly well-embedded one. As she worked, Kate found she was quite enjoying the task, running her hands over those long, muscular legs. There was an intimacy in the action. They'd touched before, friendly hugs and a companionable arm around her shoulders. But this was different, and she was almost disappointed when she declared him free of the offending grass seeds and they resumed their walk.

The path ended abruptly, the exposed roots of a giant pohutukawa grasping remnants of sandy soil where the ground had once been. The relentless sea had gnawed at this end of the beach. Alex, with his long legs, easily stepped down onto the sand. Kate stopped and surveyed the drop doubtfully.

"Jump," he suggested.

"It's still slipping away." Little showers of sand trickled beneath her feet. "I'm going to end up on my bum."

"Here." He extended a hand, steadying her as she leapt off and landed safely beside him.

It felt natural, her hand clasped in his. They sat on the sand for a moment, each silently surveying the little bay.

"Come on, let's test the water," he suggested.

They flicked off their shoes, and he pulled her onto her feet. They strolled towards the water, hands still joined in an unspoken agreement. They stood, letting the delicately frilled waves tickle their feet. Then a larger one came, and they leapt back together, laughing in delight at their escape. Another followed, drenching the edge of her dress in its chilly grasp.

As she spun away from its clutches, like a dancer, he drew her towards him. They stood for a moment, eyes meeting. His questioning. Hers assenting. He laid one hand against her cheek, trailing his fingertip down her neck to rest lightly on her bare shoulder. She closed her eyes, revelling in the touch. He lifted the hand still clasped in his, brushing it with the merest hint of a kiss.

Kate saw with sudden clarity. Their first strange encounter at the castle had been like the lighting of a fuse. In that moment, events were set in motion that would inevitably lead to this. She'd thought of him as a friend, but he was always destined to be her lover. And now the fire was ignited.

Through the delicate fabric of her dress, she could feel the lean hardness of his body as he pressed her close. He kissed her neck, her bare shoulders, her lips, and a wave of desire swamped her. She wanted to crumple under that wave, let it knock her to the ground and drown in its depths. She would have given herself over to it, but Alex drew her back.

"By god, I'd like nothing better to lie you down right here and make love to you," he said, his voice throaty. "But unlike in the movies, I think the sand might get in some rather unpleasant places, don't you think?" He raised one eyebrow, a mischievous smile on his face.

"Much as I hate to admit it, you're right," she said. "And I prefer not to risk an unexpected audience." Her glance swept along the length of the beach. "You're used to standing naked in front of strangers, but I'm a little more inhibited."

She immediately regretted that remark, hoping he would think she'd simply made an assumption that some of his roles required nudity. She knew for sure that they had. As their long distance friendship had bloomed, Kate had indulged her curiosity. She'd searched for him online, and found some of his work, including a few scenes that left little to the imagination. It was strange that she'd already seen most of his body and watched him in the most intimate of situations. It made her uncomfortable, even if it wasn't for real. She was too embarrassed to tell him she'd secretly been spying on him.

Fortunately, he didn't notice anything odd, just laughed at her comment.

"There's very little about sex scenes that's at all sexy. It's like a well-choreographed dance." He took her hands and demonstrated, moving her like a puppeteer. "Like this. I'll put my hand here, and then you put yours there and then after that we'll do this." She smiled as he placed one of her hands on his firm thigh. "Then you practice until you've got it memorised, after which you do it ten times over with the cameras rolling. And the camera operators up close to your face—or to other bits of you."

"I'd never thought about it being like that. I can imagine it's awkward. "

"Yes, it can be. But this isn't, this is just you and me." He paused and met her gaze. "Come on, let's go back to the house. If you're sure that's what you want?"

If that's what she wanted? Surely he could see that her body quivered with the wanting? But he was so bloody decent, of course he would give her the chance to change her mind. Once they crossed this line, there was no going back.

Her voice was low, but steady. "I'm sure."

They scooped up their shoes, and she led him towards the pathway.

Back at the house, Kate stood in the lounge with a glass of wine in hand, gazing out at the rippling sea. It mirrored the waves of nervousness sweeping through her stomach. He came and stood behind her, reassuringly enclosing her in his arms, and rested his chin on her shoulder. Arriving back here, they had both known without saying that there was no need to rush. It was if they'd agreed to savour these moments, the giddy newness of this change in their relationship.

Kate slid from beneath his arms and placed her glass on a coffee table. She wandered over to the sound system. She'd earlier noticed her favourite Crowded House CD in the neatly organised rack and felt the need of its soothing music to steady her nerves. Slipping it into the slot, she pressed play and turned to face him as the first notes, a soft strum of a guitar, poured gently from the speakers.

"Are you sure about this?"

"More sure than I've ever been," she said, signalling her willingness with a slow, deep kiss that resonated in every supercharged nerve end of her body. They spun like dancers, the music whirling them towards the bedroom, mouths insistent, feet moving instinctively, steps in perfect time.

He released her, and stood back, his eyes caressing her body, sweeping from head to toe, blatant desire on his face.

In return, she took a moment to admire the man in front of her. He was wearing a soft denim shirt with sleeves casually rolled back, exposing his wrists. She noticed the golden hairs glinting in the sun against the tanned skin of his arms, and also peeking out of the 'v' at the neck. She reached for the buttons and slowly undid them, revealing how the fine golden line extended down to his lightly muscled abdomen.

He reminded her of a racehorse, all lean and long-limbed. He peeled back the shirt and let it fall to the floor. She took a step back to take him in some more. God, he was beautiful. His shorts hung low, brushing his narrow hips, the sculpted lines of his body tantalising as they plunged under the waistband.

"My turn," he said, taking the strapless dress where it skimmed her shoulders, gently pulling it down to her waist, revealing her breasts.

She shivered a little as the chill of the breeze grazed her bare skin. Then another tug, and it slipped past her hips to fall in a tumble. She stood barefoot in a wreath of floral fabric, her desire banishing any self-consciousness under his gaze even though she was now only clothed in the fine lacy briefs.

"My turn," she said, reaching for his waist and unbuttoning the shorts. She slid her hand downwards, underneath it the surprising softness of his thigh. With a little gasp, he pulled her in close and kissed her, and she knew that the time for going slow had passed.

"Wait a moment." He paused to grope in the leather duffle bag lying beside the bed, producing a condom. "Don't think I was presuming anything," he said. "I didn't plan for this to happen."

"No, no," she replied. "Just as the ones in my handbag are always there, in case of the unexpected. Not because I had any plans to turn my friend into my lover. However, now that we're at that point..."

He lowered her to the bed, trailing kisses down her body from neck to thigh. His touch was gentle, but confident, as if he knew exactly how to meet her need. Long fingers explored her hidden places, at the same time his mouth swirling hot, lips sucking, tongue warm and probing, tasting her, drinking her.

"So fucking beautiful," he said, murmuring into her thigh. "The taste of you, the feel of you."

He sat back for a moment, reading her mounting arousal correctly, monitoring the response to his touch, his relentless hands not missing a beat, his eyes searching her face as she exploded with white hot sparks.

He looked down at her with a satisfied smile, pressed a kiss against her lips, the taste of her own pleasure lingering there, salty and sweet, before rolling across, his strident erection nudging at her, demanding entry. She let her legs fall open, arching her hips as she guided him forward, inviting him in.

Alex made love to her with that same unbridled joy that seemed to carry him through life, and it swept her along, an optimism in their joining that stretched off into an unknown future, while in the here and now he took her with him on a second dizzying ride, cresting the climax together, before they fell back panting and sweaty in a tangle of sheets and limbs.

He smiled across at her, pressing a finger on her swollen kiss-bruised lips, tracing the shape of them, a soothing delicate touch.

"Right now," he said, "I have to be the luckiest man alive."

CHAPTER 28

Lucky

Northland, New Zealand - December 2009

SHE LAY WITH HER head on his shoulder and traced lazy spirals on his chest with her fingertip. Alex breathed in the smell of her hair, like a fresh breeze with warm undertones of tropical flowers. It hung like a silky wave and she let it veil her face, as if to prevent him reading what it might reveal as she spoke.

"Talking of luck," she said. "Tell me..." There was cautiousness in her words. "...how, out of all those women who'd love to be lying here with you like this—how did *I* get to be the lucky one?"

"Luck had nothing to do with that. Except my good luck at being the one who happened to find you sprawled on the ground at Kisimul Castle."

"No, seriously," she said. "Why me? You must have plenty of women who'd jump at the invitation."

He lay there, wondering how to answer her. He wanted to say that it's because you're not one of those women. But to voice it as a reason for his attraction to her seemed to make him almost as shallow as the ones who wanted to sleep with him because they thought they knew him. Oh, they knew the fictional characters he played on screen, and they knew the equally fictional man of the magazine articles. So they assumed they knew him.

That she hadn't recognised him was refreshing. But that wasn't the main reason. Over the years, there'd been others who were oblivious to him as an actor and he hadn't sought them out like he had Kate. There was something in that first meeting, an ease between them that suggested they might be friends. He'd never had what could be described as friendship with a woman before. And it had morphed into this. Love. A small word that hadn't been part of his vocabulary.

He turned onto one elbow and scooped the silvery curtain away from her face to study her. He was so used to overthinking everything. In his position, it was dangerous to speak off the cuff. He understood how words could be misunderstood, misused, twisted and turned against you. It was a lesson he'd learned the hard way, and his publicist had coached him expertly so he would avoid it happening again. Sometimes he loathed the cautious person he'd become. How had he let his fear choke his spontaneity to the point he couldn't come out and tell this stunning woman how he felt about her? He took a deep breath.

"If you believed the magazines, you'd think I was bedding a different woman every week. There are pictures of me with this one and that one. Most are just partners set up for some promo event. They're usually lovely girls, but they're doing it for the same reasons as me."

"And what reasons might they be?"

"Because it suits the PR people very well. They need us to walk the line between being desirable and available. Some fans would love to see me find my happy ever after, and some would hate it. So we keep them guessing."

He leaned across and kissed her, willing her to understand the truth of it.

"So, you want to know why you?" he said, cupping her face in his hands. "Because I can talk with you, really talk, about anything. God knows we've covered some ground on those Skype calls." She laughed at that, no doubt recalling the times when she'd had to make a hasty end to a call, having noticed it was after midnight. "And that laugh. We have fun together. I think I've laughed more in these few months of knowing you than I have in years."

"Me too," she said. "It's like I see the world differently with you. You make me happy, and I needed that, because the world hasn't been the happiest place these past few years." Her grey-blue eyes were serious. "Alex, you might just be *my* happy ever after."

Once those sorts of words would have scared him, challenged the wall of caution he'd built around relationships. But not now. He rolled over further, blanketing her with his body and pressing her close. The smell of their lovemaking was still strong on her. It blended with her own scent, overlaid with a fleeting remnant of her perfume. Her breath was warm on his neck as he answered softly.

"And I think you might be mine."

Home Alone

Auckland, New Zealand - December 2009

As they walked hand in hand through the terminal, Kate noticed the way he watched the oncoming flow of people. He wore an expression of practised wariness that she hadn't seen before. When they dived off into a small bar and sat down at a table, there was an expression on his face that she couldn't fathom. Relief? Or even a hint of elation?

"What's up?" she asked, curious.

He dropped his head and said with a slight smile, "I was just thinking how anonymity is highly underrated. It's one thing I've loved about being here. No one knows me. Oh, the odd person you'll see a wee glimmer of recognition, but then it's gone. Not enough for them to be sure. Not enough for them to stop me. At home, it seems as if everyone knows me. We couldn't walk through somewhere like this without two or three fans waving me over for an autograph or a picture."

"Ah, the price of fame." She understood now. "Do you mind very much?"

"Oh no, not really. The fans are great. You know, you have to respect them. If I ever start to think it's too much, I remind myself to be grateful for what they've given me. But it's just nice to walk along with you, and not have someone snapping our pictures, or wanting a piece of me. Sometimes at home, it's like I'm in that old video game and all the little Pac Men are nibbling away at me."

She laughed. "Showing your age now. Most kids today haven't even heard of Pac Man." She thought for a moment. "So this new contract. When you come back. Things will change?"

"Yes, they will. Not for a while. But this TV series, when it's finished, it'll be a worldwide release. Even down here in quiet little New Zealand, they'll know who I am."

They picked at their food, dragging out this last meal together as long as possible. But then it was time. Beer glasses drained and plates empty, they plunged back into the busy departure hall, carried along by the crowds, heading for the door, through which only one of them could go.

And then they were there: PASSENGERS ONLY PAST THIS POINT. They stood wrapped around each other like the still centre of a spiral galaxy while the stars whirled around them. For that moment, they were oblivious to time passing by, and the scurrying people who milled around them. The blaring intercom faded into the background. All her awareness focused on the words he murmured in her ear.

"I so don't want to go. God, I can't wait to get back here before I've even left."

"And I don't want you to go, but there's no avoiding it."

She tried to sound brave, but six weeks was a long time and Skype calls would no longer suffice. She stretched up and gave him one last kiss. His lips, so soft and warm, sought her out, and she sensed his reluctance to release her. Thinking that she absolutely must not cry, she drew back and gazed at his beautiful face, as if to fix it in her mind, before he turned away with a rueful smile and headed towards security, leaving her bereft. She loved that long, leisurely way he walked, carrying his height with an unexpected grace. Then he turned, lifted his hand, tossed her a last dazzling grin, and disappeared around the corner, out of view.

Outside, she stood in line at the pay machine, draped in a sweet sadness. The past weeks had been surreal. Now, for the next two months, life was back to how it had been before. No, that wasn't possible. The universe had shifted, and there would be no going back. She would have to be patient until he returned. He would return. She didn't want to doubt it, but after years of disappointment, ugly thoughts niggled at her, threatening to take up residence in her mind. She swiped them away, sending them back to the past where they belonged.

As she climbed into the car, her phone chirped. A text.

Alex

Miss you already xx

She smiled, imagining him sitting in the departure lounge already sending her messages. She replied.

Kate

Miss you more xx

She turned the radio to full volume, a cheery companion at odds with her mood. She drove along the motorway on autopilot, her brain still consumed with him.

At home, she sat in the kitchen, sipping her tea, deep in thought. It was a robust extra-strong brew, and the soothing bitterness worked its magic. Drinking tea was a family ritual. While she usually drank far too much coffee than she should, in times of trouble, she automatically reached for a cup of tea. She could almost hear her grandmother's voice. "Sit down, love, and I'll make you a nice cup of tea. Everything's going to be all right."

Vera's tea had eased her through many problems. From fickle friends to schoolwork stresses, tea somehow helped put it all back into perspective.

The house was empty without Alex. She wondered how it could be that in such a short time this space, once wholly hers, had embraced him so fondly that it now echoed his absence back at her? After losing her grandparents, this tiny house had wrapped her in its kind arms and anchored her in its consistent warmth. She had showered it with love and care. In return, it gave her a sense of belonging, somewhere to be. This house was enough for Kate, and she had been enough for it.

But not now. After having a taste of another, it yearned for more. The house was no longer content with her solitary presence but demanded shared laughter, animated conversation, passionate lovemaking, interspersed with the languorous stillness of two. She firmly closed the door on its nagging demands and escaped to her favourite spot.

The overcast sky, with a slight glimmer of sun through the low clouds, was depressing. If it wasn't for the warmth, one could imagine it a bleak winter afternoon. On this summer day it was a disappointment, cheating her of the promised blue sky.

She sat on the matted fringe of seagrass, watching the patient waves studiously erase the beach. She closed her eyes, her only awareness the almost silent intake of breath, and a hiss as the next surge of water exhaled towards her bare feet.

The ping of an incoming text pulled Kate back from the pleasant drowsiness. Her first thought was Alex. But no, he was somewhere over the vastness of the Pacific, racing away from her. This was Tracey, checking up on her.

Tracey

> *Thinking of you home alone :(Call me if you like :)*

At least she had her friends. She would call.

The phone call revealed that Tracey and Angela had banded together, plotting to rescue her from the loneliness of Alex's departure. They had a plan and wouldn't accept any excuse.

"Going out is exactly what you need." Tracey was insistent.

"No arguments. Just accept that sometimes your friends know best," said Ange.

Although she protested at first, Kate relented, knowing they were right. Now seated in a new little bar, sipping wine and the girls deliberately keeping the conversation upbeat, she was glad she'd come.

"Guess what I heard today?"

You could always rely on Tracey to have some salacious gossip extracted from the women in her makeup chair. She had her friends' full attention as she passed on interesting titbits in a hushed tone.

"Really?" said Kate. "I'd never have guessed that of her."

She hated to admit it, but she enjoyed hearing a bit of scandal about the local celebrities. Perhaps it was because her own life was ordinary. However, this time, there was a pang of guilt. She realised this was the way people gossiped about Alex—people who didn't even know him, talking about his life as if they did. Ashamed, she diverted the conversation in a different direction.

"Tracey, is that a new ring I see? Christmas come early?"

"No—present to self—but Brett can't know." Her voice was soft, conspiratorial, as if Brett might suddenly appear and overhear her confession. "I should be saving for our holiday." That led to a detailed description of more amazing bargains to be had in the jewellery store's closing down sale.

Kate's phone rang, and she grabbed it, casually checking the caller to decide if she should answer.

"Alex," she said, her voice breathless. She leapt to her feet and stepped out onto the deck, away from the bustle of the bar. She stood there, gazing out across the harbour, her friends' eyes boring into her back, their curiosity almost palpable. Of course, they were interested in what happened next with this Scot, who had materialised out of nowhere and completely captivated their friend.

She arrived back at the table, carried on a wave of euphoria that was more than the effects of the wine, ready to face her friends' predictable barrage of questions.

"So?"

"What's up?"

"How come he rang so soon?"

"He's in LAX—and he's asked me to join him. Go to Scotland. For Christmas."

There were squeals of excitement.

"He's organising me a ticket. Business class."

More squeals. Angela waved down one of the waitstaff, her finger stabbing at the drinks menu.

"Champagne please, that one."

"Now I get to meet his family. Wish me luck."

Her stomach churned as excitement and nerves fought for control. Families weren't her strong point, not having had one.

"You don't need luck," said Tracey. "Hun, they're going to love you."

CHAPTER 30

White Christmas

Ballenaig, Scotland - December 2009

BALLENAIG WAS THE QUINTESSENTIAL small Scottish town. The modern houses and wide streets on the outskirts gave way to traditional stone buildings as they drew closer to the centre. Some were whitewashed with stark black window frames and bold coloured doors. Others, still in their natural state, revealed the craftsmanship of some long-gone stonemason's hand.

Any modern touches were deftly included without breaking the spell of the town's ancient charm. It was beautiful. Even the railway station was discreetly tucked away. A small sign pointed to its direction, the only hint of this lifeline that could have you in nearby Stirling within fifteen minutes, and Edinburgh in half an hour.

As they rounded one corner, Kate caught sight of an arched stone bridge spanning a rushing stream. They wove their way towards it, finally crossing over the river where the road funnelled them down into the main street. It was narrow and flanked by weathered stone shop fronts. Alex's driver had slowed as he entered the tight street.

Kate took the opportunity to peek into each shop. Two hair salons flanked a bakery with shelves of rustic loaves. The traditional butcher shop offered an array of meats, brilliant red, edged in creamy fat. Sausages of different hues were lined up with military precision, jaunty labels indicating their flavour. Kate was sure that the pasty-looking blob next to them was a haggis. She shuddered at the thought, knowing the ingredients of the Scottish delicacy. She hoped the MacLeods weren't serving *that* as a Christmas treat.

Around a gentle curve, the street was edged by a long row of white buildings on one side and a neatly kept churchyard on the other. They pulled to a stop alongside the church itself. With its square Norman tower, it had to be ancient.

"Here will be fine, Danny. That's us across the road." Alex nodded towards a narrow doorway. "You go ahead Kate. Reception's through the door at the top of the stairs. Danny and I will bring the cases."

She stepped out of the car's warm cocoon. As she stood there drinking in the postcard scene, she felt a delicate touch on her hair. She turned her face skywards, and her eyes widened in delight. As if on cue, feathery flakes of snow drifted lazily from the sepia sky. A white Christmas. Scotland was certainly turning on the charm.

By the time he arrived at reception, Alex's hair sported a light dusting of flakes.

"Welcome to my hometown." He bent to kiss her.

"Oh my god, your lips are like ice."

"Well, help me warm them." With a laugh, he planted them firmly against hers once more.

"Not much point, since you're going out in the snow again."

After he'd gone, Kate headed straight for the shower. She spent ages there, luxuriating in the warmth. The steady staccato beat of the droplets on her skin energised her. She emerged wrapped in an enormous white towel, soft and fluffy as a cloud, and decided to pull on pyjamas. Perhaps she'd doze a little.

She was in far better shape than she'd expected after twenty-four hours of flying. The best part of travelling on Alex's business class ticket was a seat that virtually became a couch. It was the first time she'd ever properly slept on a plane. She wasn't planning to lose that advantage by going against the accepted wisdom—don't sleep until the proper bedtime in your new time zone. But the warm bed tempted her to snuggle under the covers while reading a little of her book.

About an hour later, she heard the key in the lock. Alex was back.

"Right then-—f you think you're up to it. We're meeting them at the Tappit Hen."

Them being his siblings who were already settling into the oddly named pub at the end of the street. It was an annual tradition for the four MacLeod offspring to meet for a Christmas Eve drink at the local pub. Christmas Day with the entire family gathered at his parents' was apparently mayhem. Alex had explained how they enjoyed this chance to see each other the night before.

Kate pushed aside any feelings of jet-lag, knowing it was important to him.

"For sure, let me change and I'll be ready in five."

She was both nervous and eager to meet them. If today went well, tomorrow with the entire family would be less daunting.

"Not keen to meet my brothers and sister in your pyjamas then, are you?" he teased.

"No, sorry—not even in my stunning Christmas ones," she giggled, doing a little twirl to show off aforesaid pyjamas. While most of the time Kate didn't even wear pyjamas, she'd seen these in the vast Changi Airport shopping mall as she killed time between flights. An impulse buy. She loved their cute, playful design.

"I should make some effort to create a good first impression. Being the first Kiwi they've met, I can't let the side down."

"OK, well perhaps I can help you remove those offending pyjamas."

He pulled her close, sliding a chilled hand into the waistband and cupping her to him. Thoughts of what payment he expected for this assistance were written on his face.

"Oh god." She groaned. "It's so tempting." Her first instinct was to encourage this line of thinking. Then she envisioned the family seated in the pub. "But I suppose we'd better not keep them waiting."

She turned away from him to fling open her suitcase.

He spun her back towards him, burying his face against her neck. He drew her down with him as they both scrambled to discard clothing. His voice was low and husky.

"They can wait."

Meet the MacLeods

Ballenaig, Scotland - December 2009

KATE WIGGLED INTO A clean pair of jeans, added a plush plum-coloured merino jumper and finished with possum fur-lined boots. She'd never needed anything resembling proper winter clothes in Auckland's mild climate, but had wisely packed plenty for the Scottish winter.

Just as well, because outside snow was now falling in steady flurries, laying a delicate yet chilly blanket over the last resting place of the old ones of Ballenaig, who slept peacefully in the kirkyard across the road. She wondered if the coat, scarf and hat might be overkill for the short walk, but she wasn't taking any chances. She wasn't fond of the cold.

"They say it'll be at least minus five tonight," he said.

"Hmm, I'm definitely not overdressed then. So, what on earth is a Tappit Hen?" They were strolling down Kirk Street towards the establishment in question. "I've heard some strange names for pubs before, but not that one."

Alex laughed. "Well, back in the seventeenth century, it's what you would have drunk your ale from. One of those fancy pewter drinking jugs with a lid topped with a topknot, like a wee crested hen. A 'topped hen', so to speak."

"Oh," she replied, curiosity satisfied. "Well, that doesn't sound quite so weird now I know."

The Tappit Hen nested inside a much larger, bland white building. Its frontage glowed deep cherry red. Carriage lamps flanked two large lacey-patterned bay windows. Floral stained glass looked down from above and window boxes with an abundance of greenery overflowed below. The establishment shouted out its name in bold brass letters over the door, amplified by ornate painted flourishes on either side. The lights inside beckoned, large shining golden orbs giving an impression of wide, kind eyes and holding out the promise of warmth.

Inside, once her eyes adjusted to the gloom, Kate saw a welcoming interior common to many British pubs—lots of wood grain polished till you could almost see your face in it; a mirrored wall behind the bar reflecting a rainbow of bottles and gleaming glassware; a blazing fire encouraging her to discard her outer layers, and deep red leather booths that extended a comfortable invitation.

"There they are."

Alex nodded towards one of the largest booths. As she followed his gaze, a flurry of smiles and friendly waves met her. She smiled back, mentally doing a quick run through of Alex's earlier briefing on his siblings.

"Now Sarah's extremely bossy. Not her fault. Being the eldest, there was always an expectation she'd keep us in line. A difficult job. She can come across a bit abrupt, shades of Dad there."

Yes, she could see Sarah trying to check her out without making it obvious.

"Robbie's your typical gentle giant. He was the best big brother a kid could have. Bullies took one look at him and ran. But he's a softie. Do anything for you."

Well, he was easy to spot. The largest man in the bar.

"Andy doesn't say much. But don't think that means he doesn't like you. He's like that with everyone. He doesn't waste words. Anyway, his wife, Sam, does more than enough talking for the two of them."

Kate could see the couple. She–tiny but animated, hands flying in accompaniment to her conversation. He–watching his wife with obvious love for the little dynamo at his side.

"They're looking forward to meeting you. Though I have to warn you, you're a bit of a curiosity, so prepare for some interrogation."

"Because I'm from New Zealand?"

She could handle that. To many people it was a far off place they'd heard of but never been to, so questions about her home country were normal.

"No, because I've never brought a girl home for Christmas till now."

Her stomach lurched at that. The thought of being a trailblazer revved up her nerves even more. She hoped she wouldn't falter under their scrutiny.

"My sister's beside herself with excitement. Don't let her questions bother you. She's always asking me about my love life. In fact, she can be direct to the point of being intrusive. She means well. She only wants everyone to have the same domestic bliss that she has."

"Oh," said Kate, "that's right, she's married."

"Yes, with two little ones. My brothers are married, too. One has a wee boy, and the other with a baby on the way."

"You are the odd-one-out then."

"Yeah, this job doesn't lend itself to playing happy families. Never in one place for long. And the unpredictable work—I've had some lean times until recently. Not many fathers would have considered me a good prospect, not reliable enough to provide for their daughter. Probably would have chased me off."

These words rattled her a little. She had to admit that playing happy families was exactly what she wanted with Alex, but so far it was, at the most, a nebulous concept. He had a life very different to her own, and one that would need to change if they were to be together. And this was all too new for her to be sure that he'd want to.

The barman placed two tall glasses in front of them, both filled with beer dark as black velvet, topped with thick foam, like whipped cream floating on the surface of coffee. And her first cautious sip revealed there *was* even a slight hint of coffee overlaying the bitterness. She took a larger sip and savoured the texture that filled her mouth. And it smelled like chocolate. She'd never tasted beer like it. Perfect for a cold winter's night.

"So what do you think of our local Scottish brew?" He'd noticed her cautious approach.

"It's delicious. Different, but delicious."

"OK, well, grab it and let's go. Take the plunge."

Kate braced herself for what was to come. She needn't have worried.

A ring of smiling faces met her, curiosity and anticipation written all over them.

"Well, there you are at last. I'm Sarah. The oldest. Just as well with these three for brothers!" The tall woman extended a hand and then pulled Kate into a hug. "Apologies if we seem overly excited. It's because our baby brother always plays his cards close to his chest. We never get to meet the girlfriends." She laughed, adding, "Robbie used to think he was gay, didn't you, Robbie?"

Robbie put down his beer. "Well, if he had any leanings that way, I can see why this one would have persuaded him otherwise." He threw Kate a sheepish look, blushing a little at his own remark. Like Sarah and Alex, he was tall, but built like he could toss a caber with one hand. He stepped forward and wrapped her in a friendly, solid bear hug.

"Hi Kate. Lovely to meet you. Please forgive our sister. She's rather prone to inappropriate comments, especially after a few wines."

"Hmmph," Sarah snorted. "I just tell it like it is. And by God, I'm going to enjoy more than a few wines tonight. Have to make the most of Dom's offer to mind the kids. They have been driving me nuts since the holidays started and it's only been a few days. Tell me Kate—how on earth do you cope with kids all day?"

"Well, I have to admit that coming home to a bottle of wine helps some days."

"Oh god, wine's a distant memory," said the tiny woman seated at the end of the table. "That's one of the first things I'll be looking forward to when this baby finally decides to come out."

She placed a hand on her protruding stomach. With the vibrant orange dress stretched tight, it looked as if she clasped an enormous Halloween pumpkin in front of her.

"I'm Sam. Married to Andrew, the man of few words next to me." She offered a hand. "I'd give you a hug, but this bloody great bulge makes that a little tricky. And to be honest, I can hardly stand. Andrew has to roll me everywhere." Andrew, who could almost have passed for Alex's twin, just smiled. Definitely a man of few words.

She was obviously late in her pregnancy. How could such a tiny woman be growing such an alarmingly huge baby? Kate thought she'd be terrified at the prospect of giving birth if it was her. Or maybe it was an illusion because of her diminutive size. Either way, she needed to have that baby soon, or she was going to pop.

"So how long have you got to go?" Kate asked.

"Three weeks, three long weeks. I reckon it's a boy too, so no way he'll be early if he's anything like his father." She shot a mock glare at her husband.

And just like that, the family embraced Kate. The laughter, the banter, even Andrew, the quiet one joining in the conversation, once the effects of the whisky loosened his tongue.

So this is what it's like, she thought. To be part of a happy, boisterous family.

They sauntered back to the hotel afterwards, basking in the warm afterglow of the fireside and family, drink and laughter. He tucked her in close to his side, navigating the now icy cobblestones.

"They really liked you."

"And I really liked them. Your family is fun."

"Wait till you meet Mum and Dad—you might change your mind."

She hesitated, not knowing what to say to that.

"I can't imagine me not liking the people who produced that lot in there, and you."

"No, I'm only joking. They're great—and they're going to love you."

She hoped so. So far, this family was as comfortable as her favourite old sneakers.

"Although." He hesitated a moment, stopping in the shelter of a shop awning.

"Although what?"

"Just don't expect too much from Dad. Not till he gets to know you a little. He can be a bit frosty at first."

"OK," she said casually, despite the small ball of anxiety forming in her stomach at this warning.

"And remember, if he is, it's me he's got the problem with, not you."

"What do you mean?" Relationships with parents were another complexity of life she hadn't needed to deal with.

"Dad hates what I do. As far as he's concerned, acting's not a proper job. He has mellowed a bit as I've picked up better roles, more consistent work. But I think he's always wanted me to fail, come cap in hand needing money, so he could be proven right. And he's fairly sure in his belief that it will happen one day."

"That can't be easy."

"No, especially not when the rest of my family have all conformed. Sarah went to university, did a business degree, and then straight into a well-paid

HR career until the kids came along. Robbie got a respectable job straight out of school, then studied nights to become an accountant. Andrew's a sparky, finished his trade qualification, runs his own electrical business. And then there's me..."

"But you studied too. And you've worked hard, persevered. Surely he can see you've made something of yourself." She wanted to defend him. Hoped that she would be brave enough to do so if needed.

He choked back a bitter laugh. "The day I told him I got accepted for drama school, he practically threatened to disown me. Like I said, he's accepted it in his own begrudging way. But whenever I come home, he always gives me a hard time, at least to begin with."

As Alex swung open the heavy door to the hotel's back stairs, she was glad of the darkness that masked her frown of concern at the prospect of meeting Iain MacLeod.

———

At Christmas dinner, Kate was squeezed in between Dominic, Sarah's charming and easygoing husband, and Alex. He was acting as a buffer between her and his father, who looked as formidable as he'd been described. Iain presided over the Christmas dinner table with a quiet authority. She could see from whom Sarah had inherited her forthright manner, Robbie his bulk and Andrew his penchant for surveying a situation thoroughly before speaking. Strangely, apart from the intense blue eyes, she couldn't see much he'd given to Alex.

Although he and Alex exchanged what appeared fairly normal father-son banter, Kate couldn't help but feel a frisson of tension between them. Perhaps it was coloured by the previous night's conversation, but she noted a slight sour downturn of Iain's mouth whenever Alex responded to the others' queries about his work. There was a definite harrumph of disbelief from the end of the table as Alex described how this next project would send his career to new heights.

They were well into the traditional Christmas roast dinner before Iain addressed Kate directly, and his words only served to underline his unfavourable view of the film industry.

"Well, lass, I have to say I'm rather relieved. I've always worried he'd bring home one of those brainless painted dollies he works with. Goodness knows what we'd make of one of those plonked down in the middle of Christmas lunch. But you, my dear, you're very welcome."

Iain was built like a wrestler, incontrovertible evidence that Robbie wasn't a cuckoo dropped into the MacLeod nest. Kate imagined him as a lumberjack, felling tall trees with a single swipe of an axe. Or on a construction site hefting beams as easily as if they were toothpicks. However, the large uncallused hands betrayed his white-collar occupation. Alex had described his father as possessing a meticulous mind that was well suited to an accountant, but it also meant he didn't suffer fools. His remark suggested that he didn't consider her in that category, and she felt a little easier in his company for it.

"Thank you Iain, you've all made me feel very welcome," she replied with a smile, pleased that for once, her aversion to makeup had also worked in her favour.

"If he had any brains, he'd put a ring on her finger and make sure of that."

Sarah's quiet aside to her husband hadn't anticipated a sudden drop in the level of conversation. She flushed, realising the remark only intended for Dom's hearing had carried across the table.

"Sarah!" Eileen shot a disapproving glare at her daughter. "It's the first time the poor girl's met us. It might be the last—you'll scare her away."

Kate stared down at her plate. She tried to cover the awkwardness by paying close attention to dissecting a slice of turkey.

Alex burst out laughing. "If you think that, Mum, you've seriously underestimated her. And Kate was well warned about my sister's ambitions for me."

"Yeah, I was too," laughed Sam. "Andy said the first time I poked my nose in the door, Sarah would be planning the wedding. You too Fi?" she said, turning to Robbie's wife, who was trying not to giggle with a mouth full of food.

"Absolutely," said Fiona, having managed to swallow. "Robbie reckons she scared off a dozen perfectly nice girls before I came along, so told me to ignore her."

"OK, OK," said Sarah, throwing up her hands. "Guilty as charged. But you know I can't help it. '*Look after your brothers*' was my mantra for years. It's difficult to let you all loose on the world without me."

"Well, you still should behave yourself, Sarah," said Andy. "We can't have Kate decide to leave. How could we carry on Christmas dinner with no waifs and strays?"

They all burst out laughing at that. Kate was mystified. It must be some kind of 'in joke'. Alex choked back his unmanly giggle for a moment, turning to explain.

"Mum has always had this thing for as long as we can remember. She hates the thought of anyone being alone at Christmas. So she always encouraged us to scoop up anyone and bring them along for Christmas dinner—affectionately termed 'the waifs and strays'."

"You must have set the record for bringing someone the furthest," said Fiona.

"Oh, and Sarah gets the prize for the strangest," Robbie added. "Remember that guy from your uni hostel? What was his name?"

"Simon," said Sarah. "Yep, he was pretty strange, but harmless. And I felt sorry for him. He was always nice to me."

"Ah, but why? Probably fancied you," said Dom.

"Well, in that case, he shared your good taste," retorted Sarah. "And last I heard, he was some top-notch science researcher. He'll probably save the planet."

"No judgement on waifs and strays—all welcome, isn't that right, Mum?" said Alex.

"It's a lovely idea," said Kate. "I've dreaded Christmas the last two years since my grandmother died. Everyone's always busy with family, so if you haven't any... but in London I had friends who included me with theirs at Christmas. And then here this year—it's great."

"Well, as Iain said, you're very welcome," said Eileen, rising to refill the dishes. "And I don't think you count as a waif or stray—you're family."

Lying in bed back at the hotel, Kate felt an overwhelming contentment. Who'd have thought six months ago that she would have all of this? This family who seemed to have accepted her as one of their own, even grumpy old Iain. And this man, so unaware of how special he was, so humble in the face of the adulation he attracted, and so undoubtedly hers.

He slid across the sheets, snuggled behind her, his body still urgent, pressing against hers. She lay with his long limbs wrapped around her, breathing in the scent of his warmth and the indelible tang of their frantic lovemaking. They'd stumbled in the door, both burning with need and wasted no time in freeing themselves from layer upon layer of clothing. It had been an entire day of their relationship on show, being watched and assessed, even if it was in a kind way. It was thrilling to be alone again, just the two of them and all that suppressed energy had erupted in a frenzy.

"How about we try that again, more slowly?" His whisper against her ear sent an answering thrill of desire to the precise spot where his hand now rested, small gentle movements inviting her to match its rhythm.

"Oh yes, I think we should definitely do that again," she answered. *And again, and again, for as long as you want.*

CHAPTER 32

Fame

London, England - January, 2010

KATE STOOD AT THE enormous bay window, gazing down at the street. A tide of people surged along the pavement, Londoners flowing along the streets, their steps purposeful. Everyone on their way to somewhere, the brisk steps a stark contrast to the sluggish traffic, all but grid-locked as it passed the hotel entrance. It was a huge change from their two weeks in Scotland, with its slower, more gentle pace. But she'd lived in London for two years, and there was still an odd charm in the beating heart of a large city.

A sleek, dark-windowed Mercedes van peeled off into the parking bay. The automatic door slid open, and there he was. He unfolded his long legs with one effortless movement and plunged into the crowd. As if by magic, the fans appeared. All female.

They surrounded him with polite but insistent demands for his attention. A picture to be signed, a photo taken. She watched him at work, oozing a quiet confidence. And that lazy smile, a wave, a friendly word, meeting their eyes so that for a moment they were important, the centre of his world. He was a master of his craft.

Anyone watching would never guess he was a true introvert. He'd told her this was one reason he'd taken up acting, seeking refuge behind the characters he portrayed. In a bizarre irony, acting helped him cope with being an actor. It allowed him to slot into the persona he'd cultivated for the fandom. Like now. Only people who knew him well would understand that behind the facade he was different to the Alex out there on the street below.

Alex's agent, Becky, suggested it would be wise for Kate to keep a lower profile in London. In Scotland, they'd encountered the odd fan, but people generally gave them a wide berth and let them enjoy each other's company undisturbed. Fame did not impress Scots, unless you were a football star. She'd been told that here it could be uncomfortable. Seeing the crush below, she had to agree that it was preferable up here as a spectator.

But there was another reason that she wasn't with him. As Alex had told her, it was expected he would always project an image of being both desirable and available. It was OK for women to be interested in him, even spend time with him. Fans seeing their own desires reflected in real life could imagine that it could be them one day. But it was not OK for any one woman to be seen too often or appear too intimate. While Alex remained available, he could continue to be the subject of their fantasies, which, in turn, fuelled the cult of celebrity that was like gold to the studios.

She wondered at what point this might change. If she was going to be more than a passing fancy—and she *was* confident of Alex's commitment to her—there would come a time that they must share this with the world. Would Alex take charge? Or let others decide for him, forcing her to remain in the shadows? The questions troubled her, as did her inability to think of how she could broach the topic with him.

She wished Ellie was here. She'd meet her in a bar, spill her heart out to someone she could rely on for sensible advice. But Ellie was in Devon, having convinced the school that she was the ideal chaperone for the girl's hockey team that her now fiancée Hugh had taken away on a trip.

While she waited, the troublesome thoughts continued to lap at the corners of her mind, although she tried her best to push them away. It was Alex's arrival in the suite half an hour later that caused them to converge in a tidal wave of negative emotions that sought to wash away her calm.

As he bent to kiss her, mingled with his usual Alex smell, other unfamiliar fragrances drifted to meet her. She nestled into him, resting her face against his chest, but that smell tarnished her normal enjoyment of his embrace. The perfumes of other women hit her like a slap in the face, along with a pang of jealousy at the thought of those who owned them. She'd seen them leaning into him, hugging him, resting their heads on his shoulder, faces upturned. Anger surged within her. Anger that he'd let them into that space, a space that was hers. And anger also directed at herself for even feeling this way. It was unlike her to be so possessive. But this was not like any previous relationship.

"Quite a crowd down there."

She tried to keep her voice light and even, although still wrestling with the unwelcome emotion. But somehow he sensed that under her attempt at calm, there was a small storm brewing. Her tangled thoughts had somehow spilled into the space between them. Perhaps they were written on her face. Either way, he knew.

"Yes, unfortunately. Places like this, they'll always track me down. Now that you've seen what it can be like, it's time we talked about that."

"Oh?" She attempted to appear nonchalant.

"Up till now, we could pretend that I'm a normal person, living a normal life. But sometimes we can't do that. What we can do, though, is to be very clear about things."

"Oh," she repeated, uncertain what might come next. "OK."

"So, we've talked about this before. The people who see me on the screen, the fans with me down there—they get Alex the actor. And that's all they get. You, and our friends and family—you're the ones who get all of me. Not them out there. They only think they know me. They don't, and they never will. Promise me you'll always remember that?"

She nodded. She tried to be discreet, wiping away a tear that sought to betray the whirl of emotions that were spiralling inside. *Don't be an idiot. Don't cry.*

"Promise?" He tipped her face upward with gentle but insistent pressure, forcing her to meet his eyes.

"Yes, I promise." His eyes seemed a softer blue, projecting reassurance, his gaze soothing. Just being near him calmed the turmoil.

"And any time it's overwhelming you ..."

"Like now?" She gave him a weak smile as she brushed away another rogue tear.

"Then talk to me. I won't have all the bullshit making you unhappy. If you're not happy, I want to know. Then I can do something about it."

"OK. Thank you."

"So, is that what's made you so sad today, my pretty lady?"

"Like you said, it was overwhelming." She hesitated, then decided now was the time to go further. "And I suppose watching you with those women today it upset me that we have to be so secretive. Me hiding up here, you down there having to act as if I don't even exist. Becky seems to think I should be invisible."

"Well, to be honest, what Becky thinks is of no concern to me at all, and it shouldn't be of any concern to you. Yes, as my agent, she's got an important job to do. But it's a job. She works for me, not the other way around. So it's not what Becky thinks."

"So, what do you think?"

"I think you make me happier than I've ever been in my life. I think I'd like nothing better than to shout that from the mountain tops. But I will not do that unless I can make sure you don't get hurt in the process. The moment you come out of the shadows, then, like me, you're going to be exposed to whatever the world chooses. Some of it will be good and some of it will make you realise how damn nasty people can be. So we plan it carefully—together."

It was that last word that stuck in her mind as she sat mulling over their conversation. He'd gone back out to do a magazine interview.

"We'll go out for dinner when I'm done," he'd promised. "I know just the place. It's quiet, and the food is amazing. I'll get Becky to book."

"That sounds nice."

"Right, well, you take it easy. Enjoy this place. After all, the studio is paying for it. Meanwhile, I'm off to run the gauntlet. Wish me luck."

He'd planted a reassuring kiss on her forehead and was gone.

Of course, the diehard fans would still wait, hoping for him to appear, preparing to ambush him as he dived into the car. Kate made a deliberate choice to not watch out the window this time.

Instead, she poured herself a wine, and set to filling the enormous bath. Alex was right. Might as well take advantage of the elegant suite. She lifted the stopper off a tiny sapphire coloured bottle and the scent of roses overlaid with a smoky tobacco aroma wafted into the air. When she drizzled the contents into the swirling warm water, a froth of fragrant bubbles exploded. She parted the foaming surface with her foot and stepped in, laying back till the water lapped against her neck. Immersed beneath it, she had a sense of all her worries being washed away. She chided herself for her earlier response to Alex's encounter with the fandom. Of course, he wanted to be seen with her, but he also wanted to protect her. And whatever they did, they were going to do it together.

She heard the click of the door as she stood studying herself in the full-length mirror. The dress hugged her figure, but it revealed her body was still in reasonable shape even after the continuous eating and drinking over Christmas and New Year. It was weeks since her last haircut and the too long fringe was annoying. Although swept to one side, it framed her face quite nicely. She wasn't especially skilled at applying makeup, however, her skin had a healthy glow, the mascara had stayed put and her go-to rose lipstick suited her well.

It was a new experience, this insecurity. For the first time since her teens, the woman in the mirror questioned her appearance. But the woman in her head sternly told her she looked just fine and when the man who now stood beside her, resting his head on her shoulder murmured "God you're beautiful," while nuzzling against her, her doubts ebbed away as a blush of pleasure at his compliment spread across her cheeks.

"I've got a car waiting down below," he said. "Bottom carpark. Should be able to slip away quietly."

The lift doors opened onto the quiet grey lower carpark, and she felt a surge of relief that they wouldn't have to face the public. The driver stepped around to open the door, but before they could make it to the safe confines of the rear seat, two women intercepted them.

"Alex, we hoped you wouldn't mind...." one gushed, thrusting a poster at him.

"We're sorry to interrupt your evening, but we knew this was our only chance. We're off home to Bristol tonight."

The other woman bounced in excitement at his elbow, producing a pen and her own poster to be signed. They both cast apologetic glances at Alex, but when her eyes met theirs, Kate couldn't help but read a touch of jealousy there. They would give anything to be her. She was living their dream. But the same emotion surged in her, as he turned on the Alex MacLeod charm.

"It's no problem," said Alex. "Happy to give a few minutes to my fans."

He uttered the smooth well-practised lie while scrawling '*All my love*' and his autograph in heavy felt pen.

"Thank you so much. Our friends will be very envious. Could we just ask you for a picture too before you go?"

Without waiting for his answer, the woman thrust a small camera at Kate and they arranged themselves on either side of him. Still speechless at the cheek of them, Kate snapped the obligatory pictures and handed it back to her with a forced smile.

As they headed off with a wave, she let out a deep breath, having survived the ordeal. He put his arm around her, his touch reassuring.

"Thanks for that. It means so much to them. I just can't turn them down."

She wished he would. It made her angry that, knowing how she felt, he wouldn't brush them off for her, even just this once. But before she could tell him so, a new nightmare overtook them.

A blinding flicker of light accompanied the whirr of a camera. The photographer had appeared silently from behind a large pillar, his huge lens trained directly on them. She knew in that brief moment before Alex could bustle her into the vehicle, he would have captured images of a startled young woman, her face incredulous as she understood that while Alex had promised to protect her from all of this, it was a promise he was powerless to keep.

CHAPTER 33

Wedding

Havelock North, New Zealand - February 2010

KATE APPEARED IN THE doorway. He knew the aroma of coffee would entice her from the depths of the comfortable bed. He'd been up much earlier, a habit it seemed he couldn't shake. Just as well. They'd been in New Zealand for a month, enjoying a lull in his schedule, but the new series was set to kick off on March 1st so he'd be back to early calls.

He had let her sleep knowing that once her feet hit the floor, she faced a long, busy day. He smiled at her tousled appearance as she padded across the kitchenette. She'd only half thrown on her robe, and he glimpsed one breast peeking out before she fumbled with the ties to pull it closed. Not that it masked what lay beneath. The delicate silk clung to her curves, and he needed little imagination to fuel a rush of lustful thoughts.

"Morning," she mumbled, still in that fog between sleep and waking, as she leaned in to kiss him.

"Morning beautiful."

He meant it. He loved her like this, the warm touch of sleep still radiating from her. The smell of her, of them, a lingering reminder that only a short time earlier they had lain tangled together, the sheets flung back from the heat of the night and of their lovemaking. And hair all askew, no makeup, bare feet. Just Kate. And he loved her.

The little cottage had a deck overlooking the vines. She flung open the French doors and stepped out onto it.

"Stunning day," she called to him.

"Sure is."

He turned to join her, a cup in each hand, but stopped. She sat in a chair, her head tipped back, letting the sun caress her face. He stood with the coffee in hand for a moment, soaking in the sight of her.

"Mmmm, that coffee smells so good. Thank you."

She threw him a grateful look as he placed her regular morning caffeine hit on the table.

They sat in silence, enjoying the companionable presence of each other, sipping cappuccino and taking in the view. The leaf-laden vines confined in neat lines marched away into the distance, punctuated with little splashes of colour from a few late-blooming roses that marked the end of each row. A blissful chill lingered in the early morning air, promising a reprieve from the heat of the previous weeks. It was going to be a perfect day for a wedding.

"Hungry?" he asked.

"Ravenous. Nicky said they'll bring breakfast across from the main lodge about nine. After that, the fun starts again."

He heard the weariness in her voice and caught the hint of a grimace. Her friend Nicky was, after years together with husband-to-be Chris, including a set of nine-year-old twins, going all-out for the wedding. Yesterday she had whisked Kate off to appointments with the other girls. Kate had returned with French manicured nails and a spray tan. Nicky had insisted it was a necessary accessory for all the bridesmaids. He had to admit the bronze glow of her skin made her even more alluring when she'd stripped off her clothes to show him the result.

Today it was hair and makeup, which somehow was going to take most of the day. He knew she was only enduring it because it was her friend's wedding day.

"I'm sure you can tough it out, for Nicky's sake."

"Yeah, I can. The things we do for our friends. So, what are you going to do all day?"

"Oh, spend a bit of time on the script. Might even grab the car and go for a round of golf at that course we passed on the way in. What time do I need to be over there?"

"Wedding's at four, so best be there by about three-thirty. Lucky you. Can't say I'm rapt about the day ahead." She gave a resigned sigh. "At the mercy of an army of hairdressers and make-up artists. Much as I love Nicky, in some ways I'll be glad when it's all over."

"Don't worry. A few glasses of bubbles and you won't care."

"Yes, at least being at a vineyard, there should be no shortage of that. As long as I don't get plastered and fall over on the long walk. Which may happen anyway, as she's chosen some dangerously high heels for us. I'll need to eat lots to soak up the alcohol—starting with this." She pointed to the vehicle that had arrived. "Breakfast's here."

Alex arrived at the wedding venue at three-thirty, as instructed. He sat making small talk with two other men, who, like him, had lost their partners for the day to the bridal party's preparation.

The groom and his three supporters in formal attire stood at the front, shuffling feet, nerves evident. The marriage celebrant, dressed in a smart pastel blue suit, was joking with them, obviously attempting to dispel some of the tension. Meanwhile, his anticipation grew.

He'd missed her today, drifting from one aimless activity to the next. Since Christmas, apart from when his work commitments took him away, they'd spent virtually all their time together. It was their new normal, and he liked it.

The murmuring of the assembled guests hushed as the first notes floated across from a string quartet. 'Pachelbel Canon in D', it said on the paper in his hand. It signalled the bridal party's arrival, all eyes turning to the top of a small rise from which they would appear.

And there she stood, so achingly lovely that Alex thought she must surely outshine the bride. The dress was the colour of the ocean at night, a rippling indigo satin that swept close across the curves of her body. Her hair twisted up high, emphasised the graceful set of her neck and revealed elegant bare shoulders. The neckline dipped between her rounded breasts, drawing his eyes downward, and he felt himself harden with the memory of his lips following that line, the thought so vivid that he could almost taste her.

After a brief pause, and with a slight smile that made his heart leap in his chest, she walked towards them with slow but confident steps. The dress was split high on one side, each step providing a tantalising glimpse of one shapely leg and the dreaded high shoes that delicately ensnared her foot in a sparkle of diamantes.

The ceremony was simple, but even he was affected by the romance. However, while all other eyes were on the bride, there was only one person who captivated him. He was impatient for this to be over. He wanted to once again lay sole claim on her time and attention. For the next few hours, though, he must be thankful for any brief snippets he could snatch in between her bridesmaid's duties.

He was leaning on the bar after dinner, when the band sprang to life. He turned at the light touch of a hand on his shoulder to see she'd escaped for a moment. She leaned in to him, and he let his hand slide down the glistening satin sheath, tracing the familiar shape of her. At last, his again. The bride and groom took centre stage, close together, eyes fixed on each other. Soon, others slipped onto the dance floor, and he led her by the hand to join them.

He treasured this one slow dance. It was with regret he released her from his arms as the band launched into a more upbeat song. They joined in the crush, bodies twisting and turning, rising and falling to the rhythm, their bodies no longer joined, but their eyes staying connected.

Later she sought him out at the bar, as she returned from waving off the newly-weds.

"Home time?" He hoped she'd agree. Maybe now they could escape, all her responsibilities discharged.

"Yes, home time."

He held out a hand to guide her down the steps.

"Oh, wait." She paused, looking thoughtful. "I've forgotten my shoes."

She was barefoot, having abandoned her shoes part way through the evening in the thick of the dancing. He wandered a short way down the path. Outside, the night was still, and the sounds of music and laughter drifted from inside. It hadn't been quite the ordeal he'd expected. They were a laid back bunch, these Kiwis. It was easy to fit into any gathering. A lot like the Scots. But it was a relief to be heading to the cottage, with Kate all to himself again.

"I'm coming," she called. "Sorry, I couldn't remember which table I left them under."

She wobbled down the path towards him, the star-spangled shoes dangling from one hand. Strands of hair had escaped from the elegant updo during the dancing. She still exuded the exuberant joyfulness of the celebration. The smell of her sweat overlaid with perfume drifted to meet him. It was intoxicating. Her dishevelled appearance brought to mind the last time he had seen her hair falling over her face like that. They had been lying together, face to face, basking in the afterglow of having just made love. It stirred a desire to get her back to the cottage as quickly as possible.

"Shall we grab a car?" He indicated the line of vehicles waiting to transport guests back to their accommodation.

"No, it's a beautiful night. Let's walk."

"Are you sure?" He pointed at her bare feet, the tanned toes poking out from the sweep of her dress.

"Absolutely. If I start to struggle, you can carry me."

Her giggle spoke of too much alcohol. He'd never seen her after drinking this much, but she was an amiable, playful drunk.

"No bloody way. There's no way I'm hoisting you over my shoulder, especially not when you're a deadweight because you're drunk."

"I'm not drunk." The cute lopsided smile, slight slurring of her words and flush on her face suggested otherwise.

"Still not carrying you."

"It's OK, I can do it." She set off down the manicured grass that edged the driveway, protecting her feet by avoiding the harsh paved surface. As they strolled along hand in hand, she burbled cheerily about the day. "And you know, they are so in love. They're one of those couples that will be together forever," she finished.

"I think we could be too."

The words were out of his mouth before he had time to consider. He came to an abrupt halt, in shock at what he'd said. They'd known each other six months, together for two. The romance of the day must have got to him, causing him to go barrelling into the thought of marriage.

She turned towards him, the tiny spotlights that edged the path high-lighting confusion on her face, questioning why he'd stopped walking. Then, fighting her way through the fog of the alcohol, he saw the dawn of realisation, of understanding exactly what he'd implied in that sentence. He held his breath, cursing himself for having blurted it out like that.

Most guys were careful to pick the moment, the right time, and the right place to tell someone that you wanted to spend the rest of your life with them. That's because most guys thought it through. Made sure it was what they wanted, and were confident she'd want it too. But it had snuck up on him. He tried to read her face, wondering if he'd made a massive mistake.

She stepped towards him, but her face remained hidden in the darkness of the country night, shadows concealing her expression.

"So do I," she said.

And he let his breath out, knowing as he did, that it wasn't a mistake. He would go with his gut, and his gut said 'Marry her'. At least his sister would be pleased, he thought with a wry grin.

"So you would be happy to be Mrs MacLeod?"

"Is that a proposal, Mr MacLeod?"

"I think it is."

"In that case, I think I say yes."

He swept her into his arms and kissed her, still in disbelief at what he'd done. He hoped she wouldn't renege on the deal in the sober light of day.

"But I wouldn't like a wedding like this," she said. "Far too much fuss, and I haven't got a swag of family to invite..." She stopped. "Oh, but you have. If you think they would want it, we could have a big wedding..."

"No, one advantage of having multiple siblings is the family's already had a good run of weddings. And I think they'd just be pleased that I'd finally plunged into married life. My sister's nagging has been wearing a bit thin. We could slip away quietly and come back married. Elope." He laughed at the craziness of his idea.

"That sounds fun," she said. "Let's elope."

CHAPTER 34

Elope

Queenstown, New Zealand - March 2010

THE PLANE FOLLOWED A breathtaking route along the mountainous backbone of the Southern Alps. At times it seemed like they weren't even moving, rather lightly suspended above the sharp tips of the mountains below, an illusion created by the scale of the landscape, the higher peaks so close that Kate thought she might almost reach out and touch them.

She glanced across at Alex sitting next to her. She couldn't help the smirk on her face, and it caught his attention.

"What? Something funny?"

"You. The disguise. Honestly, if anyone was on the lookout for a celebrity trying not to be noticed, they'd look for someone in a cap and sunglasses."

He took increasing care not to be recognised. She wondered if it was only when they were together, or a general thing now. The possibility of attracting the attention of fans was certainly growing. Last year's period drama and Alex's role in it were receiving positive attention from the critics as it aired in the UK. It was due to drop onto New Zealand television soon. Once the promo trailer appeared, the advantage of his relative anonymity here would evaporate overnight.

"Yeah, but half the other guys are wearing the same thing. I blend in."

"Maybe." She was doubtful. "Well, if this doesn't work, maybe a fake moustache or beard?"

"I'll get my hair and makeup team practising. Just in case."

Finally, the aircraft wheeled around and began its descent. She could see the tiny runway far below, dwarfed by a jagged mountain range that rose steeply from the surrounding plain. And beyond, she caught her first glimpse of the lake, deepest navy, polka-dotted with small whitecaps, whipped up by the same wind that tugged at the wings of the plane. It caused the pilot to take action, steadying the unruly beast that now threatened to buck and dive as they hastened towards the ground.

"Excellent pilot," said Alex as they touched down more gently than she'd expected. "He brought that under control rather neatly."

"Yes," said Kate. "I'm not usually nervous on planes, but that drop over the side of the mountains caught me by surprise."

The airport was too small to sport an air bridge. Instead, they made their way down a set of steep and somewhat rickety stairs. Once on the tarmac, she stopped to gaze at her surroundings. She'd seen far taller peaks, but it was the way these rose steeply, looming over the small airport that made them special.

"You can see why they call them The Remarkables." They were impressive, the way they dominated the lake. "They really are quite spectacular. I can't believe I've spent most of my life in this country and never been here before. I can see why the tourists love it."

"It's beautiful," he agreed, steering her gently towards the terminal entrance. "Now, when we get inside, there should be someone there to meet us and show us to our transport. I gave them your name."

As expected, inside the sliding doors, a smartly dressed gentleman clutched a card with 'Ms Kate Moreton' written across it in bold felt-tip letters. She made her way over to the man.

"Ms Moreton. Sir." He nodded in greeting. "This way, if you please."

They followed him through a side door, then along a passageway. It was strange as it seemed to lead back towards the runway. Through another set of doors Kate realised, with a rush of excitement, beyond them was a waiting helicopter.

"Alex?" His broad smile confirmed it was indeed waiting to whisk them away.

"Another first?"

"Yes! Oh, I've always wanted to go in a helicopter. I love the way they can be on the ground one minute and up and away the next. How did you know?"

"I didn't—but I thought even if you had been in a chopper before, you'd still enjoy arriving at Arcadia Bay in style. Plus, it means less risk of some random fan spotting us at the airport and spoiling this. I want it to be exactly how we planned it, far away from the prying eyes of the world."

The only person she'd told about the wedding was Ellie. Kate knew it was too complicated to explain to everyone else all the reasons they'd decided to run off and do this on their own. It might upset some being left out of the plans. They'd expect her to reciprocate the invitations she'd received for their weddings.

However, Ellie, through her brother and his friends, had sat on the edge of the film industry for a long time. She understood. And she had her own wedding fast approaching. Having succumbed to the charms of her dashing Welshman, she was in full wedding preparation mode. Even if they'd been having guests, there was no way Ellie could take off on a twelve-thousand-mile journey. Her chosen date was in the UK summer. Alex should be well finished filming by then. They'd make it to her wedding instead.

Once aloft, Kate couldn't take the smile off her face. Like a small child at the amusement park, she was captivated by the thrilling sensation of weightlessness as the helicopter rose through the air in one smooth action. This was true flight, hovering motionless above the ground one moment, the next soaring like a bird.

"Glad that wind has dropped." Her voice sounded mechanical as she spoke to Alex through the headset.

"Yeah, it'll be a nice smooth flight along the lake."

They skimmed across the water, the darkest indigo hinting at unfathomable depths beneath. Then the pilot turned towards the mountains, their tips already dusted with snow in stark contrast to the heat of the late summer day below. Kate could see the shadow of the chopper trailing below them, a tiny dark insect outlined against the glaring whiteness, small and insignificant against the immensity of the slopes.

"I told him to take us the long way." The rippling noise of the engine forced Alex to shout. "Airport to the lodge was less than a ten-minute flight. Thought we'd make the most of it."

"Thank you," she said, her eyes wide, trying to take in every inch of the view. "It's amazing."

The far end of the lake was ringed by high bush-clad hills and at this point the pilot turned, taking them back towards their destination. He came in low over an expanse of immaculately manicured lawns to land on a small heli-pad. Kate glanced back with regret as she left the cocoon of the chopper.

"Don't worry, I've booked them to take us back as well." They made their way to where a Range Rover sat idling.

Arcadia Bay was well-accustomed to accommodating celebrity guests in search of sanctuary. They were transported to an expansive villa, hidden and private from the others on the property. Apart from the unobtrusive staff who checked they were comfortable, it was as if they had retreated into a world of their own.

Kate sat with a glass of wine, enjoying the vista of the lake framed by trees and mountains.

"It's a lot like Scotland." Alex joined her on the outdoor sofa. "But better weather—and no bloody midgies either."

"You'll have to show me more of it some time. Hopefully not in midgie season."

"Yeah, I will. Promise. Once this filming is done, we'll get back there, go to your friend's wedding, then I'll whisk you off to the Highlands. Make up for the lack of a honeymoon now."

"That sounds perfect. Now—dinner here? Or shall we go to the main lodge?"

"Well, I wasn't quite hungry for dinner yet." He leaned over to kiss her. "But perhaps a little hungry for something else?"

His hand dropped to lift aside the flimsy fabric of her dress and ventured stealthily between her thighs. She put down her glass, pressed into his chest, wrapping her arms around him to caress the lean hardness of his back. She loved the solid feel of him. To hold Alex grounded her in the reality that for the first time in her life, she had someone that she trusted to be there, to not leave her, to love her unconditionally.

He freed himself from her embrace, taking her by hand to lead her inside, into a place that could have been anywhere in the world, where only the two of them existed and time stood still.

The timber ceiling soared high above their heads. She watched as the early morning sun filtered through gauze curtains, making delicate rippling patterns on the wood. Today was the day. Today, they would be married.

"You awake?" He'd sensed it.

"Couldn't sleep, I'm so excited."

"Me too. Hopefully, all will go to plan, and within a few hours you'll be Mrs MacLeod."

Alex had been happy to take charge of the plan. He'd proven himself rather adept at organising. Even insisting Becky, his agent, simply block out four days in his diary. Becky was miffed at his refusal to reveal what he was doing. He'd decided to let her in on the secret later, and then she could wrestle with the issue of how they'd inform the rest of the world of his new status as a married man.

"Just choose what you want to wear. Let me do the rest."

What she had chosen was a simple sheath dress. Soft white satin overlaid with lace. It hugged the upper curves of her body and then cascaded away in a gentle fall to the floor. Swathed in protective tissue, it sat in its own case, patiently awaiting its star turn.

There was a polite rap on the door. It was Sandy, a pleasantly chatty local woman, whom the lodge manager assured them was well-used to remaining tight-lipped about the clients she saw there. She'd arrived to help Kate with her preparation. Although most of the time she eschewed makeup and didn't pay too much attention to her hair, she would make the extra effort for special occasions. And this was the most special of her entire life. She and Sandy disappeared into the bedroom, leaving Alex next door to sort himself.

When Kate emerged, she found Alex hadn't yet appeared from the second bedroom. She couldn't understand what was taking him so long, as surely the groom wouldn't need more time than the bride.

She stood clasping the simple posy that she'd found waiting for her on the table. It had appeared courtesy of the almost invisible lodge staff who took care of their needs. She loved how, like the flowers in her hair, it was natural, and unstructured, the florist not having robbed the blooms of their wildness as she bent them to her service. A green woodiness that hinted of the bush overlaid the flowers' delicate perfume. She inhaled its freshness, eyes closed, letting it transport her.

After a few minutes, the door swung open, but he didn't appear.

"Is it OK for me to see you now?" he called out.

"Sure, I'm ready."

He stepped out into the room. At first, she was speechless.

"Oh, my god Alex. How beautiful."

It was the only word for it. He'd dressed in full Scottish garb. He wore a kilt of greens and blues, topped by a smart black jacket accented with silver buttons, framing a crisp white shirt and black bow tie. Over his shoulder a matching plaid, draped and fastened with an elaborate pin, gave a traditional old world feel. The outfit was finished with a furry black sporran slung low over his narrow hips.

"Alex, that's stunning."

There was a huge grin on his face. He'd wanted to surprise her, and he'd succeeded.

"You're still the star of this show." He pulled her into him, taking care not to crush the flowers in her hands. He tilted her face upwards and kissed her lightly. "You're always beautiful to me, but today, well, you take my breath away."

She smiled, a little shyly. She still found compliments hard to take, even from this man who she knew meant every word. But yes, she'd been pleased with her reflection in the mirror. Her hair was loose, with Sandy's deft handiwork creating a few curling tendrils framing her face. She wore a small delicate crown of flowers, the larger blooms interlaced with tiny blue petals that highlighted the colour of her eyes. And the dress was perfect, skimming her shoulders, the sweetheart neckline following the arc of her breasts, and the colour contrasting with the honey glow of her summer tanned skin. She felt beautiful.

They walked hand in hand down to the lakeside, their steps slow as if understanding that today was important, approaching it with a cautious reverence.

The grassy aroma of the newly mown pathway heightened the freshness of the air and carried a brief touch of sadness, the smell bringing back memories of her loved grandfather. She smiled at the thought of his Saturday summer routine, each weekend zooming around the section, determined to keep it scrupulously neat. She pictured her grandmother inside baking a batch of her famous date scones, his favourite reward after the hard work. If she could ask for one thing, that would ensure the complete perfection of today, it would be that her grandparents had lived to see her find this happiness.

The mown pathway led to a small area of native plantings circling a clearing. Beyond this, through a gap in the trees, the waters of the lake formed a backdrop of brilliant blue. The celebrant stood waiting, her flamboyant floral dress giving her the appearance of an exotic tropical bird. Her smile was warm, encouraging, as they came to stand before her. Ben and Cherie, the lodge managers following behind, now moved to flank them, ready for their role as witnesses.

The celebrant extended her hand to each of them. Bedecked with a dazzling array of rings, it was as colourful as her outfit. When she spoke, she had a voice like golden syrup, oozing sweetness and warmth.

"Hello and welcome Kate and Alex. I'm Maree, and it's lovely to meet you on this day, your special day. To start with, I want to say I'm privileged and delighted to be asked to perform this marriage ceremony. Welcome also to you Ben and Cherie, who are here to witness the promises Kate and Alex make to each other today."

Just the five of them. But Kate's nervousness was equal to a crowd of thousands. She'd stood alongside friends at their weddings, hoping that she herself would have the same happiness one day. Now it was happening. She had an odd sensation. It was as if she was standing outside herself, watching another couple pledge themselves to each other. An observer, not part of the scene. She'd always been a realist, never one prone to idle daydreams and wild imaginings. But what if in her desperate longing she'd fallen prey to some delusion? What if she blinked and discovered this was all a dream?

She locked eyes with Alex, her hands clasped in his, reassuring. He radiated confidence, a surety that flowed through her, grounding her in the here and now.

"You OK?" he asked, and with the sound of his voice, her crazy thoughts evaporated and she allowed herself to be immersed in the moment. This was now, this was real.

As they spoke the traditional vows, it was if she was hearing them for the first time. To speak them out loud, to hear him say those words, so simple but holding so much power within them.

Then Maree called on them to exchange rings.

"Now it's your chance to find out what a Scot keeps in his sporran." Alex joked as he reached into it, producing the two bands. Hers, a white gold filigree inlaid with diamonds, delicate and feminine, threaded on her finger. His, of wide, unembellished platinum, sat bold and strong on his large hands.

They completed the formalities, signing the necessary papers at a small table and chairs arranged to one side. Now she could see it there in black and white, absolute proof that this was happening.

They stood once more hand in hand, the smiling Maree facing them.

"So now there's one last thing I'd like to do before we finish," she said. "It's a traditional blessing that I offer to you, as a wish for the new life together that you begin today."

She unfurled a small scroll and read:

"May the sun bring you new energy by day. May the moon softly restore you by night. May the rain wash away your worries, and the breeze blow new strength into your being. And all the days of your life, may you walk gently through the world and know its beauty.

"Now you can feel no rain, for each of you will be shelter for the other. Now you will feel no cold, for each of you will be warmth for the other. Now there will be no more loneliness. Now you are two persons, but there is only one life before you. Now go to your dwelling to enter into the days of your life together.

"And may your days be good and long upon this earth."

She rolled up the scroll and handed it to Kate.

"A little memento of the day."

"That's beautiful, Maree, thank you." Unexpected tears prickled at Kate's eyes. *Don't cry. Do not cry.* She'd never understood the concept of 'tears of happiness' until now, when they threatened to spill over despite her resolve.

"And now the words you've been waiting for. Kate and Alex, it is my great pleasure to pronounce you husband and wife. Alex, this is where you get to kiss your beautiful bride."

He scooped her up and did exactly that, at first meeting her lips passionately, final confirmation of the love they had found. Next, brushing away the two little tears that had escaped and edged their way down her cheeks.

"Let's not spoil your makeup before the photos."

Ben proved to have some skill with a camera, directing them to pose in several spots while he snapped away. Then they turned to make their way back to the villa, where a celebratory lunch awaited the little wedding party. They walked confidently now, hand in hand, stepping together into their new life. And the words of Maree's poem echoed in her mind: *now you are two persons, but there is only one life before you.*

One amazing life.

Correction

Redwoods, New Zealand - April 2010

It was a novel experience watching the hair and makeup artist at work. Kate was used to the tables being turned—Alex sitting waiting while she perched on a chair, trying to paint on her going-out face, an elusive skill that she'd failed to perfect even after all these years.

A month into his contract, the filming had moved to a location in the Redwoods Forest near Rotorua. Alex had suggested she come along to see what he did in all those hours they were apart, and she could show him some of the tourist sites when they wrapped up for the weekend.

The trailer sported a bold sign with his character name: '*Charles Pettiford*'. Opening the door was like entering Doctor Who's Tardis—it was larger on the inside than it appeared on the outside.

Here was a neat little kitchen, including a coffee machine, an essential item to ensure Alex's happiness. At one end there was a full-sized bed, with a slider to close it off, and beside that a small attached bathroom. At the other end was a rack holding his costume, and an area for Amy, his make-up artist, to work her magic. Inside this trailer she transformed Alex MacLeod, modern-day Scot, into a nineteenth century English soldier.

There was a small knock on the door. Kate opened it to find a young woman clutching a clipboard waiting at the base of the steps.

She peered in through the door. "Ten minutes Alex."

"OK, thanks Tash." He turned to Kate. "Right, time to see what I do all day. The flurry of action in between hours of waiting."

"I'm looking forward to it."

And she was. In the time she'd known Alex, she'd watched him on the screen many times. It intrigued her how, once in character, his real self subsided into the background. It must be why his career was moving along so well, that ability for a moment to step into the mind of a fictional person and become them to such an extent that others believed you *were* them. Many of his fans did, the belief feeding their obsession with him.

They stepped out into the car park. Alex's trailer was one of several. Arranged in a circle, they resembled a scene from a western movie, a wagon train clustered in tight formation for protection.

The assistant led them along a small path marked at intervals with cones, fluorescent arrows attached to the top of each, guiding their way towards the location for today's filming. Amy trudged along at the rear, hefting a large makeup case, prepared for the inevitable extra work required over the coming hours.

Partway along, Kate could hear the voices of the crew, and above them one more strident that she recognised. James Beckett. Of course he would be here. She knew James was working on this series. And she knew how he involved himself in every step of the production process.

As brother to Ellie, her closest friend in London, their paths had crossed from time to time. Not that she could say she knew him well. Or particularly liked him. At first, if she was honest, she'd actively disliked him, but she had seen a few redeeming features now and then. He'd stepped up when their mother was ill. A guy so devoted to his mother like that couldn't be all bad. She would need to make a point of saying hello to him, if she could manage it without getting in the way of his work.

"Sounds like James is in form this morning, Tash."

She could hear the humour in Alex's comment to the young assistant.

"Yeah, the pressure's on today—we have to finish by the end of tomorrow or there'll be major problems. But it's going quite well so far. He's in a reasonably good mood—for him."

As they came closer to the filming location, Kate noticed a change in Alex, even visible from behind, as she followed him between the soaring redwoods of the small forest. His relaxed gait transformed into an arrogant swagger. Perhaps it was the large solid boots that she'd earlier helped tug onto his feet as they both laughed at the ridiculous footwear. But there was a distinct set to his shoulders, too. It somehow made him appear bulkier. Again, perhaps it was an illusion of the costuming. Even on this autumn day, the heavy military jacket must be hot and uncomfortable, although authentic for the part.

He turned and glanced back at her. The smile was his smile. All Alex. But there was an expression on his face, no longer quite his own. She realised he was already deep in the character, ready to deliver what they expected from him. It was as if her Alex had disappeared. This was the magic *he* worked. Happening right in front of her.

Tash came to a halt at a small fork in the path. Two arrows, each bearing some indecipherable code, pointed in opposing directions.

"They want you down there, Alex," she said, pointing to the left. "How about I take Kate with me, and I'll get her settled so she can sit back and watch the fun?"

"Sure," he said. "Thanks for looking after my beautiful wife."

He turned to Kate. "Now you're about to find out how unexciting this all is. Hope you don't get too bored. Don't say I didn't warn you," he grinned, planting a kiss on her forehead.

"Here, give that to me," he said, taking the unwieldy case from Amy and they set off down the small path to the left, leaving Kate to follow Tash towards the voices that were now quite close.

The feeling began as she stepped into the clearing. It was odd. Coming out of the gloom of the trees and into the sunlight, the air should have felt warmer.

Kate stopped as a wave of cold prickled across her skin. She examined her arm, expecting to see raised gooseflesh, but there was none. Only a hideous sensation that made her want to claw at the chill that was taking hold of her limbs and even now pushing its way inwards through the rest of her body.

She tried to block it out. Not the time to make a scene. Not here, not now, with all these people. It was a rare opportunity to come on set like this. She couldn't embarrass Alex by causing a fuss. Whatever this was, she must control it.

And then she made a huge mistake. She looked up.

They had chosen this location for the gigantic redwood trees. A rare find in New Zealand, a country clad in subtropical rainforest, the solid trunks provided the perfect illusion that they were on the other side of the world. Now they leered over her, threatening to crush her into the mossy floor of the forest like a tiny insect.

She dropped to the ground, her arms clasped over her head in protection. Confused thoughts raced through her brain. Why was no one else moving? Couldn't they see what was about to happen? Her breathing quickened in panic. Her nostrils filled with the cloying mustiness of decaying leaves. She could taste the dirt in her mouth.

She lay braced for impact, but when it came it was weightless, although the thunderous sound of it assaulted her ears and bounced off the inside of her skull. Just when she thought she couldn't bear the noise any longer, she became aware of a hand tapping an urgent rhythm on her shoulder and by some miracle the horrific sound trickled down to a dull hum. It was over.

Part Three - Here

Return

Redwoods, New Zealand - April 2010

SHE LAY ON THE strangest bed, the mattress hard with a lumpy blanket bunched beneath her. An unusual odour, an earthy, outdoor mustiness swamped her, the smells of nature drifting in as if someone had left a door open. And she was cold, a bitter penetrating cold. Yes, maybe the door was open. She needed to move towards it, close it against the draught, and find warmth. But the sound that wrapped around her and flowed through her was pinning her down, crushing her into the ground. How could that be? Sound couldn't physically do that—could it?

Eventually, the disturbing echo in her ears subsided, and voices entered her awareness. Shrill, agitated, angry even.

"Kate! Kate! What the fuck?"

She recognised the voice, retrieved the name. James. But was unable to visualise the face that went with it, only a vague recollection, still smudged around the edges. Through slitted eyes, she could trace his silhouette, could make out his dark hair, saw his hand materialise above her before it came to rest on her cheek.

"Stand back everyone, let's give her some air." A woman's voice, quiet but authoritative. Then the same voice, more soothing in its tone. "Kate, can you hear me?"

She wanted to answer. To reach out. But she struggled to find her own voice. Still submerged under the crushing weight of the air, she could formulate the words, but they didn't want to come out yet. Slender fingertips slid down her neck, probing at first and then exerting a gentle pressure.

"She's breathing. Her pulse is good. Colour a bit pale." The woman again, still brisk in her manner, but reassuring.

"Kate, can you hear me?"

This time it was James, the desperate note in his familiar voice encouraging her to attempt a response. This time, words fought to the surface.

"I'm OK."

"Thank god." She sensed relief in his voice. "Just lie still, love. It's going to be alright." She opened her eyes a little more and her gaze met his. Although his voice suggested calm, when she stared into his eyes only inches from hers, she saw pupils dilated with agitation. Or fear? His head jerked away from her as he barked orders.

"Can we get her out of here? Tim—surely you've got something there we can use to get her up. And Kevin, get one of the vans in here."

"Not too soon." The woman continued to control the situation. "Give her some time. We don't know what caused this. Best be cautious."

She forced her eyes open wide now, to focus on the sky, white, glaring and painful.

"I'm OK," she repeated, this time with greater confidence. She took in the ring of concerned faces above her, and beyond them, soaring trees that seemed to stretch on forever, dizzying in their height.

"I'll be OK." She wasn't so sure of that, but for some reason, it seemed important that they believed her.

Kate sat curled on the hotel room sofa, a blanket wrapped around her in a vain attempt to drive away the unseasonal chill she hadn't yet been able to shake. She'd tried to wash it away in a soothing hot shower, along with the cloying odour of the forest floor. Even now, that smell clung to her hair. Donning a voluminous fluffy robe and slippers, she'd hoped to trap the warmth of the water, drawing it into the still cold centre of herself, but failed.

Kevin slumped in the chair beside her, idly scrolling through the TV channels. The big man looked uncomfortable, his arms and legs spilling beyond the confines of the tub chair. Although he'd been kind, fetching food and coffee, and tucking her under the blanket like a tender parent, she sensed his frustration.

She didn't blame him. James had selected and dispatched him as her minder. A capable sound technician, who no doubt resented being taken away from his job to babysit the boss's wife. However, she knew James, and guessed his staff didn't have the courage to question an order. James believed the brilliance his team produced was contingent on them doing what he told them, and those who didn't accept that tended to move on to less demanding studios.

It was a full five hours before he arrived to relieve Kevin from his post.

"Thanks mate, appreciate you looking out for her."

One thing about James, he always made an effort to give praise where it was due.

"No worries." Kevin looked grateful to be freed from the job, rising quickly from the chair, barely able to disguise his haste. "See ya tomorrow, OK?"

James sat carefully on the couch beside her. He drew her in close, and she drank in the warmth of his body, allowing it to push aside the nagging chill.

"So, what was that all about?" Although the question was neutral, she wondered if that was an undertone of annoyance in his voice. After all, he'd lost nearly an hour of precious time thanks to her dramatic performance.

"You tell me." After all, she'd been unconscious through most of it. "I honestly don't have any idea. Scared myself though."

"You bloody scared me, too. You read about otherwise fit and healthy people just dropping dead with an aneurysm or something. I thought you were on the way out. You were so still, and cold."

There was concern on his face, in his eyes, overriding the inconvenience she'd caused. Of course there would be. He was always so protective of her, overprotective, in fact. At times, it irritated her, an affront to her independent nature, but it was his language of love with the people who mattered to him, so she'd learned to let it slide.

"We'll get you to a doctor tomorrow, eh?"

"But I'm perfectly fine." She protested, not wanting to be subjected to poking and prodding. They'd want to do a blood test. She hated needles, ashamed of the wooziness that swamped her whenever one approached. "Apart from the huge embarrassment." This was the first time she'd come onto a set, usually leaving James to do his thing without her getting in the way. And then that's exactly what had happened.

"Nah, it was fine. Still got everything done. And they're a good bunch, really. They were worried about you, too."

"Well, I'm just a little cold and tired, that's all."

"No argument about it—doctor tomorrow." He leaned over and prevented any further protests with a kiss. "You do know that you're the most precious thing in the world to me? I couldn't bear for anything to happen to you. And you certainly scared the shit out of me today."

There were lines of tension, his mouth drawn tight as he gently tilted her chin upwards, searching her face. For a big man, there was an unexpected delicacy in his touch. He was full of contradictions. Few understood that the bold, brash, 'don't give a damn about anyone' extrovert, was behind the scenes a kind and tender husband whose love she'd never had cause to doubt, not even for one moment.

"And I'm sorry I couldn't come back here with you. We absolutely had to nail those shots today—we only have permission to use that location for two days. If I'd walked off set, bloody Jonathan would have fucked around shooting it ten different ways before deciding the first one was the best. There's no way we'd have met the deadline."

The director on this project was something of a nightmare, according to James. Brilliant but a total perfectionist, they were so alike it was no surprise they clashed. James had pulled rank several times, to the amusement of the cast and crew, who were enjoying the running battle between them, an entertaining sideshow to the main event.

"It was OK. Honestly." She tried to sound reassuring, although she had to admit to harbouring feelings of abandonment as the hours had dragged by with no sign of James.

But she'd gone into this relationship with eyes wide open, accepting how his work consumed him, how his work *was* him. For sure, some of the cast and crew would be harsh in their judgement. It wasn't a good look, bundling her off back to the hotel in a van.

She imagined the voices of condemnation from a few of the women in particular. Earlier in the day, she'd overheard one say she didn't understand what a lovely girl like Kate saw in him, as he was such an arsehole. No doubt James seeing his wife unconscious on the ground one moment and then diving straight back to work the next would be sufficient evidence to convict him of that charge. But they didn't know him like she did.

"Hopefully Kevin was a decent nurse? He's a good bloke."

"Yeah, he was great. I'm sure he'd rather have been on set than stuck here with me, but he didn't let it show."

"Right, well, I'll order some food, shall I? What do you feel like?"

"Comfort food please. Mac and cheese maybe?"

She wondered whether the hotel kitchen could produce something so ordinary. But she imagined they were used to unusual requests from their high-paying guests.

She snuggled deeper into the blanket while he called room service. What a strange day it had been, quite surreal, in fact. But tiredness subsumed those niggling thoughts. Time to figure it out tomorrow. She nuzzled into her husband's large bulk, clutching his solid shape. This was what was real, and it was good.

CHAPTER 37

Home Sweet Home

Auckland, New Zealand - January 2012

"Let's do it."

It made sense. Now that she'd cooled down, considering James's suggestion with a calm head, Kate knew it was the right decision.

One week since the blistering row, one of their worst ever, she was only now recovering from the bitter words she'd flung at her husband and the uncharitable motivations she'd attributed to him. They'd never argued much over the three years of their marriage. She was easygoing by nature and not susceptible to letting her emotions take charge.

And while James could be bloody irritating sometimes, he had an irrepressible optimism and a way of finding the bright side of even the worst situations. His work self was tough and uncompromising. But outside that, he was a chirpy extrovert who sailed through life, confident that no matter what obstacles came his way, he would find a way through. It made for a harmonious marriage.

Sometimes it worried her they didn't fight enough. Other couples seemed to. But she had come to realise one thing they had in common was they didn't sweat the small stuff. Only huge things mattered enough to argue about them. And this was one of them.

Last Saturday morning, when James was reading the newspaper as he did most Saturday mornings, he'd discovered an article in the real estate section about someone who'd moved off an old bungalow much like theirs and built a mansion in its place.

"We should think about this."

"About what?" She glanced away from her book to see him waving a page in front of her.

"This." His finger enthusiastically stabbed at the before and after photographs. "We're sitting on a goldmine here, sea views, one-minute walk down the road and we're on the beach."

"You want to sell this place?" Her eyes were wide, incredulous that he should even suggest it. "It may be a goldmine, but we don't need the money. Why would you even think of that?" She snapped at him, hating herself for it but unable to stop.

"No, no, you've got the wrong idea. Look, they moved off the old house and took advantage of the site to build something special."

"But this house is special. Maybe not to you, but it is to me." She leapt to her feet, shoving the chair back with a rough clatter on the wooden floor.

"Of course it's special. It's a lovely old place and I'm sure it has so many wonderful memories for you. But we could create something together. It would be special because it would be ours, both of ours."

"No bloody way. You are not getting rid of my house. You know James, it would be nice if just for once, you could forget about your image. I know it's not the sort of swanky place you can entertain your posh clients, like Bayswater, but it's never been a problem. Till now."

She thought they'd lived happily across the two countries and the two houses, even though the contrast between them was huge. He'd come from humble beginnings, not dissimilar to this. In New Zealand they simply went out when he was trying to woo some big-wig financier or Hollywood star.

She stalked out of the room. Snatching a coat from the hallway, she pulled on her boots and marched out the door, slamming it behind her.

She headed for the beach, the place she always went to think. The sea was a patient listener, a soothing presence. She sat in her favourite spot where a mound of seagrass cloaked a low sandy embankment, perched on the edge, dangling her feet over, her toes grazing the sand.

So many times she had sat in this place over the years. Huge pohutukawa trees anchored this end of the beach. They'd watched her when she first came here as a young girl, perhaps eight or nine years old, at last old enough to be allowed to venture here on her own. They'd also seen her as a moody teenager, mulling over ways to navigate the girly bitchiness that seemed an inevitable part of the teen years. She'd always found the answers here, eventually. After an hour or so, she headed home.

Several times over the next week, she'd found herself in that spot. She was torn. The house was old and tired, not to mention poky, with only the two bedrooms. When babies came along, they would have to move anyway, and leaving that spot overlooking the sea would be a huge wrench. Perhaps it would be easier to do something about it now. Perhaps her grandparents would forgive her for taking away the house if it meant they could still look down on their descendants playing in the yard where she'd played.

James hadn't mentioned it again all week. He had the wisdom to leave that topic well alone, fearing another violent reaction.

"Let's do it," she repeated.

"The house?" He looked up abruptly from his weekly indulgence, immersed in reading real British newspapers. He understood what she was talking about straight away. It must have been on his mind.

"I thought you weren't sold on the idea."

"No, I wasn't. Letting go of this house will be a bit like losing a family member. In some ways, I'm losing my grandparents over again."

"I can understand that. Remember how we hung onto mum's place for months? Neither of us could bear to let it go."

"Yeah, but this is not months. It's been years. It's time to move on. I have great memories of this house, but perhaps you're right, it's time for a new house—to make new memories."

"Well, you'll still be able to feel them here, I'm sure. See the same views. Our kids will play in the same street you did."

"Yeah, and I had another look at that article. How those people who bought the old house gave it a new lease of life in the country. I thought maybe it's time for this house to have new people to show it some love. Who'll make it theirs."

She could almost picture the new family. A young couple, a few exuberant kids, a playful dog. Him working nights and weekends to fix it up, her painting and wallpapering. It was comforting to think of someone treasuring it.

"OK, so I know of an architect."

Of course, James knew someone. He always did. It should annoy her he'd made plans in case she capitulated. But it was typical James to prepare for all potential outcomes.

"The guy who designed Paul and Sadie's place. You'd be hard pressed to find anyone better."

"Oh yes, their place is fabulous. Similar site too. If we go up—imagine the views."

They might even catch a glimpse of the city. Lights on the water. It would be beautiful.

"Right, well, I'll call him and see when he can make a start."

He was already heading for his phone. Now she'd agreed he was keen to move before she changed her mind.

The architect was the current darling of the local scene, with people queuing to use his services. Despite that, within three months, they had concept drawings and a rough plan. James could be extremely persuasive at getting people involved in his projects.

"Six bedrooms?" she said. "Do we need that many?"

James was inclined towards grandiose plans, with his first home, the Bayswater house sporting five bedrooms, although there'd never been more than three of them living there.

"Absolutely." He pointed to the neat outlines on the architect's drawing. "So these three upstairs, they're kids' rooms. If we get our three, then they'll want a room each. Less fighting that way."

"Kids thundering around over our heads?"

"Yep, that way you'll hear when the little buggers are not in bed when they should be. There's a bathroom—so they don't muck up ours—and a TV room so we can watch what we want down below."

She could almost see them, their faces still a little hazy, not fully formed in her mind. But three little people, clad in pyjamas, giggling and full of mischief. She knew who'd be racing upstairs to sort out the shenanigans. From what she'd seen of James with the children in his family, tumbling around on the floor, play-fighting and tickling, he wouldn't be the sort of dad who did the discipline. In fact, he himself would be a large child forever, but that was part of why she loved him. And teaching had given her enough skills that she was confident of whipping them into shape. Well, perhaps the kids; James was a lost cause.

He swished aside the huge page to reveal the ground floor plan on the next.

"Down here, guest room, our room, and this small bedroom by ours—baby room till they're old enough to move upstairs. In between, you could have it as a little study."

There was a gym room (of course), a pool (great for them and the kids) and a dream kitchen.

"Butler's pantry?" she asked. "What the hell is that?"

"A place to hide the mess when friends come over."

"Bloody good idea." They both loved cooking but dealing with the mess not so much.

He wasn't building her a house, more of a castle. And over the next year, as the plans transformed into reality, she submerged any sadness at relinquishing the house of her childhood, replacing it with excitement at watching a home that was truly both of theirs rise in its place.

Their friends trickled in from late afternoon. Sun still spilled across the decks, enveloping them in a warm hug. The saltwater pool was inviting, and those who dipped a hand in found it heated to a pleasant temperature, at odds with the early winter weather that had dared to poke its nose into May. As night descended on them, an abundance of lights bathed the group in a cheerful glow. Music floated across, buffering the buzz of chatter and softening the tinkle of glasses.

They'd spilled out onto the grass, the evening mild for this time of year. Standing under the old glossy-leafed magnolia, Kate smelled a touch of perfume drifting from its huge bowl-shaped flowers. It was a familiar fragrance linking this wonderful new house to the old.

"It's stunning. You can see why that architect won awards." Tracey had been first to arrive for the celebration, an enormous bottle of champagne in hand.

"Yeah, I feel very lucky. They say building's stressful, but honestly, with James running the show, it's been quite painless."

Kate still couldn't quite believe this magazine-worthy home was theirs. James had revelled in project managing the build. While practical tasks such as building were well outside his expertise, he knew how to gather a diverse group of people and have them do the right thing at the right time to achieve a result that was bigger than the sum of their parts. Supervising the build was a perfect job for him.

"New career option?"

"No, he enjoyed it, but you know him. He lives for his TV and movies. He's glad it's done and we can enjoy it. It's a real credit to him."

"Well, cheers." Tracey clinked her glass against Kate's. "Congratulations on a job well done. You're too modest by the way—the interior design was no small task, and it's every bit as fabulous inside as out."

"Thank you."

She'd worked damn hard, and she had to admit she was pleased with the stylish but practical result. However, it was satisfying to have Tracey recognise her efforts.

"Another mojito?" Tracey noticed her drain the last emerald drops from the tall glass.

"Just a virgin for me."

"Ooh, does that mean some good news you've yet to share? Is that gorgeous nursery going to have a little occupant?"

In fact, the nursery with its soft pistachio painted walls was the one room Kate avoided. The empty room's accusing stare made her uncomfortable. It sat unfinished, waiting for all the cute baby furnishings, an acute reminder of the one vital thing she wasn't able to supply.

"No, no baby. But I've still stopped drinking. While we're trying, it seems a good idea."

"Yeah, they say it's best. Good girl. OK, I'll be back in a minute with a lovely non-alcoholic cocktail for you."

Much as she tried, for the rest of the night, Kate couldn't put this snippet of conversation out of her head. Even after all the guests had gone and she finally made it to bed, it hung over her like a careless ink blot, spoiling the canvas of an otherwise perfect day. While we're trying. They'd been trying forever.

She flopped into bed, and James shuffled over and snuggled behind her, offering his warmth against her chilled body.

"Hope you've left the last of those dishes. I'll take care of them in the morning."

"Uh-ha." Her voice came out flat.

"What's wrong, love? You seemed to lose all your sparkle as the night went on. Are you tired?"

He was so damn good at reading her moods. She'd never have suspected that of him when they met. He'd seemed so self-absorbed. But she'd been wrong. His radar was quick to home in on anything unwanted that sailed into their territory. No point pretending. No point lying. He always knew.

"Yeah, I'm tired. But it's not that." She took a deep breath. Putting it into words frightened her. "I think finishing the house has made me realise that we've built this magnificent family home, and it's missing the most important thing of all—the family."

"Yep, have to agree with you on that one."

She rolled to face him and saw the tender concern in his eyes.

"Maybe it's time we stopped relying on hope and got some help. After all, I stopped taking the pill when we got married. It's been four years."

"Yeah, too long. It's been worrying me too, but I didn't want to say anything. Didn't want to put any pressure on you."

"Well, time's ticking, biological clock is running down as they say."

"OK, so here's a thought—how about when we go to the UK next month we get an appointment at one of the fertility clinics? We could try here, but I can't help but think there's likely to be more advanced expertise over there. Might be time for Plan B."

"Yes, thank god we can afford a Plan B. I've heard it can be hellishly expensive."

"Right, well, in the morning, I'll get started. Find a top-notch place. Set an appointment."

She drifted off to sleep after that, her mind at ease. It was one thing she loved about him, his ability to take charge, to tackle her worries head on and make her feel no matter what, things would be all right in the end.

CHAPTER 38

End of the Line

London, England - April 2013

THE SPECIALIST'S HARLEY STREET address was intimidating in itself. A discreet brass plaque directed 'Patients & Visitors' to press the small antique bell above. It didn't exactly scream welcome. But the contrast inside couldn't have been greater.

A smiling woman opened the door and ushered them into a comfortable waiting room, reminiscent of the lobby of a five-star hotel. They sank into an oversized leather-buttoned couch. A delicate fragrance of vanilla overlaid with the sweetness of cinnamon hung in the air. Kate identified the source—a creamy candle nestled in a blown-glass bowl, its tiny flame flickering, an omen of hope.

"Mrs Beckett, coffee?"

Kate nodded. "Yes, please." There was still a slight fog of jet-lag. Coffee would be good.

"And for you too, Mr Beckett? Or tea, if you'd rather?" His face showed pleasant surprise. "We have a tea menu for you to choose from. "

"Impressive," said James as she walked away. "Now you wouldn't get that in New Zealand."

"I'm hoping they're good at more than making coffee or ten different types of tea," said Kate.

"Oh yes," he said, with the confidence of someone who'd done his homework. This clinic was the best, almost impossible to get in to even if you could afford their outrageous charges. He'd waged a relentless campaign to get them an appointment, and assured her that if this specialist couldn't help them, no-one could.

After that first appointment, they'd been filled with optimism. From the moment she set eyes on him, the specialist oozed competence. If you'd asked someone to describe a Harley Street doctor, this was it. Fifty-something, slightly-greying at the temples, straight-talking, but kind.

His words soothed Kate's raging anxiety: "routine tests...," "results should be back reasonably quickly..." "within a week we will know what the best way forward is." Looking back, she was angry he'd not given the slightest warning. Nothing in his words or his manner suggested the wave of hurt that was about to descend on them.

The second appointment lasted less than fifteen minutes. That was all it took to destroy their hopes. Afterwards, they sat in the car in stunned silence, the bright spring day at odds with the dark cloud that hung between them. The trees in the street outside the fertility specialist's rooms were abundant, in full leaf, as if mocking their own newly discovered barren status.

In the back of her mind, she'd feared this journey to having a child could prove difficult. But she'd wrongly assumed that any speed bumps would be solely to do with her. While many women of thirty-six were having babies, the women's magazines were full of others who'd struggled. The last fifteen minutes had turned that assumption on its head. Kate sat replaying the conversation, the doctor's words so unexpected.

The specialist spoke to Kate first, leafing through papers and nodding in approval at what he saw there.

"Well, good news Kate. As far as we can tell, your age at wanting to start a family won't have any detectable impact on your ability to conceive normally. To be honest, for a woman of thirty-six, you are something of an anomaly. We'd expect to see a comparatively low rate of ovulation, but your body seems to have decided otherwise. So if you want to try IVF, there's a fairly good chance we could harvest eggs quite easily, no need for the types of drugs we sometimes need to use."

She had been sitting on the edge of the chair, but now relaxed back into it, the relief washing over her.

"That's great news. Far better than I expected."

James squeezed her hand and smiled. However, his smile evaporated at the man's next words.

"But now to your results, James." The specialist's face wore the mask doctors put on when about to deliver unpleasant news.

"Unfortunately, things aren't so positive. In the most simple terms, your sperm count is very low. From what the tests show, I think it is extremely unlikely that you could father a child. Whether you try by natural methods, or should you consider IVF, the chances of a positive outcome are extremely small. I'm sorry to say that in my professional opinion, I wouldn't recommend either. Time is ticking for Kate, and she needs to ensure she doesn't waste it on an option that has a low chance of success. I'm very sorry."

He stopped for a moment, letting the words sink in. Kate was in shock, but tried to keep her face from showing the crushing disappointment. This would destroy James.

"My advice is that if you are still committed to having a child, it would be wise for you to consider other options."

They sat in silence as he described the two pathways to parenthood that remained for them: using a sperm donor or adoption.

"So, I suggest when you leave here, you take time and give it some thought. Talk through the options and see what's right for you. No need for a hasty decision, but of course sooner rather than later does apply in this situation." He reached towards James, placing a business card in his hand. "And here's the number of a colleague of mine. He's a counsellor. Particularly skilled at working with couples who want help to weigh the options."

He took the card and thanked the doctor.

"We'll be in touch when we've talked it through." His voice was pleasant, exuding calm.

But Kate knew it was an act worthy of one of his best stars. They'd read up on the options for couples having difficulty conceiving. James was non-negotiable—he wanted to be a father, but only to a child that truly belonged to both of them, a child of his own blood. She couldn't see any reason that today's news would have changed his mind. Despite that, she held out a feeble hope that he might, now confronted with this reality. That hope was shattered the moment he spoke.

"So, that's the end of the line," he said, his tone matter-of-fact. "Well, for this branch of the Beckett family, anyway." He kept his face neutral, but there was a slight tremor in his voice and his hands gripped the steering wheel, knuckles white with the strain. "You could leave me, you know." He stared straight ahead, eyes glazed, not connecting with hers. "I wouldn't stand in your way if you..."

"No!" she said.

"No, let me say it. I mean it. I won't stand in the way of you being happy. If having a child by whatever means is something you need to be happy, then I wouldn't try to talk you out of it."

"Oh, so you think that's something I could do? Choose between you and a baby? What kind of choice is that?" Her voice was ragged, and her face contorted with anger.

"Please, I know you're upset." He turned towards her, placing his hand on her shoulder. She roughly brushed it away. "Kate, you must listen to me—you *do* need to think about it. Not only how you feel today, but how you might feel in ten years, or twenty years. You need to be sure that you won't end up hating me."

"Oh, I'm not upset," she spat. "Upset doesn't come anywhere close to how I'm feeling right now. You see, James, you tell me you love me, but what you've just said—it makes me think you don't even know me. You think I'm the sort of person who could simply walk away from you because you can't give me what I want? After all this time, you obviously don't know me at all."

She flung the car door open, and was half out, but he grabbed her arm, pulling her back.

"Kate, don't, please..." His voice was tiny, pleading. She sat paralysed in the seat, her face rigid, body tense, and eyes clamped shut as if by doing so she could make it all go away. "Kate, I am so, so sorry."

It was the resignation in his voice that tipped her over the edge. Defeated. James was never one to surrender. But this time, he knew it was a lost cause. The tears welled up and spilled down her face as she slumped forward, allowing the sadness to engulf her. She hunched over, sobbing to the point she thought she would choke, the pain in her chest so crippling it felt as if her heart might really break.

He wrapped his arms around her as if by doing so he could shield her from this new and terrible reality. His body shook with a grief that echoed her own. Knowing that he couldn't give her a child devastated him.

She knew she wouldn't leave him. He knew it, too. They would somehow carry on together, burying the loss of their children that would never be deep inside in a private place, only shared with each other. They would make a life together, and it would still be a good life.

CHAPTER 39

Lorelei

Auckland, New Zealand - August 2013

THEY'D BEEN BACK IN New Zealand only a matter of hours. Kate's body expected bed soon, but at ten in the morning, wisdom said she needed to tough it out if she wanted to avoid jet lag claiming her for the next few days.

"Right, let's go." He grabbed the car keys. "I've got something to show you, and no, it can't wait."

She still marvelled at how James never seemed to tire. The thought of ADHD had crossed her mind. The boundless energy, restlessness, impulsivity, the amazing creative leaps. It all added up. Gosh, Mary would have had an easier time of it if he'd been diagnosed and medicated as a child. He had a gleam in his eyes and a briskness in his manner that hinted at excitement bubbling beneath the surface. While she wore her emotions on her face for all to see, James's whole body radiated how he was feeling.

"So, where are we going?"

"I'm not telling. Knowing your analytical mind, you'll have it all worked out, and the surprise spoiled."

He was right. She inevitably wormed secrets out of him—where he'd booked them to stay for a weekend, what was inside a wrapped birthday gift, who the secret big name actor on his new project was. It was a game they'd played many times, and he knew who usually won.

"OK." She was too sluggish from the flight to pursue it this time.

"Just sit back and enjoy the ride."

The commuter traffic had subsided, and they zipped in and out of lanes with ease, finally peeling off onto the exit for the marina. The little man-made harbour bristled with masts. This marina was where the true yachties kept their craft. No ugly misnamed super yachts loomed here, only one or two weekend cruisers.

Kate loved it here. The sea still called to her, even though she had difficulty recalling the last time she'd actually sailed herself. Oh yes, they'd been on boats, cruising with the pretty, popular people. But it was no comparison to the sailing that still coursed in her veins.

She'd heard that a new cafe had opened amongst the shipwrights and sailing supply shops. Maybe James was going to take her there for breakfast. That would be a welcome treat. There was breakfast of sorts on the plane: insipid scrambled eggs on soggy toast accompanied by crusty bacon and lacklustre coffee. Business class was looking decidedly shabby lately. She could kill for a plate of good Kiwi cafe food.

She gazed with longing as James drove right on by the shiny new premises, realising that she wasn't about to be fed. He took a sharp left onto the marina proper, edging the huge SUV into one of the narrow parks. She was intrigued now.

"OK, this way." He took her by the hand and led her along a row of moored yachts that rose and fell ever so gently on the sheltered waters, breathing the soft breath of the sea. She matched her breath to it—inhale, exhale—immersing her lungs in the beguiling, salty tang.

They stopped about halfway along in front of a smart ketch. She recognised the name—*Verity*. She'd sailed with the owners when they were kids. Now they had kids of their own. No doubt they spent lots of time pottering around the islands of the gulf in this sweet little boat. Was this what they had come to see?

"Close your eyes." He was standing close behind her and she could feel the energy, the excitement, coming off him in waves.

"What?"

"Do what I say. Close your eyes."

She stood, eyes squeezed against the brightness of the day. His hands rested on her shoulders and she complied with his touch, as he turned her to face the opposite direction.

"No peeking, not till I say."

"OK, OK."

"Now. Open them."

Tied up at the jetty was a yacht of exquisite beauty, a classic racer. Her wooden kauri deck glowed a warm amber. The brass gleamed, newly polished. Although her fine livery might fool some, Kate knew this was a boat built for speed; the deck pared back to the functional. Her sailor's eye calculated the dimensions and the rigging. Yes, you could sail her with two, but to make this girl fly, maybe three to five crew. What fun that would be.

And then the realisation struck her—she knew this yacht, too.

"It's *Lorelei*."

"Yes, it is—and she's yours."

She blinked in disbelief. *Lorelei* was famous, at least in this part of the world. Everyone knew the story of how she'd been discovered in a sorry state. The enthusiast who'd poured hours of love into the task of restoring her, the man responsible for her current glory, had proceeded to win no less than three Anniversary Day regattas.

"The old guy who owned her passed away a few months ago. Very sad—there was no one in the family with any great interest in sailing her themselves."

"Oh no, he's dead?" It genuinely saddened her to hear this. "He was a legend, that guy. As kids, we all wanted to be like him. This brave little boat out there taking on the big guns. He outsailed them loads of times."

"Well, the family may not have been sailors, but they were adamant that she wasn't going to just anybody. They weren't prepared to take my money without full disclosure. You know I've had to dig around and find out all sorts of stuff about your past so I could assure them you were a suitable person to take care of her. Someone who would appreciate her. And they were keen that it be someone who would leave her here, so they can come and see her now and then for old times' sake."

"I can't believe you managed to pull this off without me knowing."

"Well, let's say those late night work phone calls weren't all work." He had a satisfied smile on his face. She hadn't suspected a thing.

"I feel terrible now. Berating you for working so much these last months."

He'd plunged himself into a new project in London, leaving her often alone in the huge Bayswater house for four months, with no friends to support her through the awful truth that she'd never be a mother. Ellie had phoned every day, invited her to come down to Brighton and stay with her and Hugh.

But Kate had made excuses. It was still too raw to sit amongst their happy little family, knowing it was the one thing she couldn't have. And so she'd stayed put, taking out her loneliness and despair on James, picking arguments over the stupidest things.

"I spoke to them so many times it's as if I know them even though we've never met. Maybe we could take them out with us sometime?"

"Ah yes, it will have to be with *us*. This lady's not a one-person proposition."

"You can teach me," he said. "I promise to be a model student. Follow the skipper's orders. You'll enjoy telling me what to do."

"And you'll no doubt make a damn good sailor." James had a natural ability with physical tasks. He could turn his hand to almost any sport. She had every confidence he could handle this.

"Well, I hope so, especially with you for a teacher." His voice took on a less flippant tone. "And I also hoped that doing something together would help. Maybe bring us closer, after the shit year we've had?"

She nodded. There was no doubt the finality of his decision about children had rocked their marriage. But their fragile relationship was beginning to heal. He was right. They needed to look ahead, live the life they were destined to live, even if it wasn't the life they'd expected. Tears spilled over, tears of grief for what they'd lost and tears of joy at his unflagging love.

"James, I don't know what to say. It's the most amazing gift I've ever been given."

He hugged her to him, laying his head on her shoulder, and his voice came low and soft in her ear. "I'd give you anything you want, my love, anything that's in my power to give."

She shrugged him off gently, brushing off the thought of the one thing he couldn't give.

"Come on then, let's check out this old girl."

They ventured downstairs into the compact cabin. Traditional wood grain on the walls and cupboards made it feel warm and cosy. It wasn't luxurious, but they'd used quality materials in the renovation and it had everything they'd need. Tucked away at one end was a snug bedroom. Kate sat on the bed.

"Is it comfortable?" asked James.

"A Goldilocks bed," she said. "Not too hard, not too soft—just right."

He plonked down beside her.

"Fancy trying it out?"

He pushed her backwards, his eyes playful. His kiss was enough to tempt her. And then when he leaned over, pressing her down with the length of his body, and she felt the hardness of his erection, any objections to the idea evaporated.

"I think we should."

She let her shoes slip off while clawing at the buttons on his shirt. He meanwhile had turned his attention to unzipping her jeans, removing them in one adept, well-practised move.

There was a spontaneity and urgency in their lovemaking that had been absent for months.

Afterwards he dozed beside her, giving in to the need for sleep after the long flight. Kate wished she could do the same, but although her body's exhaustion tried to drag her into slumber, her mind wouldn't let her.

As she lay there, she mulled over the past months, where at times they'd seemed strangers. She'd turned inwards in her grief, inside her a multitude of emotions. She'd never been sure which one would show up on any given day. Some days she was angry–at James for his unyielding stance, at herself for being too afraid to fight him on it, too much of a coward to accept the choice of leaving he'd offered her. Other days she wallowed in self-pity, at the unfairness of the world, dealing her yet another bad hand.

Her doctor had suggested a psychologist, counselling, medication. All were equally unpalatable.

Now, today, she realised that, to her surprise, she'd left that time behind. They'd faced the reality that this life was now about the two of them, and they should make the most of it. While they would never have children, they had each other. And unlike some married couples, there was still love and a passion as strong as on that first night when they'd crossed from being unlikely friends to lovers.

Later, as they stepped back onto the marina boardwalk, a family strolled towards them. A woman of about her age led the group, dressed for a day on the water, trailed by husband and children in matching sailing attire. The two little boys raced off ahead, laughing and bounding.

"Hi there," she waved. "You're the new owners?"

"Yes, we are." There was a sense of pride in saying it out loud.

"We'd heard someone had bought her. I always felt sad seeing her sitting there, not getting the attention she deserves."

"Well, I can guarantee she'll be getting lots of attention from now on."

"That's good to hear. Hope to see you out on the water soon."

"For sure," said Kate.

"You're very lucky. She's a beautiful boat. One day maybe... for now, this one is more what we need." She pointed to a cruiser moored a few berths down where the boys were scrambling aboard. "When you've got kids, there have to be a few compromises."

Kate watched her join her family. She couldn't help but wonder who was the lucky one. She loved *Lorelei*, but she'd trade her in a heartbeat for those two beautiful boys. But where once she would have felt bitterness and even jealousy, now there was resignation with a faint touch of sadness. She was going to be OK.

CHAPTER 40

Lockdown

Seven years later, Auckland, New Zealand - March 2020

OVER THE WHIRR OF the auto door closing, Kate could hear James slam the car door. Uncharacteristic of him—he loved his cars and usually treated them with reverence. Moments later, he burst through the door, tossing his briefcase on the sofa. There was a frown on his face. He went straight to the cabinet and pulled out the whisky.

"God, I need a drink." He sloshed a generous pour. "You might need one too. The world's turning to shit."

He didn't wait for her reply, but produced a second glass, splashing in a large dash of the bronze liquid.

"What's wrong?"

Kate had grown to enjoy whisky, but she couldn't help but associate its strident taste with times of trouble. Whenever things went wrong, James was quick to reach for a dram.

"One of the local guys has a contact in the Beehive. The government's under huge pressure to act on this pandemic thing. You know everyone's screaming for the border to close. But that's not the worst of it. The word on the street is that within a week we'll be in lockdown."

"So what does that mean for the studio?"

"I've no choice but to shut it down."

His face was set in grim resignation. It wasn't the first time he'd faced challenges maintaining a shooting schedule. But he'd always managed to sort it. This time, he'd be forced to admit defeat.

He leaned back in the chair, eyes shut, face tense, no doubt thinking about the huge task that lay ahead. Kate could see he was wound tight, like a coiled spring. Then whisky downed in one gulp, he sprang into action. Out came his laptop and phone and their home was transformed into a command centre.

James's call to halt production unleashed a massive operation. There were over two hundred people working on this project, more than half not New Zealanders. James and his team set about frantically organising flights home for the overseas cast and crew. Those who wanted to go.

It was a tough decision. Who knew what the best call would be? No one had lived through a global pandemic before. Some wanted to get back to family and friends, fearful of being stranded here thousands of miles from home. Others were betting on New Zealand being safe, a haven. It was simple to close the borders when you were an island nation.

By Friday afternoon, it was done. They'd delivered the last few who'd chosen to leave to the airport. Now they would sit and wait.

There was a sense of impending doom that permeated the city. People had a wariness about them. In shops and supermarkets, they flashed dirty looks if you inadvertently came too close. And if you coughed or sneezed in public, they scattered. Some people were stockpiling. There were reports from Australia of panic buying toilet paper. Crazy Australians, they said. Wouldn't happen here. But there were signs it would.

Kate and James sat on the deck, surveying the sparkling water. Summer still lingered. No one had told the season that it should move on, make way for autumn. It was the kind of day where it was hard to believe that bad things were happening.

At the neighbour's, a man in large protective earphones mowed back and forth, the roar of the motor drowning out the sea's rhythm. A fresh smell of cut grass drifted in the air. Kate breathed it in deeply. She loved that smell. The ordinariness of people going about their daily tasks was a stark contrast to the extraordinary situation unfolding around them.

"You know what? I reckon we should go out and have a bloody good weekend. If all the predictions are true, who knows when we might have another? Last night on the *Titanic*?"

"Absolutely," Kate said. "What do you want to do?"

"Dinner at the Viaduct tonight for a start. Might have to live on the memory of a good meal at Carnival for a while." He was already texting their friend Sophie to see if she could squeeze them in. "Who knows how restaurant owners like her will survive if the lockdown becomes reality? It's going to be hell for them."

"Let's go out and have a splurge then," said Kate. "The next few days' takings will have to see her through for a while."

She thought about what they required to survive a lockdown. It wasn't only the physical supplies. They had an overflowing pantry, a well-stocked bar, and an extensive wine cellar. It was their other needs that might prove difficult. She couldn't imagine how James would cope. Even on holiday, he never wanted to just sit in a hotel. He needed to be doing something. At least they had a gym and a pool, but it would be strange living their entire lives in the confines of this house.

"What about we take *Lorelei* for a spin tomorrow?" She hoped the suggestion would help to lift his gloomy mood. "The forecast for the gulf looks good."

"Perfect," he said. "Better not get hammered tonight, then. Don't want to be feeding the fish in the morning."

He stuck to his intention, and they both woke early, with clear heads. The marina was busy. It seemed they weren't the only ones wanting one last fix of the sea.

They eased *Lorelei* out of her moorings and motored out into the harbour. Sails unleashed, she sprang to life. The breeze was ideal, right in the range where she found her sweet spot. Sailing her together was comfortable, a familiar dance for which they both knew the steps and could repeat intuitively and without error.

Kate looked across at her husband. His face was alight with the thrill of wind and waves. She knew he'd see the same reflected in hers. They were happy. Blissfully so. It seemed wrong to feel this way when the world was falling apart.

CHAPTER 41

Minutes to Midnight

Auckland, New Zealand - March 2020

JAMES WAS ON THE phone with Henry Crawford. Kate adored Henry. He was the real deal, a big name movie star, but one of the most amiable and humble people she knew. James's description of him as 'so laid back he's almost horizontal' was apt, and the two had become firm friends outside of their working relationship.

Henry's uncomplicated nature was the perfect foil for that of his equally famous but highly-strung wife, Lydia. The press painted her as a diva, which was in fact far from the truth, but made better reading. Those who knew Lydia loved her rapier-sharp wit and delightful sense of the absurd. Spending any time in her company was a guarantee of fun. She was renowned for her graciousness on set, beloved by the crew who she always won over with her willingness to pitch in. One time when she'd been the lead in a West End production, they had found her down in wardrobe, famously ironing her own costume.

The two had established careers and a string of awards to their names. James had enticed them to New Zealand for the colonial era series. While the intriguing script was a draw card, Kate was sure the deciding factor had been their trust in James to deliver something worthy of their talent.

They'd brought their three young children with them. James had found the family a sprawling country home and helped with getting the kids established in schools for a planned six-month filming window. The family loved it here and were happy and settled living the Kiwi lifestyle.

When the previous week James delivered the bad news that a shutdown of the production was looming, Henry and Lydia announced their intention to ride out the pandemic in New Zealand. They had decided there was no safer place in the world to be than exactly where they were. Like the other five million inhabitants of the country, they set about preparing for an extended period of lockdown.

James wandered into the kitchen, where Kate was munching on toast. "I'm taking the last of the scripts over to Henry." Ever the optimist, James was ensuring he was prepared to resume filming at the earliest possible moment. No doubt Henry would know the scripts back to front by the time that happened. "But I think you should come too. One day of home-schooling and Lydia's already having a meltdown."

"Sure." Kate smiled at the thought of Lydia attempting to wrangle her children into completing schoolwork. "I can imagine. Being a teacher is about the last thing in the world she's suited for."

Lydia doted on her offspring and thrived on being a hands-on mother, as far as possible eschewing the nannies and tutors that other families in the industry relied on. But taking on the role of full-time teacher was one step too far.

The city was desolate, an uncanny stillness from streets almost totally devoid of traffic. It was surreal to see row on row of businesses already closed. Lights off and doors locked. Who knew when they would open again? At 11:59 p.m. tonight, they were all heading into the unknown.

They took the motorway west, then veered off onto a narrow side road winding into the hills. The unseasonably warm day and the rolling rural scenery made Kate feel like she was heading off on holiday, although a bank of cloud loomed over the western sea, a promise of rain spoiling the illusion of summer.

They arrived at a set of enormous gates that barred entry to a driveway. Beyond the gates, it disappeared into a stand of mature native bush. There was no sign of any house. No letterbox announcing that people lived here. Only a discreet button on the gatepost gave any indication that there was something beyond. Although if you searched for it, you might glimpse a reflection off the lense of a security camera discreetly peering through the trees.

The property was perfect for a family who desired privacy. Although Lydia had complained of seeing at least one drone hovering, Henry had written it off as paranoia, a figment of her overactive imagination. That no paparazzi photos of their hideaway had emerged suggested he was right.

James pushed the button, and Henry's mellow baritone issued from a speaker.

"Coffee's on, come on in."

The gates swung open noiselessly, and they wound along a small private road, eventually bursting out into sunshine and manicured lawns where the unexpected grandeur of the house confronted them. No matter how many times she'd been here, it still took Kate by surprise. Wrapped around a huge curved driveway, it was more Hollywood Hills than New Zealand. A fitting residence for the Hollywood royalty that currently occupied it.

Built for the Seaforth family, rich-lister owners of a once booming company, it still bore their name. Although the company had long since gone bust, and the family long gone, everybody referred to it as the Seaforth mansion. There'd been feature stories about the house in numerous magazines, its opulence unlike anything else in the country. Like many New Zealanders, Kate felt she knew it, even before she first visited Henry and Lydia. The ornate central building was flanked by two massive wings. Its sheer size was a testament to the millions of dollars spent on it.

Henry came to meet them at the door in bare feet and jeans. He always had a casual, even slightly scruffy air that made Kate feel she wanted to straighten his clothing. In real life, he was the complete opposite of his on-screen persona. He portrayed elegant Victorian gentlemen and suave, smart-suited Bond-like action heroes. But at home, he resembled a beach bum. He was a most unusual man, with features that could almost be described as homely except for the way his eyes bristled with keen intelligence. No one seeing him in the street would ever pick him as a movie star.

He greeted James with warmth, clapping him on the back. And then, catching sight of her, his smile broadened even further. He held out his arms.

"Kate!" His voice boomed her name in welcome. "Fuck the virus. Come and give me a hug!" He wrapped her in his large enthusiastic arms, murmuring in her ear. "Thank God you've come. Second day of home-schooling and Lydia's threatening gin for breakfast."

Kate could hear the shrillness of Lydia's voice from down the hallway. It confirmed Henry's assessment of her state of mind.

"No, Connor. You are not going to do that now. Your sister has her zoom meeting at ten-thirty." There was no mistaking her exasperated tone.

"*But Mum*, the teacher said to make up our own rhythm to go with the poem," Connor whined.

"Yes, but not now! How will your sister hear when you're banging that in the background? Do something else."

Kate walked into the room to see Connor putting down a pair of spoons—his 'instrument' of choice for the task—with reluctance and a sulky expression.

"Mum, it's not connecting." Claudia perched in front of a laptop, headset on, peering at the screen, her eyebrows knotted in an anxious frown.

"I'll sort it in a second. Let me take care of Frankie first." Tiny six-year-old Francesca, also seated in front of a laptop, listened carefully to her teacher, who was relaying instructions for a story-writing task via video.

"*But Mum*, it's almost ten-thirty and we can't be late. The teacher said it's rude to not be ready for the zoom."

"How about I help you with that?" Kate offered.

"Kate!" squealed Claudia, leaping from her chair and wrapping her in an exuberant hug.

"Kate!" echoed wee Frankie with her enchanting gap-toothed smile.

"Oh Kate, thank God you're here." Relief washed over Lydia's flustered face, a stark contrast to her normally composed demeanour. "Now I understand what drives mothers into killing their offspring," she said, her tone as dramatic as if she was delivering lines for the camera. "Or at least run away and abandon them."

Half an hour of Kate's organisational skills and all three Crawford children were absorbed in their online classes.

"You must come and have a coffee now," said Lydia. "Unless you want to join me in something stronger?" She raised one elegantly arched eyebrow quizzically.

Kate laughed. "Coffee will be just fine."

They sat in the vast kitchen, enjoying the absence of the children and the opportunity for adult conversation. They were surrounded by every appliance known to man. It was Henry's way to fit out each new residence so he could indulge his passion for cooking.

The sweet smell of baking hung heavy in the air. Today, he'd already produced a chocolate cake almost too decadent for morning tea. Not that it stopped them from devouring large chunks. James was on his third, washing it down with copious quantities of tea. Kate abandoned her resolution to cut back on eating sugary foods as he placed a slice in front of her.

The looming lockdown and the unpredictable future dominated their conversation.

"You know, you could always stay here." Henry's tone was casual, but the offer was sincere.

"Oh yes," Lydia enthused. "Join our bubble. Kate, you're so amazing with the school work, and James, the kids adore you. You're their fun uncle!"

Kate looked at James, questioning with her eyes. It wasn't necessarily a bad idea. She was sure Lydia and Henry would appreciate adult company. She would be happy to stay. And it would be great for James. Being the extrovert he was, how would he handle at least a month of only socialising virtually? She imagined he'd be pacing like a caged tiger within days. And then there was Henry's cooking...

"Nah." It surprised her to hear James decline the opportunity. "I'd love it, but I don't want to leave the house empty for all that time. There won't be any of the usual outside help come in. It seems I'm the pool guy, gardener, and most likely the cleaner for the next four weeks. Plus, there we can still get out for a walk or something."

"Yeah, now I wish I'd picked a house near the beach or with more grounds," said Henry. "Unless I get out a machete and go bushwhacking, there's nowhere to walk from here. At least there's the pool and iFit on my treadmill. Headset on and I can run anywhere in the world."

"Meanwhile, I'm out here juggling kids while you go to your happy place." Lydia narrowed her eyes, indignant at the suggestion.

"We'll survive," said Henry. "First world problems and all that."

An hour later, they made the move to head home, tempting as it was to stay and partake in thick pumpkin soup and crusty fresh-baked bread for lunch.

The girls wrapped them in exuberant hugs and plastered sloppy farewell kisses on their cheeks. Connor, deciding he was too grown-up for that, gave them a manly hug that mirrored his father's. Kate thought how bizarre it was that apart from each other, these would be the last human beings that they touched for weeks.

Henry and Lydia stood huddled under the portico, sheltering from the now persistent rain as James turned the car. The children twined around their parents, their little faces still showing disappointment. They'd hoped to persuade James and Kate to stay. Kate waved at them in encouragement.

"Don't worry, we'll call you. We can zoom."

"Take care." Henry raised a large paw in farewell. "See you on the other side!" She heard him call after them as the car plunged into the dimness of the tree-shrouded driveway.

"I'm going to miss them," she said as they waited for the massive gates to allow their exit.

"Me too," said James. "That guy, I love him like a brother. And Lydia, she's hilarious."

The car was perfectly suited to the sweeping corners and clung to the slick road with confidence. Even though he owned faster and more extravagant vehicles, the Audi wagon was his favourite. Under James's skillful manoeuvering, it dived neatly into corners and flowed seamlessly out of them.

Kate closed her eyes and relaxed back into the rhythm. It always lulled her, the controlled to and fro, the ebb and flow of the powerful engine. James was passionate about cars, seeming to understand them intimately, always demanding they give to the limits of their potential, but never pushing them beyond into dangerous extremes. It was as if the man and machine came together in a seductive dance whenever he got behind the wheel. The wipers added their own counterpoint, swiping the sheets of water to a steady beat.

"Oh, fuck!"

He screamed the words at the same time as instinctively engaging the brakes. The seatbelt caught Kate in a brutal embrace, her eyes flying open to see a truck right on top of them. There was a sickening lurch as James wrestled the car to the left, and then the screaming of metal as it skewed out of control. Kate was flung both forwards and sideways, as if trapped in a violent theme park ride. The airbags blossomed in front of her like bizarre exotic flowers engulfing her in their depths, drawing her down into nothingness. She inhaled their smoky perfume. The petals closed over her. There was darkness, stillness, silence.

Freedom

Auckland, New Zealand - April 2020

THE HOSPITAL STAFF WERE too kind, and she hated them for it. Their sympathetic faces and cautious words wouldn't bring James back. Or assuage her guilt that she'd let him go alone. No funeral, no mourners. Nor were their apologetic tones enough to compensate for her imprisonment, endless days spent in solitary confinement. Her only human contact was with strangers.

Precious phone calls were the only permitted link to anyone she knew, and they left her more distraught than soothed.

"I'm so sorry honey, I desperately want to come and see you, but we're not allowed." There was distress in Tracey's voice. "You know the moment I can, I'll be there."

Dear, tenacious Henry—he'd begged help from every influential person he could possibly think of, to no avail. "My darling, I'm so sorry. They're heartless bastards."

Because of the strict nationwide restrictions, that situation wouldn't change if she could persuade them to let her go home, but at least she would be free of this claustrophobic, white-walled room. They didn't permit her to leave it, even to stretch her legs in the bland corridors. Escape was the only solution. But to extract herself from this hell, there were two people she needed to convince.

The doctor first needed to sign off that she was sufficiently physically healed to be trusted at home. She sat in the bouffant armchair, her stomach knotted with anxiety. He hid behind a mask, choosing his words with care. She tried to read his eyes, searching for a sign that he would grant her request.

"A TBI is tricky. It's not a straightforward thing."

She knew that. Understood the jargon: TBI—traumatic brain injury. Understood the fog that descended on her without warning. Understood that her body might betray her at any moment, that she could no longer rely on it to function as expected. Understood that her brain was fickle, one moment operating as normal, the next abandoning her as she struggled to remember the most simple things.

Frustration was her constant companion. Yesterday she'd picked up her phone and tried to order her favourite perfume online, so it could be a lovely present to herself waiting there when she got home. Instead, she was defeated by an app she'd used dozens of times. Like a dysfunctional Bletchley Park code-breaker, she'd wrestled with the numbers and letters, but lacking a key element, failed to unlock the puzzle.

Summoning the concentration needed to sustain ordinary tasks, such as reading the newspaper online, was often beyond her. It had been an indulgent daily ritual. Now it was a battle. And the headaches, although lessening, could still blindside her. There was no surety from one day to the next.

"You'll have good days and bad days," he said. "We need to be sure that you're still safe on your bad days. Is there someone who can come and stay with you?"

She shook her head. "They've all got their own families. They're already struggling in lockdown. It's not as if they can turn their backs on them and come and live with me."

"What about a live-in carer? A paid nurse?"

She shuddered at the thought. She'd already been stripped bare, her muddled brain leaving her at the mercy of strangers. The last thing she wanted was another witness to her vulnerability. But, keeping her eye on the prize, she offered tacit agreement.

"That's an option. It's a big house, plenty of space. Upstairs is self-contained." She was going to grasp this lifeline with both hands. Once she was home, she could dispense with the nurse, do things her way. "And you know I can cover it, whatever it costs, to get someone."

"OK, I'll start the ball rolling. It's going to take a bit more to organise under the current restrictions, but I'll see what strings I can pull. They are keen to move people home where possible—trying to keep bed space open for a possible influx of Covid patients. So that should help your case."

"Thank you, I appreciate it."

Kate smiled, quietly triumphant. She'd won the first battle. The psychologist would be more challenging. It was harder to hide her emotional wounds.

"Kate, I won't bullshit you. You deserve the truth, not some sugar-coated version of it. But in return, I need you to be honest with me." She'd done that—allowed him in. He saw the rawness as she grappled with the reality of her fragile state. "It's normal to have these feelings of guilt." Normal didn't make it any easier to accept that she'd survived. "The grieving process is naturally going to be more difficult. There are things you haven't been allowed to do, yet are necessary."

Surely if they let her out, she could make a start on facing her grief instead of being cocooned here, away from the real world? She needed to be in their house, where he was everywhere. She needed to hold clothes that still clung to his smell. To run her hand over sheets, touch the imprint of his body captured there. Only then could she begin to say goodbye.

"Here's my number. You can call me anytime. 24/7. Don't hesitate if you need me."

He'd agreed. She relaxed back into the lumpy hospital chair. Kate had come prepared to fight, but it hadn't been necessary. She was free.

CHAPTER 43

Princess

Auckland, New Zealand - June 2020

A MEDICAL EVENT, THEY said. A ticking time bomb buried inside the body of a man. A man who climbed out of bed that morning and kissed his wife goodbye, not knowing that this was the day the bomb would go off. Loading his truck, one last delivery to the general store in a small village on the city fringe. Friendly banter with the store owner. Who knows what this next few weeks will bring? Who knows when he'll be back? Heading back to the depot, the road's not the best, but he knows it well, takes it carefully.

But no amount of knowledge or care can stop what has already been set in motion, months, perhaps years ago. He breaks into a cold sweat. Why? The day's not so warm. Then a giant invisible hand reaches into his chest, gripping, twisting, tearing. The pain is excruciating, but it doesn't last. His last flickering thought—there's a car in front of him, but there is no time to consider what that might mean.

Kate sat and stared out at the flat greyness of the sea from her glass-fronted lounge. Rain flung against the window, insistent, demanding, clawing to get in. Beyond it, the churning ocean rolled towards her, angry waves hammering the rocky shoreline below the house with thundering booms.

She was a lonely princess trapped in a clifftop castle, waiting for rescue. But her prince wouldn't be coming to save her. He'd saved her life once already, but it had cost him his own. His quick reflexes propelled the car hard to the left. Far enough to ensure it didn't take the impact head on, but not far enough to prevent the out-of-control truck crushing it, crushing him. The blankness of the concussion was a gift. She had seen nothing, remembered little. So strange how what hurt you could also protect you.

No, the only person who could rescue her from this fortress was herself. And she was even lucky to be here, thankful that somehow she'd convinced the team from the head injury clinic to overcome their reluctance and release her. The merry-go-round of physiotherapists, speech therapists, psychologists still closely monitored her progress. She put on a brave face. She told them what they wanted to hear.

The phone rang. She knew it would be Ellie, because only Ellie knew she was drowning. She phoned each day, her voice reaching out to drag Kate back, encouraging her to swim.

"Hi Ellie." Brain damage had flattened her speech, and although she religiously did the daily exercises, it still sounded mechanical to her ears. "Got the kids in bed?"

"Yes, finally."

She sounded exhausted. That was no surprise. Ellie's children had inherited the exuberant Beckett nature and their Welsh father's love of all things active. When they were awake, the house seemed to be in a permanent state of uproar. Nine-year-old Dylan and Carys, only a year his junior, launched between fighting like wild animals and raucous play. It was hard to tell one from the other. Wee James was the epitome of the terrible twos and sometimes became entwined in his older siblings' ruckus.

Kate longed to see them. To have them leap all over her with squeals of delight as they hugged Auntie Kate. But that wasn't going to happen anytime soon. The borders were closed, and even if they weren't, Ellie wouldn't risk bringing them. And should Kate find the courage to venture out of this sanctuary into the pandemic-ravaged world, she wasn't stable enough to travel that far. Although her progress back from the injury was steady, the doctors couldn't yet guarantee she wouldn't have some kind of episode. Flying was out of the question.

"Busy day?" Kate asked.

Ellie laughed. "When isn't it? So, what are your plans for the day?"

"Planning the memorial service. It's time."

"Oh my darling, you can't do that on your own."

"No, not on my own. Henry's coming over. God, I don't know what I'd do without him. And you."

"Let me help. I want to help," she pleaded. "I should help. He was my brother. Please, let's do this together. You, me and Henry."

"You're right. I'm sorry. We shouldn't be doing this without you. I don't know what I was thinking."

She sat in silence, her throat gripped tight by the sorrow. Ellie would know her tears were falling, as she knew Ellie wept with her.

"Hey, you, it's OK, it's OK." Typical Ellie, worried more about others than herself.

"It's this huge, ugly thing still looming over me." Her body shook with sobs. "And I know I need to deal with it. The psychologist—the one who's been helping me with the head injury—she said if I'm going to start recovering properly, there are things to be faced. Need to heal the mind as well as the body."

"And she's right ... We all need to do this. You, me, Henry, all of us. We need to say goodbye."

Henry was never on time. She sat with a coffee listening for the rumbling sound of the old classic Jaguar that was his favourite form of transport, its massive V12 engine an anomaly in this world of fuel efficiency and electric cars.

Her thoughts drifted to the other woman somewhere in the city, who had already faced this grim reality. Kate leapt online and searched back in the newspapers for the death notice, chiding herself for this morbid impulse, but unable to repress it. Something inside compelled her to discover more about the other side of the tragedy that had engulfed her. She found it there in the obituaries for March 28th.

KELSEY, Michael Thomas (Mike) .... Much loved husband of Beth...

Hard as it was for Kate, it was worse for her. Kate only had vague recollections of being told James had died. At first she'd drifted in and out of consciousness, with much of it a strange contorted dream she'd struggled to wake from. Four weeks in hospital created a buffer between the accident and her new harsh reality. And it was only now, eight weeks later, that she was in any state to make plans.

But the other man—his family was fully aware of their loss from the beginning. Not only that, they'd been trapped in the highest alert level. No funeral. No comforting blanket of human contact to wrap around them and ease their grief. It must have been horrific.

Adored father of Madison, Ava and Jack.

And a father, too. Three children without a father. They'd wanted three children. If life had worked out differently, she'd be the same as Beth Kelsey. A mother to three fatherless children. She'd thought the universe was cruel to deny them a baby. But it was much more cruel to rip an otherwise healthy forty-year-old man away from his young children.

Weighing her own desolate situation against theirs somehow gave her the strength to open the door in response to Henry's thunderous knock, to make the call to bring Ellie online, to make the decisions that had to be made.

CHAPTER 44

Farewell

Auckland, New Zealand - July 2020

KATE SURVEYED THE PACKED theatre, every row filled with a kaleido-scope of people, friends, and workmates whom James had amassed over the years. Most were people who'd liked him. Others didn't, but still respected him enough to attend. He who always loved being the centre of attention and thrived in a crowd would have enjoyed the memorial service. By delaying until early July when the restrictions on gatherings eased, they could extend an open invitation and masses of people came. If the borders were open, the numbers would have overflowed onto the street.

Passersby would have been forgiven for thinking there was a show playing. In a way, there was. Some of James's friends banded together to create a movie masterpiece as the backdrop for the service. The sound technicians provided an impressive soundtrack. It was a larger-than-life farewell equal to the personality of the man at its centre. Friends and family from the UK beamed in lifesize on the screen.

Her heart warmed at the sight of Julien, propped up by his partner Thomas, who made them laugh and cry with anecdotes about James. It was as if they still expected James to bound into their restaurant one evening, full of cheek and trouble.

Then Ellie appeared, surrounded by the Beckett family. Kate's throat tightened, and tears edged down her cheeks. She longed for their comforting presence. Instead, she had to settle for their beautiful tributes and kind words.

Seeing Keith there, supporting Ellie with his bulky arm around her shoulder, she wished he could hug her too. He was trying to appear staunch, but so obviously struggling to come to terms with it. James, so much younger, snatched away while he lived on. The other Beckett men stood next to him, all sculpted from the same rock, broad shoulders, rugged faces still attractive, the lines of age simply defining them more strongly, and hair thick and lush although whitened by time.

This is how the future James would have looked if fate hadn't denied him the privilege of growing old. His father was conspicuous by his absence, as he had been for much of his son's life. But Kate treasured the brief note he'd sent her. Between the lines was the regret of a man who'd always thought he'd reconnect with his son someday.

Kate spoke too, although her voice was so wispy, she didn't recognise it as her own. The time passing since his death made her more brave. She couldn't have done this a week after the accident, but now it was possible. The lockdown had given her time, not enough to heal, but enough that she could do this last thing for her husband.

Henry stood on her left, his big paw-like hand resting with the lightest touch on her shoulder. His presence was reassuring, knowing he grieved too. Tracey, on the other side, placed a gentle arm around Kate's waist, buoying her up, keeping her from being swamped by the emotion that lapped so close.

"Farewell, my love," she said. "Run free." Her hand shook as she added a single stem to the riot of flowers that blanketed the coffin; a big, bold splash of colour—just like him.

The after-match function, as her grandfather would have called it, went on for some time. The film crowd was a gregarious bunch and afterwards they ate, drank, and talked animatedly, as well as offering their condolences in person. But Kate could sense that they'd already moved on. They were already living in the post-James world, their minds on the future. Whereas she was still trapped in a strange, in-between place, like a butterfly caught in a jar. The sprawling, glass-sided house was lonely without her husband's huge personality to fill it. She was lonely.

She hadn't planned how she was going to get home. As the crowd dwindled, she stood confused, unsure of what to do. Henry, dear kind Henry, noticed her dithering and took charge.

"There's no way you're going home to your place," he insisted, steering her towards his car. "You shouldn't be by yourself, not today at least." Kate began to protest but then relented, knowing he was right. She'd exhausted her well of emotional resilience. No longer buoyed by the outpouring of good wishes, she was sinking back into her bleak reality. "It's all organised. Lydia and the kids came in her car. I'll drive us by your house and you can grab a few things."

Within half an hour, they were zipping along a winding road up into the Waitakere ranges. Henry, realising that the last time she had been to his house was the day of the accident, took a roundabout route and kept the conversation light. After a while it tapered off and Kate relaxed with her eyes closed, feeling his capable manoeuvring of the big car around tight corners. Much like James had, she thought. Always in control.

When she opened her eyes again, they were on a stretch of the road where the trees reached overhead, almost touching, blocking the sun. On both sides, the luxurious native bush crowded right out to the edges. As they swept into a tight hairpin, the car gliding with ease, Kate had the most odd sensation, almost déjà vu–but it wasn't.

This place reminded her of somewhere else she'd been. She couldn't recall where or when. She glanced over at Henry and was even more confused. For a moment, it seemed she wasn't seeing Henry at all. The profile of the man in the driver's seat was different, the same thatch of unruly sandy blonde hair, but that was all. A name flashed through her mind. *Alex*. Her stomach lurched.

"Kate? Are you OK?" Henry's quirky features returned to view, deep concern written on his face.

"Yeah, I just felt a little nauseous. I'll be fine."

"Oh my God, I'm sorry, I'll slow down."

"No, no, honestly, it's not your driving. I'm a bit lightheaded. I think I should have eaten more. So many people to talk to, I didn't have much food."

"We'll be home soon. I'll make you some lunch."

"Yes, please." She smiled, thinking of Henry's legendary cooking skills. He could make even the most simple dishes seem special. "You know, you could convince me to do anything for one of your meals. Lydia's a lucky woman."

Lydia was indeed very fortunate, since she herself was challenged by making a cup of tea without burning it. The kitchen was Henry's domain. Even the children knew it. Kate had laughed at their frantic concern one night when Henry was late home and Lydia threatened to attempt dinner.

She closed her eyes again, trying to put the odd vision from her mind. But no matter how hard she tried, it kept coming back to her, not only that day but in those that followed. It wasn't just that for a moment she'd seen someone other than Henry sitting in the driver's seat. It was the name. The same name, a stealthy intruder that had invaded her mind during the first days after the accident.

Who was Alex? Was he even a real person? Or was he a creation of her damaged brain? The niggling questions disturbed her otherwise quiet existence.

CHAPTER 45

Memory

Auckland, New Zealand - September 2020

"They've suggested I go through photographs, jot down memories. It's supposed to help me become more confident that my brain's doing what it should. That I'm remembering stuff."

"Your brain seems to be doing fine to me," Ellie said.

"Yeah, I think so too. But it won't hurt." Then she added, "Well, it will hurt. The photos are the life I had. But I have to face it. This is my life now."

"I wish I could be there."

"I wish you could too."

"How about I send some stuff to help?" Ellie volunteered. "There are loads of photos on my phone and laptop. Things we did. Some happy stuff."

"Sure, that would be great."

"I'll make a Facebook group and flick them on there."

"Cool, I'll check later on."

True to her promise, within a few hours, the invite to a private group came through. Ellie must have worked all day on this. There were so many photographs. Of course there would be—no surprise with Ellie, the queen of the selfie. She loved to record her every movement and those of others on her ever present iPhone. Even before the phone, she recalled Ellie never going anywhere without her little Nikon.

There were fifteen albums of photos here, going right back to the beginning when they'd first met in London. Some before she'd even met her friend's elusive brother. Some from the period when she thought James was a distinctly unpleasant man and marvelled how he and Ellie could have been raised by the same sweet woman. And she was there, too. Beautiful Mary Beckett decorating her beloved Christmas tree. Another captured her in the kitchen, her happy place, apron on, preparing the food that was her language of love.

Kate sat at her computer, mesmerised. Unlike Ellie's usual haphazard approach to life, she'd organised the photographs in neat chronological order. Like a student of history, Kate could track the tumultuous life and love she'd shared with James. He wasn't in the early ones, and then suddenly he was in all of them. Anyone looking at these could zero in on the time when she had admitted that, despite her better judgment, she loved him.

Hours went by and day became dusk. She only dragged herself away from the computer when she realised lunch hadn't occurred to her and she now risked missing dinner, too. Thank god for Uber eats. Food was on its way.

While waiting, she made herself a gin and tonic, deliberately flaunting the no-alcohol directive of the doctor. One wouldn't hurt–for old times' sake. The crisp flavour never failed. One mouthful transported her with a rush of clarity, back to those early London days. She'd never drunk gin till then. Just walked into a bar and thought "when in Rome" as the bored barman turned to her, his face expectant.

The takeaways didn't disappoint. She prised the lid off the plastic container and a spicy rush of steam twirled upwards, its smell tantalising and making her empty stomach growl in anticipation. She grabbed some stalks of fresh coriander from the little pot on the windowsill, chopped it roughly and sprinkled it over the top. It was her favourite dish—Pad Thai, sweet and tangy, the smooth nuttiness of the peanut garnish and the extra zing of the coriander.

Although not having eaten since breakfast, she only managed a small dent in the meal. She emptied the remains into a container, stashing it in the fridge. Maybe for tomorrow's lunch. Copious leftovers were yet another small reminder of how much her life had changed.

There was one album she'd put off opening. Barra. It was an agonising reminder that not only was Mary gone, but now her son. Be brave, she told herself, pouring another gin to provide courage. And with a click, rows of images appeared on her screen.

Scrolling through them reminded her that despite the sad reason behind that trip, there had been fun as well. The daring plane trip with James freaking out. There was one of Ellie and her, just after they'd landed. Laughing in exhilaration at having survived the disconcerting beach landing. Behind them, a young blonde-haired man smiled indulgently as they delayed him and the other passengers to get this shot. For a moment she thought he looked familiar, but then thought again and moved on. What a trip it had been. It certainly stirred some memories. Walking on beaches of exquisite beauty. A great little pub and an unexpectedly delicious cafe. The trip to the Kisimul Castle.

The castle featured in quite a few pictures, some even tourist brochure worthy. Ellie had captured it from some interesting angles. One in particular drew her in. Perhaps taken from down on the shoreline, when Ellie had left them to go fossicking.

The curtain wall loomed solid and impressive. There was a figure on the wall, with shoulder-length blonde hair, the wind whipping it into flying tendrils, but it wasn't her. Too tall for a start. It was a man. His white t-shirt and faded jeans contrasted with the sky, gloomy with threatening dark thunderheads. A last desperate shaft of sunlight stabbed through the clouds. It illuminated him, so he almost glowed with an unearthly light. She peered in at it, intrigued. She hit the magnification, hoping to reveal his features. But the image was smudgy, only a suggestion of a profile. Just enough to stir something in the depths of her brain.

It's Alex, she thought, her subconscious mind automatically providing an answer to a question she hadn't asked. In fact, her mind seemed to have totally escaped her control and was now dancing off in wild directions all of its own, as it played with the words of a raucous version of a popular song they'd all sung at drunken student parties:

Alex. Alex. Who the fuck is Alex?

CHAPTER 46

Photograph

Auckland, New Zealand - April 2021

KATE LAY ON THE sofa in her study. At first, when they'd earmarked it for a nursery, she'd avoided the room. The pastel walls projected an air of reproach, highlighting her inability to provide the occupant it desired. Even after the specialist confirmed she wasn't the problem, Kate was reluctant to put anything in there. Her subconscious mind, clinging to the slim hope of a baby, refused to let her offer the room for any other purpose.

But the day came when she'd accepted that the spare bedroom next to theirs would never fulfil that purpose, and with a swathe of white paint erased the nursery for good. In its place, she created her own retreat, surrounding herself with furniture and objects that made her happy.

Of all those special things, her favourite was her grandmother's writing desk. The desk was the only piece of furniture she'd brought from the old house. It was an anomaly amongst the mass produced and functional mid-century pieces that had populated Vera and Bill's home.

She remembered the day it came into her family. They'd been on holiday, a rare occurrence. In Rotorua, Kate tried to appear enthused about the tourist attractions. The bubbling mud and fizzing geysers were intriguing, but she struggled with the foul-smelling miasma that blanketed the town and was relieved when they loaded the Kingswood and headed for home. On the trip back, in the centre of a small rural town, Vera had insisted they stop for a nice cup of tea.

Antique shops flanked the suitable tea room she'd spotted. Bill grumbled at his wife's inevitable detour into one of them, but as usual, he indulged her in this small pleasure. She loved to potter amongst the crowded wares, castoffs from other people's lives, returning to the car with a pretty teacup or milk jug and finding a suitable spot to display it at home. Kate could still remember the surprise on his face this time when Vera climbed back into the car, announcing she had bought the most delightful little writing desk which the nice man offered to deliver the next week.

It was a beautiful but unusual piece. The oak glowed a deep warm brown, the varnished surface, unmarked and shiny from over eighty years of polishing. Even now, Kate loved running her hands over the smoothly rounded, bobbin-turned legs with their regular curves. However, what made the desk special and had attracted Vera to it were the drawer fronts. Carved faces peered out from amongst swirling leaves. The 'Green Man', according to the antique dealer. Kate had seen other representations of the 'Green Man' that were somewhat sinister, but theirs, with a cheeky expression permanently etched on his face, hinted at magic and mystery in the forest home he inhabited.

Vera loved that desk. She would sit at it writing letters home. The wafer thin paper was so delicate that you could almost see through it. Sometimes she'd send aerograms. On these she'd fill the page with rows penned in a neat hand, and then if she hadn't fitted all the news, would rotate the page writing in a circuit around the edges. Inside the desk she stored letters she'd received, birthday cards, her important papers, and photographs.

It was the photographs Kate pulled out today. She knew her memories of the earlier part of her life were still clear, not needing photos to fill in the detail. The doctors suggested that, like an Alzheimer's patient, she'd struggle with recent memories rather than those etched in her mind from the more distant past.

But it would be fun to go through these relics of her childhood. The thought of doing so brought back fond thoughts of her grandmother. Sometimes they'd spend a wet afternoon thumbing through these pictures. Vera would always say, "I must get an album to put them in." But she'd forget, and the photographs remained tucked away in their Kodak paper envelopes, arranged in strict chronological order.

The first envelope was the oldest. In these pictures, her grandparents were still young—perhaps in their forties? Not much older than she was now. One showed them relaxing on a tartan picnic blanket, fish and chips clad in newspaper spread beside them. And there was little Kate, at only six or seven, hair bleached white by the sun, as she squinted at the camera. In the background was Bill's treasured golden Kingswood. He'd loved that car, owning it right until the day he died. Probably a collector's item now. She wondered who'd taken the shot—perhaps a friend or passerby?

The next was of her at the beach below the house. She could see the Tor in the distance. She clutched a bucket and a spade and was placing the finishing touches to a lopsided sandcastle. Vera sat smiling beside her. It was hard to tell who was more proud, the sandcastle builder or the grandmother. Happy times.

There were many more tracking moments in her childhood: birthdays, starting school, a new kitten, a sports day. In the last group, she was a teenager. One picture showed her flanked by her grandparents, taller than Vera, and fast gaining on Bill. The medal around her neck glinted in the sunlight as she presented it to the camera with pride. A sailing win.

Thinking of sailing highlighted her guilt at abandoning *Lorelei*, who languished unloved down in the marina. Another hurdle to overcome, another reminder that there were so many things she would never again experience with James.

Right at the back of the stack, she came to an envelope, much thinner and newer than the rest. She read the date on the front: March 2010. Written in her own neat teacher script. She pulled out the contents and fanned through them. There were only five photographs.

The first a beach scene, perhaps Northland in summer, as the pohutukawa were in full bloom. The second showed the view across the same stretch of coastline, but this time from a much higher vantage point, as if sitting in the trees, the branches garlanded with the abundant brush-like red flowers. Postcard perfect. She sensed it was somewhere she'd been, but couldn't quite place it. Oh well, even perfectly healthy people didn't remember every minute detail of their life.

The next photograph seemed odd, out of place. She and five others seated in a pub with drinks on the table. One man raised a glass in a toast towards the camera. The walls above sported Christmas decorations, so it must have been some kind of seasonal celebration.

She couldn't identify any of her companions, including the man next to her, whose hand casually draped around her shoulder. She looked relaxed. So comfortable with the gesture that he must have been someone she knew, a friend perhaps.

It was also a mystery where it was taken. The pub had to be English and that would also fit with the time frame. Christmas 2009 before their return to New Zealand. But she had no recollection of ever being in that place. This was a shock, as her impression of the memory loss from her injury was that it was minimal. But now she wondered.

And where was James? Maybe it had been a work Christmas function. But she rejected that—too many men for it to be a group of teachers. When she looked more closely at the beaming faces, she saw a certain likeness between them. Brothers and sisters, she realised. In fact, the man beside her and one other were so alike they might have been twins.

She picked up a fourth photograph. It showed one man from the pub picture, the one who'd been next to her. And to her astonishment, he was without a doubt sitting on the little back deck of her old house, the one that had stood here. From his clothing—a t-shirt and shorts—it was probably summer. Apart from his dress, he could have been transported directly from that wintery English pub scene to summer here in New Zealand. It was as if no time had passed between the two pictures. He was staring at the camera, laughing, a beer in his hand. She peered at the label—Steinlager, probably from her fridge. And who was on the other side of the camera? Was it her?

However, while the first photos were intriguing, perhaps a little disturbing, the last photograph was incomprehensible. It featured the same man in full Scottish traditional dress, wearing a kilt, in a tartan of earthy greens and subdued blues. And while seeing herself next to him was surprising, her own outfit was even more startling.

It was, without doubt, a wedding dress. The man stood, his face tilted towards her, a look of pride and love so clearly directed at her. And the expression on her face was one of pure joy. She couldn't recall any other photos that had captured her happiness so clearly. Not even those of her wedding to James in Greece.

In the background, the distinctive peaks of the Remarkables wore only the faintest dusting of snow, suggesting summer. She was sure that this was the jetty at Arcadia Bay, the same spot where she'd stood only weeks ago when she'd gone on that holiday break with Nicky. The unsteady feeling that had come over her at the time was nothing compared to this overwhelming sensation.

There was only one person with whom she could share this discovery. Only one person who wouldn't think she was completely mad. Ellie.

Even those who didn't know her might discern Ellie's love of all things new age from her bizarre dress sense alone. On census forms in the box for indicating religion, she wrote 'Wiccan'. She believed in reincarnation, astrology, and the healing power of crystals.

Down-to-earth Hugh humoured his wife's fanciful ideas, a sign of how much he loved her. He and Kate often exchanged indulgent looks as Ellie recounted some wild theory, communicating with furtive glances as if to say *We love this woman but she is totally bonkers!* What on earth would he think of this? He would probably decide that now she too was bonkers. She'd ask Ellie to swear not to tell him. Or anyone else.

By morning, she'd changed her mind at least ten times over. Part of her needed to confirm that what she had found was real, not a figment of her imagination, not some Photoshop trick, and most definitely not a sign that her injured brain was struggling.

Part of her wanted to burn those pictures. If they no longer existed, then she wouldn't have to face the reality that the inexplicable had happened. Was happening. She didn't know which. Her world was only righting itself. It was inevitable; following where those pictures led, would turn it upside down again. And she wasn't sure she was strong enough to face that.

In the end, she resolved to talk to Ellie, but not yet. She'd leave the photographs in their secret hiding place, work on her recovery for a little longer. Then, when she judged herself strong enough to weather the storm they might unleash, only then would she act. However, that resolve evaporated within a week.

She woke each morning exhausted, reluctant to drag her still weary body out of bed. Only the thought of her neighbour's dog expecting their daily walk shamed her into moving. The problem was a crippling lack of sleep, even more annoying because it was only in the last month she'd overcome an ongoing pattern of disrupted sleep stemming from her brain injury. She'd spent countless nights listening to ambient music, calming voices of actors reading stories in soothing tones, and obediently following breathing routines. Now a man named Alex was haunting her dreams.

She stood watching the hypnotic whizz of the blender. The morning walk always left her ravenous. Nothing like a loaded smoothie to quell the gnawing in her stomach. The vast kitchen was one of her favourite places to be. It wasn't only the dazzling array of appliances and sprawling granite bench tops. Nor the drawers that glided open with a whisper, revealing high quality dinnerware in neat stacks. It wasn't the pantries with their shelves of curated ingredients representing a multitude of cuisines. No, it was the way the dramatic floor to ceiling glass doors framed the view of the bay.

To anyone it would be picture perfect, but to Kate, it was that and more. This was the scene she'd met each morning of her childhood. She remembered sitting at the Formica dining table, Vera making Milo while she chipped away at two bricks of Weet-Bix surrounded by a creamy milk moat and topped with crunchy white sugar crystals.

"Come on, love, stop daydreaming–eat up," her grandmother urged. "You don't want to be late for school."

She slipped into a daydream now, lulled by the drone of the machine. In her mind, she saw the French doors flung open, allowing the sunshine to flood in. On the little deck Bill had built was a small wrought-iron table and chairs. Not the most comfortable. But Vera had her heart set on them and so no one ever admitted to the way the unforgiving cold metal left the leaf patterns imprinted on your bum.

But it wasn't Vera she pictured sitting at that table. It was the man in the photograph. Alex: the name that wouldn't go away. Now she had an image to match it. He stalked her day and night. By the time she'd finished the smoothie, she'd made her decision.

Kate sat at her laptop, attaching the scanned photographs to the strangest email she'd ever written:

```
Ellie love, something very weird has
happened, actually has been happening
for months now.
```

I know you'll laugh, because I'm the sceptic of the two of us, and here I am admitting to something that is definitely in the realms of the unexplained. It started back in the hospital. I never told you, but when they first asked me about my husband, I couldn't even get his name right. I told them it was Alex. Odd that I should pluck that name out of the air, but I passed it off as nothing. Since then, that name has been popping up in all kinds of places, pushing its way in. And it's got worse—sometimes I even catch a glimpse of something, of someone. Strange, for sure, but I thought hey with brain injury, there's no telling what might happen, so I wrote it off as something that will probably go away. But then this happened. A week ago I found these photos tucked in the back of a drawer. You have to see them to understand why I'm freaking out here, so I've scanned them. Take a look and call me as soon as you can. I desperately need you right now, if only to tell me I'm not totally insane.

Love, K.

She took a deep breath, pushed send, and waited, knowing that on the other side of the world, soon Ellie would see them. These past months, this Alex intruding on her life had seemed the stuff of fiction. Now putting it into words, it had a strange plausibility. Especially with these images that put a face to the name.

Kate's email unleashed a flurry of phone calls back and forth. As expected, Ellie took the revelation calmly.

"Haven't I always told you, what is known is only a fraction of what there is to know." Then with her usual enthusiasm, she set to work, determined to uncover whatever strange forces were in play.

"It's simple," said Ellie. "Parallel lives. You know, like Gwyneth Paltrow in *Sliding Doors*."

"But that's fiction. And it still doesn't explain the photographs."

"No, but we know the photographs show things that didn't happen in this life. But photographs don't lie—they happened. What about *The Lake House*? Their notes to each other existed in different times. Perhaps the photos can, too?"

"Oh god, Ellie, we need more than the scripts of a few chick flicks to work out what's happening here."

She chided herself for sounding ungrateful. Desperate for Ellie's help, she should be gracious.

Ellie, however, was undeterred, as always.

"True. Which is why I've spent some time with Google. There are some pretty heavyweight scientists who would say that parallel universes are a thing. A thing they don't understand yet, but doesn't mean they're wrong. Even Stephen Hawking thought there were multiple universes. The multiverse. You should check it out."

Well, you couldn't argue with Stephen Hawking. Trust Ellie to do her homework.

"So you think that somehow bits of my other life in some other universe have become tangled with this one?"

"That's what I think. It's not impossible. Quantum physics says it's entirely possible."

"Maybe." There was hesitance in her voice.

"But the thing that intrigues me is this—if Alex exists in another version of your life, another world, does he exist in this one?"

"Oh, now you're really messing with my head."

"But you agree it's a good question?"

"It is a good question, but I'm not sure it's one I want to answer."

"Why not?"

"Well, if he does, must I do something about that? And possibly regret it? Or choose to do nothing and always wonder what might have been? It's too complicated."

"Let *me* find out. I'll do some detective work. If I find something that I think you'd want to know, I'll tell you. If not, I won't."

"Ellie, that's sweet of you. But I think that it's best we just leave him where he is for now. In some mysterious other place. Perhaps if we do that, he'll stay there. Instead of pushing his way into my world."

"If that's what you want, sweetie. Whatever you think is best for you."

"Yeah, I think that's what I want." She tried to sound convincing. "I'm going to put those photographs back where they came from. And get on with my life. This life. It's not perfect, but at least I know it's real."

And that's what she did.

CHAPTER 47

Found

Auckland, New Zealand - September 2021

KATE STOMPED HER FEET in the spongy tray, the pungent smell of disinfectant attacking her nostrils. She looked at the expectant rabble of canine cuteness, who sat poised, ready to pounce on this human.

Swinging each rubber-booted foot over the barrier, the puppies surged forward, surrounding her, an eager mass of jumping, barking, insistent paws and teeth, all scrambling for attention. She attempted to fend them off gently as she plucked sodden newspaper and scooped dollops of small but stinky poo into a large black plastic sack. A quick mop of the floor and then round two of the battle began as she attempted to layer fresh newspaper and clean blankets for the exuberant occupants of the pen.

Finally, the unpleasant tasks done, she gave into the demands of the pups, scooping each one up and revelling in the contentment as the wiggling forms relaxed in her arms, blissful faces upturned and tummies exposed for a pat. She whipped her phone out for a quick selfie with a squidgy-faced pup, and flicked it to Ellie, whose children had an insatiable appetite for adorable puppy pictures.

"Don't forget Elvis. He's been bouncing around for at least fifteen minutes. I reckon that dog has an in-built clock."

Janine's voice floated across from the laundry tub where she was furiously scrubbing feed bowls. She'd set up the rescue, and it consumed her every waking moment. "He adores you."

"Yeah, I can hear him already."

His little impatient yelps were even audible above the gushing water and the clatter of bowls. Grabbing a lead, she freed the huge, bouncy bundle of dog from his pen. Poor Elvis had been pulled from a life of misery, chained in a dirt yard, ignored and starved. With love and care, a healthy, smiling dog had emerged from the mangy flea-ridden animal he'd been on arrival.

"Come on boy, let's go."

She headed for the beach, Elvis jogging along beside her, loving this morning routine as much as she did. Daily work at the rescue gave purpose to her life. Spending time with the abandoned, neglected and abused scraps who washed up on their doorstep gave her a feeling of worth, and inspired hope that with time and love, even the most broken could become whole again.

The morning shift left her energised and ready to face the rest of the day. From a low point a year earlier, around the time of the memorial service, she'd made steady progress and was frequently amazed by the current state of both her physical and mental health. The main reason she was now out of the pit and back on level ground, back to some new normal, was her friends' relentless determination and unflagging commitment to her recovery—Nicky, Tracey, Ange—and, of course, Ellie. Wrapped in their love, it was possible to see a future, not the one she'd expected, but something beyond that terrible dark place she'd been.

And today, on this overcast morning, after a boisterous game of fetch with Elvis and an enormous stick he'd acquired, she was sitting on a bench seat at the furthermost point of the beach when she had the sudden realisation that she was happy. Not all the time, not deliriously happy, but in a small way it was definitely happiness that had crept back into her life.

She could see good in the world. And little things like early-blooming flowers that pushed their way through in her garden, the raucous call of a tui in a kowhai tree by the walkway and the company of the rambunctious Elvis, on these daily beach strolls—all brought a sense of contentment. The rawness of losing James had subsided into a gentle sadness that hovered lightly in the background. It no longer held her down as it had in those first months, where it was an overwhelming weight on her chest that crushed her until she could hardly breathe.

And she'd kept the weird flashbacks at bay. It was as if having found the photograph, pulling together the name and the face that haunted her, she could now set them aside, determined to leave whatever strange tricks time had played on her in the past. She would focus on the future.

Since the accident, she struggled with concentrating for any length of time. Work was out of the question, so volunteering at the dog rescue centre, although far from glamorous, made her feel useful. And the tiny lost and damaged souls who found their way there, yet remained full of unremitting joy in the way that only dogs can, were a constant reminder that it was possible to put adversity behind you and find happiness in the moment. The days were full and productive, but she could go home to sleep if she needed. As a bonus, it gave her something to chat about to Ellie, so the conversation wasn't all one-sided.

Ellie, a busy mother, was adept at juggling a range of activities, both her own and the children's, in her whirlwind Ellie style. There was always something happening in her life. She rang every Monday night—Monday morning in England. She'd shuffle the three older children out the door to school, settle little Jamie with some toys, and call her friend on the other side of the world.

So, hearing Ellie's voice when she answered the phone at eight o'clock on a Thursday morning, Kate was immediately on alert. Thoughts of all kinds of possible disasters rushed into her brain.

"Oh my God, Ellie—what's wrong?"

"Kate, nothing's wrong. But make sure you're sitting down. I've got something important to tell you."

"OK," said Kate, both relieved and uneasy at the same time.

"I've found him," she announced. She rushed on before Kate could stop her. "I know you told me to leave it be, and I did. I didn't look for him, but I found him anyway. And I thought maybe I shouldn't tell you, but I couldn't. Not if there might be a chance for you to be happy. I've found your Alex."

"But...I don't know. This is crazy. I don't know what happened or even if something really did happen," she protested.

"Kate, listen to me. I loved my brother so much. Losing him was hard." Kate could hear the crack in her voice. "And you loved him, and I treasure you for that. You and I will make sure that he's always a part of us. But you can't spend the rest of your life on your own. You need to find someone else to love, and to love you. And no matter how weird it is, that photograph—it shows that this someone else might be easier to find than you think. Why spend years waiting and hoping, when there's a person who at some time, in some place, you loved enough to marry him? And he loved you enough, too."

"But what if he's not the same person? He could have the same name, look the same, but be completely different. He might hate me."

"Well, that's what we're going to find out," said Ellie in her 'this is what we're doing and there'll be no arguing' tone. Typical bloody bulldozer Beckett behaviour.

"No, Ellie." Kate tried to sound adamant.

"OK Kate, I'm going to say some things that I've wanted to say for a long time. Please don't hang up. Hear me out."

Kate heard a sharp intake of breath as Ellie paused before beginning.

"First, I say this as someone who loves you. You are my sister, my friend." There was another pause as she took another deep breath.

"For as long as I've known you, I've stood by and watched you accept whatever comes your way, whatever other people have asked of you, even if it wasn't what you wanted. When you wanted a nice wedding, you let James take over and decide otherwise. He took the house you loved and replaced it with a mansion that was *his* idea of a house to love."

Kate knew what was coming next. She closed her eyes, knowing it would be said, had to be said.

"And when you wanted nothing more in the world than a baby, he put aside how much his decision hurt you. And I know it hurt you terribly. But you kept that hurt inside you and carried on. I loved my brother, but all those times I wished you'd fought for what you wanted. He always got what he wanted."

Part of her railed against these hard truths, but deep inside she knew Ellie was right. James had written the script of their life together. She'd delivered the lines exactly as expected, never improvising, never ad-libbing, never questioning. It was the price she'd paid for his love, his faithfulness, his devotion. And it was a price she'd been willing to pay for the certainty that he would never leave her. But he *had* left her.

"Kate, I know you can fight. You didn't achieve all those sailing trophies without setting your eye on the prize and going for it. And God knows, you've been in the fight of your life this past year. You want a partner, you want a family. Please—fight for it."

A second chance to love, to be loved? A second chance to have the child she'd yearned for? Yes, it was worth fighting for. She would fight.

"OK," she whispered. "I'm still not sure this is the right thing to do. But let's hear what you've found."

"I was sitting in the hairdresser's today. Getting my colour done. So while I'm waiting for it to take, she puts some magazines down in front of me. They're the usual trashy sort—full of celebrity gossip, but you know a bit of a guilty pleasure to read now and then. Well, I was flicking through one, and there are pictures of the BAFTAs. I took a closer look. Thought I might recognise some familiar faces from James's crowd. And then I see this picture of a guy from some new fantasy series they've all gone mad for. And it's him."

"Oh my god, how can you be sure?"

"I pulled up the photos you showed me on my phone. And either this guy has an identical twin, or a doppelgänger, or it's him. And the caption below—*Star of The Shadow King, Alex MacLeod, was a fan favourite on the red carpet.*' He's looking straight at the camera, and that smile. I'm sure it's him. I ripped the page out and stuffed it in my handbag. Switch to Facetime and I'll show you."

As Ellie's phone hovered shakily over the creased magazine page, Kate had to admit that the face staring back, although a little grainy, was without doubt an older version of the man she had seen in brief flashes. And the man beside her in the photographs. They'd both assumed he was just some ordinary guy, someone she'd met in London, someone who'd followed her here. But he wasn't. Well, not in this life, anyway. In this life, he was a celebrity. She'd never paid too much attention to celebrities. She and Ellie had just thought them part of James's work and apart from the odd ones, like Henry and Lydia, most hadn't entered into her world for more than brief moments. She wondered if, in one of those brief moments, this man's path had crossed hers.

"So, you agree? It's him?"

"Yes, it's him. But what do we do now? He's a TV and movie star. It's not as if I can just walk up to him and introduce myself, is it? Even if I could track him down, he's bound to be surrounded by minders to stop crazed fans getting too close."

"Well, I've already given that some thought." That sounded ominous. When Ellie thought too much, anything could happen. "I'll call you in a few days when I've done more research. Good old Google. What would we do without it?"

CHAPTER 48

Questions and Answers

Auckland, New Zealand - September 2021

TRUE TO HER WORD, Ellie invested the next few days and nights trawling the internet. She left poor Hugh to sort the kids and the dog, while she compiled a dossier of information about Alex MacLeod worthy of MI5.

It seemed that Alex's career had been a bit of a rollercoaster over the years, but was now at an all-time high with the runaway success of the fantasy series. The TV producers, having secured the rights for a whole trilogy of much-loved books, would keep Alex busy for two more seasons.

And through the books, there was a huge ready-made fanbase. The fans, delighted with the way he'd brought the title character to life, were now clambering for him to engage with them at fantasy and sci-fi conventions. And that had given Ellie an idea.

"There's a big Comic Con happening over here. You know where fans get to meet their idols. He's on the guest list. What about you use that as an opportunity to meet him?"

"Pretend I'm a fan?"

"Yeah, but once you talk to him, maybe he'll feel the connection? Realise you're *not* another fan?"

"I don't know Ellie," she said, unable to keep the doubt from her voice. "It's a long way to come for a tiny chance. Never mind that if I leave New Zealand, I could be trapped up there for months. Getting back in to the country is a lottery. And even if I *did* come, I'm not sure asking him to sign a poster and a quick photo pose is going to be enough to connect with him. It'll be a production line—meet, greet, sign, a hug for the photograph—and then onto the next person."

"Ah well, that's where the upside to this whole virus situation comes into play. Things aren't stable enough yet for the Comic Con to be in person. They're not doing the usual sessions. All of it is online. Which is an advantage. It means that even from the other side of the world, you can go to events."

"Isn't that going to make it even less likely that we can connect?"

"No, I don't think so. There's one event that's perfect—very limited ticket numbers, very expensive. I think it's your best chance. It's a panel discussion. Alex and two other stars, the producer, a scriptwriter, and the book author. Only twenty people can take part in the live event, then afterwards they charge others to watch the replay. It's a sort of conversation, much more intimate. So they talk and you get to ask them questions."

"Yeah, like *'So can you tell me Alex, what have you been doing since our marriage in New Zealand back in 2010?'* That sort of question?"

"Well, maybe not quite that direct, but surely you could think of one that might trigger some kind of recognition?"

"I don't know Ellie. It seems a long shot."

Kate didn't want to pour cold water on Ellie's idea, but she thought the chances of this being the route to connect with Alex were slim. And if she was honest, the thought of speaking to Alex MacLeod terrified her. It was one thing to look at pictures of him or watch his performances on TV. But to engage with him, one-on-one, albeit over a computer link, that was a massive step.

And all the possibilities of what might happen as a result also terrified her. If there wasn't the slightest glimmer of recognition, it could crush her. Send her back into the depths of despair so soon after clawing her way out. Or if he did recognise her, well, then she'd be heading into frightening, uncharted waters. She had no idea how she could explain the unexplainable to him without him thinking her completely mad.

"It's the best idea I've had so far, and it's better than doing nothing. If I can get a ticket, will you do it?"

She could never say no to Ellie. It seemed ungrateful turning down her big-hearted friend, especially when she was trying so hard to ensure Kate's future happiness.

"Ok, if you can get a ticket, I'll do it." She agreed, trying not to let her voice communicate the doubt and fear.

However, even getting a ticket proved to be a sticking point. All snapped up within minutes of going on sale months earlier, despite the exorbitant price tag. But with the relentless Ellie Beckett on the case, this hurdle was no deterrent. Ellie used every contact of her brother's that she could think of, and there were many. James had known everyone in the industry, and she phoned, emailed, and even had coffee with anyone she remotely thought could help. And sure enough, within two days, she was near the top of the waitlist.

Kate awoke from sleep one night, the insistent sound of her phone jarring, and only answered because it was Ellie's ringtone. Midday in the UK was midnight in New Zealand. Ellie, very familiar with the time difference, would only call for something big.

The voice screaming down the line confirmed it.

"I've got it!" Ellie yelled, her excitement outdoing that of even the most ardent fan. She had the precious e-ticket in her possession.

"I'll send it through to you now. You need to think of your question and send it to the link. There's a moderator who'll sort the questions and on the day they'll invite you to ask yours when it's your turn."

The abrupt waking, as well as the nervous churning of her stomach, left Kate feeling sick. The reality that this crazy scheme was going ahead hit her full force, leaving her unsure of what to say. But she pulled herself together and put on an optimistic voice.

"Ellie, that's amazing. Thank you for all you've done."

"You're so welcome, and the best way you can thank me is to come up with the perfect question."

That was the problem. What was the perfect question? Kate spent hours, day after day wrestling with the same impossible task, the mountainous pile of scrunched paper all over her desk evidence of her dissatisfaction with every idea of hers so far. It seemed to capture all her waking moments.

However, with the deadline for submitting the question looming, and ready to admit defeat, she awoke one morning with a clear head and a brilliant idea. There was no doubt that images of certain places triggered memories of Alex—if they were memories. She would ask a question that might induce the same response in him.

On the day of the event, Kate was out of bed at five a.m. She showered and set about doing her hair and makeup. She was out of practice but, checking in the mirror, felt pleased with her efforts. They'd cut her hair short in the hospital after the accident. Since then, she'd let it grow and now it hung at shoulder length, straight and glossy. In fact, it looked similar to what it had been back in 2009 when she had supposedly met Alex.

She kept the makeup light and natural in keeping with the time of day. She imagined the other participants, these as yet unknown women, doing the same. Although, as it was going live at seven p.m. in the UK, perhaps they'd have glammed themselves up more to suit an evening event. But no doubt they'd be busy going through the same drill: putting final touches to their outfit, checking the computer and internet connection, and ensuring a pleasant background for the zoom meeting. At least living on her own, she wouldn't have to worry about random children or animals making an unwelcome appearance.

All was quiet and still as she sat with the link in front of her, the clock in the corner of her screen ticking over the minutes with painful slowness. When it was time, she moved the mouse, making one wary click on the blue button. 'The meeting host will let you in soon,' said the message. She sipped her coffee, hoping the caffeine would help her keep her wits about her.

And then the screen burst into life, a montage of faces smiling and expectant. Seeing her own image amongst them looking far too serious, she attempted to mirror the others, rather than let the fear—yes, it was fear—show for all to see.

Next, the pictures of the panel blinked into life along the top of the screen. She recognised the cast members from her second binge-watch of the series that had rocketed Alex to his current fame.

And there he was, a dazzling smile, blue eyes sparkling in anticipation. From what she'd read, he was somewhat of an introvert, forced to make a conscious effort when the limelight shone on him, as it was at this moment. But you'd never guess it from his relaxed posture, as he leaned back in the too-small chair, his long legs spilling out in front of him.

The moderator leapt straight in with the first person. To her relief, Kate's turn was much later. The woman was skilled at her job, navigating from one person to the next with ease, questions and answers flowing seamlessly. Each speaker's image appeared larger and to the fore as they responded to the questions of their adoring fans. As the show's main character, he had to contend with more than the others. His face, almost life size on her screen, was unnerving.

Gazing at it, for the first time in ages, those odd sensations returned, as if she knew more than the face, but the person behind it. However, listening to his beautifully modulated voice soothed her nerves. If velvet had a sound, this would be it.

The minutes sped by. She caught sight of a small blinking message in the lower corner of her screen. Her question was next. She reminded herself to breathe, slow and deep. By the time the moderator spoke her name, a surreal feeling of calm washed over her.

"So next we have a question for you, Alex. And it's from Kate, who's all the way across the world from us in New Zealand."

"Hi Kate." Alex beamed at her. "I believe you're up early on my account. Hope you've got a coffee there?" His friendly smile set her at ease. She raised her coffee mug into view, smiling back at him. "Pleased to see that," he said.

"Now Kate, go ahead with your question please," the moderator invited her.

She took one last breath to steady her voice and began. She'd practised her question so many times over the past few days, she didn't need to read it, although it sat typed large and bold in front of her just in case.

"Alex, I've watched many of the different movies and series you've been in. This job takes you all over the world. What are the most memorable places you've been to, and why?"

"Great question." He looked thoughtful. "Well, you may know that I've been to New Zealand. Back in 2010, I did a series there. And it was certainly memorable. It's a lot like Scotland—but with better weather," he laughed. "But the beaches and the mountains, it's stunning. I mean, the entire country is amazing. The place that stood out for me was Queenstown—flying in over the mountains and then dropping down into that little airport, and the lake. It's pretty hard to beat."

"Yeah, I love it there," she said.

"And now you've got me thinking, hmmm, perhaps another place that I'd rate as special would be Barra—similar in that there's an interesting plane journey to get there. In fact, you land on the beach, which is disconcerting. It's an island off the west coast of Scotland. We didn't film there, but I went there to do some research for a project. It's special, spectacular beaches. Well worth a visit."

"I agree," she said quietly, unable to suppress a slight smile. "I've been there."

"For real?" he said. "Well, you know what I mean, then." He studied her, intrigued and perhaps with a hint of disbelief. She was sure fans invented stuff all the time in attempts to capture his interest. "So what are the chances that Kate from New Zealand would have been to Barra? That's a surprise."

"I lived in London for a while. Some of my friends there were MacNeill descendants. We went to visit for the family connection."

Now he accepted she wasn't bluffing. "Ah, I see. Hey that castle on the island is pretty cool isn't it? The stronghold of the MacNeills. Definitely memorable."

And then it was over. The moderator needed to keep things moving, inviting the next person to put their question, this time to the director.

From there on, it was a blur. Kate heard, but didn't process any of the remaining conversation. Her eyes remained fixed on Alex MacLeod. He appeared preoccupied, a polite smile on his face, joining in the laughter but not contributing to the banter between the panel. Had she stirred something in the back of his brain? Something that lurked there in the shadows that he himself might not yet have any conscious knowledge of? She hoped so.

There was something lurking in the back of her mind, too. The moment the video link ended, she flicked over to Ellie's albums of photographs. She went straight to the one labelled 'Barra'.

It was him. She was positive. The man in the background of their airport selfie. A younger version of the man she'd spoken to today, but there was no doubt it *was* him. And the last photo, the curtain wall at Kisimul. In this one, the photographic evidence was unclear, but she trusted her gut. Ellie had captured Alex MacLeod at the castle, at the same time she'd been wandering around it.

Two hours later, Kate grabbed at her jangling phone. She knew who it would be.

"Oh my god, that was awesome," said Ellie. "I've watched the replay. Of all the places in the world he's been, he talks about Queenstown! A place where you were with him!"

"You think so? Maybe that was just because he heard them say I'm from New Zealand. Everyone visits Queenstown."

"And then Barra. Well, that's completely out of left field. There was no reason for him to mention that, and yet you've been there too."

"Ah, well, there's something I need to tell you about Barra," she said. She herself still couldn't quite accept what the photos showed.

"What about Barra?"

"The photos you sent me last year—he's in two of them."

For a moment, Ellie didn't speak, the shock squashing her ebullience.

"For real?" she said. "Let me check."

"It's the first one at the airport, and the last one at the castle."

Kate could hear Ellie's quickened breathing and her fingers bashing on the keyboard, demanding it deliver what she sought.

"Oh, my god! You are so right. Bloody amazing. So without prompting, he comes up with two out of two. That's more than coincidence."

Kate couldn't argue with that. There had been constant challenges to her logical mind over the past year, but these were undeniable facts. This was no coincidence. Nor was the power of the sensations that washed over her when she gazed at the pictures, like a freak wave across the bow, coming out of nowhere and frightening in its ferocity.

"And he was different after that. I've watched it twice through and there's no doubt he sort of went back inside himself from there on. Kate, it was you who made the difference."

Kate didn't want to dampen Ellie's enthusiasm. She thought of other possibilities. Maybe he had relaxed knowing he didn't have more questions. Perhaps he was tired and relieved he didn't have to maintain a bright, energetic face for much longer. But the truth was in the replay. She herself had watched it and rejected those ideas. Seeing that subtle change in him ignited a small spark of optimism. Fuel for what was now a slow, burning hope.

"OK, so even if we call that a small win, we need more, a lot more. Next suggestion?"

"You need to get close to him as a person, ordinary Alex, not Alex the actor."

"Right, so how do we do that?" said Kate, suspecting Ellie had an idea already.

"We need to track him down outside work-related things. We find out where he lives, where he goes, what he does, and then make a plan to get you to one of those places." As usual, Ellie made it sound straightforward.

"OK, that's what we'll do," she agreed, trying to sound confident, but in her pragmatic way, still harbouring a secret fear of failure.

CHAPTER 49

Stalker

Auckland, New Zealand - November 2021

ALTHOUGH RELUCTANT TO ADMIT it, Kate was now a stalker. And not a very successful one. In this day and age, tracking someone down should be simple, particularly a person with a public profile. But in fact, it seemed the opposite was true. Ordinary people flaunted their every move, every meal, even intimate details of their relationships on social media for everyone to see. Public figures were far more cautious about showing themselves to the world.

In the two weeks since the Comic Con panel, she'd joined endless Facebook fan groups, followed numerous Instagram and Twitter accounts—anything or anyone with the slightest link to Alex MacLeod. Her inboxes overflowed with information about him. All it revealed was that Alex was an intensely private person who hid behind an almost impenetrable protective wall. She needed a helping hand up and over that wall if this mad plan had any chance of success.

She sat in the TV room one evening mulling it over while half-heartedly watching an old movie. Her inability to concentrate wasn't being helped by the Alex problem. No matter what, he was always prowling in the background, a clever partner in a game of hide-and-seek, taunting her playfully, but staying out of reach. Thoughts of quitting entered her head, but thinking of Ellie and how invested she was in this search, she rejected them and, with a surge of guilt, went back to her computer. When Ellie phoned the next morning, Kate could say, hand on her heart, that she was still trying. But failing.

Ellie was undeterred. "Sounds like it might be time to call in a few more favours. Leave it with me. I've got an idea."

Twenty-four hours and a few phone calls were all it took for Ellie to produce the details of where and when they could find Alex Macleod. It was staggering how easy it was when you knew the right people.

"I'm almost scared to ask how you did it."

Kate could never be sure that Ellie wouldn't take things a step too far. She wasn't the most subtle person.

"No need to fear. Nothing untoward. I just asked Rhonda to help me."

"Rhonda? As in James's PA Rhonda?"

"Yes. She's still at the production company, you know. One of the other guys snapped her up to come and work for him." Kate felt a little guilty. In the aftermath of the accident, she hadn't stopped to even think of how it impacted on those like Rhonda who'd depended on James. She was glad the company had looked after her. "But the old loyalty to James is still there. She was so happy to talk to me. Reminisce a little. You know, even though he was tough, she loved working for him. And then when I dropped in a request for some help, well, she got onto it straight away."

"How on earth did you explain it? I mean, didn't she think it was a bit weird?"

"Not at all. You have to remember, for years she's been in a job where you do what the boss asks without question. So when I said you'd been sorting through James's things and found some paperwork that you wanted to discuss with Alex MacLeod, she didn't ask any more. Said she'd put through a call to his agent's PA and get back to me."

"Wow. Just like that."

"Yes. And just like that, a message came back. Unfortunately, once he finishes his current project, Alex isn't available till somewhere in the middle of January." Kate's heart sank a little. That was three months away. "But..." Now, even in that one word, she could sense a bubble of excitement as Ellie paused for effect. "Alex will be in his hometown of Ballenaig in Scotland visiting his family for Christmas."

She hadn't realised she'd been holding her breath. It came out in a rush. She felt weak and was glad she was already lying down on the bed.

"Kate? Did you hear me?"

"Yes. I heard." Her voice came out in a whisper as her brain struggled to process Ellie's revelation.

"So you and I, my love, are having Christmas in Scotland. Our search is over."

"Yeah, although now I think I'm even more scared. The livestream was bad enough."

"Remember, you don't have to do this on your own. I'll come with you. Whatever it takes, we are going to do this, and we'll do it together."

"Thanks Ellie. You're amazing."

After they ended their conversation, Kate opened her laptop. She sought out the town of Ballenaig, flipping from the map onto Google Street View. It was an appealing little place, very traditional, with old stone buildings and whitewashed houses. And as she took a virtual stroll through the streets on her screen, the strangest thing happened. When she closed her eyes, it was as if she was still walking, still seeing. Somewhere inside her, she knew this place.

Next, she wandered back through the folder she'd named '*Alex*'. Photos, video, the replay of their Comic Con conversation, so many images of this man. And each time she saw his face, an unsettling rush of knowledge and emotion flooded in, uninvited but no longer unwelcome.

She pored over the photos of his family she'd found on Facebook, read their names, the posts about their lives, and they too seemed familiar and comforting. An echo of her past. And maybe her future.

CHAPTER 50

Waifs and Strays

Ballenaig, Scotland - December 2021

KATE SAT GAZING OUT the window at the thirteenth-century cathedral. She took a cautious sip of her tea. She always made it how James had liked it. Strong and hot, it hit the spot.

Looking at the churchyard, she had the strangest feeling. It was more than déjà vu. That was merely a passing shadow, a picture not quite in focus. This was different. Bright ribbons of memory wove through her mind, the details outlined in startling clarity. She was certain that it had been snowing the last time she had looked out on this scene. Today the ancient graves sat uncovered, but the glowering sky suggested that by nightfall they would have a blanket of snow.

Ellie lounged on the bed, still engrossed in a book she'd been reading on the journey. It was a long trip from Brighton. Kate was still in awe of Ellie's commitment to her. Not many women would leave their young family at Christmas time to go on a crazy expedition to Scotland. Particularly one that had no certainty of success.

Ellie reassured her that the kids would be fine. Hugh's mother had arrived and set about a flurry of baking and organising. Wrapped presents sat under the tree. And she would Facetime with them in the morning to share in the fun. Hugh himself was a marvel, with his calm acceptance of his wife racing off on a mysterious trip with her friend. Not delving into details of why they were going. And so she was here with Kate, Christmas Eve, Ballenaig, Scotland.

Kate's own journey to Scotland hadn't been easy. There'd been the nerve-wracking wait for a negative Covid test, the spectre of the virus threatening to derail her plans until that welcome text saying she was clear and free to travel.

Flying always took its toll, even in business class, but spending thirty hours with no respite from a mask, well, that was an unpleasant added necessity. She was glad that she'd allowed a couple of days in London to sleep off the effects before flying up here, although it had been hard rattling around in the big Bayswater house; so much James's rather than her own. But facing it had been another hurdle to get over and she'd managed.

They had done their homework over the past two months. Not that it was demanding detective work, and Kate's pursuit of the MacLeod family was relentless.

People like Alex presented a carefully curated version of themselves that, when you examined it closely, said little at all. But ordinary people, like his brothers and his sister, were willing to reveal their lives on social media for the entire world to see. Including the fact that the MacLeod siblings were planning, as it seemed they did every year, to meet at a local pub called The Tappit Hen on Christmas Eve. One simple post on Sarah MacLeod's Facebook page, a shared memory of Christmas past, had provided the answer to the difficult problem of exactly when and where they might find Alex.

"Right," Ellie said, reaching the end of a chapter. She slurped the last of her tea. "Time for me to go." They had decided that Ellie would check out the pub and report back. "It's definitely the pub in the photograph." Ellie had found the website of the little local tavern. "That blackboard with the Christmas menu behind you in the photograph—it's the same."

She headed out the door and soon Kate saw her emerge on the footpath below, her face wearing that classic determined Ellie expression. A woman on a mission and Kate knew what that mission was. Her stomach lurched with fear and excitement.

It wasn't long before Ellie came striding back up the street. Her blaze of hair, partly tamed by a knitted beanie with long strands splayed out over the jewel green of her coat, gave her the appearance of an exotic frilled lizard. She wore a look of satisfied triumph on her face.

"He's there," she blurted, bursting into their hotel room moments later.

"Oh, my god." A fluttering sensation of nausea twirled in Kate's stomach.

"Who is he with?"

"There's another guy, similar age, same hair colour, a wee bit shorter."

"Yes, his brother, Andrew."

"And there's a woman, looks to be with the guy. Short brown hair. Pretty."

"Yep, Andrew's wife, Sam. Little, like a tiny bird."

By getting close to his family, Kate knew an awful lot about him. So much so that she was uncomfortable about the folder of information that sat in her laptop. She told herself this wasn't the same as stalking a stranger or a celebrity, but still intended to delete it in the future. She could never risk him finding out the lengths she'd gone to, that engineering this meeting had consumed her for months.

Bundled in a coat and hat, she made her way down the hotel stairs behind Ellie, the nausea circling, her heart racing. They stepped out into the already dark late afternoon, the promise of snow written in the eerie colour of the streetlight bouncing off low clouds. The air was thick with the smell of dampness rising from the mossy cobbled street. They huddled close, weaving their way along the narrow path that led down a rise towards the pub, each clutching the other's gloved hand in anticipation.

A pleasant, smoky blast of warmth hit them as they swung open the heavy door. There was a vacant booth just inside, and they eased in and stripped off their heavy layers. Ellie gave a quick nod, eyes big.

"He's on his way to the bar," she hissed.

Kate glanced across without trying to appear obvious. And there he was. A jolt of recognition pulsed through her body.

"Go! Now!"

Ellie shoved money across the table at her. Kate squeezed out of the seat and cautiously made her way to stand beside him. She glanced discreetly at the tall man and a face that was so familiar looked back at her with a friendly smile and a casual nod of hello. And then his expression turned to one of curiosity.

"Have we met?" he asked. "I feel like I know you?"

"Ah, well, we've only arrived today," she replied, avoiding a direct answer.

The smile reappeared. "Oh well, perhaps in a past life," he laughed. "It's odd. Usually people say that to me—do I know you? And they don't *know* me, but they recognise me."

"Why's that?"

"Oh, it's always they've seen me on the telly. And so my face is familiar. Drawback of the job. Anyway, since we don't know each other—I'm Alex." He extended a large, slender hand.

"Kate Beckett," she said, placing hers in his, feeling a tingling thrill as he squeezed it in greeting. "And that's my friend Ellie. We're here for Christmas."

"Visiting family?"

"Ah, no. We thought Christmas in Scotland would be nice."

To her ears, it sounded rather lame, but he appeared to accept it as a perfectly normal reason. Maybe there were people who spent Christmas in small Scottish towns simply for the experience.

"And you?"

"Visiting family. Including that noisy crew over there." He gestured at a crowded table where a group of six were having an animated conversation. "Why don't you join us?"

"Waifs and strays!" the tall woman called out, laughing as they approached. She must have joined them after Ellie's reconnaissance mission. But Kate could put a name to the face—Sarah, the eldest of the MacLeod siblings.

"Could be," said Alex, "that's if you don't put them off." He turned to Kate and Ellie. "What my sister is trying to say somewhat obscurely is, if you don't have any plans for Christmas dinner tomorrow, our family has a tradition of welcoming anyone who might otherwise spend the day alone."

"And you'd be very welcome. Hi, I'm Sarah," the woman said, extending her hand.

"Kate—and this is Ellie."

"A Kiwi?" she said.

"Yes, how did you guess? Most people say Australian."

"We've employed a fair few of you over the years. My husband, Dom here owns a restaurant in Edinburgh. Kids on their OE. Good workers." The smiling man to her right was a bit of a silver fox. She imagined he was a charming host.

"Ah, glad they created a good impression," Kate said.

"Better introduce the rest of us," said the giant at the end of the table. "I'm Robbie." He held out his enormous paw. "You wouldn't know it because he's such a scrawny bugger, but I'm Alex's brother. And my wife Fiona." He nodded at the woman opposite. Her wide smile transformed an otherwise homely face, and her eyes hinted at a hidden spark of mischief.

"And I'm the other scrawny bugger—Andrew." He and Alex could have been mistaken for twins. Both had boyish good looks that belied their age.

"The spoiled baby," said Sarah.

"The runt of the litter," said Alex.

"Well, Mum stopped when she saw perfection," Andrew quipped. "As did my wife, eh, Sam?"

"Oh, you think?" the tiny woman said dismissively. "Hi, I'm Sam, the one who married this vain bastard." Her feisty attitude reminded Kate of a quote from Shakespeare she'd seen on a t-shirt: *Though she be but little, she is fierce.*

"How about you, love? From New Zealand too?" Robbie turned to Ellie, who had been uncharacteristically quiet.

"Nah, from Brighton now, but I'm a Londoner," she said, to Kate's relief. Now was not the time for Ellie to reveal her Scottish side. They'd agreed that it would be best to avoid any talk of Barra. She didn't want to risk Alex linking her to their previous Comic Con conversation. They didn't want any hint that they'd talked before. No chance he'd think of her as an ambitious fan.

"Ah, well, we won't hold that against you," he joked. "We tolerate the English here. Andy even married one."

"He knows a good woman when he sees one," Sam retorted.

Robbie turned to his wife. "As do I. Even though my one's Irish. Real United Kingdom in this family."

Fiona smiled back at him, her cheeks flushed with quiet pleasure at her husband's compliment.

Immersing themselves in the company of the MacLeod family was effortless. They reminded her of the Becketts. A patchwork of personalities, all stitched together by blood. Occasionally, the constant banter was interrupted by more serious subjects.

"So Sarah, how do you think Dad is, really?" asked Alex. "You've seen more of him than the rest of us."

"He's doing OK," she replied. "He's had a big fright, though the tough old bugger won't admit it."

"Triple bypass," Sam said, seeing Kate's questioning look. "We love the grumpy old bastard, especially the kids. Just as well they didn't lose their grandpa."

"Good we all made it home though, for mum's sake as much as his. She's had a rough time of it," said Sarah.

"She's going to love meeting you two," said Andrew. "You see, Mum views it as a sign of good luck," he explained "Thinks if she does a good deed, such as making people welcome, then the universe will somehow pay it back in kind."

"You will come?" said Fiona. "I think Eileen could do with a sign that next year's going to be a better year."

"Of course we will," said Ellie. "It's a lovely invitation."

"Who's going to get the kudos for finding them?" asked Robbie.

"Has to be Alex," said Sarah. "He brought them back from the bar. Some compensation for the fact he hasn't been around much lately." Her husband gave her a discreet nudge with his elbow. "Oh—not criticising Alex. We understand you've had so much on your plate." She was back-tracking fast.

"Don't sweat it Sarah. We both know I'd rather be here than out doing publicity if I could." He put an arm around his sister. "But I'm more than happy to take credit for finding these lovely ladies. And I'll also take responsibility for getting them home."

The barman had called the last round a while ago, and it was time for them to go. They stepped out of the bar's warm cocoon into snow.

"Here, take my arm," he said, offering one to each of them. "My boots are far more sturdy for getting up this hill. I can haul you up if I need to."

"You think so?" said Ellie, sounding doubtful.

They made their way up the rise to the hotel, arms linked as they threaded their way along the icy path. The snow clouds had peeled back to reveal a chilly, gibbous moon. Its light reflecting off the snow provided near daylight to guide their way. Anyone else who was abroad at the same time might have been alarmed at seeing the shadow of a giggling three-headed creature projected on the white-washed buildings as it stumbled drunkenly towards the hotel.

Alex left them at the doorway, checking one last time that they had the address for his parents' home.

Back in their room, Ellie was bouncing off the walls with excitement.

"That was perfect," she said. "Considering we didn't have a plan, I believe we've pulled it off!"

"And I like him, Ellie. Part of me hoped I wouldn't. Then I could take the cowardly way out of this. But the moment he spoke, well, there was no going back."

"So, lunch with the family. That's going to be fun."

"Yeah, I like them too. But wasn't it weird to meet them after doing all this background research? We have to be careful to act dumb, as if we know nothing. When, in fact, we know quite a lot."

"I decided it's best to shut up and let them talk. Difficult for me," Ellie laughed, getting in first before Kate could tease her. "Right you," she said, "get to bed. We want you all bright-eyed and bushy-tailed in the morning. You get to meet the parents."

CHAPTER 51

Outmanoeuvred

Ballenaig, Scotland - December 2021

ALEX TURNED TO THE woman seated beside him. In the daylight, she was every bit as pretty as last night, standing at the hotel doorstep, washed in the soft moonlight. Perhaps more so. She wore no make-up, but her skin glowed bronze, a beautiful sun-kissed tan. Of course she'd come from summer.

"So Kate, you said you had a yacht?"

Although her uncommon hobby intrigued him, that wasn't the only reason he asked. It was also a desperate attempt to avoid her overhearing a whispered conversation from the other end of the table. His sister was unable to speak quietly, no matter how hard she tried. It was fortunate that

Kate was on the other side of him. Hopefully, the words that had drifted to his ears hadn't made it that far. *Bloody Sarah. She never knew when to lay off.* She justified it by saying she only wanted to see her brother happy, but her attempts at matchmaking had become rather irritating.

"Very strategic of you, mum," Sarah said. "Putting the one without a ring on her finger next to Alex."

"Exactly what I thought." Sam was quick to jump in. "She'd be perfect for him. It's about time he stopped being so picky."

"You can't blame him. My brother isn't the trusting type. Too many have already tried to trap him because he's famous. But this one's different. Didn't even know who he was."

"Hush Sarah," said Eileen, "we don't want the poor girl to think we've lured *her* into a trap."

"Lock the door, I say," said Sam, giggling. "We like her."

Meanwhile, Alex had regretted asking about the yacht. There was a flutter of sadness in Kate's eyes. A slight hesitation. Then she took a small breath and carried on.

"Yes, I have. It's not what you might imagine—not one of those great big things you see in the Mediterranean. A proper yacht. With sails."

"You sail it yourself?"

"Yeah, I do. Well, me and whoever I can rope in to crew. It needs at least two. My husband, James—he was Ellie's brother—he bought it for me. For us."

It was one little word, but it might explain the sadness. He *was* Ellie's brother. So he wasn't Ellie's brother anymore? He wasn't her husband, either?

"To be honest, I've been rather neglectful. Hardly ever took her out this last year. At first, after James died, I lost all interest in everything. Sailing included."

After James died. So she was a widow. Way too young and pretty for that word.

"Plus, I was recovering from a head injury. It messes with all sorts of things. Things you've done forever, suddenly you have doubts. So even though I longed to get out on the water, for ages I wasn't brave enough."

"It sounds as if you've had a rough time."

"Yeah, I suppose I have. But time to move on now. I even took *Lorelei* out before I came over."

"*Lorelei*—cool name."

"She came with it, and some history. She's a historic racing yacht. But yes, her name suits her well."

She pulled out her phone. "Here she is."

The boat was impressive. Not big, but sleek. The shape alone hinted that she would cut through the water effortlessly.

"That's my friend Ange and her husband Tony. She and I have been messing around in boats together since we were kids." A smiling couple waved at the camera.

"We took her for a quick blast around the harbour only a few weeks ago. They talked me into it and it was fun. Ange will take care of her for me while I'm away."

"I'm sorry about your husband," he said. He didn't want to dwell on something that would make her sad. But he wanted to let her know he cared.

"Yeah, it's been hard. But after eighteen months, I've decided now is the time to get on with life. He'd have wanted it. James was never one to stand still."

Light bulbs flashed in his head. "James?" he said. "James Beckett?"

"Yes," she said. "Oh, I never thought of that. Being an actor, you may have known of him. He was a producer. Mostly TV, though a few movies."

"I more than knew of him. I worked with him. In New Zealand—over ten years ago now." He remembered James Beckett well. By reputation he was an arsehole, but Alex had found him OK. Very driven. Didn't tolerate any bullshit, but he got the job done and he did it well. "Maybe that's why you seemed familiar," he said. "Perhaps we met."

"Perhaps we did," she said, a shy smile escaping.

Perhaps they did, he thought. That would explain the faint glimmer of recognition between them when they'd met at the bar.

"I was sorry to hear he'd died. He was a talented guy."

"Alex—" Fiona interrupted them. Seated at the far end of the enormous table, next to Ellie, they'd got on like the proverbial house on fire. Having discovered lots of common ground, lively domestic chatter about children and husbands had kept them engrossed for most of the meal.

"Yes, my favourite sister-in-law. What do you want?" he joked. Fiona tossed him a sweet smile while Sam shot mock evil looks at him.

"What are you doing the next few days?"

"Nothing in particular. I thought I'd check out a few places. As my family is often pointing out, I don't spend much time in Scotland. As long as the snow's not blocking the roads, I might take a drive up to Fort William, maybe over to St Andrews. Why?"

"Well, it's just Ellie here's had a text from her husband. Seems her wee one's grizzly and miserable. Teething, no doubt. Anyway, she was wondering about whether she should head home tomorrow. But not wanting to leave poor Kate alone."

"Oh Ellie, that's no good," Kate said. "You should go."

"Yeah, I think I should," said Ellie, with a regretful look. "Hugh's fantastic with them, but Jamie will want his mum."

"I can come back with you," said Kate.

"No. It would be a shame to spoil the trip for both of us. Especially if Alex would be kind enough to take you a few places. After all, the hotel's booked and paid for."

He wasn't sure, but he thought he caught the glimpse of a wink from Ellie. However, he put it aside as he contemplated the attractiveness of spending more time with the lovely Kate. He was technically single again, so no guilt there.

It wasn't only that she was physically attractive. It wasn't just the wave of sympathy that came from hearing of her loss. He'd not met someone who seemed so easy to be with for a long time. Uncomplicated. And goodness knows his last relationship had been far from that. Kate wasn't obsessed with his fame. In fact, she was oblivious to his acting career. How often did that happen lately? It seemed a good sign.

"You should, Alex," Sarah chimed in. "Company on the drive would be good, wouldn't it?"

Usually Sarah's manipulative suggestions that he pair up with someone only provoked him to push back. She'd tried to propel women towards him before. Each time, he'd made a deliberate sidestep to avoid them. But this time, he decided he wasn't prepared to let this one go to satisfy a need to prove his sister wrong. That would be stupid.

"Kate, why don't you stay? I'd be happy to show you around a few places. Scotland in the winter is spectacular. To be honest, it *would* be nice to have the company."

"You should," said Ellie. "It would make me feel less guilty about abandoning you when we've only just arrived."

"OK," said Kate. "Thank you Alex, that sounds fun."

Everyone at the table had a smile on their face at hearing this. Even his father's lips twitched in amusement. Sarah pretended to be extremely interested in her plate, but had a look of satisfaction that had nothing to do with the Christmas pudding in it. Ellie wore a smug expression as she resumed her conversation with Fiona. Had the pair of them manoeuvred him into this? He didn't care. He was looking forward to the next few days.

CHAPTER 52

The Highlands

Ballenaig, Scotland - December 2021

KATE WAS ALONE IN the hotel room. It was quiet and empty without Ellie's large boisterous presence filling the space. And since Christmas Eve, Ellie had been even more exuberant than usual.

"Right my darling," she'd said, wrapping Kate in a farewell hug, "this is it. On your own now—but you don't need me." Her co-conspirator, Sarah, bustled her into the car and whisked her off to meet the early train to Edinburgh. By afternoon, she'd be home in Brighton with her children. And Kate would be somewhere on the road to Fort William with Alex.

Hearing another car arrive below, she looked down from the hotel window. A grey Audi wagon. Her stomach lurched. How could it be that he should choose that exact vehicle? What a disastrous coincidence. But there was no choice but to be brave. She would go downstairs, greet him with a smile, and calmly hop into the car. She liked this man. A lot. She would not let bad memories tarnish this chance at a better future.

No more snow had fallen since Christmas Eve and large signs confidently announced that all roads were open.

"So you've not been to this part of Scotland before?" he asked as they left the clustered houses of the village behind.

"No, new territory for me."

"You're in for a treat. This drive from here through Glencoe, it's my favourite place in the whole world."

She could see why. As the road wound further away from Ballenaig, the change in landscape was dramatic. Rolling fields with soft snow dusted hills behind them gave way to a row of massive mountains that rose almost vertically from the valley floor. The road snaked between them, the black-skinned surface plunging between high furrows of cleared snow.

"Can't say I'd want the job of keeping this road open," she said, noticing how high the banked snow on either side was.

"I'll tell you something funny about that," he said. "Only in Scotland."

"What?" she asked, returning his grin.

"Only in Scotland would they take something as ordinary as a snow plough or a grit truck and turn it into a joke. So—the vehicles that keep the roads open—they've given them all names. There's this app—it lets you check where they're working. And the names are bloody brilliant." She waited in anticipation. Scottish humour was akin to Kiwi humour, sometimes so ridiculous you had to laugh. "OK, down this way, they must have a Harry Potter fan. The plough—'Lord Coldermort'! And the grit truck—'You're A Blizzard Harry'."

"That's clever."

"Yeah and further north—the Bond fans have named those—'Licence to Chill' and 'For Your Ice Only'."

She whipped out her phone. "I'll Google them." Soon she was chuckling to herself as she read out more of the dreadful puns. "Oh my God, this one's brilliant—'Spready Mercury'!"

"That's a good one."

"Lew-Ice Capaldi!"

"Even better."

"Do you think they pay someone? To sit there and create them all?" she said.

"Perhaps. Whoever it is, they're bloody funny."

Kate's nervousness soon evaporated. One on one, he was even more comfortable to be with than when surrounded by his family. She was enjoying both his company and the spectacular scenery, and his pleasure at showing her his homeland.

"Even though I've seen it before, it never ceases to amaze me. I never tire of Scotland."

"I wouldn't either," she said. "It's not only the landscape. These little cottages, the villages—you get the sense people have been here forever. Where I grew up, even the old things are new by comparison."

"Let me show you something," he said as they drove into the little village of Glencoe. "A bit of history."

He eased the car into the kerb right before a stone bridge, where a lively Highland stream rushed under the road.

"Might be an idea to throw on an extra layer," he suggested. "The dash says it's three degrees outside."

Kate grabbed her puffer jacket, wrapped a scarf around her neck, and pulled on a hat. She stepped out into the crisp air. The sky was clear, but the watery sun was struggling to make any impact on the temperature.

"Up here," he said, and she followed him along a small street that wound past a row of whitewashed houses. They came to a bright signpost that announced the track on their right would lead to '*Upper Carnoch*' and headed that way. The track was deep with brown leaves, discarded by the overhanging trees. With each footfall, a musty odour wafted into the air, the smell of decay.

A short distance along, a wrought-iron fence barred their way, topped with a row of sharp white Fleur-de-Lys, a deterrent for anyone who thought they'd vault over it. Beyond the fence, atop a rough tussock hill, there was a stone cairn, also surrounded with a dangerous, pointy fence. She craned her neck, gazing at a tall, slender cross that rose from the centre of the cairn, silhouetted against the glaring blue sky.

He unlatched a small gate hidden in the fence and they made their way to the cairn past a small sign that read 'The Glencoe Massacre Cross'.

"Ever heard of this?" he asked.

She shook her head.

"Mum's a MacDonald, and they have long memories. Back in 1692, the treacherous Campbells slaughtered a bunch of our ancestors here."

Sure enough, there was another sign giving details of the massacre.

"Attacked them in their homes after they'd been enjoying their hospitality for a few days. Not a particularly nice way to treat your hosts."

As in all places where bad things had happened, even years later, there seemed to be a ghostly chill. Or perhaps it was just the wintery air.

A cheerful chirping from his phone interrupted the sombre mood.

"Didn't expect to have coverage here," he said, retrieving it from the depths of his coat pocket. He frowned when he saw who was calling. "I probably should take this," he said. "Excuse me a minute."

He wandered a little way back down the path while she sat in on a rocky outcrop, soaking in what warmth she could from the sunshine. The coldness of the stone oozed through her jeans, and she shivered, pulling her coat tighter and plunging her hands even deeper into its pockets.

Although she wasn't trying to listen, his voice carried on the clear air. And the snatches of conversation fed a growing unease.

"I won't be back before you leave. You knew that." His speech was slow and measured, as if making an effort to be patient.

"Yes, I'll take care of it."

She glimpsed him running one hand through his hair, an exasperated look on his face.

"Lauren—I said I'll take care of it."

A woman then. A faint tone of irritation had crept into his voice.

"OK, well, you do that. I'll see you when you're back. We'll sort it then."

"Yeah, I'll say hello from you. Mum was asking about you."

Someone his family knew.

"You take care. Come back safe."

His voice was softer now, kind. Someone he cared about. Kate wondered who the mystery woman was. From the lack of any women with him anywhere in the media photos, she'd assumed he was single, but perhaps he was not? And if he was not, did she have any right to be gallivanting around the Highlands with him while this Lauren was oblivious to her existence?

She decided it was now safe to make her way back down the track. She met him coming the other way, head downcast, wearing an expression of annoyance. But hearing her approach, his eyes flicked up to meet hers. She hoped he wouldn't see the troubled thoughts lurking within them.

"Sorry about that," he said. "Stuff to deal with. Shall we head back to the car?"

She nodded and fell into step behind him on the narrow path. Unfamiliar and unwelcome emotions bubbled their way to the surface. Jealousy. That someone else had a prior claim on this man. Resentment. That an unknown woman named Lauren occupied a space that could be hers.

Ahead of her, Kate heard him sigh as he trudged along, seeming ruffled by the conversation. She was glad that he was in front. It hid the tumultuous feelings set in motion by that phone call.

"Hey there's a little cafe open," he said as they arrived back on the main street. He pointed to the welcome sign a few doors along from where they'd left the car.

"Not sure there'll be too many customers today. I could murder a coffee."

"Great idea. Who knows where we'll find the next one."

The coffee was far better than one would expect out here in the middle of nowhere. The food on offer was also a pleasant surprise. It had been hours since breakfast. Normally a full English breakfast would sustain her till dinner time. Perhaps it was nervous energy. The fluffy scone topped with tangy blackberry jam and a dollop of thick, almost buttery cream was perfect.

"Excuse me again," he said, whipping out his phone again. "Need to send off a quick text. I've just thought of something." He stabbed away at his phone while she devoured the scone.

"Sorry," he said. "I'll put that away now. I hate people who are on their phones all the time. Don't want to be one of them."

"Not a problem," she mumbled through a mouthful of scone.

"It's Lauren—my ex-girlfriend," he explained, emphasising the 'ex'. "We're trying to sort our stuff. And she's off for a few weeks right in the middle of it. How on earth do people separate after years together? I can't believe how hard it's been to untangle our lives. We didn't even have a shared flat and still it's been a mission."

Kate laughed shakily, relief washing over her, a giddy happiness at his revelation

"Life gets complicated very quickly."

"It sure does. These last six months were way too complicated. It would have been easier if we had just moved in together. But we were working on the same project and Lauren has this thing about not dating her leading men. So she insisted we keep it all hush-hush. It was tiresome, to be honest."

"Is that why you broke up?"

"Nah, we finally admitted to ourselves that we'd done something we'd both said we wouldn't. We let ourselves believe we meant something to each other outside our on-screen roles. We had a real chemistry in front of the camera, but in real life—it wasn't there."

"Interesting drawback of the job?"

"Yeah, luckily neither of us was scarred by the experience. No one got hurt and we'll stay friends. I like her a lot, but I just don't want to spend the rest of my life with her."

"I'm pleased it's worked out for you." She *was* happy for him, although she was a little guilty at how happy it made her feel.

"And now I'm glad that we kept it quiet. The fans are always shipping, anyway. It would have exploded out of control if they'd known their fantasies had come true."

"Shipping?" she asked. "What's that?"

"It's when fans get obsessed with fictional characters," he explained. "So say it's a TV show couple—some fans want to believe they're together in real life. It gets out of hand sometimes. I've had friends where it almost wrecked their marriage. Their wives crumpled under the constant barrage of suggestions that they were having an affair with their co-stars."

"Wow, that must be hard."

"Yeah, you have to develop a thick skin. And try to keep your real life to yourself as much as possible. They can't do so much damage if you don't let them in."

"That sounds like the voice of experience."

"Oh, for sure. I got burnt a few times early on." Did she see pain flash across his eyes? "But I learned fast."

He downed the last of his coffee. "You done?" She nodded. "OK, let's go. Fort William for lunch."

CHAPTER 53

Serendipity

Lochaber, Scotland - December 2021

EVEN WITH HER LIMITED knowledge of things mechanical, Kate could tell there was something not quite right with the car. Alex had slowed down and now, with head tilted, listening intently to the sound of the engine. The day was growing dim, even though it was only mid-afternoon. It was especially gloomy on this forest shrouded road that wove along the banks of yet another loch.

"Don't like the sound of this car," he said. "It seems to skip a beat every so often. I'm going to pull over at the next place I can."

Outside snow was falling, though here only a few stray flakes escaped through the net of trees. There was a spot where the road widened and he swung the car into a small metalled area. As they came to a halt, the engine emitted a feeble sputter and died.

"Bugger," he said, attempting to restart the car. But although it fired, there was no spark. The car wasn't going anywhere. Neither were they.

He grabbed his phone. "No bloody signal. So much for calling out the AA."

"I don't fancy our chances of flagging down a car either. We haven't seen another vehicle for ages," she said.

"Open the glove box," he said. "I wonder if I've still got any sort of map in there. If we could work out where we are, we can see if there's any village or town nearby."

She rummaged around the debris that lurked in the small compartment, but there was nothing.

"Oh, I know," she said. "I grabbed some tourist brochures at the desk of that cafe in Fort William."

She delved into the depths of her tote bag, retrieving a small wad of information booklets that she'd taken, thinking to use them later to track the day's journey. Luckily, the most substantial one sported a map in the centre. They pored over it, now needing the torch on her phone to see.

"I'm fairly sure that was the last town we came through." He pointed to a red dot. "And see there's the loch we've been following. I reckon we must be about here."

She nodded. "Yeah, I think you're right. So not too far along, there's another town."

"Probably just a little village," he said. "Only big enough to warrant a small black dot."

"Good of them to put a scale on this map," she said. "If it's correct, that's only half a mile."

"Walkable. Thank God we wore sensible shoes."

"And that we brought coats."

"You'd make a good Scot. Prepared for all weathers."

"Got used to it at home. Four seasons in one day sometimes."

"Same as here. OK, let's grab our stuff and get going before it's dark."

Kate breathed a sigh of relief when the lights of the village came into view. Their estimate was spot on. Although she had layers of winter clothing, the chill seeped in through even the smallest gap. The muddy slush of the roadside soaked her shoes and the hems of her jeans. The thought of finding somewhere warm and dry urged her on.

One of the first buildings they came to was a small general store with a gas pump out front. There was a large '*CLOSED*' sign on the door, but a glow of light from the second storey windows suggested that someone lived there. In any other circumstances, it would have seemed quaint, almost idyllic, with the snow settling. But it didn't look like the place for an unplanned stopover.

Alex followed a pathway around behind the building, with Kate close behind. In response to his knock, the door opened a sliver. A small balding man with suspicious eyes behind wire glasses peered out at them, his face hesitant.

"Hey there, sorry to interrupt your evening," Alex began, using a friendly tone. "We've broken down—maybe half-a-mile back. We wondered if there's anyone in the village who might help?"

Taking in the pair of them and deciding they were not a threat, the man opened the door wider and his face softened into a more helpful expression.

"Alex MacLeod." Alex extended his hand in an amiable gesture.

"And this is Kate." She smiled her most winning smile, hoping to charm him into providing assistance.

"Duncan Thompson," the man said gruffly, shaking Alex's hand.

As in all small villages, Duncan Thompson's store was the hub of the town and he knew everything there was to know. They came away from the conversation knowing that unfortunately:

One, the nearest AA help was hours away back in Fort William; and two, they wouldn't come out tonight

But fortunately:

One, Dave down in the village was a pretty handy mechanic and would no doubt look at the car for them in the morning; and two, Brigid Buchanan, over the way, had a room she rented out and at this time of year would most likely not have anyone staying; and three, the small local pub was open and did a good fish and chip meal.

Brigid Buchanan, although officially closed for the winter, was happy to help them out of their plight. She ushered them upstairs, with a cheerful smile, opening the door to a large comfortable looking bed in a cosy room. It had two easy chairs and even its own small bathroom.

"I hope it will be alright. I gave it a little spruce up last spring," she said, fluffing up the pillows while scrutinising their faces for signs that the room was acceptable.

Alex looked at Kate and she at him, knowing they were both having the same thought. Mrs Buchanan's room was lovely, but furnished for a couple.

Kate jumped in first. "It's just fine Mrs Buchanan. Very cosy. Thank you so much for opening up for us."

"And you poor things, stranded here with no luggage. I'll bring a few bits and pieces for you. Some toiletries and things?"

"That's so kind of you."

"I'll get them right now in case you want to have a shower and warm up before you go over to the pub for your dinner."

Once she'd bustled off downstairs, Kate sat on the bed while Alex collapsed into a chair.

"I can sleep here," he offered.

"Don't be silly," she said, looking at his long legs spilling across the floor. "You won't be able to walk by morning if you sleep in that chair."

"I'll take the floor then."

She rolled her eyes at him. "The bed's huge, Alex. It's fine. Honestly." She grabbed one of the heap of pillows on the bed and fired at him. "If it makes you feel better, you can build a wall with these. God knows there's enough of them."

Not being the best shot, it smacked him the face. She ducked as the pillow came flying back at her, and it bounced off the headboard.

"OK, if you say so," he said. "Hope we're better at building walls with pillows than throwing them."

"Speak for yourself," she said, unleashing a flurry of them, until he leapt at her and wrestled her to the bed. She lay there, his face mere inches from hers. God, if that sparkle in his eyes wasn't so damn attractive. She felt guilty at thinking it, but she was glad his relationship with the Lauren woman was over.

"Just for that, I'm going to grab the first shower," he said, releasing her arms, just as Mrs Buchanan's hesitant knock sounded on the door.

The pub was tiny, but welcoming. It was a one-man band, with the owner manning the bar while simultaneously producing their meals from the kitchen. The potential disaster of being stranded in the snow in an isolated spot was morphing into a pleasant evening.

Duncan Thompson's assessment of the pub food was spot on. Only Alex's presence stopped Kate from wolfing down the crispy battered haddock, accompanied by satisfying saltiness of thick chips. The walk in the cold had stirred her appetite.

But as they ate and talked, something else stirred too. Sitting opposite him, she studied his sculpted face, albeit now sporting a light stubble, animated, handsome. At times, her mind strayed from the conversation, captivated by simply watching him, and then jolted back to the moment, and she awkwardly scrambled to cover her dreaminess.

Strange memories poked at the edges of her attention—the way he stroked his chin while thinking of a reply to a question; how he dropped his head modestly when she asked about his career; the comfortable pauses when neither needed to say anything, at ease in each other's company. There was a nagging familiarity.

As they strolled back to their lodgings, the snow had stopped falling. But the night was colder now, each breath of air accosting their lungs. He casually slipped his arm around her shoulders, hugging her in close.

"God it's cold. I'd forgotten how brutal the Scottish winter can be. Spent too much time in London. Gone soft."

She laughed and snuggled into him, enjoying being tucked close under his arm, the warmth of his body against hers.

"I had a great time," she said. "Couldn't have been better if we'd planned it."

"Yeah, what do they call it...? Serendipity—that's it. A fortunate accident." He paused for a moment. "Like you wandering into the Tappit Hen on Christmas Eve. I haven't had such good luck in a long time."

His voice was low as he turned to her, one hand light on her shoulder, while the other traced the lines of her face.

"Neither have I."

"Let's not go in just yet," he said, pulling her to him.

She threaded her arms around his neck. His lips were chilly at first as they made a tentative connection with hers. Sensing her assent, he kissed her again, this time firm and deep, and fire exploded inside her, its heat engulfing her body. And yet it was disorienting. She recognised this kiss, this touch. Understood the shape of this body pressed hard against hers—although this was a man she'd only known for a matter of days.

"No, let's go in," she said, her voice husky as she met his intense gaze, unable to hide the desire that surged inside her. Even in the half-dark, he must see it in her eyes.

"I think Mrs Buchanan's double room might be another fortunate accident," he said, taking her by the hand, an urgency in his stride as they headed for the house.

They tumbled in through the door, trying to suppress nervous laughter, like two mischievous teenagers as they sneaked past the oblivious Brigid Buchanan sitting in her lounge, riveted to a blaring television. Inside the room, they were frantic, stripping off the bulky layers and tossing aside the mountain of pillows and blankets.

"Just a moment."

She reached over to her handbag, lying on a chair. Bloody Ellie, always one step ahead, she thought as she pulled free the strip of condoms. She thought back to that morning. "As Mum always said, if you can't be good, be careful." Ellie's motherly advice accompanied with a wink as she'd tucked them into a pocket.

"Snap." He held up an identical packet with a grin. "Lucky I always have something in my wallet, just in case."

"In case of fortunate accidents," she said. "Although I have to admit to being rather out of practice."

"Oh, I think I can manage to deal with this."

He sat on the bed, his eyes casting an appreciative glance as she stood naked before him. Although a small heater warmed the room, she shivered in anticipation. She let her eyes rove across his body, as he sprawled back on the bed, comfortably leaning on one elbow, a small relaxed smile playing across his face, as if completely familiar with her admiring gaze.

She followed the lines of his long legs, took in the lightly muscled stomach with those twin lines of hip bones leading to the thatch of hair, where already his prominent erection left no doubt of his body's want for her.

"Come here," he said, holding out his hand. "If you're sure. If it's not too soon. After all, we've only known each other two days."

"I'm sure. It's not too soon," she said, wanting to tell him she'd known him for a very long time, but knowing it was a story too big to tell. For now, anyway.

She stepped towards him, and in one fluid movement, he pulled her down beside him. She shuddered, her need for him overwhelming as their bodies met. He moved to lie across her, taking his weight on his elbows, and she gasped a little as he fit himself against her, his body warm and hard, his kisses soft and deep.

He rolled away, trailing his hands across her breasts, tracing the shape of her body, as if retrieving it from his memories, reacquainting himself with the peaks of her nipples with the caress of his tongue and little nips of teeth.

She gasped as his fingers moved down to nudge between her thighs, insistent, locating exactly what they sought, and circling the bud of jangling nerves at her centre in an exquisite rhythm. Explosions of sensation overwhelmed her, and she gave over to him, letting him coax forth ragged breaths and the wild, guttural sounds of her building climax.

How could he know how much she craved what his hands were doing to her at the same time as his lips roughly sought her nipple? She whimpered under his touch. And how did she know he wanted her to touch him just there, as her hand found the delicate tip of his erection, her caress eliciting a deep moan of desire?

She sensed what he wanted from her, and he anticipated her need. Words weren't necessary. The experience was indescribable, making love to someone for the first time, but somehow having a memory of it. She wondered if he felt it, too. How could he not?

Without realising it, Alex possessed an exquisitely fine-tuned knowledge of how to bring her pleasure. He approached her body like a familiar instrument, his mouth and hands confident, as if playing a well-known melody.

When he entered her, her body clenched around him, as if knowing he supplied the missing piece. Once broken, now she was whole again. They found a rhythm, their bodies in perfect time. Pleasure hummed in every nerve ending, waves of arousal climbing higher towards the inevitable chorus of a shared orgasm.

After, as Alex dozed, she lay in the darkness, feeling the gentle rise and fall of his breathing, the comfort of his body close to hers, already so familiar, but in some ways still a stranger to her.

Thoughts of James pushed their way forward. He had been a creative and assertive lover. She'd enjoyed allowing him to be in charge, even experiencing a little thrill of danger sometimes when he took control. But with

Alex, it was different. Yes, he'd taken the lead, and she'd willingly handed over her body to him. But when he'd made love to her, it was if he could see into her soul. And with that, he had lifted her up from a dark place, freeing her from the shadows that lurked, threatening to drag her down once more.

He stirred a little, turning to wrap one arm across her, his body nested comfortably against hers. A flood of contentment washed over her, and she relaxed, allowing sleep to take her in its embrace.

She woke a while later, in response to her body's insistent need for the bathroom. Extracting herself from the bed, taking care not to wake Alex, she stepped into the chilly adjoining room. She should have just done what was necessary and hurried back to the inviting warmth of the bed. But now awake, her brain buzzed with the enormity of what had happened between them.

She didn't regret it. Certainly the opposite. It had been a long and difficult journey to find him. And he was all she'd hoped for. But sitting on the side of the huge claw-footed bath, in the dark, naked, cold, another emotion simmered below the surface.

Guilt. It was unbidden, but perhaps not unexpected. Perhaps it was natural to feel disloyal at the possibility of loving someone else. Especially when James, always surrounded by beautiful women, had only ever had eyes for her. Loyal, faithful. Always. But would he forgive her for choosing love, choosing happiness? Overwhelmed by the conflict that raged within her, tears came. After a time, she calmed, and finding the answer to the question inside herself, tiptoed back to bed, to Alex.

He stirred in his sleep as she tried to slip back under the blankets. He stretched out a hand, finding her in the darkness.

"Oh my god, you're like ice. Come over here. Let me warm you up."

She eased herself alongside him, melting into the protective hollow of his shoulder, and let sleep take her once more.

They woke late, only disturbed by the sun as small shards of light pierced a tiny gap in the curtains.

"Do you really have to go and see Dave about the car?"

He stood naked beside the bed, the early morning light illuminating his body. She unashamedly let her eyes run over the long limbs and the muscular curves. He was in great shape for a man in his forties.

She was pleased that she felt no self-consciousness about her own body as she slid out of the bed to rub herself against him, hoping to persuade him back between the sheets. Sure, she was a little curvier now than before, but somehow she felt sexier and more attractive for it. In her youth she'd revelled in the lean hardness of an athlete's body, proud of what it could do. Now this was a woman's body in full bloom, and she wanted to give it over to him again if he wanted.

And he did. "Perhaps Dave can wait?" he suggested, his voice husky. "Can't presume he's an early riser."

"Hmm, but looks like you are," she said, grinning down at the hardness of him. She let her hand drift down, taking hold and guiding him with a firm touch, so that there could be no doubt about what she intended him to do about it.

CHAPTER 54

Back To The Future

Lochaber, Scotland - December 2021

THERE WAS NO TOW truck in the village. Alex clambered into the passenger seat of an aged Range Rover alongside Dave, the mechanic. Dave sported an enormous shock of curly red hair that fell to below his shoulders. The matching russet beard was long and tangled. Alex was sure if you examined it at close range, there'd be remnants of Dave's last meal trapped in its depths. His broad smile made him look like some kind of benevolent Viking.

"Thanks for this," said Alex, holding his hands against the welcome stream of warm air chugging from the grills in the dashboard. "Sorry to get you out on a holiday morning."

"No worries, mate," Dave replied. "One day's much the same as the next out here, you know. As long as you don't expect me up at sparrow's fart, I'm always happy to help."

They rumbled along the road, back towards the abandoned Audi. Alex hoped it was still in one piece. It'd be just his luck some bastard had stolen the wheels, or smashed it up for the hell of it. He liked the car and though he could easily afford to replace it if the worst had happened, it would go against his basically frugal nature to do so. It was a carryover from his upbringing. They'd never been poor, but Iain's accountant's brain and Eileen's homemaking skills had left a lasting impression on all of them.

He was determined they'd get back to Ballenaig today, one way or another. Only because they had nothing but the clothes they stood up in. With the generous hot water supply at Mrs Buchanan's, he'd put a clean body back into dirty clothes. Not that he minded the faint mingled smell of him and Kate that lingered on them. In fact, he'd gladly wear this reminder of their lovemaking for a week.

In an ideal world, they wouldn't go back. He hungered for more of her, more time with only the two of them, keeping the world at bay. Not that he needed time to know he wanted her like no one else before. He'd thought love at first sight was some ridiculous plot line that inhabited the type of romantic chick-flicks he'd fortunately avoided so far in his career. Now, it seemed his life was turning into one. The moment she'd walked into that bar, a switch had flicked inside him. Not love, but an unexplainable connection.

"This it?" said Dave, jolting him from his thoughts.

To his relief, Alex saw that apart from a crusty coating of snow, the car was the same as he'd left it.

"Right, we'll give her a try, shall we?"

But the car gave a brief hopeful splutter and then died once again.

"OK," said Dave. "We'll throw the tow rope on and get her back to mine. Can't look at it properly out here."

The trip back to Dave's was short, but precarious. The moment he leapt back into his vehicle, Dave seemed to forget that he had another car tied on behind him. They took off with a roar.

Alex was grateful that there was only one serious corner on the route back to the village. It was like being a stunt driver. Wrestling the car as it slingshotted around the bend and then surged ominously towards the back of Dave's vehicle was not a manoeuvre he'd care to repeat. He wasn't sure he could pull it off more than once.

Back at his workshop, Dave attacked the problematic vehicle with gusto.

"Where'd you last fill up?" His voice echoed from under the bonnet of the car.

"Ah, not sure, some small town maybe thirty miles back."

"That explains it," said Dave. "Picked up some dirty fuel, I think. That cheapskate bastard back there. He knows the tanks are stuffed, but he doesn't want to do anything about it. You're not the first one to have a problem after filling up there."

"So is it fixable?"

"Yeah, usually flush it right out and start again with some clean stuff. Sometimes these flashy European engines don't respond. Depends how far the crap's moved through the system. But I'll give it a try."

Alex hoped Dave could work his magic. If they could get on the road by noon, they'd be back home at a decent hour. And then what? He wasn't sure what shape it would take, but he sensed that from now on, his life would be better for having Kate in it, which was entirely possible.

She'd said she planned to stay around for a while, since even for Kiwis, getting back into New Zealand was a lucky dip. And she had a house in London. Convenient, as he did too, and would spend time there with the next series of 'Shadow King' kicking off again in February. He was lucky to have work that didn't force him to navigate travelling in this tricky new world.

He sat in a small, glassed room, its windows bleary with a layer of grime and cobwebs clutching at every corner. There was one chair, uncomfortable and a little shaky, but at least it gave him somewhere to wait. Pinned to one wall was a traditional mechanic's girlie calendar, pages curling and dusty around the edges. Two years out of date, a laughing, scantily clad woman blew a kiss at him. He shook his head, smiling at the incongruity of finding such things even existed in 2021. It was unbelievable that they were less than three hours from a major city. It was like stepping back in time, these little villages, doggedly holding onto a way of life that didn't exist anywhere else.

After much huffing and harrumphing, Dave pronounced the car ready for a test drive. He leapt into the driver's seat, calling out the window "If I'm not back in five, you better bring the Rangey," then sped off back down the road.

It was right on midday when Alex finally parked outside the pub where they'd agreed to meet. As she sauntered out the door, eyes bright, her cheeks flushed fresh from a seat by the blazing fire inside, he thanked whatever god had delivered Kate Beckett to Ballenaig on a snowy Christmas Eve.

CHAPTER 55

True Lies

Edinburgh, Scotland - December 2021

"RIGHT, MATE, HERE WE are then," Eddie announced, easing the vehicle into the drop-off zone.

Although the distance between the central Edinburgh hotel and the cordon wasn't far, calling on his driver to ferry them to the edge of the barriers allowed a more discreet arrival. And far easier with so many streets around here closed in these days leading up to New Year. He was looking forward to introducing Kate to this most Scottish of celebrations. You'd not experienced a true New Year until you'd done Hogmanay.

"Thanks mate, appreciate it."

And they *were* mates. Eddie was not only the driver Alex always called on when working in the UK, but his friend. Over five years and many miles on the road between hotels and sets, they'd become close. In fact, Eddie knew him better than anybody. He was the kind of guy you could trust to have your back. And he was damn good fun, with a ridiculous sense of humour. He'd become famous for his online banter with Alex. Started as a way of entertaining themselves while Alex sat around bored between takes, 'Ready Eddie' had been elevated to a minor Twitter celebrity alongside his more famous passenger.

"No bait trail today?" said Eddie.

"Probably not wise," said Alex. "Not with Kate here. If it goes wrong... don't want to spoil the night."

Astute fans had realized that wherever Eddie was, they could often find Alex, leading the diehards to use him as a tracking device. It was a game of cat and mouse that Alex and Eddie thrived on and usually won by throwing out red herrings or delaying tweets till they were tantalisingly just out of reach. But now and then they'd overreached themselves, with Alex finding himself surrounded by women begging for photos and autographs. It was too soon to expose Kate to the circus of his other life. He hoped that buried in layers of coats and a hat for the cool evening, he'd be anonymous in the crowd.

"Call me later if you want a lift back. I'm only going home to watch the footy."

"Nah, we'll be good thanks Eddie. Not far to walk."

"Well, if you change your mind, give me a bell."

Eddie manoeuvred the nondescript grey Range Rover back into the crawling traffic, and Alex grasped Kate by the arm, steering her through the throng of people towards the VIP entrance.

"Good afternoon sir, tickets and bands please."

Alex presented his phone to the green-uniformed security guard. Barcode scanned, they pulled back their sleeves to reveal the lilac coloured bands encircling their wrists. A means of denoting the wearer as vaccinated and Covid free, they were essential to gain entry. Only these precautions allowed the event to take place at all, albeit in a vastly different form from previous years. In the past, the fire festival wound through the streets of the Old Town, free for anyone to join the crowd. But the rules had all changed. At least they could celebrate, unlike the previous year when the city had observed New Year in deathly silence, the streets empty of the usual thousands of revellers.

Inside the gate, they encountered the first of a dazzling array of buskers. As expected, many of the acts involved fire. Later, the performers would merge to parade along the winding pathways of the gardens before the night culminated in a concert on the main stage.

A myriad of sounds filled the night air—layers of melodies, pounding drums, the melancholy drone of the pipes, a racing fiddle, undulating voices joined in harmony. It should have been a dreadful cacophony. Instead, it was a joyous chorus celebrating their first proper taste of freedom in a long time. He could sense Kate's exhilaration echoing his own.

A tantalising smorgasbord of smells, sweet and spicy, familiar and exotic, drifted across from the food stalls, where vendors displayed offerings from a rainbow of cultures. Although they'd slept late and eaten a generous brunch, the aromas tempted him to suggest they venture over to find dinner soon.

"Wow, this guy's good," Kate said, pointing at a juggler tossing flaming torches into the air with a confident flair. The trails of fire traced elaborate spirals around him, the clubs threatening to break free from their dance, but their escape always thwarted by the master as he regained control.

The reflections of the flames bounced off her hair and illuminated faint hints of red amongst the gleaming blonde. Her eyes were alive with wonder and her face alight with both the cold and excitement. Beautiful.

"What about her?" he said, turning towards a woman walking towards them. In defiance of the chilly air, she was scantily clad, her costume revealing an expanse of bronzed skin. She wore an elaborate tribal headdress, mimicking the appearance of some exotic tropical bird. In each hand she clasped a rope that twirled in hypnotic circles, the blazing poi on each end spinning rapidly, so it seemed as if one continuous stream of fire surrounded her like a force field.

Kate laughed in delight.

"Now—I bet you'd never have guessed I could do that as a child."

"For real?"

"Well, sort of—no fire," she admitted. "But I was pretty skilled with the poi. Our school had a kapa haka group–a Māori performing arts group. Nowadays, most schools have them, but back then we were an oddity–especially as half of us were blonde-headed, not Māori."

They ambled along the pathway. Around each turn, small crowds gathered, enthralled by the entertainers. Dotted in amongst the more carnival-like buskers were traditional Scottish performers. A band of bearded drummers, reincarnations of their Viking ancestors, played a relentless primal rhythm, muscular arms protruding from sleeveless leather jerkins that topped low-slung faded kilts. A young woman performed a Highland dance, her body erect, hands held aloft in an elegant curve, and dextrous feet propelling her back and forth between the crossed swords. The wailing sound of a piper accompanied her, rising and falling alongside the dance.

"Oh, look," Kate said. "They're wearing the MacNeill tartan. Ellie would be so excited to see that. Perhaps they'd let me have a photo with them when she's done."

As the last notes of the pipes trailed off, the dancer took a bow, not the least bit breathless after her exuberant dance. Kate thrust her phone at him.

"I'll ask," she said, making her way through to the resting performers.

He could see them nodding agreement, looking modestly pleased at her request. She waved to him, beckoning him forward. As the trio arranged themselves for the photograph and Alex stood waiting, a thought niggled at him. The MacNeill name sounded familiar. Why was that? Perhaps Ellie had mentioned it at Christmas dinner? Seeing the group posed, he brushed the question aside and turned his attention to snapping the picture.

"Thanks," said Kate, pocketing the phone again. "I'll message Ellie later. Show her the fun she's missing."

"So tell me," he said, "what is it with Ellie and the MacNeills?"

"Her mother was a MacNeill. The family originally came from Barra. I went there with them once…"

She paused abruptly, and her eyes grew wide. And in that moment he knew, he remembered. The Comic Con panel. The girl from New Zealand. Who'd been to Barra.

"It's you," he said, his voice quiet in disbelief. "From the panel."

Her face was pale and the blatant fear in her eyes confirmed he was right. She spoke, but he didn't register the words. He was in shock. How could it be? This woman who'd completely captivated him was just another fan. But a fan like no other. There had been a few stalkers over the years, but none of them, *none of them,* had ever come this close. For fuck's sake, he'd practically taken her into his family!

And it wasn't only that she'd got to him physically—although the sex had been amazing. No, it was way more than that. When their bodies joined, he'd connected with her on some other level in a way he'd not experienced with anyone else before. It had gone well beyond simple desire. And outside the bedroom, there was a warmth and companionship that he'd sorely lacked. He'd been on the point of admitting to himself that he loved her, crazy as it seemed, after only a week. What a fucking disaster.

"Alex, I can explain," she pleaded, a note of desperation in her voice. "It's not what you think. There's so much more to this that you need to know."

"You lied to me," he said. "I don't need to know why. You've made a bloody fool of me. But that stops right now."

He had to get out of there. She'd humiliated him with her lies.

"But Alex—" He heard her call after him, as he pushed through the crowd, striding towards the gate, the phone in his hand already dialling Eddie's number. He cut a swathe through the waves of people still surging into the gardens, pushing against the tide. Even with his height, he struggled to make his way forward. Once he glanced back and he caught sight of her, still rooted to the spot while the mass of people swirled around her. A still point of unhappiness amidst the trails of bright faces.

He leapt into the vehicle before it had come to a complete stop.

"Let's go to yours, eh? A few beers and the footy is just what I need."

"What happened, mate? Did she ditch you?"

"Something like that."

"Ah, that's a shame. She seemed nice. Bit of a looker too."

"Yeah, well, let's say a wolf in sheep's clothing," he said bitterly.

Eddie knew him too well to push for more. As they drove through the streets, he felt a stab of shame at having abandoned a woman amongst strangers, after dark, in the middle of a city she didn't know. God, what was wrong with him? Did she really deserve him to be such a bastard to her? He should tell Eddie to turn around, go back and find her. But she was a grown woman, capable and confident. And a paralysing disappointment at her deception replaced his initial flash of anger.

No, he wouldn't go back. She had the room key. He'd get himself blind drunk at Eddie's, erase the evening. He didn't want to think beyond that.

A dull thud next to his ear brought a rude ending to the only decent bit of sleep he'd snatched in the entire night. An excess of alcohol did that to him, left his limbs so heavy with tiredness yet his brain wired and unable to submit to unconsciousness.

"Time to face the day, sunshine."

Shards of light assaulted his eyes as Eddie ripped back the curtains with a flourish. He scrunched them shut tight against the pain.

"Last day of the year. You can't spend it wallowing around on the couch all day."

Bloody Eddie. He was almost twenty years Alex's senior but always matched him drink for drink, and by some magic was no worse for wear in the morning.

"Bugger off Eddie," he moaned. "At least shut those fucking curtains. The light's bloody blinding."

"Now, now, that's no way to greet your host. Especially not after he's provided you with drinks on the house, a bed for the night, and a morning coffee delivered."

Shit. Bloody Eddie. It was always the same. Alex would drag himself out of bed for some ridiculously early-morning call, bleary-eyed and dishevelled, and Eddie would be there looking dapper and chirpy as hell. He'd open the back door of the vehicle for Alex to sprawl on the bench seat so he could squeeze in a few more minutes of sleep before hours trapped in a chair submitting to the attentions of his make-up artist. How the man did it remained a mystery. Must be genetic.

With reluctance, Alex abandoned all hope of retreating under the pile of blankets, swung his feet over the side of the couch and sat contemplating the coffee sitting beside him. The drummers from last night had followed him home and were now pounding out their relentless rhythms in his head.

Eddie seated himself comfortably in a battered armchair opposite and leafed through a newspaper, intent on the last stories of the year. He was old school in that respect. No way you'd catch him reading the news on his phone. His spiky thatch of white hair was damp. He'd attempted to slick it down, but as always, it sprung back irrepressibly, giving him the appearance of a well-used toothbrush.

"Once you've had that, get yourself in the shower. You'll feel much better, I can tell you."

"Thanks Eddie. You're a good man."

"Well, it seemed you needed a mate last night."

"Yeah, I guess I did. Thanks."

"Have you heard from her?"

Alex reached for his phone. The screen was blank. No phone calls. No texts.

"Nah, not a thing." He felt a faint tinge of worry. What if she hadn't made it back to the hotel?

"I need to get over there, check if she's OK. I shouldn't have left her like that."

"No, not your finest moment." Eddie paused for a moment, his face thoughtful. "Look, mate, you know I don't poke my nose into your business. But..."

"I know. I know. I need to sort myself out."

"Yeah, remember you're not twenty-five anymore. You're not some kid thrust into the limelight all of a sudden. And she's not that little bitch who tried to stitch you up."

Eddie was right. It had been a knee-jerk reaction to Kate's unwitting revelation. After all these years, he was still letting the past rear up and dash him to the ground. And this time, he'd taken her down with him. It was time to man up and take control. He needed to get his butt off this couch, down a handful of paracetamol, and head over to that hotel.

He hesitated at the door to the room. Should he knock first? Deciding that she might still be asleep, he swiped the plastic card in the reader and, taking a cautious step into the hotel room, was relieved to see her there. At least she'd made it back safely.

In the cold, hard light of day, he regretted storming off, abandoning her. Apart from being a shitty thing to do, he chided himself for his hasty action. On his overreaction. He was letting the events of twenty years ago fuel a lurking paranoia.

Sure, she'd spoken to him on a zoom. So what? And perhaps she'd been embarrassed to admit to it, scared to own up to the truth, thinking he might react in exactly the way he had. Was it such a crime? Yes, she'd tricked him into breaking one of his rules—never date fans. But then he'd broken the 'no bedding your co-stars' rule with Lauren and although it hadn't worked out, it hadn't been a total fuckup. They'd still emerged as friends.

She sat at the table, hunched over a mug of coffee. When she turned to face him, her eyes were puffy, the dark, bruised-looking skin underneath suggesting she hadn't slept. She looked like a flower burned by a blast of frost. What an arsehole he was. He'd done this, put her through hell for a tiny transgression. A sin of omission.

Meanwhile, he'd drunk himself into oblivion, snoring on Eddie's couch. The painkillers had yet to kick in, and his head throbbed with a well-deserved hangover. Nausea swirled in his stomach, and his mouth tasted like a sewer. He stroked the stubble on his chin, unsure of what to say.

She stood, wrapping the bulky wool cardigan protectively around her. It made her appear so fragile, tiny. He had done this. Diminished her somehow.

Her face had a grey tinge, almost matching the garment that cocooned her. He'd done this. Dimmed her sparkle. She was a shadow of the vibrant woman he'd spent the last week with. Seeing her like this, his mind struggled for words.

She spoke first, solving the problem for him.

"Alex, there's something you need to see," she said, her voice almost a whisper.

She padded across the room, dainty bare feet poking out the bottom of baggy sweatpants. Even her feet were beautiful. Hesitantly, he followed. She took her MacBook from where it lay on the desk, tapped in a password with deft fingers, then clasped it against her chest, obscuring the screen.

"Before you look at this, I can tell you I do have an explanation for why I didn't tell you we'd met before. But it's got to do with what's on this screen—and I don't have any explanation for that." She pulled out a chair. "Perhaps you should sit down. "

Intrigued, he did as she suggested, and took the proffered computer. She stood behind him, her breathing quick and shallow, watching, waiting, close but not touching him, still preserving the gaping space that he'd put between them.

There was no rational explanation for the images in front of him. His own face smiled back at him. A younger him. A younger Kate. In one, his siblings clustered around them. In the other he wore the MacLeod tartan, Kate beside him also resplendent in simple white, both their faces lit with a glow of inner happiness.

One could be forgiven for thinking it a camera trick or Photoshop wizardry. But when he looked at her he knew that, fantastical as it seemed, this was no elaborate hoax. The truth was written in her eyes, those mesmerizing eyes the colour of a stormy sea, now welling with tears. Even though it was a truth he didn't understand.

He stood and took her in his arms, tucked her in close, rested his chin gently on her glossy head, while she sobbed uncontrollably. He stroked the shaking shoulders, letting her melt into him, holding her until she stilled.

After, they lay entwined on the generous couch, his arms cradling her, attempting to radiate reassurance of the return of his trust, her body relaxed against him, eyes calm now, having released the expression of wariness and agitation that had met him earlier.

He sat caressing her silken hair in a soothing gesture while trying to find a similar calm within himself, but his mind still churned with knowledge that turned everything he thought he knew on its head. She'd lived with this for longer; over a year. How had she processed it, accepted it, learned to live with it? He needed her help if he was to do the same.

He kept his voice soft and low, as if approaching a wary horse, not wanting to spook her, induce a fight-or-flight response.

"You've had time to think about this, what happened, what it means." She stiffened a little, the tension returning. "I'm not questioning it," he said. "Just trying to understand it."

She relaxed again at that, but her voice was tight and small, crushed by the enormity of this conversation.

"Yes, I've thought about it a lot. How could I not?"

"Who else knows?"

"Only Ellie."

"And what does she think?"

"That I should thank the universe for giving me another chance with you. That I should grab hold of that chance and not let go, not give up. And she's held my hand every step of the way, except those times she was standing behind me, urging me forward even when the possible outcome terrified me."

He leaned and kissed her hair, recognising the risks she'd taken, the courage she'd summoned, and shame at the devastation his actions had wrought.

"Ellie was the right person to tell. She's open to possibilities. We've talked about it over and over, trying to make sense of it."

"Tell me then. What's it all about?"

"Time," she said, her voice now taking on a softer, dreamy quality, like a storyteller recounting a tale of old. "A trick of time."

"You think you've time travelled?" In spite of what he'd just seen, the words still sounded ridiculous, in the realms of the impossible.

"No, not in the usual sense."

He smiled at that. "And what exactly is the 'usual sense' when it comes to time travel?"

"Well you know, *Back to the Future*, *Outlander*, people going back and forth, jumping in and out of the flow of time. Like it's something linear. But what happened to me, it's as if there are lots of different threads of time. And I now think that maybe at any time our consciousness, the knowledge of our existence travels along one of those threads, but there are others, parallel threads, other lives.

"Somehow this thread, this life I know, tangled with another for a while—not the past, not the future, a parallel time, a parallel life. Where I wasn't married to James. Where you were the person I fell in love with. And then for some reason it corrected itself, untangled, catapulted me back to my first life, with those photographs the only evidence of me ever being away, hidden for all those years."

He listened but didn't speak, not wanting to interrupt the flow of her voice, just a light kiss brushing her forehead, encouraging her to go on.

"That was until the accident. Afterwards, at the hospital, when they asked me about my husband, it wasn't his name that came to me. It was yours. I pushed it away, but you were relentless, returning again, and again, whenever I least expected. Images I saw, places I went—you were there. You've been haunting me, Alex MacLeod."

A small smile played around her mouth.

"I'm very sorry that I've disturbed your life," he said, answering her smile.

"I'm not," she said, squeezing his hand. "Not at all sorry. I'm glad. You saved me."

He stood and returned to the computer, and she followed. Drawing her onto his lap, he once more pulled up the photos while she cradled her head on his shoulder.

"Don't we look all bright and shiny? Bit of an alcohol-fuelled glow happening there," he said, as he clicked the image of his family at the pub, allowing it to fill the screen.

"Except for Sam, look at that protruding stomach. God, she must have been almost due."

"Yeah, young Liam was an enormous baby. Big lad now too."

"You haven't changed much. None of you."

"Nor you. Looking at you there, I'd swear it was taken last week. In fact, I thought it was at first. But yeah, Sam's tummy gives it away."

"And this one," he said, flicking onto the beach scene. This was the one that had unexpectedly caused a flood of emotions to overwhelm him, despite it being devoid of people, simply a photograph of an azure summer sea, framed by trees laden with bright red flowers. "Believe it or not, this one triggered something more than the first. I was certain I'd been there before. Where is it, do you know?"

"Northland, New Zealand. I looked through loads of photos and I'm pretty sure it's a place called Aurora Bay. Private beach you can only get to by boat, unless you own one of the houses up above it."

When he moved on to the next photo, one of him standing on a small deck, beer in hand, she gave a little sniff, and he glanced down to see a single tear edging its way down her cheek as she now choked back a slight sob.

"This is my house, was my house," she said, her voice trembling. "It's gone now. I loved living there."

"Looks like you made me very welcome," he said, trying to lighten the mood. "Is that a Kiwi beer in my hand?" He peered in at the screen.

She smiled at that. "Yes, looks like a Steinlager. You must have been doing something right if I shared my beer with you."

And then, with one more click, *that* picture appeared. He'd never married, not even come close. But in some strange other place, some other life, things had been different.

"By god, that girl's so beautiful you know I think I'd marry her. If she'd have me."

It was crazy. He'd known this girl sitting on his knee for just a week, and yet the thought of marriage, once so foreign, now had an unusual appeal. Perhaps it was because he'd unknowingly tried it before and liked it. Anyway, he didn't regret the impulsive words.

"You never know, she might. Have you, that is."

She tilted her head towards him, and in their kiss, they found acceptance of their past and a promise of their future.

Confession

Edinburgh, Scotland - December 2021

AT FIRST THEIR COMING together was gentle, hesitant, both seeking forgiveness, both giving it without need for words of apology. As their bodies moved in rhythm, it unleashed a passion driven by both joy and relief at setting aside what had divided them, along with an unspoken promise it would remain in the past.

As he thrust deep inside her, Kate welcomed him to her, welcomed him home. Last night fear had gripped her, fear that he'd abandoned her like all the others before him. Even James, her loving loyal James, had left her in the end. No, the others were gone. But Alex was here, making love to her, loving her, inextricably joined to her in this life, not only in the past.

Afterwards they lay, limbs tangled, in a peaceful doze. Eyes closed, she languidly let her hand drift across his stomach, the skin so soft but taut over his muscled torso. With one light finger, she traced the line of hair that stretched downwards from his chest. He stirred at that, untangling his legs and rolling away from her to sprawl on his back. He lay saying nothing, staring at the ceiling, his eyes blinking as troubled thoughts rippled across his face. With a look of resolve, having obviously weighed up what needed to be said, he spoke.

"I owe you an explanation. I'm not trying to excuse my behaviour. But I thought you should know—know it's not your fault what happened last night."

"If you want."

The old Kate would have brushed it aside. Accepted his reasons were his to keep. Would have feared letting him appear vulnerable in case he might hold her knowledge of his vulnerability against her in the future. But allowing him to own his behaviour seemed right, and she felt no fear.

"Back in the early days, when I got my first decent role, I learned a very hard lesson. I've thought about it a lot over the years. How I got to that point. And I suppose it stems from even earlier, when I was in high school. I was painfully shy, geeky looking, not comfortable in my own skin."

She smiled, finding it hard to imagine this attractive man as an ungainly teenager.

"Yeah, fortunately I kind of grew into my body," he said, grinning at the way her eyes were instantly drawn to it, roved across his nakedness, imagining how the ugly duckling teen had evolved into this. "But back then... Well, you know teenagers, they're on the lookout for targets. Sure, I had friends, but they were a lot like me. We were never part of the cool crowd. More often, we were the butt of their jokes. I hated school. The only thing that kept me there was this one teacher. He taught drama. I think perhaps he saw his younger self reflected in his students, and spotted potential we weren't aware of. He encouraged me to come along to the lunchtime drama club, after school workshops. I didn't think it was my thing, but I was curious. And although I was an introvert, somehow I enjoyed it.

"Soon I was in productions, at school and the local youth theatre too. So when it came time to decide what to do when I left, it was natural for me to try for drama school. I was lucky—accepted into a good one and spent three happy years before being thrown out into the harsh reality of life as a young actor. It took me almost five years to get that breakthrough role. But when it came, it was big."

"What was it?"

"A TV series. A group of young people living in London, you know, the sort of thing that appeals—left home, challenges of life and love, alcohol and drugs thrown into the mix. Anyway, my character was one of those bad boys that the girls are all attracted to."

She smiled again. This Alex had no hint of the bad boy about him.

"Well, overnight I had fans. Lots of them. They'd appear everywhere I went. Sidle up to me in bars, corner me in the supermarket. There'd been a few girlfriends. But I suppose because I was shy and immersed in whatever work I could pick up, I'd never had much female attention before."

He cleared his throat and took a slow breath, delaying the telling of it.

"It went to my head. And my dick. They offered themselves to me and I took them. I was young and naïve, but that's no excuse. I'm not proud of it. I was old enough to know better."

She rolled over, placing her head on his shoulder, stroking his chest to offer reassurance.

"So what happened?" she asked, keeping her voice low and calm, inviting his confession.

"The inevitable." There was a tremor in his voice, his body tense. "One girl I'd slept with a few times got pissed off with me—rightly so, because I'd moved on to bonking her best friend. Anyway, she threatened me. Made noises about how she could get me into a lot of trouble. End my career. She never spelled it out in so many words, but it was obvious she was toying with an idea. She planned to say I'd forced her. I didn't—I might have been a jerk sleeping around, but I didn't force her to sleep with me, or anyone else. I didn't need to."

"Oh, my god. That's awful."

Kate struggled to reconcile the young actor, taking advantage of his stardom, with the humble man she'd spent these days with, a man with no hint of arrogance. Imagined the fear, the realisation that he'd brought this on himself.

"I went to my agent. Back then, it was a woman named Stella Shadwell. I thank god that I did. She was older, a sort of mother figure as much as an agent. Had been in the business a long time. Knew what to do. Starting with giving me the dressing down that I deserved. I emerged from that room, vowing I'd never be such an idiot again. And I made a rule—I'd *never* date fans. And I've stuck to it."

"You thought I'd tricked you. Into breaking your rule."

"Yes," he said, his voice regretful.

Now she understood his anger, and knew what had driven a man who cared for her to in an instant find her repellent, what had driven him to run.

There was a discreet knock on the door.

"Room service," said a voice from the other side. Damn, they'd forgotten to flip the 'do not disturb' outside.

"Sorry, not now," he called. There was a click as the door opened.

"Not now," he yelled, and this time the mystery visitor retreated with a polite "Sorry sir".

They lay back giggling, the near miss breaking the serious conversation. Now the tense set of his mouth morphed into a wicked grin. With one powerful arm, he rolled her onto him, his other hand already cupping her buttocks and his leg nudging between her thighs.

Later, when they summoned room service again, it was to deliver food. Now showered and clothed, she opened the door to the neatly-attired staff member who wheeled in a laden trolley. Kate's empty stomach growled in anticipation. She couldn't recall eating anything since yesterday. Only numerous cups of strong sweet coffee had sustained her.

With a flourish, Alex lifted the covers to reveal platters piled high with meats and hot vegetables. "Oooh haggis," he said. "You must try some."

She regretted admitting she'd never sampled this bizarre Scottish delicacy. The sight of crumbly sausage meat spilling out of a long wound in the side of a rounded greyish mass confronted her.

"Come on, you can do it!" he urged.

She wrinkled her nose and scrunched her eyes shut as he delivered a steaming fork full into her open mouth. She opened them, blinking in surprise at the unexpected pleasantness of its coarse oaty texture and warming peppery flavour.

"Here, wash it down with some of this if you don't like it," he said, offering her a glass of the champagne that he'd requested.

"No, no, it's fine. It's actually quite nice. As long as you don't think about what's in it."

She took the glass anyway, and sipped at it, savouring the bursts of acidity as the tiny bubbles exploded in her mouth.

He raised his glass, and she mirrored him.

"To us, past, present and future."

"To us."

Later they stood on the balcony, watching colourful searchlights play across the castle walls, the historic and the modern blending in a spectacular celebration to mark the fast approaching New Year.

"I wonder where we spent it?" he said, his fingers brushing his chin in that way he did when mulling something over.

"What?"

"New Year. That New Year. When we were together. Before."

There were so many unanswered questions. Strange questions. Most likely unanswerable questions.

"Wherever it was, I think we were happy," she said.

"Like now," he answered, turning to kiss her as the thunder of fireworks echoed across the ancient battlements, and bouquets of bright stars bloomed in the midnight sky.

Epilogue

Kate

Ballenaig, Scotland - December 2023

KATE WASN'T SURE WHAT was more delightful—the sight of her precocious nine-month-old daughter displaying her newfound ability to walk in random wobbly steps, or the doting look of the little girl's grandfather, his face a wrinkled smile as she toddled towards him like a happy drunk.

Unable to sustain the movement for more than a few paces, Sorcha flopped down in the middle of the lounge with an audible plop. Insulated by the padding of her nappies, she didn't produce tears, simply sat in dazed surprise at finding herself once more on her bottom.

Kate's father-in-law was the stereotypical dour Scotsman, with a critical eye and sardonic wit. Iain didn't suffer fools. His tendency was to make quick assessments of people, and he found most of them wanting. It was a rare occurrence for anyone to measure up to his exacting standards.

But he and Kate had hit it off from the beginning. His brusque manner with outsiders reminded her of her grandfather. And this small person enchanted Iain MacLeod. Sorcha had everyone, including him, completely in her thrall. He contorted his face into a silly expression while she chortled and waved her little hands in excitement.

Alex appeared in the doorway, the scene captivating him as well. There hadn't been a baby in the family for some time, and Miss Sorcha was the star of the show this Christmas. He met Kate's eyes, and they exchanged smug looks of pride in this perfect being they had created.

"So you're going to be a good girl for Granny and Grandad?"

The little girl's eyes widened at the sound of her father's voice and she turned towards him, making small pleading gestures accompanied by indecipherable gibberish; a baby talk request for him to pick her up. Alex stooped down and swept her into the air with a flourish as she giggled with glee. Kate thought to herself that the laugh of a baby was one of the purest sounds in the world.

Alex's mother, Eileen, came into the room.

"Now don't you be getting her too excited, my boy. How will she ever settle to sleep after you've been tossing her around like a wee dolly?" She extended welcoming arms towards them. "Come to Granny, my love."

Alex handed over the squealing bundle, and his mother eased herself into one of the generous armchairs and snuggled Sorcha to her.

"You two should get ready," she urged. "Go on, she's fine here," she said, lowering the baby to a blanket amid an assortment of toys. Sorcha immediately grasped one in her hand and sucked on it, strings of happy drool dripping from her mouth.

"OK," said Kate. "Then we can try to put her down as we leave. Hopefully, it will give you a few hours' peace."

She and Alex climbed the stairs, both radiating the same warm contentment at the blissful scene in the room below.

"Shall I jump in the shower first?" she asked, heading into the bedroom.

"I think there's something else I'd like you to do first," he said, not able to help the flicker of a smile.

He shut the door behind him with a firm clunk.

"And what might that be?" she asked, knowing full well the meaning of that cheeky expression on his face.

"Well, it is Christmas," he said. "The giving season. And there's certainly something I'd like to give you, and perhaps you've got a gift for me in mind too?"

She laughed as he steered her towards the bed.

"I don't know if we have enough time for you to both unwrap and enjoy it," she said, raising one eyebrow quizzically.

"Oh, I'm pretty sure I can have a wee play with it now, and then tuck it away for more fun later," he replied. "But I'm not sure if it's going to be too noisy and disturb them downstairs?"

"Noisy?" she protested. "I'm not noisy!"

"Oh yes, you are, my love. Moans and squeaks and heavy breathing."

She laughed and gave him a playful slap as he drew her to him. They made love quickly, and quietly, and with an immeasurable joy at this wonderful gift of each other that life had given them.

Afterwards, they lay face to face, saying nothing but everything in the meeting of their eyes. With reluctance, but knowing that they *did* in fact need to get ready to join the rest of the younger MacLeods at the pub, he broke the moment with a smile and a tap on the nose.

"I think you need to get into that shower. You're sticky and smelly."

"And whose fault is that?" she said, poking him in the chest with an accusing finger. "Yours!" Adding, as she sat up and swung her legs over the side of the bed, "Yours, and that little monkey downstairs. I'll have to wash my hair as well. It's got mushed vegetables in it."

Sorcha was at the stage where she took equal delight in both eating and playing with her food. Lifting her from the highchair, Kate had felt grubby little hands scrunching themselves in the back of her hair. Motherhood was a dirty, messy business.

"That little monkey downstairs is the best thing that's ever happened to me, that and meeting you." She knew he meant it. The man who kept his private life so hidden from his fans was like an open book to his family. "I can't believe that I didn't want a child until you convinced me otherwise."

"There was a time there when I didn't think you'd come around to the idea."

"It was a tough time. All those doctors and tests ... if it wasn't for you pushing me, I'd never have seen it through. But it was worth all of it. To have her, and to have you happy."

Soon Kate had showered, snuggled into a warm robe, and was sitting in front of the mirror, her hair wrapped in a fluffy towel. She gazed at her reflection. Not bad, considering she was nearly fifty. Life hadn't left as many marks on her face as one might expect from this rollercoaster ride. It had been a wild ride, for sure.

The highs had been exhilarating, but the lows had been incredibly hard. Losing James was still the hardest. But she'd survived. That little jagged piece of loss still tucked away inside her would always be there. But slowly and surely she had wrapped it in careful layers, like protective cotton wool, that had diminished the pain. Time was one, each year making it that bit more bearable. Alex was another.

Their marriage was different, the product of a gentle, more constant love and a meeting of equals. Loving James had been challenging. It hadn't been easy living with a force of nature, a man with a driving need to push their lives forward in whatever direction he thought best. The old Kate had accepted it, allowing herself to drift in the tide, with James steering the ship.

But she wasn't the same person as she'd been then. Forged in tragedy, she was a stronger person, knew what she wanted and what was good for her. And Alex was exactly what she needed at this time in her life, both friend and lover, a true partner. The child they shared was the greatest joy she had ever experienced.

But the thing that really allowed her to hold James tight at the same time as letting him go was a thing for which there was no explanation. However, she knew it with absolute certainty. She knew it wasn't simply a figment of her imagination, some delusional creation of her damaged brain. Nor was it a lie she had invented to soothe her grief. The reason she knew it was true was because Ellie knew it, too, as did Alex.

Tucked away in an old envelope were photographs that, if they didn't quite prove it, provided some strong evidence: this life she was living was just one life, and somehow, somewhere, sometime, there was another—a second life. Maybe there were others too. But she was certain of that one.

And in that life, James still lived. She smiled, thinking how in *that* life he would most likely be preparing for the famous Beckett Christmas. She hoped there was someone who loved him by his side.

The light press of Alex's hands on her shoulders brought her back to this life. His breath on her neck tickled as he leaned forward to kiss her behind one ear.

"I love you Kate MacLeod," he whispered.

They closed the front door behind them with a quiet, careful click so as not to wake the precious sleeping child they'd entrusted to the loving care of her grandparents. Kate and Alex stepped out into the already dark late afternoon.

There was a hush, all sound dampened by the layer of snow that blanketed the town of Ballenaig. They walked down the narrow road, gloved hands clasped in a tight grip, as they steadied each other on the slippery cobbles.

The lights of the small pub beckoned them as the snow drifted casually from the brooding clouds, caressing their faces as gently as the touch of a lover's hand.

If you enjoyed this book, I'd appreciate it if you have time to leave a review on your favourite retailer, review site, or social media.

And if you'd like to read more about Kate, James and Alex, why not check out Tangled Thoughts, a free short story available on my website along with other bonus content.

Filming is done. The wrap party is all that stands between Alex and his flight home. Back to the people and places he loves. A welcome escape from the actor's life that has made him a success. So why do his thoughts tell him there's something, or someone, trying to keep him here?

www.carolinecorvin.com

While you're there, sign up to my newsletter to receive future updates and information on new releases.

For details on all books in the series, turn over a few pages to see more from Caroline.

Acknowledgments

Writing may be an individual pursuit, but it doesn't become a published book without a wonderful support team. I've been fortunate to have just the right people surrounding me at this time. My heartfelt thanks to my editor Jacquelin Cangro, whose wise advice calmed my nerves and gave me the confidence I needed to go forward with this book. The talented Jules who captured the mood and the mystery of the story in the beautiful updated cover for this edition. To the team at Grenwyvern Publishing, I am so grateful for your work navigating the publishing process. To the members of my tribe, the romance writers who read my work and gave me unfailing support, you rock! And finally to David, who reminds me every day that happily ever afters don't exist only in books.

Caroline

About The Author

Caroline Corvin

When not writing, you can usually find Caroline with her nose in a book from any one of an eclectic mix of favourite genres. While officially a resident of Auckland, New Zealand's stunning City of Sails, she has become adept at juggling her love of writing alongside her other magnificent obsession of travelling the world. Caroline didn't set out to write romance, but her characters took control the moment she let them loose on the page, reminding her that finding happy ever afters are the reason she's one of those people who sometimes reads the last page first, just to be safe.

Follow Caroline Corvin on all your favourite social media or review sites!
Visit her website: www.carolinecorvin.com

More From Caroline

Caroline's Tangled In Time series takes time travel
romance and twists it in a new direction. Each book can
be read as a satisfying standalone, so if you haven't already,
check out the other titles.

Find the links to purchase on her website.

The prequel novel, Tangled In Time is available free!

www.carolinecorvin.com

Tangled In Time

**A free-spirited artist, a wandering astronomer,
and an instant connection.
Is their future painted in the stars?**

Landscape painter Blair Silvestri hasn't time for stargazing —or love. It's her immediate, more precarious situation that she needs to focus on for now. Daniel Tremayne spends his life looking skyward. Maybe that's why he's made such a mess of all his relationships so far. A trick of time throws them together, but also threatens to tear them apart.

Tangled Paths

**"In a world full of limitless lives,
of endless possibilities, I will always find you."**

Sarah Mitchell always put family first. Now, freed from self-imposed exile in her hometown, she's ready to jump back on the academic path she sacrificed for others three years ago. It's her time to choose a path. Or is time going to choose for her? When Sarah's future seems destined to be defined by loss, will time's tangled paths deliver her a second chance at happiness?

Tangled Hearts

Two loves, two lives. One heart shattered.
Can a love from another time heal the pain of the present?

Young emergency room doctor, Layla Angell, is living the dream: in the perfect job, surrounded by friends who are like family—including the man she's always wanted to be more than a friend. Life is full of potential. But the future is never promised. Caught in a time-twisted love triangle, Layla's connection to two men, across two parallel lives, offers a second chance at happiness beyond tragedy—if she can learn to accept the impossible.

Tangled Past

**When the past holds you in its power,
is love enough to set you free?**

Cassiopeia Tremayne isn't looking back at her sleepy hometown. Facing the future, all she can see is her dream of being a writer, just there on the other side of her final high school year. But Cassie's future also includes navigating the turbulent waters of two parallel but intertwined lives, forcing her to confront truths about herself, her family and the men she loves in two separate worlds. And when those worlds collide, will love give her strength enough to rewrite the past and become the hero of her own story?